Ahab

CONSTANCE HEAD

BROADMAN PRESS • Nashville, Tennessee

© Copyright 1979 · BROADMAN PRESS
All rights reserved
4273-09
ISBN: 0-8054-7309-2

Dewey Decimal Classification: Fiction
Subject heading: AHAZ, KING—FICTION
Library of Congress Catalog Card Number: 79-50340
Printed in the United States of America

The Scripture quotations are by the author and are based on the
Revised Standard Version of the Bible.

DEDICATED TO THE MEMORY OF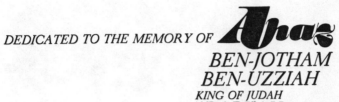
BEN-JOTHAM
BEN-UZZIAH
KING OF JUDAH
AND ABIJAH THE WOMAN
WHO LOVED HIM

The king is a leper. For three days now the city of Jerusalem had been astir with the terrible news. "What will become of him? Will he still be king? Where will he go?" Hundreds of times the questions had been asked, and now gradually small bits of information filtered down to the people of the city from the great palace on Mt. Zion. The stricken King Uzziah, even in the first stunned horror of discovering his illness, knew that there was only one course of action open to him. As a leper he was an outcast from society, but he was still Judah's anointed king; and though his body was afflicted, his mind was as clear as ever. With a few servants to attend him, he retired to a secluded house in the country and his favorite son, Prince Jotham, whom he could count on to obey his orders, was installed as regent.

Still one question remained unanswered, the one which Uzziah's bewildered subjects asked most of all. "Why? Why did our God let it happen?"

If the king had been an oppressive ruler like so many kings of the past, it would not have been hard to find an answer. But Uzziah of Judah, far more than most sovereigns, was greatly beloved by his people. Many of the folk of Judah had no memory of any other king, for Uzziah, who was now an old man, had ruled since his early youth. His genuine concern for his subjects was obvious. Throughout his long life he had striven to estabish justice. He had heard countless cases brought to him by humble petitioners, and while assuredly he could not please them all, his sincere striving for fairmindedness was famous throughout the land. Military victo-

7

ries over the neighboring states of Ammon and Edom had added to Judah's prosperity, but Uzziah preferred peace to war. In the last years of his reign, he had concentrated on the building of his seaport at Elath and the extension of trade with other nations. The kingdom of Judah prospered under Uzziah's leadership and those who knew the chronicles of the nation's past agreed that rarely in the land's long history had there been a king so genuinely devoted to his people and, equally important, so steadfast in his worship of Yahweh, Judah's God.

Unlike some of his predecessors, Uzziah had no use for the other gods: gods like the fertility deities Baal and Ashtoreth, worshiped by so many Judeans, or the fierce Ammonite Molech, the lord of the glowing fires. No, King Uzziah, while he did not doubt the existence of these rivals of Yahweh, gave his whole allegiance to the God who had chosen Judah as his special people and who had promised kingship forever to the house of King David. Uzziah was the eleventh in the direct line of David's descendants, the living symbol of Yahweh's promise to his people. And still, in spite of this, Uzziah the king had fallen victim to that most dreaded and feared of all diseases. As long as he lived he would be unclean, shunned, an exile from his own house, a victim of a fate more terrible than anything which had befallen any king who had ever ruled the kingdom.

Why?

It was the priests at Yahweh's Temple who were first to offer a definite answer. Certainly, they declared, with a tone of finality that would brook no opposition, Uzziah must have done something to offend Yahweh. And what could that have been? Why, on the very morning that his illness was discovered, he had been in the Temple burning incense upon Yahweh's altar. Presumptuous, that was what Uzziah was. Not content merely to be king, he would take upon himself the prerogatives of priest as well. Clearly, Yahweh was not going to tolerate such overbearing pride. The King's leprosy was the sign of Yahweh's wrath, the punishment he would have to bear for the rest of his days.

8

So be it. Who is to dispute that which so plainly seems the will of Yahweh?

And the nation resigned itself to Uzziah's unhappy fate, feeling inwardly assured that somehow in spite of what the old king would suffer, life in the kingdom of Judah would go on much as it had before.

Yahweh's will . . . indeed. There was in the finality of the answer a sense of comfort for a people seeking to understand the inexplicable, and the words of the priests were repeated innumerable times. But to those who really knew Uzziah, to his family who loved him not so much because he was king as because he was the center of life itself to them, the glib explanation of the men of the Temple was like salt in a deep wound. Yahweh, the just and merciful God, had dealt a blow that passed understanding, and the confidence of a family long schooled to trust their God without question was shaken to its foundations.

There was no one in all the world who adored Uzziah so much as the Lady Jerusha, his wife. Jerusha was a fervent woman. Through her long and prosperous life she had always been strong in her loyalty to Judah's God. Now, when faced with the fact of her husband's incurable illness, she could only cling to the hope that Yahweh would relent of his harsh judgment and work the miracle of healing upon her beloved. *If only Yahweh could be sufficiently moved to mercy* . . . Jerusha thought. And so, in alternate paroxysms of tears, screaming, and deathly silence, for three days now, ever since the terrible news had come, the king's wife had lain in sackcloth and ashes before her own private shrine to Yahweh, imploring him to heal Uzziah. On the first day, cautious attendants approached her with food, but she drove them away in a burst of tears and rage. "Be gone, you dogs, and let me alone till you have word that the King is well. You heard me. Out!"

So they left her in solitude.

At every footfall in the corridor, her heart quickened. *The news is coming . . . he has been healed.* Hope so sweet as to be almost unbearable would lay hold of her, only to vanish again as the sound

9

of steps receded into the distance. And now on the third day, the frenzied woman had reached a point of utter despair. Yahweh seemed oblivious to her prayers and wailings. This could only mean one thing: He must want more. "Oh Lord, oh Lord," she moaned in a frantic cry of agony, rising and staggering half-blindly to a little table nearby. Here was her jewel chest and in it a dagger. "Oh Yahweh, Lord, see how I pour out my blood for him!" Deliberately and without hesitation, she cut a deep gash in the soft flesh of her forearm. "My blood for his healing! See, see!" Twice, three times, she drew the sharp blade across her arm. Then shuddering with pain and fresh hope, she dragged herself back to the little shrine and collapsed before it on the floor, the dagger still in her hand.

For what seemed an eternity, the room was utterly silent save for the woman's faint yet labored breathing. Then . . . "Grandmother . . . ." It was a tiny whisper. A small boy on soft slippered feet had entered Jerusha's room and was kneeling by her side. The old lady opened her eyes and stared up at him as if he had come from another world. In these past days, her mind had somehow completely blotted out the fact of her grandson's very existence. But now here he was, her son Jotham's little lad, whom she had adopted as her own child since his mother's death the year before. He was seven years old, a deeply sensitive child, at times so much like herself in temperament that it amazed her.

Someone, perhaps one of the maids, had dressed him in a robe of sackcloth and smeared dark streaks of ashes upon his forehead as a sign of mourning. "I've been praying, too," he said. "Praying and praying, but I don't think Yahweh is going to do anything."

"Jehoahaz!" Jerusha's hands fastened like claws around the boy's wrists. "Don't you ever dare to say such a thing! Ever! Ever! Would you have Yahweh smite you too?"

Panic was written large in the child's wide brown eyes. "No, no, I didn't mean it," he gasped.

"Jehoahaz, do you love your grandfather?" The tone of Jerusha's voice suddenly changed from anger to pleading.

"Oh yes, oh yes." Since that terrible day when his mother died

10

giving birth to his little brother Maaseiah, there was no one in all the great palace whom Jehoahaz loved and trusted so much as Uzziah the king. His father, Jotham, visited him only rarely, and when he did there was an air of remoteness about him that all the little prince's longing for affection could not penetrate. As for his grandmother, she was so unpredictable he could never be sure if she would shout at him or caress him. Even when she was in one of her good moods, she was likely to torment him with her incessant reminders that he was a "half-breed," half Judean and half Ammonite, as if he were to be blamed for it. Oh, but with his grandfather . . . that was something different. Who had held him and comforted him on the night his mother died? Was it not Uzziah? Who came to see him almost every day? Who told him wonderful stories and brought him presents? Who took him down to the great audience hall and let him sit beside his royal throne while all the men of the court came and bowed before them? Oh surely, in all the world there was no grandfather so kind and good as King Uzziah. "I love him more than anything," said Prince Jehoahaz.

"Then if you really want to help him and want Yahweh to make him well, stay here and pray with me." Jerusha lifted the dagger. "Hold out your arms, Jehoahaz."

"No! No! Don't cut me!" He jerked wildly to free himself from Jerusha's grasp.

"Yes! You want Yahweh to feel sad and have mercy, don't you? You know, Yahweh can do whatever he chooses. If he sees us both shedding our blood for the king, Yahweh will certainly answer our prayers. See, I have already done it."

"Will it really work?"

"You must try. You must not doubt Yahweh's power," she answered. Deep chills ran through the little prince's body as his grandmother spoke. Yahweh was so great. . . . The boy ceased his struggling and looked at Jerusha with absolute trust. "I believe you," he said, closing his eyes and holding out his arms toward her. "I'll try to be brave."

"Pray child! Pray with all your heart!" Jerusha urged.

11

Once, twice, upon each arm the boy felt the sharp agony of his grandmother's dagger. He screamed wildly and great tears rolled down his cheeks. There was no shame in weeping, only he must not let himself continue to cry aloud for his own pain. Yahweh was looking and Yahweh was going to help.

"Pray, Jehoahaz!" Jerusha said sharply.

"Oh Lord our God, make my grandfather well, please, please! And when he is well, I will tell him how I helped him." The words flowed naturally from the boy's heart. "Please, Yahweh, please." And with all the unshaken confidence of early childhood, Jehoahaz collapsed on the floor before his grandmother's shrine to wait for Yahweh's answer.

It was long moments, perhaps half-an-hour later when the message from the king arrived. The bearer of the letter was Azrikam, a pleasant young man and one of Uzziah's most trusted household officials. Three of Jerusha's maids accompanied him into the precincts of her apartment, where ordinarily he would not have dared to venture.

"I have a message for my Lady Jerusha from His Majesty."

"He is well?" She sprang up from the floor with the grace and agility of a young girl. "Oh Yahweh! Oh Lord! Oh Lord!"

"My lady, no. He is no better. It would be a miracle if he were healed."

Jerusha and little Jehoahaz looked at the messenger in stunned silence. "Would you read his letter?" Azrikam held out the missive to Jerusha who grasped it eagerly and broke the seal, then stared unseeingly at its contents.

"You should know I can't read! Here, read it to me, Azrikam." She handed the letter back to him, her hands trembling violently.

And Azrikam read: "Uzziah the king to his Lady Jerusha: I feel certain that you have heard that my counselors are urging me to abdicate. I want you to know that that is something I shall never do. I do not know how long I shall live," Azrikam read on, "perhaps a few months, perhaps many years. But this I know. I must never see you or come near you again, for I am unclean and I would not have his affliction come upon you also. Jerusha,

12

my wife, if you would have release from the vows of our marriage, I grant it to you freely."

"After all these years," Jerusha gasped, "what does he think?" In the wake of that dreadful pronouncement, all her fervent hopes for Yahweh's mercy vanished. Deep sobs wracked her body and over and over she cried her husband's name.

At last, after long moments, she regained a semblance of composure. "Tell him this, Azrikam. . . . Tell him I have no desire for release. Tell him I will come to him and take care of him and live and die with him. Tell him I am not afraid of his uncleanliness."

"Aye, my lady, I will tell him."

Azrikam bowed respectfully and withdrew, while Jerusha returned to her place before Yahweh's shrine. "No more will I trust you, Yahweh! Never again! Never! Never!!" Her angry fists beat at the wall.

Jehoahaz watched the scene in wide-eyed horror. His grandmother had forgotten his presence, and, as her violence mounted, a stream of curses so terrible as to make him shudder flowed from her lips. He knew that he must get out, away from this dreadful place. Fearful, but determined, he stole a last glance at the frenzied, wailing woman who was his grandmother. Then, without a sound, he eased himself up from the floor and tiptoed across the room to the open door beyond. Outside, a wide expanse of the flat palace rooftop beckoned invitingly. Around a corner he sped, out of sight of his grandmother's apartment. Here was the bench where his mother sometimes used to sit on still, warm summer afternoons, drying her long hair in the sun. Such beautiful hair it was, he remembered, closing his eyes, gleaming fiery auburn like his own. Terrible waves of loneliness crept through his small body, loneliness for that precious mother whom he would never see again, loneliness for his grandfather, the king, who had suffered a fate worse even than death. *Now there is no one who cares about me*, he thought. The gashes upon his forearms throbbed. Unutterably sad, he threw himself down beside his mother's bench, hugged the cold stone, and wept.

And then, into the stillness, came thoughts so frightening as

13

to be almost unbearable, terrors that no little child should have to bear. In his sheltered, carefully protected life, the young prince had never seen a leper. But in these last three days he had heard so much that he was able to visualize a thousand horrors of the disease. He could see his grandfather deformed, blind, and helpless as he surely would be in time. *Yahweh did it*, he thought. *And Yahweh refused to hear our prayers to cure him. Oh, how can anyone know what God wants when he does things like this? What if he should strike me with leprosy too?* This last thought was perhaps the most dreadful of all.

If there had been anyone in the world whom Jehoahaz could trust, he would have run to that person and poured out his fears. But he knew there was no one.

Overhead, the spring sunshine beamed down in golden radiance, but little Jehoahaz neither saw nor felt it. He was icy cold and he was utterly and completely alone.

* * * * *

How long he stayed there, he never knew. Probably it was just a matter of minutes but it seemed an eternity. He was still there when Ushna the Ammonite found him, a disconsolate little heap of coarse brown sackcloth and auburn curls.

"My prince . . . ." The boy looked up shyly at the Ammonite stranger who knelt beside him. "You are my Prince Jehoahaz, are you not?" Ushna said, laying his hand upon the child's curly head. Of course, there could be no doubting it; the boy's features were the image of his mother's. *The son she might have borne me*, Ushna thought, and a piercing memory of the Ammonite woman who had been Jotham's bride darted through his mind.

For a moment Jehoahaz said nothing; his eyes were intent upon Ushna's face. It was an ugly face, fat, smooth, and beardless. A few straggly wisps of black hair fringed the Ammonite's head; otherwise he was quite bald. There were very tiny golden earrings in his ears. His eyes were jet black, round and beady, gleaming with a look of ill-disguised smugness. Yet, despite his looks, his voice was not unkind.

"My mother called me Ahaz," the boy said at last. Tears hovered in the corners of his eyes, but he was making a great effort to hold them back.

"Ahaz," Ushna repeated. "Are you hungry?"

"No," only the slightest shake of his head. Ushna's little display of kindness after all the dreadful things that had happened lately was too much for him. "I don't feel good!" he sobbed, throwing his arms around the Ammonite's wide waist. "Yahweh wouldn't . . . ." A great sob convulsed him and the words would not come. If the childless Ushna was nonplussed, it was only for a moment. *Molech, my god, what is this opportunity you have sent me?* he thought. *The heir of the Crown Prince Jotham.*

"Look at me, my boy," Ushna said aloud and his hand beneath Ahaz's chin forced him to look up. "Yahweh is not the *only* god. You have Ammonite blood in you, Ahaz, and there is a god of Ammon who watches over his own." The priest's voice was very solemn and Ahaz tingled with excited fear.

"Molech," he said. "My mother had him in a little box and she used to pray to him, and I did too. But when she died, my grandmother found Molech and broke him." A sudden vivid memory came to him of Jerusha's smashing the little statuette which had been found among his mother's possessions. "But I'm not an Ammonite," he added in protest. "I'm a Judean." As much as he had loved his mother, Jerusha's jibes of "half-breed" made him quick to disclaim any connection with the land of Ammon. "See, I have the Star of the House of David on me." Ahaz held out his arm, pointing proudly to the unmistakable symbol of Judah's royalty. In accordance with a centuries-old custom, the symbol had been cut into his flesh just slightly above the veins of his left wrist and darkened in order to leave a permanent mark. "My father put it on me a long time ago," he explained. "It is a sign that I am a prince forever—a prince of Judah, not Ammon."

Ushna scarcely looked at the royal mark. He saw instead the

15

fresh gashes of Jerusha's dagger. "You've been hurt," he said. "You come with me and I'll put some ointment on these places so they will heal fast."

"My grandmother said Yahweh would see our blood and have mercy," he explained, as they walked across the rooftop and down to a courtyard below.

"And it did not work, did it?"

Ahaz shook his head. "I think Yahweh must hate us. He does. I know he does."

"Indeed so," said Ushna. "He is angry with the entire House of David. But when we get to my rooms, I have a secret to tell you."

The fear in the small boy's heart began to give way to hope. Now across another courtyard and through one of the long, seemingly interminable covered walkways that joined the scattered buildings of the great palace under a single roof. Then, more stairs, up to the top of a great tower. As Ushna unbolted the door to his apartment, a world of undreamed-of wonders opened before the boy's eyes. Ahaz was accustomed to royal splendor, but he lived in surroundings where light and brightness prevailed, where rooftops and windows and open porches welcomed the rays of the warm Judean sun. Ushna's apartment was different. It was very dark and the air was heavy with incense. Shelves against the walls were laden with jugs and bowls, full, no doubt, of the most diverse and marvelous medicines. Mysterious instruments ("for probing into the secrets of the future," Ushna explained) were scattered about, and there were boxes upon boxes full of scrolls and clay tablets. There was something frightening about the place, yet the magnetic presence of Ushna so dominated the scene that there appeared no need to fear.

"Did you know my mother?" Ahaz whispered.

"From a distance only," Ushna answered. "She was a great princess of Ammon and I only the humble servant of Ammon's god." It would not do to tell the prince too much.

Ahaz thought back and it seemed he could remember his mother speaking of Ushna. "He is a great wise man; very skilled in secrets

16

of medicine and astrology. Very wise and very lonely." Was that what she had said? She had been gone so long now, it was hard to remember. Ahaz's eyes roamed the shelves of Ushna's mysterious treasures.

"Come here now and let me rub something on your arms," Ushna was saying. He fumbled about for a little vial of healing oil, then seated himself on a low couch in one corner of the room and motioned Ahaz to his side.

The priest's hands upon Ahaz's arms were gentle and the ointment soothing to his hurts. "Now would you know my secret?" Ushna asked. Ahaz nodded, and the Ammonite went on in a voice marvelous to hear. "I was praying before Molech just a little while ago, my Prince, and as I prayed Molech spoke to me, a message about you. He said, 'Ushna, my servant, go up on the roof and there you will find my child, Ahaz. Go and bring him to me.' "

"And so you came?"

"I came." Uneasily, Ushna felt in his girdle the crackle of a small, neatly rolled sheet of papyrus. It was a message he had been on his way to deliver to the chief of Jerusha's household staff. It could wait; it would have to. "I always obey the voice of Molech," he said.

"Does Molech ever do cruel things?" Ahaz asked. "Like . . . you know . . . ." He could not bring himself to utter the words, but it was clear that he spoke of his grandfather.

"Never, if you serve him faithfully," Ushna replied solemnly. "To those who dedicate themselves to him, who give him what he demands, he is always merciful."

"Then I will dedicate myself to him," said Ahaz, the prince of Judah. "He will be my god forever."

Ushna's beady eyes glistened. This triumph was easy, almost too easy. The child must be made to understand that his acceptance of Molech was no game; it was a serious matter, serious as life and death. For the next few moments, Ushna talked on in his soft, solemn voice of Molech's ways and his not-to-be-doubted interest in Ahaz's welfare. Even as he spoke, Ushna could feel the words taking root in the boy's mind. "And now," Ushna said at

17

last, "are you ready to go in and see Molech yourself?" He rose from the couch and moved toward the heavy draperies at the far end of the room. "We will go in together, and I want you to kneel before him and consecrate yourself to him. I will tell you the words to say."

Obediently, without a word, Ahaz rose.

The inner room of Ushna's apartment was windowless and completely dark save for a little fire that burned before a small bronze idol. Ushna's voiced dropped to a whisper. "The great one of Ammon sees you, my child, and he is ready to accept you as his own." The priest's hand grasped the hand of the little prince of Judah and placed it upon Molech's feet.

Through the darkness, Ahaz fastened his gaze upon the eyes of the statue and the god seemed to be looking into the depths of his heart. "Repeat after me," Ushna intoned. "Oh Molech, Lord of Ammon, I, Ahaz ben-Jotham, give myself to you and you alone, flesh and spirit, while my life endures." There was security and hope and indescribable excitement in the words and the child whispered them gladly. "If I turn from you, may I be smote with misery and early death . . . ."

"Hear him, oh Molech, and receive him," Ushna added imploringly; then gazing through the darkness he murmured, "You have been heard, my son."

"I will never fail him," Ahaz said, rising.

The two of them left the shrine and Ushna led Ahaz to the exit. "Of course, you must not tell your grandmother about Molech," he commented, with a note of dismissal in his tone.

"Oh no!" Ahaz understood that perfectly, but he ignored the Ammonite's obvious desire for him to leave. "Ushna, let me stay with you forever! My grandmother's going to go out to my grandfather, and the maids don't want me. They always have so much to do, taking care of my little brother . . . ." For one glorious moment, he allowed himself to think that Ushna would agree, but the Ammonite of course could consent to no such reckless promise.

"You come to see me whenever you can," Ushna said, "and

18

don't forget wherever you are, whatever you do, Molech will always be your protector from this day on."

"Always and always," said Ahaz, and he meant it with all the sincerity of his young heart.

* * * * *

The silence hung heavy in Ushna's apartment when little Ahaz had gone. The Ammonite priest sighed heavily and turned his steps back to the shrine where he knelt before his god. He did not pray; but his mind whirled with a thousand thoughts of past and future, of Ahaz's mother whom he had loved, and of her son who would one day be king of Judah and who might well become so dependent on Ushna's counseling as to make him a tool in his hands. The Ammonite was a complex man. He realized his longing for power and he did not try to deny it. But he felt too, in his concern for the son of his lost lady, there was a chance to do some service for that lady's memory.

Perhaps, from the dim reaches where her spirit wandered in the nether world of Sheol, the princess of Ammon had intervened to see that her little son would grow up with an awareness of Ammon's god. And for this service, she had chosen Ushna. She, who had rejected him in life, was calling to him now from beyond the grave, giving her child into his care. Ushna felt a deep sense of self-satisfaction and vindication.

Not for a moment would he have admitted, even to himself, the emotion that ran still deeper in his heart: a covert hatred both of Ahaz's mother and of Ahaz himself, the one because his love for her had led him only to shame and disillusionment, the other because he was the child borne by his lady to another man. Unable to pray, Ushna at length rose from before the idol of his god, haunted by ominous forebodings.

19

Time passed. The months turned to years. Uzziah, the leper king, still lived on in his lonely seclusion, while from the splendid palace on Mount Zion, Prince Jotham the regent ruled over the land of Judah. The long hot summers and gray rainy winters followed each other in monotonous succession. The land was at peace, and in spite of the old king's incurable illness, people said that Yahweh had smiled again upon his chosen people. And as the years passed, the child Ahaz grew to young manhood. His natural longing for affection suppressed, he had become very reticent to express his feelings. His inwardness was such that not even Ushna, who believed he knew the boy well, really guessed the emotions that stirred in the young prince's heart. Ahaz was haunted by fears: fears of his own future and of the mysterious power that had stricken his grandfather with the most loathed of all diseases. But all these were things too horrible to mention to any living soul. Only to Molech, the fierce god of the glowing fires, did he dare to turn with all his deep longing for love and protection. Molech was the god of Ammon, god of the mother he would never forget. As he grew, Ahaz had learned to take a fierce pride in his Ammonite blood. Like his fiery auburn hair, it was a part of his heritage from his mother; something that set him apart from most men of Judah, and made him special in Molech's eyes.

Ushna taught Ahaz about the many gods and remained amazed at the boy's obviously sincere and singlehearted devotion to Molech. Most Judeans who were untrue to Yahweh followed the old native fertility gods: Baal and his consort Ashtoreth. In groves and at "high places" throughout the kingdom their worship with all its lewd, orgiastic rites, had gone on for hundreds of years. Zealous reforming kings like old Uzziah had tried to stop it with little visible results. Yahweh's prophets for generations had preached against it. "It is a part of nature," Ushna would say. "It can no more be stopped than the winter rains and the summer drought."

Ahaz agreed: Baal and Ashtoreth must have their place as divine guardians of fertility in man and beast and field. Yahweh had a place, too. Ahaz never denied that. Yahweh was Judah's national protector, a great help in battle, or so it was said. The growing prince had to study the military arts. He practiced his swordsmanship and his archery, exhibiting considerable skill, and silently prayed to his Molech that he might never have to go to war at all.

This hope, at least, seemed likely to be fulfilled, for the years of Ahaz's early adolescence were a peaceful time for Judah. For the folk of the court, the seasons were best marked by the regent's daily walks. In the summer one could see Prince Jotham daily pacing up and down the winding walkways in his inner garden and in the winter round and round his royal council hall.

Such daily walks were routine with Jotham. He was a man capable of boundless energy, an energy that hated to confine itself to long hours with his council or in the audience chamber. He would have vastly preferred to be leading the armies of his nation on some rich plundering expedition against neighboring territory. But directives from Uzziah urged him to keep Judah at peace, and Jotham was a dutiful, obedient son.

And now, nine years of Jotham's regency had come and gone. It was a dry, still afternoon like countless other afternoons beneath the hot Judean sun, and the prince regent was walking in his garden. At his side was his mother, Jerusha. Heedless of her pleas, Uzziah had never permitted her to join him, and through the long years of her semiwidowhood, she had found a solace of sorts through cultivation of an avid interest in affairs of state. The whole court stood a little in awe of her, for in spite of the apparent frailty of her aging body, the regent's mother was as strong willed and determined as a young warrior. Jotham's decisions were never made

21

without first seeking her approval, and indeed her hold upon the government of Judah was such as to cause the frequent whisper that the true regent was Uzziah's wife and not his son.

"I am weary, Son." Jerusha sank down on a little bench and pushed a few loose wisps of lifeless gray hair beneath her veil. Jotham sat down for a moment at his mother's side, but then was up and walking again, the long skirts of his robe rustling vigorously. Jerusha stared up at him with a piercing gaze. She had borne several children to Uzziah, but Jotham was the only one to reach maturity. In many ways he had always been a riddle to her. She loved him, yes, but there was much about him that was rather disappointing. *So unprincely,* she thought. Jotham was a big man, strong and powerfully built, and with a bit of effort he could have been magnificent. Indeed when he was younger, he had been strikingly handsome. But during his years as regent, he had let himself become fat and seemed to have lost all interest in his appearance. Jerusha's eyes roved from the traces of dirt beneath his fingernails to a few spots of yesterday evening's wine that soiled the front of his ill-fitting robe. *So unlike his father,* she thought.

"Jotham, tell me the truth," she said aloud. "You look worried, and there's not a thing under the sun that you should be worrying about." Her voice trailed off without enthusiasm.

Jotham was willing enough to unburden himself once Jerusha had opened the matter. "It is Ushna the Ammonite. Jehoahaz seems to be spending far too much time in his company. I have thought about ordering the fellow out of the country, but I am afraid it would cause repercussions."

"And what is wrong with Ushna?" Jerusha countered halfheartedly. "He's the only one around here who has ever been able to do much with our Ahaz. As you know, he's made him into quite a scholar, taught him to read and write, taught him astronomy, and now they are in the midst of this sun-clock project. Is there anything so wrong with that?"

"You've seen what the two of them put up on the roof beside my son's apartment?"

"Molech," Jerusha smiled. "So Ushna and Ahaz have finally

22

set up a little idol of their god in broad daylight. Ah my son, there was a time when I would have been most distressed over that, but really when you stop to think, there's no harm in a man having some sort of god to rely on if he can. At least Molech has never done anything against us."

"But Molech is a god of Ammon, not Judah! A foreign god on the roof of my own house!"

"Well, your son's half Ammonite himself, you remember. And as for Molech, he's been there several weeks. Are you just now seeing him? Besides that, this thing has been coming on for a long time, years I'd say. You don't think those two spend all their time talking about sun-clocks, do you? A boy like Ahaz is going to wonder about many things, about the gods, and you can guess what Ushna must have told him."

"You should have let me know." Jotham was clearly shaken. He almost never visited his son and consequently had discovered the idol's presence only that morning. A look of haggard confusion crossed his face. "I do not dare to risk offense to the god of Ammon." His voice dropped to a whisper. "Molech is powerful, you know that."

Jerusha shrugged. Jotham was by practice a loyal son of Yahweh, but his theology was not uncolored by cautious respect for any and all other gods. "Then it seems to me that what Ahaz really needs is something to get his mind off of Molech," Jerusha said.

"A military expedition? He's nearly sixteen. He's certainly old enough to have seen a little service in the field." The regent's tone brightened tremendously. "We've gone to such trouble to see that he's had thorough training in arms, and to tell you the truth, while he's able enough, his teachers tell me he's most unenthusiastic about it all. I think it would be a different matter if he could get a taste of real combat. The Ammonites keep raiding along the Dead Sea."

"No," Jerusha said with finality. "You know that the king says to preserve the peace. However, there is another possibility. We could get Ahaz a woman." The last sentence was spoken lightly. The old lady's dark eyes sparkled with enthusiasm.

23

"Our Jehoahaz!" Jotham almost shouted. "Mother, you forget how young he is!"

"My son, you know well enough that you were as young as he is now when you had your first one and so was your father. It's about time Ahaz was getting someone to keep him happy. He is young; chances are we wouldn't want him to take her as a legal wife, but there will be plenty of time for that later. All he needs now is some fascinating little creature to take his mind off of Molech and Ushna."

"I suppose that you have someone in mind as a likely prospect," Jotham commented unenthusiastically.

"No, I'm afraid not. Son, how can you expect me to know anything about the eligible young ladies of Jerusalem when I never go out any more? I never see anyone outside this palace." The smile faded from Jerusha's face and her voice rose in a high-pitched, self-pitying whine.

Jotham forced a polite laugh. "As if that's not enough. This place is swarming with people every day." His plump, bejeweled hand tugged thoughtfully at his beard. "I am getting an idea, Mother. Zechariah the priest was telling me a few days ago about his daughter. She's about the same age as Jehoahaz, and if she is all her father describes her to be, she must be a real beauty."

"Hmmm, Zechariah." Jerusha knew him well. He was one of the priests at Yahweh's Temple, dutiful but pleasant, perhaps a bit too talkative, but with enough good sense never to mention the worship of Yahweh in her presence. "They are a suitable family," she commented. "Not so rich as to protest selling us the girl or expect we'll make her his chief wife, yet not so poor as to be common. We could at least investigate. Coming from that background, she is probably a firm believer in Yahweh, but one that young can have her mind changed easily enough."

Jotham did not reply immediately. He did not share his mother's antipathy to the time-honored religion of Judah, but he had learned never to express opinions which ran counter to hers. It was no use, he had discovered long ago. "I'll tell Zechariah I am interested in getting the girl for Jehoahaz," he said at last. "And I'll have

24

him bring her here where he can look her over."

"Well, enough, do it," Jerusha's voice brightened again. "Speak to him about it tomorrow morning. No, wait. I have a better idea. You could send Azrikam down to have a look at her. If she's not, let us say, suitable, we won't have committed ourselves and can look elsewhere."

Jotham seemed pleased. As always, Jerusha had been more practical and foresighted than he. He was glad enough to accept her suggestion.

"It will be good to have another woman about for me to talk to," his mother was saying. "My son, you cannot imagine how lonely I am sometimes. Of course, there are those concubines of yours, but . . ."

"I know, Mother." It was a familiar refrain. Jotham had not taken a legal wife since he had lost his Ammonite princess years before. He kept a small harem of slave girls, all of whom seemed uniformly unable to get along with the domineering Jerusha and avoided her as much as possible. It would probably be the same with any girl they would get for Ahaz, but that was a problem that could be tackled later. "Yes indeed, Mother," he sighed. "I'll send for Azrikam right away and he can get a look at Zechariah's daughter this evening."

Thus were spun the first threads of the web of fate in which Abijah the daughter of Zechariah and Prince Ahaz ben-Jotham were so soon to be entangled.

* * * * *

Meanwhile, on the roof of a far wing of the palace, young Ahaz, the principal subject of Jerusha's enthusiastic planning, relaxed, half-sitting, half-reclining on a couch laden with a huge pile of pillows. Jotham's son was an attractive youth. Though only of medium height, he was well-proportioned and possessed a princely grace that bespoke his royal background. His hair, which according to current fashion hung almost to his shoulders, was a cloud of magnificent wavy auburn framing the finely-molded features of his

25

face. Most striking of all were his eyes; they were a deep radiant brown, with just the faintest hint of golden lights in them, sparkling like rare jewels when he was happy.

Ahaz was happy today. Propped against his knees was a large board spread with a thick coating of wax on which he was carving patterns for the designs which would adorn the walls of his sun-clock. "I'm almost finished, Ushna," he said to the Ammonite who lolled luxuriously on a nearby couch. There was nothing that gave the young prince more pleasure than artwork. What if it were an unsuitable occupation for one of royal birth? What if it were properly the work of hired artisans or slaves? Ahaz possessed a definite knack for creating pictures, and who was Ushna to stop him? The sun-clock they proposed to build would be a tall, stair-like structure in the outer courtyard, with a gnomon at its top for measuring the shadow of the sun. Its flat sides would be ideal for carved reliefs.

"Look." Ahaz lifted the tablet and held it across to Ushna.

"Excellent, magnificent." The Ammonite was scarcely looking at the youth's work.

"This just shows one panel," Ahaz explained, rising and hovering over his work protectively. "See, this is the procession marching up to the sanctuary of Molech. Only my father will think it's a sanctuary of Yahweh." Ahaz's fingers, touching the carved tablet were long and slender. A ring with a deep green stone, the only jewel which he wore, sparkled on the little finger of his right hand. In the center of the stone, letters of gold spelled out his nickname, *Ahaz*, which he so vastly preferred to the true name his father had given him.

Ushna smiled up into his young master's eyes. "Magnificent indeed. And Molech never doubts our good intentions, even when they must remain secret." The Ammonite's voice was solemn. Ahaz's fervor for Molech was much more intense than his own, and sometimes it was hard to keep the façade of being Molech's humble servant. Ushna sighed. He thought back through the years to the day when he had first won the trust of the young prince of Judah. How much had happened since then! Ushna had soon

26

learned what to expect from Ahaz and how to remain in his good graces. The boy was quick-tempered and easily given to anger, yet these sudden storms usually passed rapidly, for Ahaz possessed a deep longing to please those around him. Ushna was aware also that there were certain subjects which Ahaz could never bring himself to mention. One was his grandfather's illness. Another was the tragedy of Ushna's own past, a story which he told Ahaz when the prince was still very small.

Ushna was a eunuch. The dreadful penalty of castration had been inflicted upon him when he was a young man, by order of the King of Ammon, for Ushna had been caught trying to enter the apartment of the princess, that princess who shortly thereafter was sent to Judah to be Prince Jotham's bride. "And although she was lost to me forever, I followed among her servants to her new country." Ushna remembered how difficult it had been to try to explain to the young prince why, in spite of all that had happened, he had felt himself drawn to Judah. Ahaz seemed horror-stricken by the story and had never questioned him further on the matter.

"By the way," Ushna remarked, suddenly recalling his thoughts to the present, "has your father said anything about our shrine?" Across the rooftop stood a little altar for incense and before it the small, highly polished bronze idol of Molech that had aroused Jotham's ire just that morning.

"Nothing," said Ahaz. "He was here this morning, but you know how he is. He never knows what is happening."

Ushna turned his attention back to the tablet and tried hard to banish the sense of impending catastrophe which had suddenly come over him. Jotham was a mild man and not one to interfere with the gods, he reminded himself. As for Ahaz, it would take more than a little fatherly disapproval to break Molech's claims upon him. Had Ushna not worked diligently for nine years to inculcate in him devotion to the god of Ammon? And was not Ahaz a most willing devotee of his heavenly patron? In these assurances, Ushna took comfort, never dreaming of the very human rival so soon to enter the contest for Ahaz's heart.

27

* * * * *

"It is understood then, Azrikam?" Jotham's satisfaction with the well-planned scheme was obvious. Before him stood his most trusted officer, Azrikam, who had once carried Uzziah's letter to Jerusha and who now had risen to the post of royal steward, "commander of the palace." Azrikam, a man of great dignity and courtly elegance, had donned the simple garb of a shepherd and was ready to perform his master's orders. "You will be at the well by the north gate this evening at the time when the women go out to draw water," Jotham reiterated the plan with thorough enjoyment.

"I understand perfectly, sir." Azrikam smiled knowingly. "Then I ask one of the older women if the daughter of Zechariah the priest is there, and if she is, I will observe whether or not she seems suitable for our purposes."

"You must not let her realize who you are," Jerusha reminded sharply. "Not under any circumstances."

"Of course, my Lady." Azrikam realized his responsibility thoroughly. During his years at the court, he had performed numerous missions for the royal family, but never one which promised to be as uniquely interesting as this one. "I am reminded," he said, "of the old story of how our forefather Isaac met Rebekah. He sent a servant to the well to watch for her."

Jotham smiled vaguely. "Let us hope Zechariah's daughter is there," he said. "That priest has assured me innumerable times that he does not let his children shirk their responsibilities. And now, I would say, Azrikam, it is not too early for you to be on your way," Jotham added solemnly. "May Yahweh go with you and grant you success."

"Yes," Jerusha commented. "May *all* the gods help you, that is, if they help anyone."

Azrikam withdrew from the hall, too intent on his mission to be much disturbed by Jerusha's bitterness. It was no secret that Jerusha in anger and disillusionment over her unanswered prayers for Uzziah had rejected the ancient God of Judah and Israel and had made up her mind to live the rest of her life without relying upon any god. *Strange,* Azrikam mused as he trudged along the dusky street in the direction of the north gate, *that she and Jotham would pick out a priest's daughter for Ahaz.* But then incongruity was a basic part of Jerusha's nature and something simply to be accepted without question.

Oblivious to the plans which so soon would involve her, Abijah, the daughter of Zechariah, went about her chores as she did every evening. Zechariah was rich enough to have servants; there were several in the household. But, as he so often reminded anyone who would listen, he was old-fashioned enough to believe that work was good for his children, too. Abijah shouldered a clay water jug cheerfully, grasped another in her hand, and started toward the neighborhood well, humming a little tune to herself. As the oldest of Zechariah's children, she had long been accustomed to bearing responsibilities. Scarcely fifteen, she was mature beyond her years, a second mother to her seven younger brothers and sisters, all of whom adored her.

No one had ever yet told Abijah that she was beautiful. Delicate as an early spring flower, she was entirely unaware that she was unusually pretty. Her face was a perfect oval; her eyes a warm, deep brown, sparkling with a rare attracting radiance and accented by long dark lashes. This evening the heavy mass of jet black hair, which was coiled in careful braids around her head, was covered by a transparent yellow veil.

So this is Abijah. From a safe distance, the commander of the palace watched the girl who had been pointed out to him. She had seated herself with a number of other girls on the old stone bench that circled the outside of the well. Azrikam heard their lively chatter but made no attempt to catch the import of their conversation. He saw Abijah smile; he saw her gesture gracefully, happily describing some little event of the day. *She is exquisite,* he thought, *perfect for Prince Ahaz. Or is she?* His delight in his discovery of the lovely girl was suddenly eclipsed by the thought of the changes that would be wrought in her by life at the palace. She would be deprived of friends and family and closely guarded. She would spend her days with no other company than the grouchy

29

old Jerusha or Jotham's harem girls. And, most perplexing of all, what could a radiant girl like Abijah possibly have in common with the temperamental, overly sensitive, frequently moody Prince Ahaz? Of course, no one dared to consider these factors, Azrikam told himself sternly. It was a great honor for any girl to be bought as a prince's woman, especially his first one. Ahaz just might develop a special partiality for her, especially if she bore him a son before he had the chance to take other concubines or wives. *Who knows?* thought Azrikam, *through her Yahweh might choose to work great things for the kingdom of Judah.* And the thought was most steadying.

* * * * *

"Abijah, that man over there is staring at you." One of the girls nudged her, knowingly.

"Don't be silly. He would not be looking at me," Abijah said, hastily pulling her veil over her face at the same time for the sake of caution. "Which way?" she added in a subdued whisper.

"Over yonder," the other girl nodded as Abijah cast a quick glance in Azrikam's direction. The staunch commander of the palace hastily averted his gaze and turned to leave.

"Who is he?" Abijah asked.

"How should I know?" her companion giggled. "Anyway, Abijah, he's old enough to be your father and he's probably got a wife or two and flock of children already."

"I was just wondering." Abijah's voice was cool. "A girl can wonder, can't she?"

"If I didn't know better, I'd say it was the regent's henchman, Azrikam," a third girl volunteered. "Of course, he wouldn't be down here by the well, but I saw him once up right close and it looked just like him."

"No, it couldn't be," Abijah spoke confidently, as if dismissing a story too fantastic to deserve any further consideration. But her eyes followed him as he trudged off down the road and a strange, foreboding feeling churned her heart. The walk home seemed unusually long that evening and the water jugs unusually heavy. Abijah's brain whirled. What if the stranger had been Azrikam? What was he doing disguised as a simple shepherd? Why had he turned to leave so quickly when she looked in his direction? *Abijah, you are a foolish girl,* she told herself, half-aloud. *He was only some boorish country fellow. Stop thinking about him. You'll never see him again, and you wouldn't want to, anyway.*

* * * * *

Azrikam's report when he returned to his royal master the next morning was glowingly enthusiastic. Jotham and Jerusha lost no time in planning their next move, and a letter was drawn up to be dispatched to the priest Zechariah. Azrikam himself, this time accompanied by several slaves, was entrusted with delivery of the royal missive.

When the chariot of the commander of the palace pulled up before Zechariah's house that afternoon, Abijah was watching through the cracks in the window lattice. And the memories of the stranger whom she had seen by the well the evening before came flooding back into her mind. The elegant, splendidly dressed man in the chariot was indeed identical with the shepherd she had seen hovering about the well. With her heart fluttering wildly, she rushed to the door to admit him.

"Tidings from His Highness, the Prince Regent, for Zechariah the priest," announced Azrikam bowing ceremoniously.

"I will call him." Abijah's voice was low-pitched and gentle. Once again, Azrikam felt a wave of uneasiness at the thought of this lovely girl's possible induction into palace life. What was this thing he had done, telling Jotham and Jerusha that she was most suitable?

Abijah disappeared into the curtained-off chamber adjoining the entry hall. A moment later Zechariah emerged alone and accepted the waxed tablet bearing Jotham's message. Azrikam could not help but smile at the look of frightened astonishment which crossed the priest's face. "Do not fear, my friend," he said. "This may

31

be the greatest honor that has ever come to your house. I shall be waiting for you by the outer gate of the palace at the appointed time tomorrow." With that, the regent's messenger withdrew as suddenly as he had come.

The moment Azrikam left, Abijah and her mother, who had been watching the whole scene through the curtains of the adjoining room, rushed back into the entry hall. "What does it say?" Zechariah's wife inquired fearfully. "Read it!"

Still half-dazed from this unexpected turn of events, the priest read: "Jotham ben-Uzziah, Prince Regent who is over the House of Judah, to Zechariah the priest, greeting and peace be with you. It has come to our attention that you have a virgin daughter, Abijah by name. It is our royal wish that you present her at the palace tomorrow afternoon. We are considering the purchase of a concubine for our son, Prince Jehoahaz."

"Not really!" Abijah's mother, who could not read, peered unbelievingly at the tablet in her husband's hands. "Jehoahaz. He is the handsome one with the auburn hair. We have seen him in processions. Remember, last year after the New Year festival, when he rode with his father through the streets and everyone cheered so? Oh my daughter, I cannot believe it! How do you suppose Jotham knew about you? Zechariah, have you been talking to the regent about Abijah? Do you think they'll take her after they see her?" Abijah's mother fluttered about, too excited to stop for a breath. "Oh my little one," she said hugging Abijah tightly. "This is so wonderful, such unhoped-for good fortune."

"I cannot believe it," Abijah said. No one noticed or seemed to care that her voice lacked her mother's enthusiasm.

"I suppose you can hardly wait to tell everyone." The proud mother was fairly bursting to share the news. Glorious visions of a rich, luxurious life for her eldest child floated through her mind.

"No," Abijah replied. "Not really. I would rather wait to see what happens tomorrow."

But it was impossible to keep a secret. Hearing the excitement, Abijah's younger brothers and sisters came scurrying in from all parts of the house and inner courtyard. Within an hour, all the

32

neighbors knew of Abijah's forthcoming trip to the palace and were exclaiming with enthusiasm to equal that of the delighted mother. A thousand questions were being flung at Abijah. "Is he going to marry you?" "Will there be a big wedding?" "Will you live in the palace?" "Is he going to send you a lot of presents?" On and on. Abijah's brain whirled.

"Let's say we don't really know anything until tomorrow."

"But what *is* a concubine?" demanded one of Abijah's little sisters, persistent and not to be easily silenced.

"It is just like a wife," the mother tried to explain. "Except instead of having a betrothal and a wedding, the man just gives the girl's father some money and signs a contract of purchase. Oh, there are many different ways to do it. The regent will work it out."

It is not just like a wife, Abijah thought miserably. *A prince, a king, takes many concubines, and when he grows tired of one she is locked away in the harem and forgotten.* All her life Abijah had looked forward to the day when she would be a wife and mother like her own mother, the center of a warm and loving family. But the message from the palace suddenly had shattered the dreams she had cherished and raised a most unhappy vision in their stead. Riches did not matter to Abijah. She knew what she wanted and now, if she were accepted at the palace, it was beyond her reach forever. She longed to weep, but instead she merely sat silent while excited family and neighbors chattered on happily.

Only Abijah, it seemed, of all people who knew of the regent's request, failed to exhibit pleasure over it.

But then, Prince Ahaz himself still knew nothing of the plan.

As Jotham had commanded, the day after Azrikam delivered the message, Zechariah brought his daughter to the palace. Abijah was arrayed in her most elegant finery—a new dress which she had planned to save for the forthcoming New Year festival, elaborately embroidered around the hem and the edges of the sleeves. It was the serene blue of the Judean sky, with a sash of soft rose pink. A veil of light blue covered her hair and draped over her face. Only her deep brown eyes and her dainty hands were visible as silently she moved down the streets of the city by her father's side. Zechariah in his priestly robes was a splendidly impressive figure. The fatherly pride radiating from his face was a sharp contrast to the icy shivers that penetrated Abijah's heart.

Azrikam met them at the outside gate of the palace, bowed low with all the formality of a well-polished courtier, and asked the traditional, polite questions about Zechariah's health. To Abijah it seemed forever before the commander of the palace reached the all-important purpose of their visit. "The Regent and the Lady Jerusha are waiting to see the young maiden," he said at last. "When you go in," he turned to Abijah, "you must bow before Prince Jotham, like this." He prostrated himself upon the ground. "And stay till he tells you to rise," he added, springing up with admirable agility and grace. Abijah trembled. She was grateful for her veil and hoped Azrikam could not see the fear which she felt was plainly mirrored in her face.

"You know about the Lady Jerusha," Azrikam continued in an undertone. "She is not nearly so fierce as she sounds, little lady.

34

Just do not mention Yahweh and all will be well enough with her."

"But . . ." Abijah began to protest.

"Trust in him all you will," Azrikam pronounced with finality. "Only keep it a secret."

The chilled feeling that gripped her seemed to tighten its hold. Azrikam and Zechariah were moving on; slaves rushed to open the great carved folding doors of the royal audience chamber.

At the far end of the hall, high on a raised dais, were two thrones where Jotham and Jerusha sat side by side. It seemed an eternity before Abijah and her father and the commander of the palace reached the end of that long hall and made their bows at the regent's feet. Jotham promptly summoned Azrikam and Zechariah to rise but made no remark to the frightened girl. Abijah did not dare to move.

"Your Highnesses may see the maiden I have brought you," Azrikam announced ceremoniously.

Jotham nervously tapped his fingers on the arm of his chair. "Arise, girl," he said. "Take off that veil."

Abijah stood; her fingers fumbled nervously with the little clasp that held the veil in place. "Come now, how can I see your pretty face if you keep it covered up?" Jotham laughed loudly.

The veil dropped from Abijah's face and floated to rest upon her shoulders. "Hmmm . . . not bad," the regent remarked, studying her features intently. "What is she good for, Zechariah, besides the obvious, of course? Can she sing, play the lyre, dance, weave, embroider?"

Jotham had descended from the dais and was circling Abijah with a curious yet appreciative gaze. "She is very skillful, your highness," Zechariah was saying. "See the dress she is wearing—she made it herself; wove the cloth, stitched it, worked the embroidery. And her singing—like the sweet birds of springtime," the proud father continued. Abijah did not try to listen to his typically extravagant boasting. Her heart was beating far too wildly.

At that moment old Jerusha, who had hitherto been silent, opened her mouth. Her voice was loud, high-pitched, and extremely

35

shrill. "Has this daughter of yours any blemishes, Zechariah?" The words seemed to fill the great, almost empty hall. "We certainly don't want a woman with any defects to lie with our prince."

Zechariah was strongly shaking his head to indicate his daughter's lack of blemishes, but Jerusha apparently was not to be satisfied with mere parental assurance. "Come with me, child; I must be sure."

Startled, but respectful, Abijah followed without a word to a tiny curtained-off chamber adjoining the audience hall. "Disrobe," Jerusha commanded, and Abijah obeyed unquestioningly. The old woman scarcely glanced at her youthful but shapely form and flawless skin. "What do you think of the gods?" Jerusha intoned shrilly, laying her bony hand on Abijah's bare shoulder. *So this is why she wanted to get me off to herself,* the frightened girl thought. Azrikam's recent warning rang in her ears; she felt speechless, unable to answer.

"Come now, my girl, certainly you must think something, or would you have me believe you are like some other empty-headed women who never think at all?"

Abijah swallowed hard. "If what I have to say offends my lady, I am sorry. My lady knows that I am the child of a priest of Yahweh, and in our home no other god has ever been worshiped except the God of our nation." There, she had said it, and now perhaps Jerusha would turn her down and let her go home!

"Ha! You are still young and you do not know the ways of the gods, my dear," Jerusha was saying. "Now if Yahweh had dealt with you as he has dealt with me . . . ." The old woman broke off. Abijah was listening breathlessly. "When I was young, I believed as you," Jerusha began again. "But I have found out differently. You will change, too, in time, my girl." She gave a high, witch-like laugh. "In the meantime, I doubt if you'll do much harm to my Ahaz. He believes in his Molech; I believe in nothing. You can't change him any more than you can change me."

Abijah bent to pick up the dress that had fallen in a dejected blue heap upon the floor.

"When you're a woman of the palace, you'll have maids to dress

36

you every day. You'll have nothing on earth to worry about . . . ."
Jerusha's voice trailed on as Abijah fumbled with arranging the
soft folds of her skirt. *They are going to take me after all,* Abijah
thought.

"Now wait here, girl." In the next few moments Abijah was
left alone, while Jerusha returned to Jotham and Zechariah and
the three of them decided on the term of the contract. After a
time, Abijah heard her father calling her back into the hall.

"We are pleased with you," Jotham said, "and I trust my son
will be."

The dreadful finality of the regent's words gripped like hands
of ice about Abijah's heart. Something within her wanted to scream
out in protest, but one did not scream to the prince regent, even
when obedience meant, as now, the destruction of every hope and
dream of her young life. Meekly she sank once more in a low
curtsy before the regent's feet. "I am greatly honored," she said.

It was not until Abijah and her father returned to their own
house that either of them spoke again. The whole family had gathered to hear of their adventure at the palace and the excited happiness mirrored in their faces was too much for her. The misery
she felt could be held back no longer. "Oh, father," she said, slowly
and deliberately, her dark eyes blazing fires. "Please, can't you go
back and tell Prince Jotham that you think I am too young? Tell
him I was already betrothed to somone else. Tell him anything,
father, but don't make me go . . . ." Her voice broke. She was
very near to tears.

"Now, daughter, do you honestly think I can lie to the regent?"
Zechariah sighed. "And you are not too young. Most girls are
married by your age. As you saw yourself, I did not have any choice
in the matter; you must go." He was trying to be stern, but his
voice was filled with ill-concealed emotion.

"My little one, you must try to be proud that you have been
chosen." Abijah's mother put her arm around her and gave her
shoulder a reassuring pat. "After all, you do not really have to
love your prince. Just please him and he will give you everything
a woman can wish for."

Of all things, this was not what Abijah wanted to hear. "No, no, you do not understand. I want to love him, but how can I, when I know he will grow tired of me and take other women and I will have nothing? And besides that, he worships Molech." Abijah's mother ignored this last remark. "You'll have children," she bubbled on. "You're sure to have children. Look how many I've had. And think, daughter, *they* will be royalty!"

"Yes, and I no better than a slave! Oh, I don't want to go!"

Zechariah turned and faced his daughter sternly. "Child, it is time that you learned that women in this world do not say what they want to do." There was anger in his voice, an anger that covered his own burning resentment of the fact that even had he willed it, he would have been powerless to oppose the regent's choice. "You will belong to Prince Jehoahaz forever. They are giving me twenty silver shekels for you, and that is not a bad price these days. This makes you the Prince's property, his possession. Now you must accept that fact and make the best of it."

It was as if the walls were closing in on Abijah. Her face buried in her hands, she ran from the hall and threw herself down on her bed. The room was perfectly still except for her deep breathing. Moments that seemed like years passed.

Out in the kitchen, her mother and the younger girls were making ready for the evening meal. The distant murmur of their voices drifted into the little room. Outside, the soft hues of twilight filled the garden. A little breeze stirred the cypress trees in the inner courtyard and rustled the thin draperies at the window. At last, the girl sat up and gazed out the window. There was a peaceful greenness out there in the garden, touched by the pink-gold of the setting sun. The sight was so lovely that Abijah felt another twinge of tightness about her heart. And then, suddenly, a new thought swept over her, a thought so wonderful that the grief she felt about going to the palace seemed to melt away and in its place tingled a kind of excitement. "Yahweh wills it!" she said aloud. "I would not have been chosen at all were it not part of God's great plan!"

And the thought was most appealing. The strange turn of events that would make Abijah a prince's possession no longer seemed the end of everything. Instead it was an opportunity to carry out God's will. "O Yahweh, my Lord," Abijah knelt before the window. "Only help me to serve you without wavering!"

* * * * *

The day that the bargain for Abijah was made was the same day that Ahaz had the idea for the roof garden. "Ushna, why don't we have the slaves bring up some long boxes and plant shrubs and flowers in them up here on the roof? We could make a garden around Molech's shrine."

Of course Ushna had approved heartily of the idea and added his own suggestion that the expanded shrine would also be an ideal place to set up some of his astrological equipment. All afternoon the prince and the priest had worked enthusiastically drawing diagrams for the arrangement of their glorious scheme.

It was growing dark when a slave came to summon Ahaz to his father's audience chamber. The young prince was frightened. "He has seen Molech," he said, half to himself, half to Ushna. "He is going to make us move him."

"Do not fear," Ushna replied. "We know your father will not risk tampering with the god of Ammon." Ahaz walked to the interview with a prayer in his heart for Molech's protection.

One glance at his father's face told Ahaz that his fears had been needless. "Jehoahaz, my son," Jotham began with a twinkle in his eyes. "Your grandmother and I have a present for you."

"A very special present," Jerusha cackled.

Ahaz smiled vaguely. His grandmother was forever bombarding him with meaningless little gifts, most of which he had no earthly use for. "Should we make him guess?" Jerusha was saying. There was a childishness about her that irritated Ahaz tremendously at times.

"I have no idea, Grandmother."

Jerusha laughed. Ahaz did not know it, but for these few brief moments her almost constant grief for her husband Uzziah had left her mind completely. "I will give you a little hint," she said. " 'Tis something alive."

"A horse!" Now there was something he would really be glad to receive. There were dozens of horses in the royal stables, but not one that was really, specially his. Without wanting to Ahaz had blurted out a guess. Jerusha and Jotham both rocked with laughter and delightedly Jerusha seized upon the mistake.

"She has big brown eyes and a long black mane." The old lady was obviously enjoying adding to Ahaz's bewilderment. "And her name is Abijah."

"Abijah!" The name signified "child of Yahweh." It was an exceptionally popular name for both men and women, Ahaz knew. But for a horse! It would be a sacrilege. Even if one were not devoted to Yahweh, there was no use to provoke him. "I'll not call my horse such a thing," Ahaz declared.

Jerusha chortled with glee. "Abijah is a woman, my son," Jotham explained. "The daughter of Zechariah the priest." The prince's face went white; anger and disgust welled up within him. His grandmother laughed more loudly than ever. "We really fooled him, didn't we, Jotham? You did not expect a concubine, did you, Ahaz? Well, she's prettier than any horse, I'll wager, and a great deal more fun."

Ahaz did not answer immediately. Certainly he was not so young that he had not felt strange, restless longings stirring inside him; not so young that he had not looked with tingling gratification at the graceful figure of some passing slave girl and wondered what it would be like to press a woman in his arms and feel the warmth of her body against his. There were times when he would awaken in the dark stillness of the night when he allowed such thoughts to whirl unrepressed through his brain. Yet, forever creeping in to spoil the pleasure of such dreaming was the image of Jerusha, the woman he knew best, Jerusha, the high-strung, whining bundle of complaints and self-pity. Some dreadful prompting told him that all women were in a measure like his grandmother, and the thought was utterly repellant. "How soon am I to have her?" he said at last. He knew that was the thing to say, even though he

40

wanted to scream, "I will not take her!"

"We have yet to consult the Temple," Jotham answered, "for the omens. But it will be soon, I assure you."

"So be it," said Ahaz. "And now if my royal father will excuse me . . ."

"Are you not even going to thank us?" Jerusha whined. "Here we give you the most exciting present a man can receive and you do not even seem grateful."

"Indeed, I thank you both."

"But do you mean it?" Jerusha would not be satisfied.

"I think he is overcome with surprise," Jotham said, and Ahaz was infinitely grateful.

Once out of the audience hall, Ahaz hurried to find Ushna. "A woman!" he exclaimed over and over. "Oh, Ushna, it seems at least they could have told me what they were planning and let me see her first. And a priest's daughter at that! Can you imagine?"

Ushna was comforting. He knew what the young prince wanted to hear and he would say it. "After all, Ahaz, a woman is just a piece of property. Enjoy her, fondle her, lie with her whenever you wish. Then when you are tired of her, ignore her. There is no bond on earth that can hold you to her when you no longer want her."

The words sounded good to Ahaz, for more than anything else he feared that which was unalterable. He closed his eyes and felt himself wondering if Abijah was really pretty.

"Only do not let yourself fall in love with her," Ushna added. "For once you *really* love a woman deeply, you can never completely forget her. I know, my prince."

Ahaz smiled uneasily. He must not let Ushna mention the subject of his lost love. "Could you imagine me really deeply loving *anything* my grandmother picked out?" he said with a laugh.

"I am not worried," said Ushna. But it was a cold lie.

41

Much to Ushna's satisfaction in the days that followed, Ahaz appeared to give far more thought to his roof garden than to the arrival of the girl, Abijah. Moreover, his interest in completing the shrine to Molech almost eclipsed the resentment and anger he felt about his grandmother's choosing him a concubine. Of course, preparations for the ceremony, at which the woman's purchase from her father would be legalized, called him away from his prime interest occasionally. There was a long ritual at Yahweh's Temple which involved consulting the omens. And still more time-consuming, gifts had to be selected for the maiden he had never seen but who soon would be his own.

At last, yet all too soon, the day of the ceremony arrived. According to the custom of the centuries, the documents of purchase were to be signed at the girl's house. By midmorning the royal party was ready to leave the palace. Prince Regent Jotham, in his purple robes of state, rode in the first chariot. Immediately behind him came Ahaz, magnificently garbed in a white robe which had been lavishly embroidered in gold and purple and red. The morning sun shone brightly and his auburn hair seemed to burn with fires of hidden gold. He was splendidly handsome, and even his lack of enthusiasm lifted a little when he heard the cheers of the people who had gathered to wish him well. Perhaps this was to be a wonderful day after all.

To Abijah, waiting at home for the arrival of the royal party, the time seemed to drag by endlessly. Waiting in her own bedchamber, she could hear the noisy chatter of the early arriving kinfolk, but it seemed to be coming from another world. Her thoughts were only of the man to whom she would be given that day. Slowly, almost reverently, she fingered the ornaments which he had sent her for this important occasion; long dangling earrings and a pair of golden bracelets, encrusted with jewels. *What will he be like? Can I ever please him?* she thought. Longings stirred within her; strange longings that would not be still even when she reminded herself that he worshiped a foreign god. *Tonight I will lie in his arms.*

And now the house was growing full of people: relatives, neighbors, priests from the Temple. In the spacious inner courtyard the servants had spread the tables for the feast that would follow the ceremony. *Will he never come?* Abijah's heart beat with rapid excitement. *O Yahweh in heaven, bless this day,* she prayed again and again.

Then at last, Ahaz and all his royal party arrived. Abijah heard the shouts of welcome followed by the shuffling feet of those hurrying to bow as Jotham entered the doorway of Zechariah's house. *Who would have ever dreamed that such a thing as this would have befallen our home?* Abijah thought.

And now, Zechariah had come to take his daughter by the hand and lead her to the prince's side. The next few moments were breathtaking. The crowd was hushed as Abijah entered; all eyes turned to gaze at the lovely maiden, graceful and shapely, garbed in a gown of softest lavender, a transparent veil floating about her face but scarcely hiding her radiant countenance. Her eyes sought out Ahaz, standing motionless beside his father. He alone of all the people in the room seemed not to be seeing her, as his eyes stared down at the floor. Fearfully, chilled with apprehension, she proceeded to the center of the room where Jotham and Zechariah had spread out the contract of purchase.

* * * * *

She is too beautiful, Ahaz's brain whirled. The mysterious realm of women which had hitherto been closed to him was now coming so enticingly near. Deep inside him stirred an almost indescribable sensation, a desire to take this delicate, captivating creature away from all the noise of the crowd and to discover with her the depths of love. Ushna's warnings were forgotten. *But what will I ever say to her when she is mine?* Ahaz thought, as he glanced at the maiden Abijah across the table.

Their eyes met. Abijah returned his gaze with warmth and tenderness, the words of her father echoing in her heart: *You shall belong to him forever.*

Then when the contract had been sealed, they proceeded to the inner court where for hours there was dancing and singing, feasting and drinking. Ahaz and Abijah were placed far apart at separate tables; there was no opportunity for them to say even a word to each other. But again and again, his eyes sought hers.

When the time for departure came at last, young Abijah bid her family good-bye bravely, without tears, and seated herself in the magnificent litter chair that had been prepared for her trip to the palace. Then they were off, through the winding streets of the city to Abijah's new home in the royal residence on Mt. Zion.

The evening sun was sinking far to the west when they reached the palace. Slowly, so slowly, the procession moved up the great ramp, up to the gates of the palace. Abijah watched wonderingly through the thin curtains of her litter chair. And now they had stopped, and Azrikam himself was there extending his hand to help her to the ground. A flurry of excited female slaves clustered about; the air was tense with waiting.

"The Lady Jerusha wishes to conduct you to the Prince's bed chamber," Azrikam whispered softly. "Remember all I have told you, my lady."

Abijah nodded, and the little group stood in hushed expectation. To her dismay, Abijah noticed that Ahaz himself was nowhere to be seen. The moments that passed before Jerusha arrived seemed like years, but at last she came, glittering in a gorgeous outfit of red and gold that only made more evident the fact of her advancing years and vanished beauty. "Come, girl," she said brusquely, almost roughly. Her thin lips were forced into a smile. "Not you," she

44

added, motioning to the slaves. "You stay here." And Jerusha and Abijah walked alone in silence through the lamplit halls of the palace.

Ahaz's bedchamber was empty when the two women entered. Abijah stared at the lavish furniture in wide-eyed amazement. The prince's bed, a magnificent thing of carved ivory, stood in a raised alcove at the far end of the chamber. "Tomorrow, I will show you your own suite, where Ahaz shall come to you henceforth. But tonight, the first night, you will stay here." She chortled.

"Yes, my lady," Abjiah said.

The room was oppressively quiet. Jerusha sank down wearily on a little ivory bench, but she gave no word for Abijah to sit and the girl did not dare to do so of her own volition. "Where is my Lord Prince?" Abijah asked at last after long moments.

"If I know him, he's out on the roof," Jerusha said, "with his Molech. He'll be in soon enough."

Abijah did not answer. A chilled feeling of apprehension ran through her; *that foreign god.* How often in last few days had she tried to convince herself that the prince's professed devotion for Molech was merely perfunctory and could easily be broken. Yet, when he might have been with her. . . .

"Don't you ever do anything to interfere with Ahaz's god," Jerusha was saying. "As long as he can trust in something, it is better than nothing, so let it be."

Another great stillness followed.

"Girl, I think I will be going," Jerusha said at last. She sighed deeply. "No doubt he is waiting for me to leave, and I'll not be so stubborn as to sit here all night."

Abijah sank in a curtsy at Jerusha's feet. "Farewell, my lady."

"Farewell, girl. Make him happy now."

* * * * *

No sooner had Jerusha departed than the folding doors against one wall of the Prince's room slipped open and he entered, alone. He gave no formal greeting. "If you will come with me, I will

45

show you something wonderful," he said. He seemed shy.

Wonderingly she followed him to the open rooftop where his array of astrological devices was set up between neat rows of boxed shrubs. His face glowed with enthusiasm. "Ushna just finished getting all the equipment set up yesterday afternoon. We have been planning it for weeks."

Abijah was almost too surprised to notice that Ahaz did not even express joy at being alone with her at last. If his first words to her were not what she had hoped, what could she expect next? She felt a strangely sinking feeling, a fear that she would never think of the right things to say or do. *What do I know of Ushna's astrological equipment?* she thought helplessly. The last rays of sunset filled the west. The sky was a vivid golden panorama of breathtaking beauty, a sight far more delighting to Abijah than the peculiar instruments which apparently so engulfed the Prince's attention. Abijah's eyes darted over the odd assortment of Ushna's equipment, and then, suddenly, she was aware of the presence of Molech. The various pieces of apparatus stationed about the idol seemed to be whirling. Abijah was dizzy; deep inside her an icy grip of dismay seemed to take hold. *I will not look at that thing,* she told herself, staring hard at her feet.

"This roof garden was my idea," Ahaz was saying proudly. "At least, mine and Ushna's. You can see that we have a fine collection of instruments for probing into the secrets of the future. We thought the roof would be the best place to put it all."

Abijah was not looking at the instruments, for to look at them would be to see Molech also. She walked over to the railing and gazed out across the roof tops of the city. "You can see so far from up here," she remarked uneasily. "The whole city—why, in the broad daylight, I could probably find my father's house."

In an instant, Ahaz had come to stand beside her. "Yes, and if it is a very clear day, you can even see the pool of Siloam beyond the wall."

The Prince placed his hands on the railing, and Abijah saw the symbol of the royal family cut into the light brown flesh of his wrist. "The Star of the House of David," she said, more to herself than to him, as reawakened awareness crept through her

46

that this young man who had entered her life so suddenly was a prince of royal blood.

Ahaz glanced down at the mark casually. "My father put it on me when I was just a little boy," he said. There was something bordering on apology in his tone. "We all have it—all the princes of Judah. It is supposed to be a sign of the covenant."

Of course, Abijah knew this. It was a custom perhaps as old as the kingdom itself, for the covenant of which he spoke was Yahweh's promise to the great King David at the beginning of the kingdom's history, the promise that his family would enjoy sovereignty forever. A delighted thought crept into Abijah's mind that in spite of Molech's presence on the rooftop, it was Yahweh's sign that Prince Jehoahaz bore on his body. "It is a fine and noble thing," she said aloud. "Something you must be very proud of."

Ahaz nodded, but he seemed eager to change the subject. "As I was about to tell you, Ushna and I are designing a sun-clock. It is going to be built down in the main courtyard. But it will be a long time before we get all the details completed. You know, the sun is a strange thing. Ushna says some people worship it as one of the gods and maybe they're right. What do you think?" The prince's tone grew suddenly lighter, more conversational.

"My Lord Prince Jehoahaz," she spoke cautiously. "Since you have asked me, I must answer truly. To me there is only one true God and that is Yahweh."

"So be it with you if you wish. So it was with my grandmother, too, but she changed in time. And, oh yes, you will call me Ahaz and I will call you Abi."

"As you say. 'Tis well with me."

"You might as well realize from the very beginning that I am not a devoted worshiper of Yahweh." He was growing bolder. "Jehoahaz indeed!" He growled his name contemptuously. "It means 'Yahweh holds fast'. Hmmmph! As if my father thought that he could make me better by calling me such a ridiculous name! Disgusting, isn't it?"

"My lord Prince!" Abijah felt her hopes of a few moments before shattering.

"You must learn right away that I plan to say what I think,"

47

he continued. "Now the name of 'Ahaz,' 'the Possessor.' It is much better for me, don't you think?"

The frightened girl did not reply, but merely looked out unhappily over the rooftops of the city in the direction of her own home which lay somewhere out there in the distance. She longed desperately to be safely back in her father's house, away from the court and all that it stood for. But over and over again, she heard her father's words ringing in her ears: *It is unlikely that you will ever be home again, Abijah. You will belong to the prince.* Half fearfully, half hopefully, she cast a shy glance up at the young man beside her. There was a look of discomfort in his wide brown eyes that mirrored her own uneasiness.

"Ahaz," she began softly, almost in a whisper. "I want more than anything else to make you happy. After all that is why they brought me here. Really, I'm going to try to please you. But, you know, these last few days have been so full of changes. And now, they have taken me away from everyone I love, and here I am in a strange new place. I know I shouldn't say these things," she broke off suddenly.

"No, Abi, go on," he sighed. "You are honest, and it's good to hear someone speak the truth for a change. This whole palace seems like a maze of duplicity, everyone trying to deceive someone else, from my father the regent on down to the lowliest slaves. And my grandmother! She most of all!"

"Ahaz!" Again Abijah started in surprise at the prince's evident disrespect for his family.

"Don't let what I say surprise you," Ahaz laughed. He reached out and grasped her hands in his. "After all, you and I are in this thing together now."

"Yes, so we are. I hadn't thought of it that way." Abijah answered.

In an instant he was pressing her tightly against him in a fervent embrace. Abijah's heart beat with overwhelming rapidity. Behind them, the idol Molech stood, surveying the scene with his cold ruby eyes. But the young couple, lost in the warmth of each other's arms, were oblivious to his very existence. And with joy surpassing all he had ever dreamed of, Prince Ahaz led Abi to his bed.

Three weeks had passed since Abijah had come to the palace, and Ahaz remained happier than he had ever been in his life. It was a strangely wonderful feeling, quite incomprehensible. There were times even when he was away from her, perhaps when he sat at his father's council table or rode in his chariot through the streets of Jerusalem that the thought would suddenly rush upon him: *Abi, that delightful little thing, is a human soul even as I, and she loves me!*

The whole court knew, of course, for there could be few secrets at court, that young Prince Ahaz was deeply enamored of the beautiful daughter of Zechariah. Many among them smiled with predictions of, "It cannot last long. He will grow tired of her soon enough."

No one seemed the least concerned, except Ushna. To him, the vague forecasts of how Ahaz would tire of her were already too long in being fulfilled. Whenever Ahaz and Abi were together, Ushna feared, there was the chance that the young woman might be deliberating with her prince on the glories of Yahweh, her soft, coaxing voice whispering anathemas on Molech, undermining Ushna's influence. So he feared. But he feared without foundation, for Abi dared not risk speaking to Ahaz about his god. Out of these groundless fears grew Ushna's hatred of Abi, hatred that went deeper, no doubt, because she was giving Ahaz pleasures that he could himself never know. He made up his mind that he must speak to Ahaz at the first possible opportunity, and if possible speak in such a way as to make Ahaz turn against her.

Ushna had planned his strategy carefully, and when Ahaz appeared one afternoon at the roof shrine, the Ammonite was waiting for him. "You love her," Ushna said. "Do not deny it, Ahaz, you are beginning to love that little wench your grandmother bought for you." The Ammonite's tone of voice clearly indicated that he expected Ahaz to protest vigorously, but the prince sat perfectly still. "I am warning you," Ushna continued. "You must not let this happen. You were meant for better things, foreign princesses. The priest's daughter is nothing but entertainment for the night. Something your royal grandmother has dreamed up to keep you away from brothels. That's all a concubine is, just a respectable harlot."

"Ushna, you lie!" Ahaz shouted. The Ammonite priest was his friend, but suddenly, momentarily, Ahaz hated him. *Ushna is a eunuch; he does not even know what he is talking about,* he thought. "Abi belongs to me, only to me," he declared, "and she will be mine forever. And I do love her! I am not ashamed to say to you, even to the whole court: I love her more than I ever loved anything in my whole life!" The words came very hard to Ahaz, yet even as he spoke them, shudders of fierce joy ran through him. His eyes were blazing fires.

"I only want you to be careful, my Prince. The wench is a follower of Yahweh, and you have pledged yourself to Molech. Do not forget she could lead you into danger."

"What God she worships is her own business," Ahaz answered hastily. "It is nothing to me." And he walked away with a sudden uncontrollable impulse to counter Ushna's venomous words by an act which would lift Abi irrevocably above the reach of the Ammonite's criticism.

The fire in Ahaz's heart had not abated any when moments later he strode into his father's private garden. Jotham looked up, surprised. He was engaged in one of his inevitable afternoon walks. "What brings you here, my son?"

"It is about the girl, Father."

Jotham eyes twinkled. A coarse remark formed in his mind, but

50

something in the earnest expression of Ahaz's face caused him to hold it back. "Does she please you?"

Ahaz nodded. "I have a request to make. I want her legally married to me."

The remark took Jotham by surprise. "But, Son," he protested, "her purchase from Zechariah has already been completed. She already belongs to you legally, as you say. You make her your wife and you would only be binding yourself."

"Father, Abijah was purchased as one buys a slave. There was no holy pledging of vows, no marriage."

"She has been wheedling you, no doubt."

"No, she has said nothing. We have not spoken of it. But I know it would make her happier than anything I could do for her. Someday, perhaps, I shall be king, and I want her to be my lady."

Jotham laughed loudly and watched his son's face turn crimson. "I said things like that, too, about my first one, but I changed in time. You will too. I know you will. No, not the woman, poor silly thing. Most likely, she'll love you till her dying day."

"My father, . . ." Shivers of uneasiness seized Ahaz's body. "I will love her, too, till my dying day, as you have said. She is lovely and precious and wonderful. I want her bound to me with such ties that all the world can see that I love her and none will dare to speak slightingly of her."

Jotham did not seem disposed to comment on his son's profession of loyalty to Abi. "An ordinary man, you know," he said solemnly, "is free to divorce a wife if she no longer pleases him. But a prince is bound by honor to keep the women he marries. You may in time grow to hate her. You may put her away, ignore her completely, but as your first legal wife she will still have certain rights. And I ask you, are you willing without any further looking about to take her as your first and chief wife, to be bound to her in alliance which can never be dissolved regardless of the favorites you may have later?"

Ahaz nodded. "I am willing," he whispered almost inaudibly.

51

"It is what I want more than anything on earth."

Jotham sighed deeply. It seemed ages before he spoke. "So it shall be done," said Jotham at last. "Before Yahweh and all the nation."

The decision was sealed, and Ahaz knew there could be no turning back, nor did he wish it. He who had always feared the unalterable had chosen willingly to be bound to his love forever.

* * * * *

Ten days later, Ahaz and Abijah were officially married in the courtyard of Yahweh's Temple, amid all the pomp and ceremonialism befitting a royal wedding. To Abijah, the hours of preparation before the vows were to be said seemed endless. It seemed an eternity since she had seen Ahaz, for since the night he had told her that they would be officially married, he had absented himself, according to the dictates of time-honored custom.

But now at last the day of the wedding had come. Unable to sleep, Abi had risen early and whiled away the long, long morning trying on her new dresses and brushing her hair. Old Tamar, the chief of Abi's maidservants, fluttered about impatiently all the while, urging Abijah to let her begin decking her in the bridal apparel. At last the young woman yielded to the old slave's request. She was ready much too early, and this last time of waiting was the hardest of all.

But at last the hour came for the procession across the covered walkway which connected the palace and the Temple. Arrayed in a soft, flowing gown of springlike green and bedecked with jewels, Abijah was a beautiful bride.

And now the ceremony was beginning. A delighted, tingling sensation penetrated to the very depths of her being as she walked to the appointed place on the Temple porch. She thought of Ahaz, of his wonderful courage in requesting that they might be legally married when his father and grandmother no doubt expected him to reserve the dignity of chief wife for some foreign princess. The fears, the sorrows she had felt scarcely a month before about her

52

future seemed now only distant and vague memories. Her love for Ahaz was boundless. She knew she could have been his concubine forever without complaint. But now, oh miracle, they would be wed in the eyes of Yahweh and bound by a covenant which, as Ahaz himself had promised her, "can never be broken."

Zechariah radiated fatherly pride as his priestly voice began to intone the time-honored words of the marriage covenant. *I am glad he is a priest,* Abi thought to herself. A wedding was not a religious ceremony in itself, but Zechariah as the father of the bride, conducted the pledging of the marriage vows with the same solemnity with which he officiated in sacred services at the Temple. It was with a deep sense of reverence that he placed his daughter's hand in Ahaz's.

The bridegroom's hand was icy cold. Abi squeezed it reassuringly. *After all, we're in this together now,* she remembered how he had said it that first evening on the roof.

Then there was the marriage covenant to be signed. Three copies of this contract beautifully inscribed on scrolls of papyrus were spread on a table before them. Abi felt herself wondering how the bridegroom would sign his name. *If he writes 'Ahaz' I will have to write 'Abi',* she thought uneasily, fearing that the use of nicknames on the holy covenant would be displeasing to Yahweh. Slowly, Ahaz dipped the pen into the inkhorn. For a moment his hand wavered as if he were thinking the same thing; then he signed in large uneven letters: Jehoahaz ben-Jotham ben-Uzziah.

And deep in her heart, Abijah felt a hopeful feeling that there was still left in him some loyalty to the God of Judah. The thought was strangely out of harmony with the occasion, but Abi felt warmed by it. Perhaps even in this matter of the gods, their gravest difference yet one which they had never really discussed, there was a chance for harmony.

* * * * *

Side by side upon the couches of honor they sat now for the wedding feast. "Abi," Ahaz reached for her hand beneath the table.

He pulled his ring from off the little finger of his right hand and pressed it into Abi's palm. "As a token of our covenant," he whispered.

It was a gorgeous thing, one of Ahaz's most treasured possessions. The central set was a deep green stone, in the center of which was engraved "AHAZ" in letters of gold. The band was carved with pomegranate blossoms, Judah's national flower. "I shall treasure it forever," Abi said, slipping it upon her finger. The stone sparkled like green flame in the flickering lamplight.

"You will remember me whenever you see it," Ahaz said, reaching for her hand.

"Yes." The comment took Abi by surprise. "I mean, if I ever needed to be reminded of you, but then I would not ever need that." It was an awkward sentence, Abi knew, but Ahaz did not seem to notice. He pressed her hand gently in a manner that spoke more than words, and offered a silent prayer of thanks to his patron deity, Molech, for giving him Abi as his bride.

* * * * *

The feast was long. To the young couple it seemed forever before they might be by themselves. There was so little they could say here with the eyes of all the court upon them. To pass the time, Abijah tried to count the people in the banquet hall, but it was an impossible task. Her eyes swept over the sea of faces in the hall to the head of the royal table. There, lolling on a couch, was the Regent Jotham, his frequent bursts of loud, raucous laughter reverberating through the room. Beside him on the right was his closest friend the Prime Minister Elkanah, whose remarks were causing much of Jotham's amusement. On the left was the serious, dutiful Azrikam, commander of the palace, who registered a look of utter boredom as he thoughtfully twisted the stem of his wine goblet.

Abijah paid little attention to the multitude of courtiers who filled the places up and down the royal table. Far down at the opposite end of the table sat the aged Lady Jerusha, glittering in

54

an array of jewels and a fiery red gown (red was apparently her favorite color), yet looking older and more haggard than usual. Beside her was Maaseiah, Ahaz's ten-year-old brother. The little prince's face was glowing with excitement over the privilege of attending the wedding festivities. *He is nothing like Ahaz*, Abi thought. Maaseiah was dark and round-faced like his father. *But Ahaz must favor his mother*, she decided, feeling a sudden pang of wonder about the long-departed Ammonite woman, who had also been a prince's bride.

Lost in her musing, Abi was startled when suddenly a voice rang out in the hall, a deep melodious voice, lifted in song. Throughout the great room, people stopped their talking and looked toward the singer. He was a young man, certainly not much older than Ahaz, tall, very thin, not really handsome, but strikingly attractive, and endowed with a magnificent voice. He was singing an enchanting marriage ballad, every note outpouring the deep enjoyment of the song which he felt in his own soul. "Set me as a seal upon your heart . . . ." It was an ancient song, so old that people liked to say it was first sung by King Solomon. "Love is as strong as death, and jealousy is cruel as the grave . . . ."

"He is wonderful, Ahaz," whispered Abi. "Who is he?"

"My cousin, Isaiah ben-Amoz," Ahaz replied. "Prince Isaiah." There was sarcasm in the way he said the word "prince."

And Abi noticed that when the song was over, Ahaz did not join in the cries for an encore.

Neither, for that matter, did Ushna. The Ammonite eunuch, much in his cups by now, was lying sprawled out on his couch with an empty goblet in his hand, a most disgusting sight. Isaiah had begun his encore by now, but Abi's attention for the moment was fixed upon Ahaz's great friend. The slaves, and even old Jerusha, had been warning her about Ushna, but this was the first time she had caught more than a fleeting glimpse of him. She stared at him with contempt, unable to comprehend why Ahaz seemed to admire him so. "Isn't that Ushna the Ammonite?" she whispered. "The one who helped you build the roof garden?"

"Oh yes, Ushna," Ahaz nodded. "Poor fellow, he's been drowning his woes in wine since morning. He is so worried that my little bride will try to win me back to Yahweh. And as many times as I've told him, 'She's a woman, not a priest!' he still seems to think you are dangerous, Abi!" Ahaz paused and then went on. "But of course, what would a little thing like you know of the ways of the gods?"

Abijah felt herself growing uneasy, but she must not let anything spoil this day. "Let us not even speak of such things," she said, "not today."

* * * * *

It was only a few moments later when the doors of the great hall opened to admit Joah, one of the palace scribes. "I bring a message to Prince Jehoahaz from His Majesty the King," he said, bowing low before Ahaz and his bride. The scribe held out a little scroll.

Ahaz drew back in terror. "Fool! Do you think I'll touch that unclean thing? Read it to me!"

"But, my Prince, His Majesty told me, it is for your eyes alone. Let me assure you, the King's hands did not touch this note. He can no longer write even if he would. He sent for me this morning, and I sat outside and listened to him through the lattices. Would you have the whole assembly hear it?"

Ahaz did not answer but turned instead to his bride. "Can you read?" He looked at her intently.

"Yes," Abijah nodded.

"Then read it softly so that all this crowd will not hear it."

Fearlessly, without question, Abijah took the scroll, unrolled it, and began to read:

"Uzziah ben-Amaziah, in the fifty-first year of his reign, by Yahweh's grace King of Judah, to Ahaz, his beloved grandson. My child, they brought me word today of your wedding and my soul was made glad by it. With the eye of my heart I can see how happy you must be this day. My old eyes are blind now, my son, and it has been almost ten years, I think, since I saw you face-

56

to-face. Yet even in the darkness, your likeness is often before me. Do you remember in the old days when you were just a tiny boy, how you used to run down the great ramp to meet me? Do you remember how I would lift you up into my chariot and we would ride up the ramp to the palace gate together? I used to tell your grandmother that in all the kingdoms of the Westlands there was nowhere such a handsome little prince as our Ahaz. Perhaps you have forgotten those days, my child, but I shall never forget. Sometimes I say to myself 'Uzziah, you would not know him if you could see him, for he has grown to manhood.' But then I know, my son, that your brown eyes must sparkle as they did when I held you up in my arms so long ago. And I know I would know you if through some miracle I might see you again.

"Now, Ahaz, about the young woman, treat her gently. Nothing on earth can be more precious than the love of a good woman. She is your possession, surely enough, but never forget she has a heart and soul even as you do."

Abijah paused. Embarrassment swept over her, mixed with overwhelming emotion at the old king's words. "Go on," Ahaz said. He did not look at her, but stared hard at the table.

"Tell Jerusha if you think it is wise, that in my heart she is with me always. I, Uzziah the King, speak these words, recorded by the hand of Joah, a brave and loyal scribe. May the blessings of all powerful and all righteous Yahweh rest upon you and your bride forever."

"Is that all?" Ahaz asked.

"That is all."

Ahaz seemed lost in thought. "He was always so good to me," he said at last. "Do you remember him, when he was well, I mean? He liked to put on a great show, the more pomp and ceremony, the happier he felt. Yet, for all of that, he was the kindest man I ever knew."

"My father always speaks well of him," Abijah remarked slowly. To her King Uzziah had always seemed a distant shadow, a figure of past history rather than a living man. Suddenly she realized the full impact of the fact that he was still alive, and that, in spite of his terrible affliction, he had not forgotten those he loved. It was difficult to think of the right things to say. "It was thoughtful of him to write to you," she said after a moment. "Does he write often?"

"No," Ahaz replied. "It has been years since he did anything like this. Oh, he keeps in touch with governmental affairs, but he's never sent any word directly to me. When he was first taken ill, he used to send my grandmother a message every day, but he stopped when he found out how it upset her to hear from him. She would have to get someone to read to her, and she would wail at the top of her voice. You have never seen anything like it, Abi. Grandmother can be a very demonstrative person at times."

"She loves him very much, doesn't she?" Abi said, half-wondering how there could be any feeling of love in Jerusha's stony heart, yet knowing somehow it was true.

"Far too much," replied Ahaz. "You see what it has done to her."

* * * * *

The warm summer days that followed the wedding were happy ones for the young couple. Sometimes they would spend their time in Abi's spacious apartment, with slaves to bring them their meals and seemingly nothing in the world to worry them. Perhaps Abi would sing, for Ahaz loved to listen to her gentle voice, though he could never be coaxed into singing himself. Or perhaps, Ahaz would read to her from one of the scrolls that Ushna had acquired from far-away lands, strange tales of gods and goddesses hitherto unknown to Abi. Then, sometimes, they would ride out from the city to Jotham's summerhouse, where they would rise early in the morning and walk through the fields, stopping to examine anything lovely that might catch their eyes—tiny wild flowers, or strange rocks, or the cool, clear stream which flowed along the border of Jotham's land.

Then again, there were days when Ahaz did not come to Abi at all, and the young woman would be left in her huge apartment,

58

alone and lonely. At times like this, she often sought out Jerusha and the two of them would sit in the great hall of the women's apartments. Jerusha had grown unexplainably fond of Abi, perhaps because Abi was a good listener. In the young woman's company, something of the old woman's perpetual gloom lifted a bit. Always busy with some kind of fancywork, Jerusha would talk by the hour of the memories she held most dear, of the days when Uzziah was well and the palace had been to her a happy, blessed place.

Often, young Maaseiah came to sit at his grandmother's feet to plead with her for stories about his own mother, who of course was Ahaz's mother too. Abi was continually fascinated by these tales of the fiery-tempered, willful Ammonite princess. "She was a beautiful woman," Jerusha always remarked at the end of these reminiscenses, "but she was not one of us. I always told Jotham it was a mistake to take a foreign bride."

Abi marveled that Maaseiah never seemed the least perturbed by these comments that inevitably accompanied the tales of the mother he had never known. He was indeed a very mild-mannered child, with little to say in his grandmother's presence. Yet as the weeks passed, he grew warmly fond of Abi and came to look upon her as a special confidant. And Abi, who missed her own brothers and sisters, was glad of his company.

* * * * *

Then sometimes there were the very lonely days, days when perhaps Jerusha and Maaseiah had gone out to the country place and Abijah was left with only dreams of Ahaz to keep her company. She knew that even when he failed to come in the daytime, the arrival of evening almost always brought him to her side.

But, occasionally, as the months passed by, (and this was a thing which distressed Abijah deeply) there were nights when Ahaz would awaken crying in terror. Then Abi, the quiet and gentle one, would hold him till he slept again, whispering softly soothing words of love. It was one of those nights when he tried to unburden the deepest secrets of his heart, a still, moonlit winter night, when the air in Abi's bedchamber tingled with a crisp chill. It was well past midnight when Abi was awakened by Ahaz's terror-stricken screams: "No! No!"

"Ahaz! My darling!" She touched his hand. It was chilled though the bed was piled high with warm coverlets. He sat up, gazing frantically into the dim light.

"Abi, are you there?"

"Why, yes, certainly. You know I would not leave you."

A sense of relief ran through him. "It is all right," he whispered, trying desperately to seem brave. "It was just a dream, I suppose."

"Lie down, my love."

He submitted meekly, sinking down on the pillows as if in pain. "I am sorry, Abi. It was a dream . . . horrible things . . ."

Abi did not answer. She held him tightly as if he were a frightened child.

"Always the same . . ." he muttered incoherently. His words were a mystery to Abijah but she sensed something of the agony in his soul and her heart ached for him. "You will never know; I cannot tell you," he said.

Her gentle hand touched his forehead, smoothing back his soft auburn hair. "My love, you can tell me anything. How can I belong to you completely if I do not know everything about you?"

Ahaz sighed deeply. "It was long ago, when my grandfather became . . ." he broke off. "Became a . . . you know . . . a leper." Abi felt him shiver all over as he spoke the word. "Grandfather had gone over to the Temple, and it was while he was over there that the priests first noticed it. There were some white spots on his forehead and priests made him leave the Temple. They said that Yahweh sent him the disease because he burned some incense and only the priests were supposed to do that. Right at first after that, we were praying for a miracle, my grandmother and I. We were there in that same hall where you sit with her now so often. Anyway, then Azrikam came and told my grandmother there was no hope and she went wild. Oh, Abi, you can never know."

It was difficult for Abi to imagine the hard-faced Jerusha showing any emotion, but she remembered that Ahaz had mentioned his grandmother's weeping scenes before. "Did she ever get to see your grandfather again?" Abi asked.

"Oh, no, none of us has ever seen him again. He went out to that little house where he is to this very day." Ahaz's voice quavered.

"I am so sorry that it had to be that way. I know he was, I mean he *is*, a good man. Remember the letter he sent you on our wedding day, Ahaz. In spite of everything that has happened to him, he loves you. He would not want to see you so sad."

Though Abi's words did not even begin to reach the agony in Ahaz's soul, the feel of her warmth against him was comforting and he felt impelled to speak on. "There is something else. You see, my grandmother told me that if we prayed and humbled ourselves that Yahweh would certainly heal my grandfather. So we prayed and fasted and she drew blood from my arms." Another deep sigh.

"Oh Ahaz, I'm sorry." With the eye of her heart she could see the scene spread before her. She could hear Ahaz's frightened sobs as his grandmother forced him to extend his arms that she might make the gashes thought to be so placating to Yahweh's wrath. She could see the frightened little prince, hungry and sore, lying on the floor with old Jerusha beside him. No wonder that he felt no great love for his grandmother. "It is all over now," she whispered. "And you know, my dearest, I do not believe that we should blame Yahweh for what happened. So many people pray for miracles, and then they are so disappointed when the miracle does not come. I believe we should just ask Yahweh for strength to bear whatever must be borne. If he wills to send a miracle, he will, but we cannot count on that. We can always depend on him for strength in these times of troubles." Abi spoke with conviction; with all the sincerity of her young heart. "I have never known such great trouble myself," she admitted, "but I do believe that Yahweh can help us through whatever happens. Ahaz, please try to believe that."

"No," he protested. "Maybe, I'm not sure, but just listen to me, Abi, please listen."

"Whatever you want to tell me, I will always listen."

"I must tell you this; I have never told anyone." Ahaz's heart was beating rapidly and fiercely. "When my grandmother did not know it, I slipped out and went up on the roof." The tone of his voice revealed more than his words. In all-too-vivid memory, he was reliving the unforgettable tragedy of his childhood. There were no words to tell Abi, or anyone, of the sense of heartbroken loneliness he had felt on that dreadful day. "And I was up on the roof, and Ushna came walking by," he said.

Ushna! The man whom Abi disliked so intensely! The Ammonite scoundrel! The priest of Molech.

"I did not know him then," Ahaz went on. It was getting easier for him to talk now. With Abi's arms around him and her head resting on his shoulder, he related the story of this strange event of his childhood. Ushna had been kind to the frightened little boy. "He took me to his apartment and tended to my wounds. And he told me all kinds of things about Yahweh and the other gods. He told me that if Yahweh was cruel, I should turn to Molech, the god of Ammon, my mother's god. And I made a covenant with Molech that I would serve him forever, that I would give him whatever he demands. And if I fail him, he will strike me down, but I have never failed him yet. Oh Abi," Ahaz's voice suddenly rose in sharp anguish. "Do you hate me for it?"

"I could never hate you, my darling," she answered. Molech's hold on Ahaz was deep-rooted and sown in fear, and she knew she could not win him away from his foreign god by condemnation. "Just lie still and rest. It does not matter about Ushna. Nothing that he could ever say or do can make me stop loving you." It was so simple, so easy to say these words that seemed to bring him so much relief. Gradually his breathing was more regular. At last he was asleep in Abi's arms.

But Abi herself lay sleepless. A thousand thoughts crowded her brain. The horrible image of the Ammonite Molech upon the roof hovered above them all. *'Give him whatever he demands,'* the words were ominous. *Surely my Ahaz cannot really love a god like that,* she told herself. *Someday, somehow, soon, I must lead him to Yahweh.* But how she might accomplish it, Abijah did not know.

Then came a day Abi and Ahaz would never forget. It was late winter, that gloomy season when there were heavy rains for weeks at a time. Gray clouds hung about the palace like an oppressive weight. Abi sat weaving at her loom in the great chamber of Jerusha's apartment, as she so often did on these long dreary days. Old Jerusha sat beside her. They talked very little this day, yet the aged woman seemed to find some comfort in Abi's presence. Jerusha's fingers worked frantically at a piece of embroidery work. She was always busy; the idea of rest never seemed to enter her mind.

Somewhere below them in the great council hall, Jotham was holding a meeting with envoys from the neighboring kingdom of North Israel. Because of the importance of the occasion both Ahaz and Maaseiah would be present.

Abi was humming softly, thinking of Ahaz's evening visit and wondering when the rains would cease. Suddenly, the peaceful atmosphere was shattered by the sound of running footsteps in the corridor.

"Grandmother!" It was little Prince Maaseiah, flushed and out of breath, his usually happy face clouded with an air that bespoke bad news. He bounded into the hall, and then abashed by his grandmother's stern, reproving stare, stood before her with downcast eyes.

"For the gods' sake, Maaseiah, what is it?" Jerusha's tone was ridged with acid.

The boy hesitated. "I was down in the hall with my father and Ahaz just a moment ago and a messenger came and uh . . . ."

He stared hard at the floor, trying to avert Jerusha's piercing gaze. "And then what?" she questioned sharply.

"The messenger was one of my grandfather's slaves. He said that my grandfather, that is, the king had . . . uh, just died." A sudden sob shook the boy's body. "Abi!" he gasped looking pleadingly into his sister-in-law's serene, lovely eyes. She held out her arms, and he rushed to her.

"It's all right, Maaseiah, it's all right." She held him tightly. Tears came to her eyes and she did not try to hold them back.

Jerusha sat motionless, for a moment, just a moment; then her high, unearthly laugh shattered the air. "So," she said, flinging her embroidery work to the floor, "so it is Maaseiah and Abi who weep for him. You who did not even know him. And I . . ." another burst of weird laughter, "I loved him more than my own life and I cannot weep at all." Hysterical sobs racked her frail, bent frame. "Not at all!" she gasped incoherently, staggering up from her chair as one who was drunk.

Maaseiah lifted his tearstained face in wonder, too afraid to cry any more. "I'm going, Abi," he whispered, with an air of adroit withdrawal for one so young.

The little prince's exit went unnoticed by Jerusha. Grasping the arm of her chair, the old woman tottered dizzily. "Jerusha, my lady, let me help you," Abi reached out a sympathetic hand, but Jerusha brushed it away.

"Be gone with you . . . you wench!" she groaned. "Leave me alone! Leave me alone!"

It was at that moment that Jotham and Ahaz entered, unaware that young Maaseiah had already delivered the tragic news. One glance told them the situation; Jerusha wailing, screaming in agony, while Abi stood helplessly beside her. Jotham, with unexpected tenderness, put his arm about his mother and led her to a nearby couch. Her sobs subsided; she breathed heavily. "He is at peace now, Mother," Jotham said. "His suffering is over. He would not want you to grieve so."

"Down into Sheol," Jerusha muttered, as her son propped several little pillows behind her head.

"Shall I go and call Ushna?" Ahaz volunteered.

Jotham nodded. That detestable Ammonite would at least have some kind of sleeping potion to slip in a goblet of wine.

"Mother," Jotham drew up a chair beside her. "It had to be."

"I shall see him no more," she gasped. "And I had always hoped. . . ."

"Perhaps in Sheol, Mother." He laid a comforting hand on her forehead, but his voice trembled. "Some of the prophets say in Sheol we shall all meet again."

"No . . . I don't believe it! The realm of the dead is gloomy and cold, and the spirits do not even know each other. Jotham, leave me!" Another deep sob shook Jerusha's body. Jotham sighed, but he did not leave. It seemed only an instant until the filmy draperies parted, revealing Ushna with a goblet of wine in his hand.

"A sleeping potion for the queen," he said bowing low. Ever aware of the niceties of protocol, he had remembered to give Jerusha her new title of queen; the title borne only by the reigning king's mother, never by his wife.

Jerusha glared at him.

"It is the finest secret of the Babylonian physicians," Ushna said, extending the goblet. "To bring forgetfulness and ease from every agony."

Jotham took the cup from the Ammonite's hand. "Drink this, Mother," he urged.

"No," she said weakly.

"You will sleep; you will forget."

"I do not want to forget him. Leave me alone!" she screamed.

Dejectedly, Jotham rose. "I shall leave the cup here for you and when you wish to sleep take it."

* * * * *

The long night passed, and the cup upon Jerusha's table remained untouched. The next day dawned as gloomily gray as the one preceding. Ahaz rose early to go with his father to consult with the priests and make plans for Uzziah's burial. The old King could not be buried in the royal Judean tombs because of his leprosy. Probably they would bury him in the garden of the little house where for so long he had lived in isolation. Abi lay abed lazily, thinking of these things and wishing she could drop off again into sleep. The sound of the rain beat heavily in her ears. The wind moaned through the lattices, recalling the sobs of Jerusha.

Abi tossed restlessly. Tap, tap, tap. She was not aware when the sound first entered her consciousness. Tap, tap, footsteps on the pavement of the walkway below her window. She rose, opened the lattice and peered out into the driving rain. There she saw old Jerusha, pacing back and forth madly under the little roofed walkway which circled the inner court. Her long gray hair hung tangled and stringy about her shoulders. The wind whipped furiously at the coarse sackcloth gown which she wore.

Up and down the walkway, back and forth. Abi could see Jerusha's lips move but she could not hear her words.

* * * * *

The unrelenting beat of the rain on the tile roof echoed in Jerusha's mind. "It is better," she muttered to herself. "He is at peace." Then turning fiercely as if to shake off every vestige of this thought, she exclaimed in a loud, wild voice, "No! No! While he lived there was yet hope, but now there is nothing!"

Abijah watched from the window in weird fascination. The scene before her scarcely seemed real. This frantic, rain-drenched Jerusha was not the hard, stern woman she knew. It was as if the news yesterday had transformed her into a madwoman.

Abi could not help but feel a sense of pity, a longing to help, even though she remembered Jerusha's fierce reproaches of the day before. "There is nothing I can do," she sighed to herself. By now old Jerusha had turned a corner and was out of sight. Abijah turned away from the window. *She will certainly come in soon*, she thought.

No one saw Jerusha when she fell. The pavement was wet, and the old woman lost her balance. In a split second, she who had been pacing with such furious vigor lay on the cold sidewalk. Frantically, she struggled to pull herself up, but unrelenting pains shot through her. "Help me!" she screamed. "Abi!" But the wind and rain drowned out her feeble voice and Abi did not hear. Painfully Jerusha dragged herself along the cold pavement for a little space, but it was an impossible effort. Time that seemed an eternity passed, and the aged woman lay motionless. The rain and wind beat against her, but she did not stir.

Abijah could never explain what prompted her to look for Jerusha. Was it merely a sense of pity, or was it a genuine love for the old lady who was Ahaz's grandmother that directed Abi's feet toward Jerusha's chamber? *Surely she has come in by now*, Abi thought. But Jerusha's apartment was empty. And now a sudden fear seized Abijah. Mindless of the weather, she ran out into the courtyard. Her eyes surveyed the rain-drenched scene. *She is not here*, she thought hopelessly, darting around the inner court to the far side. And there she found her, lying motionless. *She is dead*, Abijah thought. *O Yahweh! O Lord!* She knelt in terror at Jerusha's side and pressed her hand.

The injured woman stirred. Her eyes opened. She spoke feebly, but the sharp tone of her voice was still the same. "Get me up from here, child." She coughed deeply.

"Are you hurt, my lady?" Abi glanced about feverishly for help, knowing that she herself lacked the strength to lift her.

"Yes, I'm hurt. Why else should I be down here?"

"I'll go get help," Abi said, trying to sound comforting.

Jerusha groaned.

Abi hurried as swiftly as she could, but the walks were slippery and she could not run fast. *Where is everyone?* she sighed, and even as she thought it, it dawned on her that the palace slaves were probably all gathered somewhere for public mourning for Uzziah. She knew she must find someone—a strong man—who could lift Jerusha and who would know what to do for her. Ushna! She hated him, but he was knowledgeable in such matters. Forgetful of all protocol, Abijah sped to his apartment. "Help me!" she shouted, standing outside his door. The startled Ammonite appeared. "Come quickly! It's Lady Jerusha, on the walkway of the inner court. She's hurt."

* * * * *

Jerusha opened her eyes at the sound of the approaching footsteps. "Oh, it's you again." She glared up at Ushna, taking no pains to conceal her distaste. "Well, get me up from here and start praying to your Molech that he'll help me."

Ushna was tactfully silent as he reached down and cautiously scooped up the fragile woman in his arms. She was not visibly hurt, but when he lifted her, she screamed loudly.

"What seems to be the trouble, my Queen?" His tone was smoothly solicitous.

Jerusha only moaned.

They brought her to her apartment. With what seemed unusual gentleness, Ushna placed her on her bed, hovering about her attentively. "If my Queen would let me examine her," he suggested, "perhaps . . ."

"No!" Jerusha let out a piercing scream. "Don't touch me! Don't you dare touch me, you dirty Ammonite!" A fit of coughing shook her or she would have said more.

Humbly Ushna withdrew. Who was he to dispute the word of Queen Jerusha?

Later that day, however, when Jotham returned to the palace and learned of his mother's accident, he sent other physicians to examine her and she submitted tamely enough. Their diagnosis was grave; the old lady apparently had broken her hip. Recovery for one of her age seemed unlikely.

Jerusha heard their pronouncement with a calm that was as startling to Abi as the wild mourning of hours earlier. "I am ready," she whispered. "Soon, I will *know*."

And for several days, she, who had almost forgotten how to pray, lingered in agony, praying for death. Through those long days and nights someone always kept vigil beside her. Abi was there much of the time. Ahaz, too, came when he could, and

68

Jotham. The plans of the old king's funeral hung in abeyance.

Through the days that she lingered, Jerusha made almost no effort to speak to those about her. Then on the fourth night after her accident, suddenly, in a clear voice, she called her son's name, and Jotham bent attentively over his mother's bedside. The old lady's eyes opened; her brain whirled; her vision blurred. The face above her in the flickering lamplight was not that of her son. "Uzziah! My beloved!" A hint of a smile played about the corners of her mouth. "I shall be with you after all." Her eyes closed again, and in radiant peace such as she had not known for many years, she died.

They buried Uzziah and Jerusha side by side in the garden of his little house where she had never been permitted to visit him. At the palace and throughout the nation, people mourned the death of the good king and the woman who loved him. During the long weeks of official mourning, Prince Ahaz, in sackcloth and ashes, walked daily with his father to the Temple to offer prayer and sacrifices to Yahweh. It was a perfunctory task. Through he bowed in apparent sincerity, no prayer that he prayed was unclouded by the dreadful belief that it was Yahweh who had been the author of Uzziah's illness and Jerusha's years of heartache.

Could he only believe in God's lovingkindness with the certainty that he believes in his wrath, Abijah thought. *But this is not the time to try to convince him.*

* * * * *

Then when the period of official mourning was over, a splendid coronation ceremony was held for Jotham on the porch of the Temple, and he, who had borne the burdens of government so long, was officially anointed as King. Imbued with new vigor, he decided without anyone's advice to undertake a campaign against the Ammonites when summer came and began making preparations for his departure. A reprisal raid, he called it, for those frequent skirmishes instigated by the Ammonites along the frontier between their two countries. It would be a perfect opportunity, too, Jotham added to all who would listen, for the Prince Jehoahaz to learn firsthand the business of warfare. Azrikam, the commander of the palace, would direct affairs of state in the absence of the king and the crown prince.

The days that followed were filled with busy preparations for the Ammonite campaign. Jotham's call for volunteers produced an overwhelming response and to the confident king, Judah's victory seemed a certainty. With an enthusiasm for ceremonialism and pageantry which had lain dormant throughout his regency, Jotham scheduled a magnificent service at the Temple and a lavish banquet to take place on the day before the army's departure.

He even invited his half-brother, Amoz, though he knew when he sent the invitation that Amoz would not come.

Prince Amoz, Uzziah's eldest son, was a meek, retiring man, fearful of the palace where by all rights he should have lived. He was fearful, too, of the half-brother who ruled the kingdom which, but for a strange turn of fate, might have been his own. Once indeed Amoz had been regarded as heir to the throne. His mother was a woman called Zillah. She had been Uzziah's concubine when that king was very young, before he had ever fallen under the spell of the fervent Jerusha. Zillah had borne him several daughters, but only one son, and then still in her early twenties she had died giving birth to her last child.

The kings of Judah had never held to a hard and fast law of primogeniture. When Jerusha's son Jotham was born some ten years later, Amoz was ousted from his place as crown prince. But except for this one life-shaping blow, Uzziah had dealt generously with his firstborn. When Amoz married, his father granted him a magnificent and spacious estate just outside the city. In the years that followed Uzziah bestowed upon Amoz a vast amount of wealth in lands and possessions. No one ever denied Amoz's right to the title of prince, but no one ever considered him a candidate for the kingship.

Nor did the mild-mannered Amoz seem to regret the shift of fate that had made him what he was. Quietly and serenely, he lived the life of a prosperous gentleman farmer, having as little to do with the court as possible after Uzziah's illness brought Jotham into power. He cared not at all for the glitter of life at the palace.

Jotham knew this, and for the most part ignored his half-brother's very existence.

There was, however, one thing in which Prince Amoz was very insistent. He had a fine family of sons and daughters, nine in all, and while he sought no personal dealings with Jotham, he was most eager to see his sons accepted in their rightful places as princes at the Judean court.

Amoz's eldest son was Isaiah, the one who had sung at Ahaz's wedding feast. At nineteen, young Isaiah showed every promise of fulfilling his father's dreams of his becoming a great prince. Everyone admired Isaiah's beautiful, deep voice. He could sing so sweetly that even his Uncle Jotham readily praised him and often called upon him to perform at royal banquets. Moreover, it seemed that poetry flowed from Isaiah's soul. When he sang of trees and woodlands, of vineyards and palaces, and of the love of beautiful women, more often than not the words were his own, rising spontaneously from the depths of his heart.

Isaiah was a distinguished-looking young man, strangely attractive, though not handsome. He was tall, a bit too thin, too bony. The hair that swept back from his forehead was light brown; his skin was fair and his eyes a grayish-green. Thin, finely arched eyebrows and high cheekbones lent an aristocratic air to his face, but his nose was unfortunately long and curved like the beak of an eagle. "He looks like a Hittite," Jerusha had been wont to say, "even if he is one of us."

Still, whatever he may have lacked in good looks, people soon forgot, for Isaiah ben-Amoz was a magnetically fascinating figure. He liked to talk and he liked to listen—to anyone, rich or poor—it made little difference. Not that Isaiah didn't thoroughly enjoy the magnificence of being a prince. The son of Amoz dressed splendidly. He rode to court in a superb chariot drawn by horses almost as fine as those of Jotham himself and was lavish with everything he did.

Ahaz hated him. Not only was Isaiah slightly older, much taller, and distinctly more talented than his cousin, but he seemed able without any difficulty to gather about himself a larger circle of

72

admiring friends and flatterers. "When I am king, I will put Isaiah in his place," Ahaz often confided to Abi and to Ushna, though he never seemed too sure what this would involve.

* * * * *

Now on the day that Amoz and his family received Jotham's invitation to the festivities which would celebrate the departure for Ammon, their old stone mansion in the country rang with unaccustomed excitement.

Amoz was opposed to the Ammonite campaign. When the call for volunteers had gone out several weeks before, Isaiah had been eager to enlist and Amoz had forbidden it. But the Temple ceremony and the farewell banquet were another matter. Isaiah must be sure to put in a good appearance, see and be seen, and come home with a full description of the festivities for his father.

So it was that Isaiah went up to the city and to Yahweh's Temple. And there, while he knelt in the ancient sanctuary, amid the awesome magnificence of the ceremony, something happened to him which would change his whole life.

* * * * *

When the service was over, Isaiah walked down the hill from the Temple with a sense of almost overpowering reverence in his heart. All around him was the noisy clamor of voices, happy laughter, crisp talk of business, here and there angry shouting.

"Aren't you coming to the banquet, my Prince?" a suave, polished voice called out. It was Ushna the Ammonite.

"No," Isaiah hesitated. The sickening memories of Jotham's coronation banquet which he had attended and others before it flashed through his mind. Heavy drinking, sultry, scantily-clad dancing girls, the loud, raucous laughter of Jotham and his courtiers. And the singing; surely they would expect him to sing as he always did. Isaiah trembled as the recollection of some of his own songs floated through his brain.

73

"No, I'm going home," he said at last to the inquisitive Ushna who was still standing at his side.

"Don't you feel well?"

"I am quite well," he replied slowly. *How could I ever tell him?* he thought.

"I will tell the king you are indisposed," Ushna offered.

Isaiah ignored him. A few moments later he was in his chariot, driving furiously toward his home, away from the court and all it stood for.

Once outside the city gate, he slowed down. The afternoon was a soft gray-green, quiet and still. The only sounds were the familiar clop of his horses' feet and the incessant creak of the chariot wheels as they rolled along the rough road. *I will go up to the north field where it will be quiet,* he told himself. *I must have time to think.*

* * * * *

Prince Amoz, looking down from the flat roof of his secluded house, saw his son's chariot in the distance. Isaiah! He would not come home so early were he not sick or hurt or in trouble. Worriedly, the old man rushed down the stairs and out toward the gate.

"My son!" he called, waving his arms vigorously. "My son! Are you all right?" Isaiah slowed his chariot to a halt and stepped down.

"Yes, Father."

"Then why did you come home?"

"Hasn't there ever been a time when you felt you didn't want to stay at the court?" he replied evasively, knowing well his father's feelings on that subject.

"King Jotham will be angry." Amoz's voice was crisp.

"He probably will not even miss me," Isaiah replied.

"My son, are you in trouble with the king or with Ahaz?" A thousand fears rushed through Amoz's mind.

"Oh, no, not at all. I just thought I'd go up to the north field for a while and . . ."

"Isaiah, what under the sun is the matter with you? If you have insulted your cousin Ahaz . . ."

"Father, please don't suspect me of something I have not done." *I must tell him,* Isaiah thought. *It will not be easy, but he will understand me.* "Today has been the most wonderful day of my life. Today, in the Temple, at the festival, I saw Yahweh and I heard him speak to me."

Shocked horror crossed the old man's face. "You saw him! Why, that's absurd!" he exclaimed. "No one has ever seen Yahweh, not even Moses when he went up on the holy mountain. Don't you know that?"

"Perhaps Moses did not look for him in the same way that I did," Isaiah replied.

Anger flared in Amoz's eyes. "Go up to the north field then! Go up there and pray that Yahweh will forgive such a blasphemous thought, such audacity, such a lie to your old father! And don't come back till you've come to your senses!" Amoz stalked away, burning with rage.

* * * * *

Soft lavender twilight had descended upon the earth when Isaiah strolled back down to his father's house. Inside the rambling limestone mansion, Amoz's wife, Maacah, and the little girls began to light the lamps while Amoz and his neighbor Yosef sat contentedly by the hearth. Outside in the garden, Isaiah's little brothers played, their happy shouts and laughter echoing faintly on the air. It was like countless other early summer evenings, yet to the young man who had heard Yahweh's voice, nothing could ever be the same again.

"I'm still not sure why Isaiah has been acting so strangely today," he heard his father remark to Yosef. Amoz did not sound angry any longer, only puzzled. "I expect he's restless because I didn't want him to join the army."

Softly, Isaiah went to his bedchamber and closed the door. From a chest near his bed he took a few pieces of broken pottery such as he often used to write down the songs he sang at Jotham's banquets. Ink, a pen . . . Isaiah sat on the edge of his bed.

"In the year that King Uzziah died, I saw Yahweh sitting upon a throne, high and lifted up . . ."

Slowly the words came at first and now more easily as again the vivid memories of those moments in the Temple flooded back into his soul:

"and his train filled the Temple. Above him stood the seraphim . . ."

Isaiah was certain about the seraphim. They looked exactly as the priests had always said they would look; just like their statues in the Temple:

"each had six wings; with two he covered his face, and with two he covered his feet, and with two he flew. And one called to another and said: "Holy, holy, holy is the Lord of hosts; the whole earth is full of his glory." And the foundations of the thresholds shook at the voice of him who called, and the house was filled with smoke. And I said: "Woe is me! For I am lost; for I am a man of unclean lips, and I dwell in the midst of a people of unclean lips; for my eyes have seen the King, Yahweh of hosts!"

Isaiah knew well, as his father had reminded him that afternoon, that no one had seen Yahweh. The priests always said that a man who saw Yahweh would die; *but that is not so,* Isaiah declared to himself, as his soul relived the moments in the Temple.

"Then flew one of the seraphim to me, having in his hand a burning coal from the altar. And he touched my mouth and said; "Behold this has touched your lips; your guilt is taken away, and your sin forgiven."

This was the most difficult part to describe. Isaiah read over that which he had written and frowned pensively. The writers of his

76

nation through the centuries had always delighted in symbolism. Meaning beyond human description often hid behind the written words. It would have to do.

"And then I heard the voice of Yahweh saying, "Whom shall I send, and who will go for us?" Then I said, "Here I am! Send me!"

Send me . . . Isaiah stopped writing. Yahweh wanted him as a prophet, a spokesman for God at the court of Judah. *I am a prince by birth and yet I am also to be a prophet,* Isaiah thought, *and that is why he has chosen me: because I can go into the palace itself and speak for him.*

There had never been a prophet in the royal family of Judah. Never, so far as he knew, had any well-born aristocrat chosen this way of life. Prophets, most of them, lived a life of wandering poverty. Sometimes listened to with respect and interest, these days it seemed they were more often mocked and scorned by their audiences when they spoke for Yahweh. Sometimes they made predictions (though Isaiah knew well that foretelling the future was not supposed to be a prophet's major concern); sometimes the predictions came true, and sometimes not. In any case, once committed, a prophet was never really able to renounce his calling, for upon pledging of his soul to God's service, the prophetic candidate submitted to having a holy sign of Yahweh branded upon his right hand with a red-hot iron. It was the sort of brand that slaves had borne in the old days, and it stood for slavery to Yahweh. It was quite a different matter from the royal star which Isaiah, like all the princes of Judah, had imprinted on his arm. The star was a sign of great honor: of Yahweh's love for King David's family. The prophet's slave brand was a sign of humility: of the prophet's love for Yahweh, and his absolute commitment to his vocation.

The prospect of this irreversible act held no terror for the young man who had answered God's call in the Temple. He was ready to accept completely the discipline of a prophet's life. His only problem now was how he should begin. He had never even known a real prophet.

77

"The Colony!" Suddenly he remembered that there was a group of holy men living in a camp on the road north of Jerusalem. Surely, they would understand his calling; certainly, they would help him discover how he might best begin his service to Yahweh.

In the early morning, well before daybreak, while all the family slept, Prince Isaiah ben-Amoz slipped away from his home and went to seek the prophets.

* * * * *

When day came and the family discovered he was missing, Maacah had no doubt where her son had gone. "Amoz, you should have let him join the army when he first wanted to," she declared despondently. "Now he has run off to go with the men into Ammon anyway."

Amoz accepted his wife's judgment without comment. It was logical and likely. As he remembered Isaiah's strange remarks on the previous day, he assumed that whatever the young man thought he'd seen and heard in the Temple, it must have had something to do with joining the king's forces. Ah well, so be it. Perhaps every prince should know what it was like to be a soldier.

* * * * *

Oded had lived at the colony of prophets for years; now in his old age he had risen to the place of master. It was a good life. Though sometimes on their trips into the city, prophets were mocked and insulted, everyone knew the ancient law that a holy man of Yahweh had freedom to speak and act as he pleased. Even the king, it was said, would not dare to interfere with the activities of the prophets, for such interference would surely bring the wrath of Yahweh upon the whole nation.

Oded had seen many young men come to the prophets' colony in his lifetime. Most of them were very poor, seeking, he knew, an easier life rather than feeling any real longing to serve God. A surprising number of them stayed, at least long enough for a period

78

of training which culminated in the ritual of commitment and the branding with Yahweh's sign. Then many of them left to harrass villagers in other parts of the kingdom. Others, usually those with less incentive, stayed at the camp forever.

But, never in all his years had Oded seen a prospective holy man of the sort that stood before him this morning. The aged master prophet was accustomed to taking in the most pitiful creatures, ragged, starving, poverty-stricken peasants seeking a better life. But this young man, whose deep-set eyes looked into his own with such earnestness, was not poor. One glance at the clean and expensive clothes he wore revealed that. But even had he attempted disguise, his smooth, graceful hands were silent testimony that he had never known hard work.

"I have come to be a prophet," the young man said simply. "I have heard the voice of Yahweh in the Temple."

Oded eyed him suspiciously. "Inside the Temple?" Who but the priests and the highborn noblemen ever saw beyond the outer courts of that splendid sanctuary? "Who are you?" Oded asked.

"My name is Isaiah."

"Just Isaiah?" The master prophet clearly expected him to indicate his parentage, but the young man merely nodded. *There is a prince by that name*, the old prophet thought. Impulsively he grasped Isaiah's left arm, twisting it to reveal the mark upon his wrist. "The Star of King David!" proclaimed the old man with an air of self-satisfaction. "You cannot deny it; you belong to the royal family. No doubt you are the grandson of his late majesty," Oded went on. "Do you honestly think, my Prince, that we could take you?"

"Why not?" asked Isaiah.

"This is not the life for a rich man," Oded stammered. "That is, we work. It's summer now, of course, the planting season is still some weeks away; but when fall comes, we till our fields and sow our crops. Prophets have to have their sustenance."

"Do you think I cannot work?"

"No, my Prince, I only meant it will be so different for you. We have never had a nobleman here."

79

"It seems to me," said Isaiah, "that when one has heard the call of Yahweh, it should make little difference if he is rich or poor."

"You will not be happy with us." Oded's protests were growing weaker.

"I shall not be able to agree or disagree with that until I have stayed a while," Isaiah replied. "So I shall stay. Not forever; do not fear that. I have work that I must do in the city, but this time of training, of discipline, has to come first. I must know more of what Yahweh expects of me, and I must receive his sign upon my hand." The prince's voice was compelling; he spoke with determination and certainty. "While I am here," he added, "it might be well to forget that I came from the royal family."

"Yes," Oded promised, though he could scarcely wait to spread the news to every inmate of the camp. "We shall forget it completely, if we can."

* * * * *

It would have been as impossible to hide the fact of his noble birth as it would have been to hide a thunderstorm. It was in vain that Isaiah wrapped a torn strip of cloth around his wrist to cover the royal star. Before the morning was half-gone, the whole camp knew that their newest member was a man of the nobility, King Jotham's own nephew. This fact promised to add immeasurable variety to the prophets' daily routine.

In the days that followed, the men of the camp questioned him incessantly: while they ate, while they worked, even while they were supposed to be having their silent meditations. And Isaiah, who loved to talk, would supply vivid answers to their questions of life at the palace. He spoke with complete honesty. His uncle's court, he declared, was far from the ideal that Yahweh must want for his chosen nation. There was too much luxury, vast wealth in the hands of a select few. Every night, the king and his courtiers dined for hours, never giving a thought to the hundreds of poor folk in the city who went to bed hungry. And this war against the Ammonites! What was it but an aggressive quest for plunder? Isaiah had lost all desire to be a soldier. Though he knew he would gladly give his life for Judah *if* the land was attacked by enemies, he would never willingly take part in war for the sake of conquest and plunder. "Someday," he said, "men will no longer want to fight. Nation shall not lift up sword against nation, neither shall they learn war any more."

"When will that be?" said Oded dubiously.

"I do not know," Isaiah answered, "perhaps very soon."

But to have true peace, there must be justice, and Isaiah admitted there was little justice in the land. With his own eyes, he had witnessed trials where the favorable verdict went to the man able to offer his judges the largest rewards. Elkanah, the prime minister whom Jotham trusted with such extensive powers, had built up his personal fortune through the shadiest of practices.

"Our leaders mislead us," Isaiah reflected. Still, he remarked, Uncle Jotham was a good sort in many ways. He was full of potential for tremendous good, if only he and his ministers could be made to listen. And they will!

Oded began to wish fervently that he had not revealed Isaiah's identity with such eagerness. The prince was proving to be a most distracting influence.

But then the nobleman was good for something. He knew how to read and write. He was appalled at the gross ignorance of most of the inmates of the camp and began teaching a group of them the simple fundamentals of literacy. "A prophet should be able to write down his thoughts," Isaiah insisted.

"They say, and I suppose it is true," Oded remarked, "that some prophets in the North Israel have tried to do some writing. But never in Judah."

"Someday it shall be done," Isaiah answered. "Soon."

* * * * *

Of one thing, everyone seemed certain: Isaiah would not stay. *Regardless of what he says, his heart is still at the court,* Oded assured himself. *He will never be able to give up the pleasures of a nobleman.*

Indeed there was much about the camp that displeased the young prophet, though he did not say so. He had no liking for living in a small, hot tent and sleeping on the hard ground. The simple meals at the colony seemed extremely meager in comparison to the delicacies which had been common fare at home. Most of all, he who had always taken pride in presenting a fine appearance was distressed by the prophets' general neglect of cleanliness.

But the weeks rolled by, and time allotted to a prophet's training was drawing to a close. Still Isaiah stayed on. No one, and certainly not Oded, understood the plans that had formed in the young prince's mind. But to Isaiah himself, the course of action that he would follow was growing increasingly clear. He had determined that he would stay at the colony only until he had received the brand of Yahweh upon him, for it was a thing expected of every man who committed himself to God's service. *Then, after that, I will go home,* he thought, *and to the court. I will be of no service at all to Yahweh if I stay here much longer.* Thus, looking upon the days at the camp as merely a prelude to the truly great things yet to come, he endured the hardships of life there with remarkable patience.

And he dreamed of the future. In rosy hues he pictured himself standing before the court, admonishing King Jotham and all the nobility in such moving tones that they would undertake a great reform. The idols, all of them, the Ammonite Molech and the dreadful local fertility gods, Baal and Ashtoreth, would fall from their pedestals. The king and his courtiers would return to Yahweh wholeheartedly, and in their reborn zeal, would attempt to deal more justly with the ordinary people whose lives were in their hands. It would be a wonderful, blessed time. It would a time when as Isaiah liked to say to himself, "The earth shall be full of the knowledge of the Lord as the waters that cover the sea."

He dreamed; he wrote some of his verses on scraps of potsherds. And he waited for the weeks to pass till he had completed his time of testing.

Then, one almost unbearably hot afternoon, when all work had ceased and the prophets were free to rest or meditate as they pleased, Isaiah set out to look for Oded. As he approached, he heard from inside Oded's tent, the voices of the master prophet and one of the other men. What they were saying made Isaiah stop and listen, for they were speaking of the very problem he had come to ask about.

"He is ready for the commitment ritual," Oded remarked in a worried tone. "But I cannot permit it. I know he has done surprisingly well here. I know he seems sincere, but still I do not believe he could ever really be a prophet. No doubt, his whole experience here has been just a grand adventure to him, something to talk about when all his noble friends and kinsmen return from Ammon. I would be a fool to let him mar his princely body with the mark of a committed prophet."

"You are right, Oded," said the other. "We really should send him away from here, the sooner the better."

"O Lord, I must show them!" Isaiah breathed a silent prayer. Despondency swept over him as he turned away from Oded's tent and sought out his favorite spot for meditation, a secluded cluster of trees on the outskirts of the camp. There he fell to the ground in prayer. "O Yahweh, they will not take me," he wept uncontrollably. He did not dream that Oded had seen him and followed him, and that even now the old master prophet listened incredulously from his hiding place in a thick clump of bushes nearby. "Speak to me again, O God! Tell me what I should do!"

The place was completely quiet, no birds sang, no breeze whispered in the branches, and no heavenly voice stirred in Isaiah's heart. There were only the deep waves of anxiety sweeping over his own very human soul, frustration in finding himself barred from what seemed to him God's will.

"He is sincere," Oded, decided, walking noiselessly away.

* * * * *

Was it an answer to prayer that evening when Oded summoned the prophets together before the campfire and announced that Isaiah ben-Amoz of Jerusalem was ready to take the vows of final

83

commitment? Prince Isaiah was taken by surprise but this was not the time to show hesitation. Fearlessly he repeated the prophet's vows. Then, for the irrevocable sealing of those vows, he knelt before the campfire and held forth his right hand that Oded might burn upon it the holy sign of Yahweh's service.

The glowing iron touched his flesh and pain staggering beyond his wildest expectations ran through his entire body. "O God, O God, help me!" he moaned and collapsed upon the ground.

Oded helped him back to his tent, and for what seemed hours, he could think of nothing but the intensity of the pain. His brain was whirling. His hand seemed to be on fire and shudders of agony wracked his whole arm. "Lord, forgive my weakness," he prayed, desperately ashamed that he was not able to exhibit more physical stamina.

How long he lay there in such agonizing misery, he never knew. At last, he felt something cool touch the burning wound; it was Oded's hand with healing oil upon it. Isaiah looked up at him gratefully through the darkness. "I was thinking," the young prince said slowly, "Over and over it keeps coming to me, the message that Yahweh spoke to Samuel the prophet long ago: 'Man looks on the outward appearance, but God looks on the heart.'"

"So now my Prince is feeling regrets," replied Oded emotionlessly, as he continued rubbing the wound. "I need not remind you it is too late now to change your mind."

"I have no regrets," said Prince Isaiah. "I wanted this done to me, *because* I want the world to see that I intend to give my whole life to Yahweh, and certainly I shall never be ashamed to bear the mark of Yahweh's service. But, what I wonder is if the Lord *really expects* such a thing of his prophets."

"Isaiah, I fear you tamper too much with tradition," Oded said, and he withdrew.

When his wound had healed, Isaiah left the camp of the prophets and started for home. His heart beat fiercely as he trudged up the long road toward his father's house. The surety of purpose that had possessed him at the camp still burned in his heart, but it was not unmixed with fear of his father's reaction when he learned what he had done. Perhaps this was the hardest obstacle he would ever have to face. Isaiah had always been a dutiful son. He loved and respected his father, and he had obeyed him without question all his nineteen years. Now there was likely to be difficulty, for Prince Amoz, though a staunch follower of Yahweh, was very much the aristocrat. *But he will understand me,* Isaiah thought. *When I am able to explain, he will understand and he will give me his blessing.*

Amoz was walking across the field when Isaiah glimpsed him in the distance. At almost the same moment Amoz saw him, and came running down the road toward him. "My son!" he cried joyfully, and then as he came nearer, he saw that Isaiah was dressed in a rough sackcloth robe such as prophets wore. And he saw the brand on Isaiah's hand.

"My son!" he repeated, this time in a voice heavy with dismay.

Shakily he leaned against a tree. One look at the tragic expression that crossed his father's face told Isaiah more than any words Amoz might have said. "I thought you had gone to Ammon." Amoz's lips trembled and his voice quavered. "Oh, Isaiah, what have you done? How could you?"

"I am sorry if I hurt you, Father. But I knew what I had to

do. I know I have heard Yahweh's voice and I am ready to do his will. I have only made a beginning."

"Yahweh's voice, indeed! 'Honor thy father!' That is Yahweh's voice!"

"Have I dishonored you?"

"Dishonored!" Amoz exclaimed with a fury Isaiah had rarely known in his gentle father. "How am I to explain to our family and our neighbors and to the king when my son comes home with the mark of a fanatic upon him and a fanatic's ideas to match. Such shame as you have brought upon your father's house!"

"The sign on my hand is the outward symbol of my commitment to Yahweh. Surely there is no shame in that," Isaiah answered firmly, gazing down at the deep scars burnt into his flesh. "I bear the mark of Yahweh as proof to all of what I am."

"You *were* a Prince of Judah. A son of the House of David. You were even in the line of succession to the throne. And what have you done? Thrown your life away on some foolish whim, some absurd imagining." Amoz's voice grew louder. "Isaiah, the time will come when you would give anything to remove that mark of commitment, as you call it, from your body. How will you ever explain to people? As long as you live, you will have to hear them say, 'That is Prince Isaiah who, when he was very young and very foolish, imagined himself to be a prophet of Yahweh.' "

"I am not imagining, Father. I *know* I have heard Yahweh's voice. He called *me.*"

"You had such a magnificent chance," Amoz continued, ignoring Isaiah's last remarks. "You could have been a great power at court, honored and respected. And yet you choose to make yourself Yahweh's prophet. Don't you realize that there is no harder life? Don't you know you will be mocked and despised by the very people who were once your friends?"

"Who has said that a prophet cannot be a power at the court?" This was the whole basis of Isaiah's hope; if he were not to serve at the court, the entire message of his calling had been an illusion.

Amoz did not answer, but shook his head sadly. He could scarcely hold back the tears that were welling up in his eyes.

Neither father nor son saw Maacah coming down the path towards them. Isaiah's mother stared at him. She saw the brand. She saw the sackcloth robe he wore. She saw the fire of determination in his deep, expressive eyes. And she saw her husband's look of utter misery. Maacah could be very brave when there was a need for it. "You must be quite weary, Isaiah," she said. "Come into the house and I will give you something to eat." She was trying desperately to act as though nothing were amiss.

"Maacah!" Amoz practically screamed. "Can't you see what he has done?"

"Yes," she replied, "I see. He has hurt us both deeply, but he is still our son." She grasped Isaiah's scarred hand and side by side they started up the slope to the house, while Amoz followed with downcast eyes. "It is not what I wanted for you, Isaiah," Maacah said. "And though I'd try a hundred years, I could never understand why you would deliberately choose such a life. But now there can be no turning back and I can only pray that you will serve our God worthily." She glanced up at his face and at that moment, the realization of the long years that he must live with his commitment vibrated in her consciousness. And at that moment, Maacah's courage broke. "Oh, my son!" A little gasp; then a deep sob. The unhappy mother ran up the path alone.

* * * * *

This was only the beginning. The days that followed were agonizing ones for the young prophet.

His mother, now that the first shock had subsided, determined to ignore his commitment and tried desperately to act as though nothing had happened. Life would go on just the same, she told herself. Isaiah would really be no different, she thought, refusing to face the future.

Old Amoz, however, could not ignore what Isaiah had done. "Whatever will we do with him?" he was heard to remark to Maacah numerous times a day. "What will I do when the king finds out?" The question seemed unanswerable.

87

Neither of Isaiah's parents was willing to listen to him. Maacah, the busy housewife, always managed to seem preoccupied with the younger children and the household chores. Amoz avoided Isaiah almost altogether, and when he looked at him, it was with a look of withering sadness. Isaiah's little brothers and sisters and their young playmates were thoroughly horrified yet fascinated by the brand upon Isaiah's hand. "Does it hurt?" "How did you do it?" "Did you cry?"

The house was noisy; it was hard to think, hard to feel close to Yahweh, almost impossible to know his will. Closing the door behind him, Isaiah would spend long hours in prayer and meditation without finding the answer to the problems burning in his soul. "When shall I go into Jerusalem? When? When?"

He had no doubts of what he would say; often in those days just as he had at the camp, he recorded his thoughts on broken scraps of pottery. It was just the matter of actually going that disturbed him. The nights were sultry and still. Isaiah tossed restlessly, sometimes drifting into a sweet dreamless sleep, only to awaken to the ever-present reality of his commitment. *I cannot go on like this,* he told himself. *I must go up to the city, tomorrow.*

But tomorrow after tomorrow passed and Isaiah continued to postpone his trip to Jerusalem. He wrote, he meditated, he planned, but he did not act. *Father will be too deeply grieved,* he rationalized. *I must not hurt him again so soon. I will wait until the king comes back from Ammon.*

* * * * *

Meanwhile, on the Ammonite frontier, through countless little villages on the east side of the Jordan, King Jotham's forces swept down like a horde of devouring locusts. As long as he lived, Ahaz would look back on the Ammonite war as a continuous series of nightmares: heaps of dead and dying upon the field of battle; soldiers searching the bodies of the fallen foes for spoils; harmless civilians crushed beneath the chariot wheels of the onrushing Judeans; cottages blazing into rubble; strong old fig trees hacked to the ground.

Destruction and death were everywhere, and King Jotham and his chief of staff, Ben-Tabeel, were in their glory. Whenever there was Ammonite resistance, and almost every village put up something of a struggle before surrendering, Prince Ahaz was in the thick of the fighting, laying about sword blows with scarcely any comprehension of what he was doing. That he killed several Ammonites he was certain, while he suffered nothing but a few minor bruises and cuts himself. He fought fiercely, and hated every moment of it.

Worst of all were the disquieting thoughts when he tried to rest. *These people did not want war.* Night after night as he lay alone, bone weary but unable to sleep, in his royal tent, the thought returned to haunt him. *There have always been Ammonite raiders along the border, but we are fighting the civilians, the ordinary people. We are killing them, burning their homes, seizing their meager possessions as plunder.*

"Why must we do it?" Unable to contain the burning unrest in his heart, he at last approached his father with the question that seemed unanswerable. It was early morning. In the king's tent, slaves were preparing breakfast for Jotham, Ben-Tabeel, and Elkanah. Another of their interminable conferences was about to get under way and the Crown Prince Ahaz, as always, was invited, though until now he had been a silent observer.

"What's that you say, Jehoahaz?" Jotham was obviously more interested in the plateful of summer fruit piled before him than in his son's question.

"I don't see why we have to keep fighting."

"Because we're winning!" Jotham laughed loudly. "The King of Ammon has asked for terms you know, and we'll not let him off easily. A hundred pounds of gold, I'm asking, and five hundred of silver. And of course the cattle we've taken, the men will divide among themselves. It's been a most profitable little expedition. You've not done badly yourself, Jehoahaz. Ben-Tabeel tells me you killed three of the enemy in last week's foray."

"I did, I think I did; and I am sorry," Ahaz said slowly. "In the night, their cries haunt me. The enemy we call them, but

89

these people are as much my people as the Judeans are. I am an Ammonite myself; the law of Judah declares that a man bears the nationality of his mother. If I were anybody else but *your* son, it would be recognized: *I am one of the enemy.*" As he spoke, his voice had grown more nervous and excited.

"Stop talking nonsense, Jehoahaz. You're overtired. You're not getting enough rest, but that's no cause to start raving like a maniac."

"Does it mean nothing to you that my mother belonged to this people?"

The question took Jotham by surprise, and for a moment he was silent. "No," he said slowly. "It means nothing. Do you know what I think you must be, Jehoahaz? You are a coward, looking for excuses. I expected better of you, and I'll not hear any more of this wild talk. Ben-Tabeel and Elkanah will be here in a moment, and I'll not have you shame me before them. Ammonite, indeed! You can't even remember your mother. I raised you as a pure Judean, Yahweh knows!"

Ahaz saw that it was no use to speak further. Already he had dared to say too much. Across the table, his father sat placidly eating figs and dreaming, no doubt, of his hundred pounds of gold and five hundred pounds of silver. *At least,* Ahaz thought, *if the King of Ammon is talking of terms, this miserable business will soon be over, and we will go home. And if I survive till then, I will never go to war again.*

* * * * *

In late summer Jotham's forces returned triumphant from Ammon, laden with spoils and burning with zest for celebration.

A victory banquet was held at the palace, and as a matter of course, Prince Amoz and his son Prince Isaiah were invited. Contrary to their usual practice, it was old Amoz who attended. Though Isaiah longed to go, longed to seize the opportunity to begin his prophetic mission at the court, he could not.

Amoz, his father, had forbidden it.

Indeed it seemed now that the king had returned, Amoz spent most of his time trying to hit upon a plan which would permit Isaiah's "commitment" to remain forever undiscovered by the court. Maacah, his wife, offered him no help at all, still pretending unrealistically that nothing was amiss. Amoz grew more despondent than ever.

Sometimes in the dusky twilight a few neighbors would gather around the hearthside in Amoz's hall. When they did, the old man would always launch out on that most unforgettable subject. "It is one thing for a poor man to be a prophet," he would say over and over again. "But my son!"

In the next room, separated from the hall only by a beaded drapery, Isaiah sat one evening on a bench in the shadows. Apparently unaware of his nearness, Amoz continued. "I told Maacah that I think the best thing to do is to give him some of my land, farther out from the city, where he can stay away from the court. Poor Isaiah! He'll live to regret his commitment, as he calls it," Amoz added. That was the worried father's favorite theme; he must have said it a hundred times or more in the past weeks. "I believe," he continued, his voice heavy with grief and shame, "that I would rather have seen my son dead than for him to have made himself a prophet."

Yosef, the neighbor whose land adjoined Amoz's, listened sympathetically. "Amoz, my friend, you have deep trouble, I know. But at least, the prophet in your family is a son." His voice dropped lower, almost to a whisper. "Now I have a daughter. You know

Naamah. I had not wanted to tell you, but she believes she is a prophetess."

"She has not made the commitment?" Amoz asked, with a genuine note of concern.

"If you mean does she have the prophet's brand on her; no. I doubt there's any way a girl could contrive to have that done. But she's committed just the same. She has been talking about having a 'calling' even before Isaiah started on that subject. I kept hoping it was just a passing fancy, but it seems not. I have never seen anything like it."

Isaiah's heart stirred. The agony of his father's cutting words subsided and something closely akin to happiness swept over him. Naamah. When they were both very young, they had played together under the great trees of her father's lands. She was a quiet, gentle girl, not really pretty but good-natured and kind. It must have been several years now since he had seen her up close without a veil or talked to her without a great crowd of relatives present.

Could it really be that Naamah, the little neighbor girl whom he had known since childhood, knew the strange burning fire of Yahweh in her soul? Could it be that so close by there was a young woman who felt the prophetic call, even as he? It was surely not impossible for Yahweh to call a woman. Isaiah knew the stories of the great prophetesses like Miriam and Deborah. But Naamah!

And Isaiah was determined that when morning came he would find the daughter of Yosef and discover for himself if this wonderful thing could be true.

* * * * *

She believes she is a prophetess. I have never seen anything like it. Yosef's words echoed in Isaiah's heart. The night air through the filmy curtains was cool. The world outside was bathed in silvery white moonlight. Isaiah stood at the open window gazing across the fields toward the house where she dwelt, drinking in the beauty of the night before he lifted his eyes in prayer. "Grant me but this, O Yahweh, that I may know when I see her if she is sincere

92

in her conviction. And if she is, give her to me."

The young man slept deeply, with a freedom from heavy concern that he had not known since before those days at the prophet's camp. It was not yet daylight when he arose. He dressed simply, neither in the sackcloth of a prophet nor the magnificent garb of a courtier, but in a plain robe of brown linen.

The morning was perfect. Far to the east, the sun was breaking through the clouds, its rays casting a reflection of pink and gold in the sky. A gentle breeze rustled the treetops. Almost unconsciously, Isaiah directed his feet toward the low stone wall that separated his father's land from Yosef's. In the early morning stillness, Yahweh seemed almost as close as he had that day in the Temple. "O Lord, make her mine, and make me worthy of her," Isaiah prayed, confident that God would answer his prayer.

"Naamah!" His heart sang her name. He tried to remember how she had looked when last he had seen her, but somehow that seemed so long ago. Lost in reverie, he sat down upon the wall at the border of the lands. How long he sat there, almost motionless, he did not know.

"Isaiah!" The voice calling him was very real.

"Naamah!" He rose and held out his hands to her.

The girl Naamah was certainly no beauty. She was very small in stature, and just a little plump. Her hair, black and straight, was wrapped in a tight knot. She wore a dress of plain blue linen, no veil, no jewelry. But her voice was like the voice of an angel. "I had to find you," she said, as they sat down side by side on the low wall. Her dark eyes were fixed upon him in something akin to rapture. "I have looked for you every day since I heard that you had returned."

"I, too, had hoped to find you. I heard your father speak of you only yesterday."

"Oh!" gasped Naamah. "I fear he spoke harshly."

"Not so much as my father speaks of me."

Naamah smiled, searching for the right words to say. Here he was, now at last after all her days of searching, the wonderful man who had heard Yahweh's voice and had dared to follow his call.

93

"Tell me," she began slowly, "how can you really be sure you heard Yahweh?"

"You are the only one who has cared enough to want to know." His smile and the tone of his voice spoke more than the words. The strangeness vanished, and they talked of the day in the Temple and of the weeks at the prophets' camp. Without hesitation, Isaiah found himself telling her of the heartbreaking reaction of his family to his calling and of the inner fire of God that would not die despite all his father's efforts to extinguish it. Here at last was someone to whom Isaiah could open his heart, one who did not laugh at him or feel sorry for him or try to convince him that in time he would come to regret what he had done.

"I am a prince of Judah, a son of the House of David," he said slowly. "Yet my own father is ashamed of me and wants to hide me out in the country."

Naamah was not disturbed. Her small hand closed over Isaiah's, covering the indelible brand of Yahweh. "You have done right," she said. "And now, if your father sends you from his house, it shall be because Yahweh wants to guide you into some place where you can serve him better." Her words radiated simple confidence. "Next, of course, you must go to see the king."

"Yes," replied Isaiah, "yes, I must. I had thought it would be so easy and it is proving to be so hard. Of course, Jotham is my uncle and he has always been kind to me, but I cannot imagine what he will do when I go back to court." Isaiah paused. Why was he letting this young woman who so evidently admired him see his hesitation to follow his calling? Would he have Naamah to think he was a weakling?

"What does your father say when you talk of going to the city?" Instinctively, she seemed to know the root of his reluctance.

Isaiah sighed deeply. Those terrible words which his father had uttered echoed in his heart. "He said he would rather see me dead than to have seen me throw away my life as a prophet."

"Yahweh is testing your willpower," said Naamah.

"So is my father."

"And you will triumph," she pronounced with confidence. "With

94

Yahweh to give you strength there is nothing which can defeat you. I understand your reluctance to hurt your father, but I know also that Yahweh has called you for a very special reason. No prince of Judah has *ever* spoken God's word at the court. Isaiah, you shall be something that no one else has ever been and your name shall be inscribed in the annals of our nation forever."

"You believe a man can be a prophet and still remain a prince?" Isaiah remembered Amoz's doubts on this subject.

"Of course." Naamah had no doubts. "Yahweh has called you because you are a prince and you know more about the court than a poor man could ever know. You know what they are doing there that is displeasing to God. And you can go into the very palace and tell them."

It was exactly what Isaiah believed himself before he'd met so much discouragement.

"Ah, yes," Isaiah answered. The girl's voice brought back vivid recollections. "Naamah, if you could only see what I have seen at the palace, the great show of piety and underneath it, the dishonesty, the selfishness, the deceit, the corruption. And running after personal pleasures! Those courtiers, most of them, have only an empty allegiance to Yahweh. They love the elaborate sacrifices at the Temple merely because of the feasting and the drinking afterward. And that idol Molech that my cousin Ahaz has put up on the roof of the palace!" One thing seemed to lead to another.

"Idol!" This was a surprise to Naamah.

"The god of Ammon, it is, and the king does not even make him move it. Oh Naamah, I tremble to think of the days when Ahaz will rule this land. Sooner or later, they say, though perhaps it is just a rumor, Molech demands human sacrifices."

The awful import of Isaiah's words was ignored by Naamah. "But Ahaz is not king yet," she said. "Jotham is still young and will reign for many years, we trust. You know for yourself there is much good in Jotham. He believes in our God, even if he does tolerate idols, too. And Isaiah, with you to urge him, just think what he might accomplish in the service of Yahweh."

The fire which had burned in Isaiah's soul in the Temple and at the camp was burning again. "I shall go up to the city today," he declared, "to the palace of the king. Also," he added, "Very soon, I intend to make you my wife. Our fathers have been neighbors for many years. I see no reason why they should not both be pleased and relieved to have us settled." He smiled. "That is, of course, if you will have me."

"I will love you as long as I live," Naamah said simply. "I could ask no greater reward on earth than to be the wife of the prophet Isaiah."

For a few moments he held her in his arms. Custom said a bridegroom was not to come near his bride until his wedding day, but he and Naamah were not children of custom. Marriages, more often than not, were plotted by well-intentioned, if sometimes hopelessly unfeeling, parents, but the love of Isaiah and Naamah was created by Yahweh's own hand.

"Tomorrow morning," he said at last, rising to leave, "I will see you and tell you what happens at the palace." Whatever happened, he knew she would want to listen.

* * * * *

Late that afternoon Isaiah rode alone into Jerusalem in his magnificent chariot. He had dressed as a prophet was supposed to dress, in a short garment of coarse sackcloth. He wore neither shoes nor cloak. But upon his arms were the golden bracelets of nobility and upon his bare chest sparkled a jeweled medallion which had been a gift from his Uncle Jotham. The crisp autumn wind tossed his hair and indescribable exhilaration filled his heart. People looked up and gasped as he went by: "It is Prince Isaiah!" "No, it can't be!" Stunned amazement turned to querulous disputation among the bystanders who saw him pass.

Isaiah did not stop, staring only straight ahead, ignoring the people's remarks. Past the marketplace he drove; past growing crowds of astonished spectators, straight up the road, up the great ramp to Jotham's palace. The slaves waiting at the outer gate bowed low when he approached; they had been taught to ask no questions of the king's relatives.

Isaiah stepped down from his chariot, and leaving the slaves to take care of his horses, walked resolutely up the wide steps of the king's house.

Jotham and a group of courtiers were at supper in the banquet hall. Isaiah found the doors of the hall open, with Azrikam doing the honored duty of standing guard. The older man scrutinized the young prince in amazement. "Is this a jest, my Prince?" Azrikam was solemn. "If it is, I would certainly not advise it."

"Have you ever known me to make light of our God?" Isaiah replied.

Azrikam protested no more, but allowed him to pass through the wide doorway while he announced in his most ceremonial tone: "Prince Isaiah ben-Amoz."

A gasp of astonishment swept the room. The courtiers, reclining on couches, sat up as if with one accord. Silence, complete silence, hung heavy in the air as Isaiah walked slowly toward the raised dais where Jotham sat. Surprise was mirrored on every face in the hall. Isaiah saw Ushna grasp Prince Ahaz's arm, almost as if afraid. He saw Ahaz's fists clench angrily and his mouth twist in contempt. He saw the amused smile of young Maaseiah, who plainly thought the whole matter was some elaborate jest.

The prophet walked slowly, too slowly. "Come here!" Jotham commanded.

Isaiah bowed at his uncle's feet with all the grace of a true prince. Then fearlessly he looked up into Jotham's eyes and held out his hands. The light from the torches shone full upon him and the King could not help but see that Isaiah bore the brand of Yahweh.

"No!" Jotham screamed, rising from his place. His mind envisioned his nephew as the victim of some highwayman's sadistic violence. "Who has done this to you, Isaiah? Tell me, and I will search them out, have them tortured . . ."

"Nothing has been done to me save of my own free will," Isaiah said rising to face the courtiers. "I have come to this court as a prophet of Yahweh."

"He's a prophet of Yahweh!" someone shouted mockingly.

"Just what we needed! A prophet!" echoed another. "Go on then, prophesy!"

Isaiah stood still before them.

"Do not forget that Isaiah is my nephew and a prince of royal blood," Jotham's voice rose weakly, but only a few of the courtiers even heard him.

"Can you still sing?" someone called.

"Yes, we'd rather hear a singer than a prophet. Come on, give us the vineyard song!"

Isaiah knew it. It was a popular ballad, really much better if sung by a woman for it was a song of a young peasant maiden to a rich landowner.

"What's the matter? Can't you sing?" someone called again.

Certainly, no one expected he actually would.

And then, without even a moment's hesitation, Isaiah's deep, melodious voice rang out in the song and once again the courtiers sat in hushed silence.

"Let me sing for my beloved
    a love song concerning his vineyard:
My beloved had a vineyard
    on a very fertile hill.
He digged it and cleared it of stones,
    and planted it with choice vines;
he built a watchtower in the midst of it,
    and hewed out a wine vat in it; . . ."

The courtiers were listening in hushed amazement when Isaiah stopped the song and cried out in a dramatic voice:

"He looked for it to yield grapes,
    but it yielded *wild* grapes!"

The courtiers murmured among themselves and Isaiah went on:

98

"For the vineyard of Yahweh of hosts is the house of Israel, and the men of Judah are his pleasant planting. And now I will tell you what I will do with my vineyard. I will remove its hedge, and it shall be devoured. I will break down its wall, and it shall be trampled down. I will make it a waste."

"So Yahweh is going to destroy us!" Ushna called out. "Go on and say so then, prophet, and don't bother us with your allegories!"

"Quiet!" cried King Jotham, but nobody at all listened to him. The room was growing very noisy. Isaiah raised his voice and looked straight toward the Prime Minister Elkanah.

"Woe to those who rise early in the morning that they may run after strong drink, who tarry late into the evening till wine inflames them! They have lyre and harp, timbrel and flute and wine at their feasts; but they do not regard the deeds of Yahweh, or see the work of his hands."

Effortlessly the words flowed from Isaiah's soul. He was not organized, but he went on, denouncing every injustice of the court that came to his mind. He certainly felt no awareness of the presence of his uncle the king, until Jotham's voice rang out, louder than before: "Stop, Isaiah!"

Isaiah did not question the fact that he must obey the king and he stopped still. Jotham's next words were a surprise to everyone. "We might all do well to listen to the things Isaiah has said to us. However, I regret that he has thought it necessary to interrupt our meal with his message. Come to us again, Isaiah, but choose a more auspicious time."

There was no mistaking the note of dismissal in the king's voice. Isaiah bowed to his uncle, then turned and left the hall.

Perhaps they were not really moved this time, he thought *but the next time, things will go better. And it will be soon.*

* * * * *

Conversation at the banquet tables for the rest of the evening centered around Isaiah's erratic behavior. "I cannot believe it,"

Jotham said. "Of all people, he was the most unlikely sort to be a holy man of Yahweh."

"He will not be able to stay with it," Ushna predicted. "Our prophet will have had his fill of prophesying before winter comes, I'll wager, though of course he'll have to bear that little memento on his hand for the rest of his days. He'll grow weary of his "calling" soon enough when he sees that no one really listens to him."

"I hope you are right," Ahaz sighed. "But I do not think Isaiah is one who gives up easily." He dared not say more, for his father was listening and it was all too clear that Jotham was not in the least angry with Isaiah. The storm brewing in Ahaz's soul must remain hidden until the feasting was over. Then he would tell Abi, and she, the patient and gentle one, he knew would understand.

* * * * *

"You could never guess what my cousin Isaiah has done now!" Ahaz stormed into Abi's bedchamber with fury burning in his eyes.

"No?" Abi called, pulling back the curtains from around the bed where she lay. Ahaz kicked off his sandals and flung himself down beside her. "He has decided to become a prophet for Yahweh. He has gotten the slave mark of Yahweh branded on his hand and this evening he came to the banquet hall dressed in sackcloth and made us a long speech about how the court had forsaken the Lord. What do you think of that, Abi?" Ahaz clearly expected her to echo the disgust which was evident in his every word, but she could not.

"I think it is splendid," she replied, quietly.

"Splendid!" Ahaz sat up and nervously began pulling off his jewelry. "Abi! Can't you see what a position this places us in? It is bad enough for an occasional prophet to come into town for a little while. But if I know Isaiah, he will spend his days hanging around the court and we can do nothing to stop him because he is a holy man of Yahweh. It is revolting, sickening, and yet, you lie there and say it is splendid!" The anger was rising in Ahaz's voice.

"Do you really expect me to condemn a man because he has given his life to the service of my God? I would as soon expect you to condemn Ushna for his service to Molech."

"Abi, I have never in all these months, more than a year now, thought you were really serious about Yahweh."

There was scarcely anything that Ahaz could have said that would have hurt Abi more deeply. "Nothing in all the world is more serious to me," she said. "But I have never believed that any argument between those who love each other can be pleasing to any god. I love you very much, Ahaz, and I will not argue. Let's forget about it." She reached out her arms to embrace him, but he rose and escaped her grasp.

"You refuse to agree with me, yet you say you won't argue!" he shouted like a spoiled, petulant child. "Let me alone then, and dream of your Yahweh and his prophet!" And he stalked away.

Abijah would not let herself be too hurt over Ahaz's mood. Tomorrow he would be sorry, she felt sure. He was always sorry when there was a little disagreement between them. Somehow he would find an indirect way to tell her, for he would never make an outright apology. Tomorrow he would send a gift and perhaps a little note saying how he loved her and not a word of any unpleasantness. And tomorrow night, if not sooner, he would come back. That was how Ahaz was, she told herself, pushing him out of her mind.

Then snuggling deeper beneath the coverlets, she closed her eyes and contemplated Isaiah's heroic acts. A vague image of the son of Amoz floated through her mind. She tried to remember the times she had seen him. Of course, he had sung at the wedding feast. She had seen him kneeling in mourning before old Uzziah's tomb, and then, too, he had been at the Temple for the ceremony before Jotham went to Ammon. Prince Isaiah, a prophet in the royal family. Never before had Yahweh bestowed a greater blessing upon the house of David than this. Imagine the courage it must have taken for a fine nobleman to have allowed the mark of Yahweh's service to be branded indelibly upon his body. Abijah shuddered, but it was not an unpleasant shudder. *And what if it had been my Ahaz who had heard the call of God? Would I be happy?*

101

Would I be proud? Oh, I would be so proud, no words could tell!

* * * * *

It was several weeks later that the court received invitations to the wedding of Isaiah and Naamah. "I pity the poor creature who has to marry *him*," Ahaz remarked bitterly. "His father probably had to pay a tremendous bride price."

Abijah ignored Ahaz's all too apparent dislike for his cousin. "We will go though, won't we?" she asked, eager for the chance to see the prophet and the woman who would be his bride.

"Are you a fool, Abi?" Ahaz shouted. Somehow it seemed he was growing more irritable lately, or was it only when the prophet came into the conversation? "Do you think I would actually seek out the company of that unspeakable Isaiah? Besides," Ahaz added, "he didn't invite Ushna."

"I should have known better than to think of going," said Abi, humbly.

* * * * *

The wedding went on quite well without the presence of Isaiah's royal cousin. For the time being, the proud fathers, Amoz and Yosef, who were both delighted by the match, made a special point of ignoring the fact that the bridegroom was a prophet and the bride-to-be a prophetess. "What if Naamah does have pronounced ideas about the call of Yahweh? So much the better," Amoz and Yosef told each other confidently. "Will she not thus be better able to abide with Isaiah's peculiarities?"

The marriage was celebrated with all the pomp befitting a prince of Judah and his bride. And when the ceremony and feasting were done Isaiah and Naamah journeyed to their beautiful new house in the country, Amoz's wedding gift to the young couple, where he hoped they would be content to stay, safely away from the glittering palace on Mt. Zion.

Nothing could keep Isaiah in the country. Naamah loved the house, and would have been content to stay there forever, but to Isaiah the country estate that his father conferred upon him was a distinct disadvantage to the practice of his prophetic vocation. Not that he was ungrateful for his family's wealth. He truly appreciated the fact that income from the family lands gave him the means to provide a comfortable home and servants for Naamah. There was no reason for a prophet to despise the worldly blessings that Yahweh had conferred upon him, and the house, large and spacious, was a true blessing. But, it was three miles outside the city wall, and for Isaiah this meant almost daily journeys back and forth to Jerusalem. Sometimes he drove in his chariot; but in good weather he usually walked, often singing as he went. And in the city he preached wherever he could find an audience.

In the weeks immediately after his first appearance at Jotham's court the prophet prince was a sensation. He spoke in the Temple courtyard; at the city gates; in the palace itself, and he was always surrounded by a throng of listeners. He spoke with deep conviction, of the need for the people of Judah to return to Yahweh's ways, "Come now, let us reason together," he pleaded. "Though your sins are like scarlet, they shall be white as snow."

Yahweh stood always ready to forgive the repentant, always ready to receive those who earnestly sought him. Isaiah knew, for had he not been an unthinking, intensely selfish young man himself until that day when Yahweh called him in the Temple? Once all he had cared about, really, was having a good time, enjoying life to the fullest. Perhaps he'd not done so much to displease Yahweh as some did. He had never followed Baal and Ashtoreth as so many of his young friends did. But, he'd had no real concern for Yahweh's world in those days, and now he did. He cared very much. And, because he cared, he wanted his fellow citizens to fulfill the ideals of Yahweh's chosen people. It was not enough to follow the right rituals at the Temple. King Jotham did that unfailingly while the land cried out with injustice.

But while the crowds seemed to admire Isaiah's oratory, the great reawakening he hoped for did not come. The men of the court, especially Elkanah and Ben-Tabeel, Ushna and Ahaz, mocked him behind his back, and sometimes to his face as well. Jotham the King remained detached. Isaiah, as a prince of royal blood had the right to a seat at the King's council table, and as a prophet he had the right to speak whatever he pleased. Jotham would not have dreamed of denying him either privilege. When Isaiah spoke, however, in the King's council, Jotham scarcely seemed to hear him. Isaiah warned repeatedly against entangling foreign alliances, yet he knew that King Jotham was in the thick of a plot with King Pekah of North Israel, with the objective of helping Pekah's kingdom break free from its Assyrian overlords. Isaiah did not know the details. No one did except perhaps Jotham's closest confidants, Elkanah and Ben-Tabeel. Isaiah did know, however, that secret envoys traveled back and forth from Jerusalem to Samaria with great frequency. Something ominous was shaping on the horizon. Peace was not so near at hand as he'd once believed.

If Isaiah were discouraged, he would have never dreamed of letting the world know it. The very fact that there were so many who predicted he would abandon his prophetic vocation gave him firmness. But as months passed, his heart grew heavier. "How long, O Yahweh?" he often cried out in secret, "how long must I speak to those who will not listen?"

And in his heart he knew Yahweh's answer: Forever. Isaiah was not yet twenty. Should he live to the good old age that Yahweh sometimes granted, there was a half century or more ahead of him, a long time to labor without visible results.

"There are *some* good people in the land," he thought to himself as he walked home one evening in the late autumn rain. "Only there's such a *few* of them. Whatever makes us think Yahweh could love this rebellious, stiff-necked people?"

He was tired, cold, and miserable. He thought gloomily of the miles that he had to cross to get to his house. That house would always be something of an obstacle to him Why couldn't he simply go home and stay there; take a good long rest, and forget about Jerusalem and the court?

By the time he reached home, he was in the gloomiest sort of mood, and Naamah sensed it instantly. "Come and sit with me by the fire, my dear one," she said.

He tossed off his rain-soaked, mud-spattered mantle on the floor, and Naamah bent to retrieve it, and spread it on a bench by the fireplace. He watched her in silence. *If I had not insisted on being a prophet, we could be a happy, normal aristocratic young couple,* he thought. *A prince of Judah and his bride.* He stood by the fire, and stared at the brand of Yahweh on his hand. *Commitment is forever. Here I am. Send me.*

"Isaiah, my love," Naamah's voice was happy. "What are you thinking?"

He could not tell her, much as he wished he might. But perhaps she knew instinctively; so often, she seemed to know his thoughts. He put his arm around her. "I have given you a hard life, Naamah," he said.

"Oh, no, don't say that."

"Sometimes I wonder why Yahweh wanted me. Why does Yahweh care at all for Judah? The people are hopeless."

"No, Isaiah."

"No, no, not everyone, but almost everyone. Elkanah was so drunk at the council today he scarcely knew what was being said. And King Jotham raised taxes. He's appointed Elkanah to see to it that the ordinary farmers pay an extra portion of their crops to the king's men when the harvest comes around next spring. You know yourself, that some people simply can't pay any more. And what is his purpose? To build up the army; apparently to help

105

out old King Pekah in Samaria on some harebrained scheme of his. A scheme that can't possibly help Judah, except the soldiers, who'll get their hands on the spoils of war.

"And then, something else today, Ahaz invited *me* to go to the feast of Molech that he's holding out in the valley of Hinnom on the south road."

"Does the king know?"

"Oh yes, of course he knows, and he doesn't care. He knows that hundreds of people in Jerusalem are sacrificing to Baal and Ashtoreth, too. I suppose he thinks Molech is a lesser evil than those two. I really don't know what he thinks." Isaiah sighed deeply. "Oh, if only my father had been king."

"And you were the crown prince? Yes, Isaiah, why couldn't it be? I've asked myself a thousand times. All I know, it was not Yahweh's will."

"Jotham is Yahweh's anointed; and after him, it will be Ahaz, and what will I be? Yahweh's prophet to a people that won't listen."

"As long as there is anyone left, even one, who will listen, you have not labored in vain. And there will always be a remnant of the faithful."

A remnant. *What a strange way of saying it,* Isaiah thought, *but she is right. Yahweh loves his whole land of Judah for the sake of the faithful few. If the majority does not listen to his prophets in this generation, there will still be the remnant who will follow Yahweh.* Somehow he felt much better. Naamah truly had the gift of prophetic insight, perhaps more than he. Yahweh had given him a precious blessing when he gave him Naamah.

"Isaiah," she whispered his name softly. "I have some wonderful news. I am pregnant."

The announcement, the complete surprise, brought the young man's thoughts rapidly down to earth again. He was happy beyond words. Ecstatically he embraced her, then stood back and looked into her radiant dark eyes. As much as he loved her, he had always admitted to himself that plain little Naamah was far from pretty: but, now, all of a sudden, she was beautiful.

106

* * * * *

The following summer, when Naamah's son was born, Isaiah called his name Shear-jashub, "A Remnant Shall Abide." People laughed when they heard it but Isaiah did not mind. Few could resist asking why the boy had been given such a strange name, and he was eager to explain. For months now he had been speaking to all who would listen about the idea of Yahweh's remnant who must keep alive the covenant with Judah's God, and now in giving his child this name, he had made him a living symbol of his dream for the future of Yahweh's people. The faithful remnant was the hope of Judah.

11

Another year went by, and another: three years since the death of old King Uzziah. For three years, Jotham had ruled alone over the Southern Kingdom of Judah. Most people said that his reign was good. For though taxes were high the nation was prosperous.

Abijah was almost nineteen now, more beautiful perhaps than when she had been a bride. For four years she had been Ahaz's wife, and the whole court commented on his surprising faithfulness to her. He apparently gave no thought to taking other wives, which he could have done anytime he pleased. But Abijah's happiness was marred by the fact that she had borne no children. The prayers she offered daily went unanswered, and at last her cries began to echo the ancient cry of Rachel: "Give me children, or I shall die!"

Why, she often thought, as the months turned to years, *does Yahweh refuse to answer me?* She thought of old Jerusha, praying for Uzziah's miraculous recovery and failing to receive an answer. *We must not ask Yahweh for miracles.* So Abijah herself had tried to tell Ahaz when he wept with incomprehension over his grandfather's illness. *But is praying for a child really asking the impossible?* Abi wondered. *I am young; I am strong and healthy. I have a husband who loves me, and I want to give him many children? What is wrong, oh Lord?*

Meanwhile, Ahaz continued to offer his daily devotions at the shrine to Molech on the roof. At one time Abi had hoped Jotham would make him move the idol, but after a while it became amply clear that the king had no intention of offending the powerful god of Ammon. *Perhaps it is just as well,* Abijah sighed to herself with pretended resignation. *As long as Ahaz loves me and I love him, what should it matter about the gods?* But it did matter, deep in Abi's heart. Perhaps, she thought, the real cause of her childlessness lay in Yahweh's displeasure that she had failed to win Ahaz away from Molech. It was a most disturbing thought.

* * * * *

In the winter of the third year of Jotham's reign, envoys from the neighboring kingdom of North Israel arrived at the court of Judah to finalize the proposed alliance which would affect the history of both kingdoms forever. Jotham had never met King Pekah of the North face-to-face; but he knew a great deal about him. North Israel, Judah's sister kingdom, had never succeeded in establishing a long-lived dynasty like Judah's House of David. Pekah ben-Remaliah was the most recent in a series of usurpers. He had seized the throne of Israel some years before by assassination of his predecessor.

Intently, Jotham listened to the envoys' glowing descriptions of their royal master. Pekah, it seemed, lived and ruled amid a constant flurry of plottings for his further self-aggrandizement. Now, they reported, his anti-Assyrian plot had the enthusiastic support of King Rezin of Damascus, as well as the king of Edom and the rulers of the city-states of Philistia. Certainly, Pekah's officials made it clear, their royal master expected no further hesitation from Jotham of Judah.

There were hours of such discussions. Numerous details had to be determined. Jotham had favored the planned uprising from the first time he had heard of it but was not one to make a commitment without thorough planning. It was a fascinating prospect, the overthrow of Assyria and the downfall of that pretentious gardener who had seized the Assyrian throne and called himself Emperor Tiglath-pileser.

At length, after many days, King Jotham of Judah placed his royal seal upon the Contract of Alliance.

On the evening of the same day that the contract was sealed, Jotham summoned Ahaz to the royal council chamber. "Jehoahaz, my son, I must explain to you about the alliance with North Israel and Damascus." Jotham stood before the littered council table where he had conferred with Pekah's envoys earlier that day. From amid the pile of scrolls and tablets, he selected one freshly prepared document and unrolled it flat upon the table. "Here," he said, "is a copy of the Contract. Read it for yourself."

The prince picked up the scroll and glanced at it. "I, Jotham ben-Uzziah, King of Judah, do solemnly pledge to render full support to the alliance under command of Pekah ben-Remaliah, King of Israel. . . . *So there is to be war.* Ahaz trembled inwardly, but he was determined to act unconcerned in his father's presence. Rapidly, he skimmed over a lengthy section involving the numbers of infantrymen, archers, horsemen, and charioteers which Jotham would supply. He ignored the details regarding the meeting place of the armies and the appointed time for their march against Assyria, for one sentence toward the end of the contract had caught his eye. "Failure to comply with the terms of this agreement shall be looked upon as treason to our common cause."

The foreboding that had seized Ahaz was growing deeper, a cold, gripping sense of the needlessness of it all. He could understand why Pekah and Rezin wanted to crush Assyria. For years now, North Israel and Syria had been vassal states of the Assyrian emperor, paying heavy annual tribute into his coffers. But why Judah? Judah was an independent kingdom, not subject to any foreign overlord. Judah had nothing to gain and everything to lose. Why provoke Assyria and risk destruction when one might just as easily have peace? He was about to say something in this regard when Jotham laid a hand upon his shoulder and said slowly, "I can guess what you are thinking, Jehoahaz, but when Assyria collapses, it will be to the mutual benefit of all the Westlands. You must understand that."

"I really do not understand it, and I do not want to fight," Ahaz said simply.

"Well enough, you needn't fight in person if I am still here when spring comes. But if I should be gone by then, my son, you must know what to do." The King's voice was heavy with grief. "I shall not live forever, you know."

"Father! Whatever makes you say such a thing?" Ahaz looked unbelievingly at the plump, round-faced King. He was too fat, but otherwise he appeared the image of good health.

"My son, sometimes—quite often lately—I have felt pains, like a knife under my heart," Jotham said. "My time will come too soon, I fear, and when it does you must be ready."

For a long moment Ahaz did not answer. "You will be better when spring comes," he said at last, "when you have taken to the field."

* * * * *

A few weeks later, while he was in the banquet hall eating his evening meal, King Jotham of Judah toppled from his couch and lay motionless upon the floor. Solicitous courtiers, thinking him merely to be drunk, made a vain effort to arouse him.

But Jotham the King, not yet forty years of age, was dead.

That night, as they knelt around his father's bier, Ahaz wept inconsolably. Abijah wrapped her arm about him in wordless consolation and listened as he sobbed: "Why so soon? I am not ready." For he wept not so much for the loss of his father as for the sudden grave responsibilities which had been thrust upon him.

* * * * *

Jehoahaz ben-Jotham was king. Nay not Jehoahaz, but Ahaz. When they anointed him with holy oil of consecration on the porch of Yahweh's Temple, he had taken "Ahaz" as his lawful name, the name which would be inscribed upon his royal seal and written in the chronicles of his nation forever. Even to mention the word *Jehoahaz* in his presence would be considered an offense to the King's Majesty.

111

He was not quite twenty years old, willful and headstrong. The land of Judah trembled and waited for spring.

Most ominous of all, Ahaz seemed to have little interest in his government. While the punctual, well-organized Jotham had spent time every day preparing for the forthcoming anti-Assyrian campaign, Ahaz much preferred to work with Ushna on the plans for the sun-clock which was at last, after several years' planning, being erected in the outer court of the palace. This imposing contraption, which consisted of a set of steps and a shadow-casting gnomon, was unlike anything ever seen before in the kingdom of Judah. By noting the place of the gnomon's shadow on the steps, one could calculate the time of day. Ahaz seemed as delighted with the clever contrivance as a small child with a new plaything. He rushed out to look at it several times a day and spent hours drawing and revising the designs which he wanted carved to embellish its sides. That some of these designs plainly reflected the cult of Molech did not seem to bother anyone, but the fact that the king allowed himself to be occupied with what was properly the work of artisans was perplexing indeed. Ahaz's subjects possessed no understanding of their young monarch's artistic inclinations. And as for his inordinate interest in telling time, that was a most baffling thing to a people who had never seen a clock of any sort before.

When it was not Ushna's sun-clock, or Ushna himself and his Ammonite Molech absorbing Ahaz's attention, it was the Lady Abi. In the eyes of certain of Ahaz's subjects, the influence of his wife was more disturbing than all his other shortcomings combined. Clearly, heaven had rejected Lady Abi by failing to send her a child. So why did the king not reject her, too? Why did he not take another wife who would produce an heir? But instead, it was reported that he spent hours of idle ease with Abijah almost every day. If he was concerned over their childlessness, he gave no indication of it. "Heaven will bless me with a son in due time," he was often heard to say in a tone of great piety which he hoped would impress his courtiers.

112

But when, if ever, would the king direct his attention to Pekah's alliance? The Royal Council wrung their hands, sighed impatiently, and went on with their plans for alliance as if the young King did not exist. Ahaz, they were eventually to discover, did most of his thinking when he seemed not to be thinking at all. Through the weeks that he ignored the council, a plan for breaking free from the ominous Contract of Alliance was crystalizing in his mind. Then, one afternoon, when he felt that the time had come, he met with his father's old counselors. For long moments he sat still listening to them report the progress in preparation for the alliance. They all took it for granted that Ahaz would follow Jotham's policy.

Ahaz sighed deeply. To extricate himself and his country from Jotham's anti-Assyrian plot clearly would not be easy under any circumstances. The difficulty was compounded by the fact that the most enthusiastic of the warmongers was Elkanah, his prime minister. Silently, Ahaz glanced around the council table. Isaiah was there; Ahaz had not dared to exclude him from the Royal Council. As in the days of Jotham, Azrikam, commander of the palace, and Elkanah, the prime minister, were in their honored places on either side of the King's chair. There were others around the table, too: Urijah, the gentle-mannered, aging chief priest; Zechariah, Ahaz's father-in-law; fourteen-year-old Maaseiah, Ahaz's brother, eager to learn the arts of government and war. Then, too, there was that strange fellow, Uzziah ben-Tabeel, who had never been known to say a word of advice in the council hall, but whom Jotham had honored with a place in this inner circle in reward for his splendid service as a general in the Ammonite campaign.

Because he bore the name of the late King Uzziah and because to have called him by that name would have seemed somehow an infringement upon the royal memory of Ahaz's deceased grandfather, Uzziah ben-Tabeel was always merely "Ben-Tabeel," as though he had no name apart from the patronymic of his father. To Ahaz, he was one of the least problematical members of the council, silent and unassuming. For a moment, Ahaz's eyes rested upon the old warrior's stony face and the thought crossed his mind that here perhaps was one among his father's council who would offer him little opposition.

And then, of course, there was Ushna, Ahaz's only new appointee to the council. The Ammonite flashed Ahaz a look of radiant confidence that spoke as clearly as any words: *You are king. You are greater than any of them.*

Still, Ahaz sat silent.

In the days of Ahaz's absence, Elkanah the prime minister had thought through his strategy carefully and now was determined that it would be he who should make clear the intricacies of the alliance to the young King. He had brought with him a formidable looking map showing the proposed line of march and now was unrolling it enthusiastically before him. "Now if my King will give me his royal attention for just a brief moment," Elkanah's voice was smoothly ingratiating. Talk of this sort irritated Ahaz to the utmost. "The troops will assemble outside Jerusalem and march northward to Bethel." The absurd Elkanah, fat, well-oiled, lavishly attired, the very image of courtly ease, was glowing with eagerness for a good war as if he were a young recruit. "My royal master, I fear, is not listening."

"I am listening!" Ahaz's voice rose sharply in answer, as he shoved the map angrily to the floor. "And I want you to tell me one thing, Elkanah, why are you trying to get my country into this hopeless plot? Any king who thinks he can overcome Assyria is a fool, and that means Pekah and Rezin and anyone else ignorant enough to join them!"

"Your late father . . ."

"My late father included! He was a reckless, over-bold adventurer and all of you know it! But as for me, I don't want war in this country. I don't want the Assyrians pillaging our land, killing our men, taking our families as slaves!" Ahaz pounded his fist on the table with great force. "I love my country! I want her to survive!"

114

"The uprising is not to be in Judah, my King," Elkanah protested. "As I have pointed out before, your troops will march north to join the forces of Pekah and Rezin." The prime minister bent to retrieve the rejected map from the floor. "If you will just consider the line of march . . ."

Ahaz ignored the map. "You seem so certain that we would be victorious." His voice was loud and full of desperate pleading. "Has it never occurred to you that it is more likely we will be defeated and pursued back to our own lands, hunted out, and killed or taken as slaves?" Ahaz breathed heavily. "Do you want to bring that upon us, Elkanah?"

"It is strange indeed to hear such a brave young warrior as our king speak in such discouraging tones." Flattery had always worked wonders with Jotham in moments of hesitation, Elkanah knew. It was worth trying on Ahaz.

But it was a mistake. "I am not a warrior! Elkanah! All of you! The sooner you learn that about me, the better it will be for all of us. I fought in Ammon because I had no choice. Now I do have a choice and I have no desire to lead my nation into war."

Loud murmurs of discontent were heard around the table. "Perhaps then," suggested Azrikam, "you will entrust command of the Judean forces to some skillful general."

"There will be no Judean forces!" Ahaz shouted.

"What of your father's contract with Pekah?" The silent Ben-Tabeel, seemingly stirred by momentary visualization of himself as commander in chief, raised his voice humbly. "If my king would care to trust me . . ."

"Wait! Hold!" It was the voice of Isaiah. "The king has spoken wisely." Ahaz, startled at support from such unexpected quarter fixed his gaze intently upon his cousin.

"Speak on, Isaiah," the king commanded.

Isaiah rose from his place at the table. There was a glow of prophetic fire in his eyes, and everyone, even Ahaz, felt prepared for one of his typically lofty dissertations. For a few seconds, he stood silent, as if breathing a prayer for Yahweh's guidance and rapidly trying to collect his thoughts. When he spoke, it was not

115

with the voice of a holy man pleading for changes that might never come, but rather that of a calm, clear-thinking statesman, more reasoned indeed than anyone in the council hall. "We all know that Assyria is the mightiest nation on earth. Tiglath-pileser will doubtless come against all lands which join in the alliance against him. Judah must remain neutral if we are to be preserved as a free nation."

Ahaz smiled a smile of deep self-satisfaction. This cousin Isaiah might prove to be a very useful man to him after all.

"In quietness and in confidence there is strength," Isaiah went on. But Ahaz was not really listening. He glanced across the table toward Ushna the Ammonite.

"Would you have me draft a letter to Pekah informing him of our withdrawal?" Ushna knew instinctively what the king wanted to hear.

Ahaz nodded. "And to carry the message to Samaria?" He looked about the council table for a likely person to undertake this task, but saw no one.

"My king will excuse my presumption." For the second time that day, Ben-Tabeel lifted his voice. "I would be honored to serve as your envoy." At that very moment, beneath his humble exterior, a plot of preposterous dimensions was forming, but who would ever suspect a staunch old veteran like Ben-Tabeel of disloyalty to his king?

Unenthusiastically, Ahaz nodded his approval. Ben-Tabeel would do well enough, he supposed. "You may go and make preparations for your journey. Return promptly and we will have the letter ready for you."

Beaming with satisfaction, the king's newly appointed messenger did as he was told.

* * * * *

Pekah ben-Remaliah sat in state in his ivory palace in Samaria and listened with alternating bursts of fury and amazement to the report of Uzziah ben-Tabeel, the ambassador from Judah. Pekah

116

was an unkingly man; born a peasant, living for years as a hunted outlaw in the plains of Gilead, he had risen to power by a course of reckless, desperate daring. With his own hands he had killed his predecessor. Even now, there was still a rugged, uncouth air about him that not all the splendor of his surroundings could erase. So Ahaz, that despicable young weakling in the south, was deserting the cause. Unconsciously, the king's rough hand grasped at the hilt of his dagger. "May Yahweh strike him dead!" he muttered, more to himself than to Ben-Tabeel.

"Your Majesty," the Judean's voice dropped to a confidential whisper. "Just because Ahaz will not fight, my lord Pekah need not think that the people of Judah support him in his madness. They hate Ahaz, let me assure you of that."

Pekah smiled shrewdly. "A cowardly king is easily disposed of, isn't he, Ben-Tabeel?"

Pekah's willingness to cooperate was remarkable, thought the Judean. "I merely meant to imply," he protested aloud, "that our people have no great love for King Ahaz. There are hundreds, nay thousands, who fought for me in Ammon, and who will rally to me again."

Pekah did not need to hear further. Without another word to the cringing Judean, he called for his royal scribes and set about dictating the revised plan of action and issuing letters to his allies in Damascus and Philistia and Edom. "The withdrawal of the kingdom of Judah from the Contract of Alliance must not go unpunished!" he decreed in a dramatically powerful tone. "Your name is Uzziah, is it not?" he added, turning again to the messenger from Judah.

"Aye, Your Majesty."

"Named, no doubt, for his late Majesty of Judah?"

"If it please you . . ." Ben-Tabeel swallowed hard. He was none too proud of his name.

"Yes," said Pekah smiling. "It pleases me well, Uzziah the Second."

117

It was not long until all the court at Samaria was buzzing with talk concerning the king's decision. With the aid of his allies, Pekah ben-Remaliah would launch an early spring invasion of Judah, and the uncooperative Ahaz would be deposed. The people would rush to acclaim Ben-Tabeel as king, while Pekah himself, as the new king's sponsor, would become overlord of the Southern Kingdom. From there, they would proceed with plans against Assyria.

It was less than a fortnight after Ben-Tabeel's arrival in North Israel that Pekah and Rezin were on the march against Judah. When the word of Ben-Tabeel's treason reached Jerusalem, young Ahaz seemed at a loss to know what course of action he should follow. "What shall we do?" he moaned, burying his face in his hands and giving his council a most unkingly demonstration of despair. "The people will follow Ben-Tabeel."

"No, my King," Azrikam protested eloquently. "You must not forget that you are the son of the House of David; you are the living symbol of Yahweh's promise to the Judah. Our people will give their lives for you if the need be."

Azrikam spoke with the grace of an experienced courtier, but there was much truth in what he said. Yahweh's covenant with King David was a sacred thing to the people of Judah. There was not one among them who had not heard from early childhood of the Lord's word to that magnificent monarch who had ruled at the dawn of their national history: "Your house and your kingdom shall be made sure forever before me; your throne shall be established forever." Loyalty to this glorious tradition meant uncondi-

118

tional loyalty to the king, whoever he might be, so long as he was a member of the royal line. For nearly three hundred years, the succession had passed from father to son according to Yahweh's holy plan. Ahaz sat very still thinking of these things, feeling, as he had never felt before, a part of that mystic covenant. Slowly he removed his gold bracelet and looked at the Star of King David, imprinted on his arm in his childhood, so long ago now. The wonderful promise of the Davidic covenant was what the sign was supposed to symbolize. *Yahweh has chosen us. Yahweh has chosen me.* Who was to say but what Yahweh would indeed be gracious to him in this time of terror for the whole kingdom? Molech was Ahaz's special god, but Yahweh was the lord of the old covenant. And at this moment, Yahweh might well be the most likely source of divine help. Waves of longing penetrated Ahaz's soul, an unexplainable desire to be a king worthy of his people's love. He hated his weaknesses. The Ammonite campaign had been dreadful beyond words, but perhaps the greatest horror of it was its needlessness. Now, with Pekah and Rezin marching south, Judah was in an entirely different situation. This was a matter of defending the homeland, and suddenly Ahaz was determined to do his duty as king, no matter how unpleasant. *I will do it; I will go out with the army,* he was thinking when the voice of Elkanah shattered the heavy stillness in the council chamber.

"I can explain to our forces that it would be foolhardy for you to risk your life when you leave no son to succeed you." The prime minister was trying his best to be diplomatic; he knew the young king was not an enthusiastic fighter. How could he have guessed the sudden burst of determination that for a moment had inflamed Ahaz's soul, and even now in the wake of his words was dying out again?

"I shall trust you fully, Elkanah," Ahaz said, sighing deeply.

* * * * *

Before the afternoon was over, their strategy was formulated. As rapidly as possible, troops were to be mustered. Within a week's

119

time, Elkanah and Azrikam should be ready to march north at the head of the Judean forces. All reports indicated that they should encounter the main body of Pekah's army somewhere near the border. If they were successful in crushing the might of the invaders at this point, Jerusalem would be safe. The men of Judah were confident of victory.

Prince Maaseiah pleaded to go with them. Unlike his brother, he visualized going forth to battle as the greatest of all adventures. Ahaz, with what seemed an unusual stroke of cleverness, not only permitted him to go but made him nominal commander of the royal army. After all, it was high time he was learning the arts of war, and he might be able to do a great deal in preventing rivalry between Azrikam and Elkanah. The latter was sure to accomplish his duties as actual commander to the best of his ability, while Azrikam would be trusted with the position of special bodyguard for the youthful prince.

"You will take good care of him, Azrikam?" Ahaz's concern for his brother went deeper than he allowed himself to express. "Keep him out of real danger."

"My King, you may feel assured I will defend Prince Maaseiah with my life," the commander of the palace promised.

And with their banners flying proudly, the brave little expedition of Judeans marched away to its doom.

* * * * *

It was less than a week later when the news arrived of the drastic defeat outside of Gibeah. There had been a surprise attack upon the Judean camp before daybreak. The list of dead was stupendous, with scarcely a family in Jerusalem spared from the loss of some loved one. Ahaz and the remainder of the Royal Council sat stricken as they listened to the names of the casualties, Elkanah, the prime minister; Azrikam, commander of the palace; Maaseiah ben-Jotham, prince of Judah.

"I prayed so hard," Ahaz said bitterly. "To Molech *and* Yahweh and they both have failed me. I prayed that they would protect

120

my brother and grant our army victory." The king and Ushna had withdrawn and were now alone in Ushna's study, that same dark, mystic room where Ahaz had first pledged himself to the god of Ammon long ago.

"You must not blame Molech," Ushna said. "My King, it grieves me to say so; you have only yourself to blame. Molech is displeased with you."

"But why? What have I done?"

"You give open recognition to Yahweh. Molech is jealous. You even admit you prayed to Yahweh yourself."

"Yahweh is the national God of Judah," Ahaz protested. "And he is powerful. I don't understand him, but he is the God of our covenant. And I thought maybe he would protect Judah for the sake of his promise to King David. It was no use though; Yahweh has never listened to me. And Molech must know that *I* am not Yahweh's, I am his."

"Perhaps," said Ushna, "the time has come to prove it."

"Oh, yes!" Ahaz whispered in relief. "I will do anything so that he will not forsake me, so that he will keep me alive through this war. I'll build a public shrine in the valley of Hinnom."

"Wartime is not the time for shrine building. Molech would no doubt be pleased, but there is something you can give him which will please him far more." Ushna's voice was very solemn.

"Yes?"

"Your firstborn son."

"Ushna!" Ahaz gasped in horror. He had heard tales of the human sacrifices to Molech that went on in the land of Ammon. But such things did not happen in Judah. Yahweh's law forbade it.

Instinctively, Ushna seemed to be reading Ahaz's mind. "So it has not been done in Judah! So it is against the Law of Yahweh! Are you not the king? Are you not above the Law? Ahaz, listen to me: what gift could show your loyalty to Molech more deeply than the fruit of your own body?"

"I have no children," Ahaz protested weakly. "I do not think Abi will ever bear a child."

121

"The infant need not be Abi's. She need never know. Lie with some slave girl, my King, get her pregnant, and when the infant is born he can be spirited away and offered to our god." So Ushna spoke, yet even as the words fell from his lips, his mind stirred with the fascinating likelihood that Abi was already pregnant. While Ahaz was mourning for the losses at Gibeah, Lady Abi reputedly lay ill in her apartment, sick with the queasiness that anyone could readily identify. Ushna had his confidants among Abi's household staff; he had the report of her symptoms on good authority.

If she bears him a son and he destroys it, it will be the end of whatever bonds have held them together, Ushna thought with great self-satisfaction. His hatred of Abi was boundless. For four long years, it had rankled within him. Now, Molech had sent him the opportunity he longed for, the opportunity to alienate Abi and Ahaz forever.

Ahaz sighed. Fear and desperation and utter weariness hung heavy upon him. Within a few days the forces of the enemy would be encamped outside the walls of his capital. Within a few weeks he might well be dead or, what would be still worse, a captive king without a throne. If ever he needed the beneficence of his god, it was now.

"A bargain, Ahaz! A bargain! If Judah be spared from conquest by the enemy, give Molech your child! Swear it!" Ushna's voice rose in terrifying fervor. "It is your only hope."

"I swear," said Ahaz, sinking to his knees before Molech's shrine. "My lord and my god, I swear it. If ever I have a son, I shall offer him unto you in return for your protection."

* * * * *

For the next few days, Ahaz continued to wander inconsolably through the halls of the palace, clad in robes of sackcloth with ashes streaked upon his forehead. He clipped his hair and shaved off his splendid auburn beard; he fasted; he prayed to his Molech for hours on end. But of his vow, he said nothing.

Tales of the undaunted courage of Azrikam on the battlefield drifted back to the court. The commander of the palace had died defending the tent where Prince Maaseiah lay. Ahaz listened to the story over and over again from various survivors and wept each time he heard it. "My only brother! Why did I let him go?"

And the courtiers despaired of relieving his mind. Even when old Tamar brought word that Abi was very ill, he would take no heed. "You know what to do for her better than I," he muttered with a wave of dismissal.

Then at last, on the fourth day, he took time out from his mourning to call for a skillful gem cutter who would prepare a seal for Elkanah's successor. It was to be an elaborate thing, a deep red carnelian stone, intricately and beautifully carved. The inscription upon it, however, was brief, composed of only a few simple words: Ushna, Prime Minister of Ahaz.

The men of the court, even those who detested Ushna, took heart. The King was at least ready to begin business again. But for the unhappy Lady Abijah, lying in her apartment, ill and neglected, there was no such hopeful sign.

*　*　*　*　*

It was the day after the news arrived of the battle of Gibeah that Abi had first awakened with sickening chills. Ahaz was not with her. *He must have passed the night down in the hall with the mourners,* Abi realized, *and I should have, too, only I was so weary.* She thought of the long hours she had spent kneeling the day before, her voice lifted in the slow, mournful dirges that through the centuries the people of Judah had sung to wail the loss of their loved ones. Maaseiah, Ahaz's little brother, so soon grown up and now lying dead on the field of Gibeah. Abi moaned and told herself that the sickening feelings inside her must be the result of yesterday's tragic news. She breathed a prayer to Yahweh for strength.

But now, almost a week had passed and still each morning the chills and sickening discomfort lay hold of her, and she knew it was not the loss at Gibeah that had caused her weakness. With

123

tear-filled eyes, Abijah stared at the dancing spots of sunlight reflected on the floor beside her couch. It seemed impossible that the sun could be shining; impossible that through the window lattices she could catch a glimpse of green leaves and blue sky and hear the early morning chirping of the birds in the courtyard.

Waves of almost unbearable discomfort ran through her; she was very cold. Miserably, she pulled the light woolen coverlet closer about her and huddled among the pillows. "Oh God, why now?" she moaned. "Why after four years of unanswered entreaty? Why, when our country is torn by the ravages of war, did you decide to send me a child?"

Silent tears ran down her cheeks. Abijah was not the sort of woman who cried easily, and she must not allow herself to weep now. Her body ached with longing for Ahaz; desire to feel the warmth of his arms around her and to hear his voice speak words of comfort and love. *If he comes today, I will tell him*, she promised herself, and for a split second the thought brought relief. It seemed an eternity since she had been with him. Closing her eyes, she breathed her husband's name over and over: "Ahaz! Ahaz! Come to me!"

It would not have occurred to Abi to unburden her anxieties on anyone else, but the old slave woman Tamar, who all through the last days had waited on her with unprying patience, could plainly see the frightened girl's unhappiness. And now, in the early morning stillness, Abi suddenly became aware that the slave woman was pressing her hand with motherly gentleness. "Don't you worry, my lady," Tamar said when Abi looked up into her eyes.

"But," Abi protested, "You do not know. I am pregnant, now when the enemies are pillaging the country and killing our men. Yahweh only knows what will become of me."

"So it is a little one, is it? I suspected as much, and my lady, let me say that surely the coming of the child at this time is a wonderful omen, a sign that God is with us." The aged voice radiated enthusiasm. "And think how happy your mother and father will be when they hear! Their first grandchild, is it not?"

Abi nodded and a flicker of a smile lighted her face. "God is with us," she repeated. "I will send a note to my father at the Temple," she added after a moment, rising weakly from her couch. She was infinitely grateful that she had learned to write. So many women had to depend on scribes if they ever sent a letter at all, and Abi would not have cared to trust a scribe with this message.

The note to her father was cheerfully impulsive, stating the news simply and briefly. Abi rolled it, then opened it again and scribbled a little postscript at the bottom: "If it is a boy, I think I will call him Immanuel, meaning 'God is with us,' for surely he is."

"Shebnak will take it across to the Temple," Tamar remarked as Abi rerolled and sealed the little missive. "I'll find him. Ah, my Lady, I can see the joy in your father's eyes now! Grandfather of the future king of Judah!"

"It will be a boy. You know it will!" Abi said emphatically.

"Oh, for certain it will! And he will be as handsome as his father. I wish you could have seen Ahaz when he was a baby!" Tamar fluttered about with excitement.

Abijah smiled. "Take the note to Shebnak. Hurry! So my father will get it before they start the morning ritual."

Singing lightly, Tamar went on her way to obey her mistress's orders.

* * * * *

The priest Zechariah had long been fearful that his daughter would never bear a child for the king. He had listened to the popular complaints against the fruitless union and shivered with apprehension whenever the suggestion was made that the king put Abi away and take another bride. Now it was with trembling hands that he broke the seal on the little scroll. *Ahaz is rejecting her,* he thought and a feeling of utter helplessness engulfed him. Then he read, and his fears were transformed into exaltation. His heart fairly bursting with relief, the aging priest sank to his knees and cried aloud his thanks to God. Abi carried the king's child. Zechariah could scarcely wait to share the wonderful secret. The idea that he was betraying his daughter's confidence never entered Zech-

125

ariah's mind. *Surely Ahaz already knows,* he thought, if indeed he thought at all.

The first to hear the news was the chief priest, Urijah, already a proud grandfather many times over. "To think that my own grandson may someday be king of Judah!" Zechariah pronounced with pride. Old Urijah smiled. The secret would be safe with him; he was not one to gossip like a tattling female.

And then Prince Isaiah came to the Temple, as he did almost daily and he too was informed of the imminent birth of the royal child. "Abijah has even chosen a name for him," Zechariah went on proudly, divulging all the contents of the letter. "Immanuel. Isn't that splendid? Just think, Prince Immanuel of Judah, my grandson. . ."

The prophet listened courteously but with little interest for his mind was on other things. This was the day he was moving his family into their new city home, for all Jerusalem was buzzing with the rumor that within a day or two the city would be under siege, and inside its strong walls, Isaiah hoped to keep his family safe from the oncoming tides of Pekah's forces. That King Ahaz was at last about to be blessed with an heir to the throne seemed a matter of small importance in comparison to this.

* * * * *

Tonight Ahaz will surely come and I will tell him, Abi promised herself all that morning, as she tried without success to still the waves of concern which continued to shake her. *After all he has been mourning now for five days.*

Ahaz came sooner than she had thought, indeed before the morning passed, but he was in no mood to hear Abijah's news. "I must tell you something horrible, Abi. Before tomorrow morning we will be besieged!" The young king leaned in the doorway of his wife's bedchamber. His face was a deathly white, but he was making a noble effort to keep calm.

A thousand thoughts raced through Abi's mind at once. Her heart beat wildly. The fears she had not dared to entertain pressed upon her. Siege, then perhaps hunger, defeat, slavery, no!

"My scouts have sighted the enemy troops encamped less than a day's march from our city walls," Ahaz continued. "The people are all blaming me for this, but what could I do? If I had joined Pekah's alliance, the Assyrians would have killed us all."

"You were right not to join them," Abijah spoke with pretended conviction, not daring to think of the full significance of Ahaz's words. The steadiness in her voice surprised her. She must not let him see her fear. Gently, she took his hand in hers, led him to her ivory couch, and urged him to lie back upon the soft mountain of pillows. *Twenty years old and all the weight of a war-torn kingdom upon him! And he not even a soldier! It is too much!* Abi felt a deep longing to help Ahaz escape the responsibilities of royalty, but it was a feeling of weakness which she could not allow herself. *In his hour of deepest need, Ahaz has come to me,* Abi thought. "Jerusalem will withstand the siege," she said aloud.

"Yes, we will if we can. But Pekah has already killed off my best men at Gibeah. And besides that, the Edomites have crossed the southern border and destroyed our garrison at Elath. Our seaport, our only seaport! It was my grandfather's pride and joy. I just received word of it this morning. Abi, we have practically no army left!"

"But we have a strongly walled city and if we can just hold out long enough, our enemies will have to withdraw. It is impossible to take Jerusalem. Everybody says so." Abi felt a surge of confidence and prayed fervently that she had imparted some of it to her husband.

Ahaz's face brightened. "The food situation will not be so hard to handle, thanks to my grandfather's storechambers." Years before, Uzziah, a strong believer in preparedness, had ordered construction of a number of grain warehouses in Jerusalem to be stocked yearly as reserve for such an emergency. "Our greatest concern is water," Ahaz went on. "Something will have to be done about seeing to it that the water supply is safe. Now if we can just get enough water into the city reservoir before the siege actually begins, then we can close up the conduits and hold out indefinitely."

127

How often had Ahaz remarked in more serene times that Jerusalem's greatest weakness was in the antiquated system of bringing water along conduits into the reservoir! "You will have to send someone to inspect the situation immediately. See about closing up the tunnels in the city wall."

"I'm going myself in just a few moments," Ahaz answered. "Ushna is readying things now." The King's long graceful fingers toyed with a gold tassel on one of Abi's pillows. He did not look into her eyes. Abi sensed he had something more to tell her, but for long moments neither of them spoke.

"Abi," he said at last, "our resistance simply is not going to be enough. I am going to send an appeal for aid to Tiglath-pileser."

Tiglath-pileser of Assyria, the most powerful ruler on earth. Abi was aghast.

"Ushna says it is the only real solution," Ahaz went on. "I will try to persuade the Assyrian to invade Rezin's territory in Syria from the north and our enemies will have to withdraw to fight him. Judah will be left in peace. Ushna assures me it will work."

Ushna! Why must Ahaz forever be listening to him? What does he care for Judah? What does he really care for anything except his own selfish soul? An appeal to Tiglath-pileser would have to be accompanied by a lavish bribe. In some mysterious way that she could not begin to fathom, Abi felt sure that Ushna intended to work the entire situation for his personal profit. Her mind worked frantically to produce an alternative to the Ammonite's plan. "Don't you think we could wait a while and see if we are really going to need help?" she said weakly.

"If I wait, I may not be able to get word through the siege. The appeal must go today. Abi, I tell you, I do not like the idea so much either, but it is the safest way. Oh, and what if it should fail?" Ahaz tossed the tasseled pillow aside. "Why was I born to be king, Abi? Heaven knows, it is not what I would have chosen for myself."

In moments like this one, Abi's only care was for the man she loved. Her hatred of Ushna, her fear of the besiegers, even the awareness of the child she was carrying, all these left her. "My

128

dearest," she whispered, her lips against Ahaz's ear, "you do what you think is best, I've a feeling that someday, they will write in the annals of Judah how the wisdom of King Ahaz saved his country from the hand of the enemy."

Ahaz turned to her and swept her close to him in a powerful embrace. Here lay the healing balm for his torn and shaken confidence. He held her close, not dreaming of the unspoken agonies that racked her own heart at the same moment. "For you, my beloved, for your sake, I cannot let them conquer us."

Abi gazed up adoringly into his dark, troubled eyes. *The child I shall bear,* she thought, *shall be a living sign of my love for this man. O God, O God, may he be born into a land at peace!* She surpressed the fiery longing to tell Ahaz of the child. "Come back to me when you return from the conduit," she whispered, after long, precious moments of wordless ecstacy.

"Indeed, I shall," he promised. Then sighing deeply, he rose and was on his way.

* * * * *

Beneath the perfect blue of the spring afternoon sky, a little party toiled up the road toward the city of Jerusalem. Two men, one a prince and the other the prince's servant, trudged along beside a sturdy donkey cart which was piled high with odds and ends of furniture and other possessions. Isaiah, prince of Judah, like countless other refugees on the road that day, was tending to the heartrending task of moving.

Already that morning, he had brought his wife Naamah to their new quarters in the city and now there was just the business of transporting the cartload of possessions. When the besiegers came, and well did Isaiah know it might be that very night, he and his family and the few treasures Naamah had insisted on bringing with them would be safely within the city.

Perched high on a large wooden chest which contained his mother's clothes sat little Shear-jashub, the prophet's son. As the old, two-wheeled cart rumbled and creaked and jolted over the rough

129

road, the boy atop the load bounced happily. To Shear-jashub, the business of moving was a glorious adventure. "Look, Father!" The thought had just popped into the boy's mind to play that the donkey cart was a royal chariot, and he clambered to a precarious standing position atop the great box.

"Jashub!" In an instant Isaiah had pulled him down again. "Do you want to fall in the road and break all your bones?" the prophet said in a voice that clearly indicated his disapproval. "Now sit very still, for we'll soon be in the city and I want to tell your mother how good you've been."

Obediently, Jashub settled down again in his place, and Isaiah patted his head lovingly. The boy adored his father; to him there was nothing at all strange in the fact that the man whom people called Prince Isaiah more often than not dressed in a coarse robe of sackcloth, when he could if he chose, array himself in garments of royal splendor. Jashub knew only that his father was gentle and kind and that he loved him very much. "Father," the boy said in a plaintive tone after a few moments, the incident of his standing up in the cart forgotten, "sing me a song."

The people of Judah through the centuries had been as much inclined to singing in times of sorrow as in times of rejoicing. The boy's request was a good one, Isaiah thought, lifting his voice in a song of fervent hope, one like so many which he sang lately, telling of Yahweh's unfailing love for Jerusalem and his eternal protection of the Holy City. "As the mountains are round about Jerusalem, So Yahweh is round about his people." The prophet's deep and beautiful voice rang out confidently in the ancient psalm which had its origin in the misty dawn of Judah's national history.

But even as he sang, Isaiah's mind was on a piece of almost incredible news which he had heard from the high priest Urijah that very morning. The old man had whispered to him in strictest confidence, pulling him aside after his colleague Zechariah had finally had his fill in telling about the Lady Abi's pregnancy. "Ahaz is planning to send an appeal for aid to Tiglath-pileser!" Urijah had had it direct from the slave Shebnak when he brought the note from Zechariah's daughter. Shebnak, rest assured, had heard it from one of Ushna's own men.

130

Isaiah's first impulse had been to deny the rumor as absurd. Certainly Ahaz must realize that as soon as Tiglath-pileser got wind of Pekah's anti-Assyrian plot, he would march against the rebels without any need of a summons from Ahaz. On the other hand, if Ahaz sent to the Assyrian for aid, he would be obligated to send a heavy tribute also. Any clear-thinking monarch in Ahaz's position would, of course, prepare for the siege and then wait for events to follow their natural course. But was it safe to count on Ahaz to think clearly? Isaiah wondered. *If I could only see the king*, he told himself, *I could show him that it is not Yahweh's will for Judah to seek alliance with foreign powers.*

Suddenly, the sound of hoofbeats and chariot wheels in the distance entered Isaiah's consciousness like an answer to prayer. The song he was singing with only half-awareness broke off, and he gazed down the road toward Jerusalem and saw coming toward him a cluster of horses and chariots. As they approached the place by the fuller's field where the conduit ran parallel to the highway, the men dismounted. Clearly they were persons of rank, Isaiah thought, coming closer. Surely the king would not be riding out in the country today of all days. Yet who was the figure whose fiery auburn hair Isaiah could make out even at this distance? Clearly, unmistakably, it was Ahaz.

Quite without warning, the prophet exclaimed "Stop," to the manservant who was leading his donkey cart. "Wait for me here under this tree. Jashub, my boy," he continued, "you and I are going to see the king."

Ahaz did not see them approaching, for he and his advisors were engrossed in talk about the conduit. "I believe," the king was saying, "that the workmen we left at the city wall must have closed the gap where the water enters the city by now. Ushna! The measuring rod for the water level! Ah yes! And presumably the rest of the men are now at the reservoir. Someday, I'll declare, when this siege is over, I'm going to have a tunnel dug underground."

"Our king is very wise," said Ushna, who had had the idea for the tunnel in the first place.

By this time Isaiah had come within speaking distance. He saw

131

that no one was noticing him and called out in his finest courtly manner: "Hail to my lord, the king!"

"Good day to you, cousin," Ahaz said as civilly as he could. "I trust you come in good health."

Isaiah would waste no time on the formality of greetings. "I come with the word of Yahweh," he said, and there was no doubting the sincerity in his voice. "Take heed, O Ahaz! Do not fear, do not let your heart be faint!"

"What do you take me to be, a craven coward, a weakling?" the king interrupted angrily. "I am doing all I can to save Judah! The alliance with Assyria is our only hope!"

So he is indeed seeking alliance with Tiglath-pileser. The full reality of the King's plan trembled in Isaiah's consciousness and the desperate urgency of it impelled him to speak more boldly than he had ever done before. The enemies, Pekah and Rezin, he proclaimed were but "smouldering stumps of firebrands."

A cold, thoughtless remark, thought Ahaz, *when their armies have only recently slain my brother, and my generals, and several thousand of my men.*

"If you do not trust in Yahweh, your rule shall not be established!" Isaiah finished in a burst of exclamatory indignation.

Ahaz stared down wordlessly at the slowly flowing waters of the conduit. *What does Yahweh care for me?* he thought. *Why should I trust him when he has dealt so harshly with all of us?* As usual when Yahweh was mentioned, his mind turned to the painful memories of his grandfather's disease and of the shattering of his grandmother's once fervent trust. For an instant, Ahaz felt tempted to speak out about these things, but a deep-rooted sense of caution held him back. For after all, for good or ill, Yahweh was irrevocably the God of Ahaz's kingdom and of the Davidic covenant. Moreover, Yahweh was extremely powerful and there was no need to risk his wrath.

For a moment the stillness was so heavy that there was no sound at all but the faint tossing of the wind in the tall cypress trees in a lonely border at the side of the field. The prophet fixed his gaze on the windswept trees. *That is the way the king's heart is shaking,*

132

he thought, *as the trees of the forest shake before the wind. O Yahweh, my Lord and my God, give me the power to save him and our nation from disaster!* Isaiah's soul burned with love for Judah and longing to preserve Judah's freedom that no words could express. *Surely, Yahweh, you will not let the land and people of your covenant become subject to that foreign despot. Lord, I am your instrument! Give me power!*

And he felt a sense of heavenly power sweep through him. "Ask a sign of Yahweh, your God!" Isaiah's voice shattered the stillness with glorious defiance. "Let it be as deep as Sheol, or as high as heaven."

A sign. He thinks he can prove that it is wrong for me to appeal to Assyria. Ahaz had no doubt of Isaiah's ability to produce a sign if the need be. *Yahweh, indeed all the gods of heaven, perhaps even Molech, are against me,* Ahaz thought. Somehow an answer came to him, a splendid answer, and he spoke in a voice as boldly defiant as the prophet's. "I will not ask. I will not put Yahweh to the test!"

Isaiah's reply was fearlessly stinging. "Hear then, Ahaz! Is it not enough that you weary men? Must you weary my God also?"

The king's face reddened with rage. His hands clenched into fists, but he did not utter a word. He was remembering the words Azrikam had spoken scarcely a week ago before he marched off to die in battle, words about how he, Ahaz, was the living symbol of Yahweh's eternal covenant with the House of David. *Heaven knows,* Ahaz thought, *Yahweh and all the gods know I love my land with all my soul. I would rather die than see Judah conquered. I am even willing to submit myself as a tributary to the Assyrians to save my kingdom from the ravages of the enemy. What greater love could any king show for his kingdom than this?*

Still Isaiah was raving on—something about the birth of a child who would be called Immanuel. Ahaz was scarcely listening.

"Isaiah," he said at length, in a cool deliberate voice, "I am not interested in your prophesying and you do not sway me at all. Now go your way." His hastily controlled temper was rising. "Who are you to interpret Yahweh's will anyway? I am the king, not you. I am Yahweh's anointed one, and were it not his will I would not have been born to the kingship. Say what you like; the God of Judah works through his anointed one!"

These were high-sounding phrases. *A choice rebuttal to the prophet's criticism,* Ahaz thought . But deep in his heart he had small confidence in his own claims. Fired by the heat of his own oratory, the king did not even notice when the prophet gathered little Shear-jashub up in his arms and turned back to his cartload of furniture.

"I am Yahweh's chosen one!" Ahaz exclaimed again with great fervor, and suddenly he felt Ushna's gentle tapping on his shoulder. Looking up, he realized that the prophet had not even stayed to hear him out.

Ahaz reached home still fuming over the scene with Isaiah and he was distinctly in no mood to listen to Abijah's news. She sensed immediately that something had made him very angry when he came in and flung himself down dejectedly on the couch. "That prophet!" he muttered. "He seems to think that he has some sort of divine commission to go about criticizing his king. If he were not a holy man of Yahweh, I'd . . . I'd . . . . " Ahaz stammered.

"What did he do?" Abi asked half-heartedly. *Why must we talk about that prophet when I would tell him about the child?* she thought.

"It was the most insolent thing he has done yet, telling me not to worry. 'Take heed, be quiet, do not fear!' And then all that nonsense about a sign from Yahweh. Does he think I am so easily led about that I would put off my appeal to Assyria just because he claims it is displeasing to his God? Can you imagine that, Abi? Whatever makes him dare to talk so?"

Abijah did not try to grasp the import of her husband's complaints. "Ahaz . . . ." A gentle whisper. She rose from her chair and seated herself on the edge of his couch. "There is one wonderful thing in the midst of all our troubles." She laid her soft hand on his arm.

"Don't preach to me about Yahweh!" He drew himself away and sat upright. "Don't tell me to have confidence and trust in the Lord!" His voice rose angrily.

Abi's eyes welled with tears. "I didn't say that," she began. "Have I ever tried to force Yahweh on you?"

135

"Well, what is it then?"

The tension in Abijah's heart mounted to a feverish pitch. "I wanted to tell you I am going to have a child."

"Abi!" Ahaz's face registered a look of utter agony, for a reason that Abijah never dreamed of.

"Don't worry, my love, it is a wonderful omen, a sign of hope. Darling, I have waited so long." Her arms were about him, her deep brown eyes looking up into his with inexpressible pleading.

"Molech!" he whispered, and Abi could feel the frantic thumping of his heart.

"Ahaz, Ahaz, tell me you are happy!"

Great tears welled up in Ahaz's eyes, but he did not speak. No threat of the enemy, no fear of losing his kingdom and his life could equal the horror of this new development. He had sworn to Molech a vow which he dared not break. Yet fulfilling it would break the heart of the woman who was dearer to him even than his god. He could not bring himself to speak, and after a long moment it was Abi who broke the silence.

"It will be a boy, I know. It just has to be. And I thought we might call him 'Immanuel,' 'God is with us.' "

"Oh no!" Ahaz drew away. With that statement all the discomforting memories of the afternoon's meeting with Isaiah came flooding back. "Not that . . . anything but that!" He almost screamed. "That must be what Isaiah meant today about a sign from Yahweh . . . that you were with child! How would he know before me? And the name Immanuel!" The horror in Ahaz's face had turned to rage; his hands were on Abi's shoulders. "How would he know, Abijah?" he shouted, shaking her violently. "Explain that!"

"Why, Ahaz, I can't imagine it." Her voice was weak and terribly frightened. "He would have no way of knowing." The surprised innocence in her unhappy eyes should have been convincing. "Maybe he had a revelation from Yahweh," she added. She did not doubt for an instant that such a thing was possible. "Tell me what he said."

The suggestion was repellant to the king. "I do not care to discuss it," he said and stalked away.

"Ahaz! Please!" she called after him, but he ignored her call. In an instant his fear over his reckless vow to Molech had been replaced by one yet more agonizing: *The child she will bear is not mine, but that prophet's.*

Desperate, he ran to the little shrine that he and Ushna had built upon the roof in happier days and threw himself at the feet of the great god of Ammon. There was no desire for life left in him.

* * * * *

How long he lay there before Ushna came Ahaz never knew. The threatening siege of Jerusalem, the appeal for help from a foreign power, and now, most sickening of all, the fear that the wife he so deeply loved had been untrue to him. For eternally long moments, his eyes fastened on the edge of the roof. It would not be hard to jump, the misty haunts of Sheol would be welcome relief. *But I have no heir,* Ahaz moaned to himself. *Isaiah, that unspeakable man, is first in line of succession now that Maaseiah is gone.* Isaiah's own father, Prince Amoz, had died suddenly the year before. A picture of Isaiah as king floated through Ahaz's brain. And this thought, if nothing else, fanned the flame of his will to live.

"Give me strength, Molech!" Ahaz's hands clung desperately to the hard bronze pedestal at the idol's feet. "God of my mother!"

Somewhere in his consciousness he heard soft approaching footsteps and knew that someone stood silently watching him, but he did not move.

It was not to Ushna's liking to interrupt one so deeply plunged in supplication to Molech, but after all, the appeal to Tiglath-pileser had to go out today and it could not go without the King's seal. "Ahaz, I have the letter for the Assyrian," he said at last.

"Oh," Ahaz breathed. Slowly he raised himself to a sitting position and pushed back the wavy auburn wisps that hung low on his forehead. Ushna could not fail to see the disconsolate droop of his shoulders.

137

"You are worried about the siege," he said. "Aye, it is well to come to Molech for guidance, but we cannot spend all our time in moaning."

"Would to heaven it were only the siege!" Ahaz replied. "In that, at least, I know where to turn for help, but this . . . this . . ."

"The prophet? He is nothing. Just a restless, headstrong braggart, craving publicity!"

"And my wife is pregnant with his child!"

"Ahaz! What are you saying?"

"You heard it with your own ears, Ushna, this very afternoon. 'Yahweh himself shall give you a sign . . . The young woman shall bear a son and call his name Immanuel . . . .' Then, when I returned I went to Abi and she told me she is pregnant," Ahaz paused, waiting for Ushna to comment, but the Ammonite did not speak. "And . . . and . . . she told me she wanted to name him Immanuel! Oh Ushna, how else would that prophet know unless she told him? They even contrived together what they would call him."

Frantically Ahaz was hoping that Ushna could think of something to disprove his suspicions, but the priest's cold silence banished any such glimmer of hope. Ushna was puzzled. Perhaps Ahaz was correct, perhaps there was a liaison between Abi and Isaiah. It seemed unlikely. But what did it matter, so long as Ahaz believed it?

For long moments, Ushna merely stared at Ahaz with his black beady eyes, supressing with effort the flicker of a smile that almost escaped his lips. The young king was not looking at Ushna. His eyes were fixed upon the fiery ruby gaze of the idol.

"Surely Molech will not want the bastard," he said at length. "Has he done this to me just to torment me?"

"To test your strength perhaps," Ushna replied suavely. It did not matter to him what cause would drive Abi and Ahaz apart, so long as something happened to produce that end. If Ahaz decided to accuse her of adultery, she could be stoned to death. So much the better. "Now, my king, the letter to the Assyrians," he said

138

aloud. "It cannot be delayed any longer. If you will but come and sign it."

The king rose with difficulty, leaning heavily on the priest's shoulder. "Our strategy against the enemy will make you the hero of our nation," Ushna predicted enthusiastically, but Ahaz paid him no heed.

"Let me sign the letter and then mix me some sleeping potion and good strong wine," Ahaz said.

"Well enough. I will go and prepare it and meet you in the council hall."

"The council hall . . . ." Ahaz repeated as he watched Ushna hurry away.

* * * * *

It was at the landing of the stairway that led down to the inner court that the King came face-to-face with Zechariah the priest. "My Lord and king!" Ahaz's father-in-law had a habit of speaking in the high-flown phrases that had so pleased Jotham. "I rejoice with you in the news of your child to come." He did not notice the unusual paleness in Ahaz's face, a pallor which was turning even now to burning rage.

"Who told you?" Ahaz was trembling so violently he could scarcely speak the words. "That cursed prophet?"

Amazement was written on Zechariah's aging face. "Isaiah? Why, no, I told him, this morning. Abijah sent me a letter herself. My king!" Zechariah broke off for suddenly Ahaz was embracing him with all his youthful vigor.

"My father! My father!" Tears rolled down his cheeks. "Can I believe you?"

"Would I lie to my king? Here, I have the letter. Read it yourself." Abijah's father freed himself from the king's frantic clutches and pulled the tiny scroll from his girdle. "If perhaps I spoke hastily this morning, I can only beg you will forgive me. It never occurred to me that you would not want Isaiah to know. I was so pleased."

Ahaz did not wait for him to finish. "I will forgive you anything,

139

Zechariah! Go out, break all your laws of Moses at once and I'll forgive you! You have given me my child!" Without a sign of warning, he kissed the older man lightly on the forehead, and then clutching Abi's note tightly in his hand, he ran down the stairs of the palace to the audience hall to share the good news of his heir-to-be with anyone and everyone who would listen.

When Ushna finally coaxed him to the council chamber, the young king was still glowing with an enthusiasm that made the priest of Molech quiver. "Ahaz, what under the sun?" He could not contain his amazement.

The king smiled enigmatically. In the moments that Zechariah had spoken to him on the roof everything had become clear. The whole agonizing cycle of events was the work of some divine hand, intervening to release him from his vow to Molech, sparing him from destroying the child that Abi would bear him. And who could that divine rescuer be but Yahweh? Yahweh whose priest Zechariah was? Yahweh to whom Abi herself had prayed so long for a child? Ahaz's heart sang with gratitude. What did it matter if Ushna believed the child to be a bastard? A power mightier than Molech was whispering in Ahaz's soul: "Heaven wills the child shall live." *In due time I shall acknowledge Yahweh publicly*, Ahaz was thinking, *but not so soon that Ushna would suspect.*

"I have had a revelation from Molech," the king said at last, lying boldly. "He has told me that I must forgive Abi and accept her child as my own, and if it is a boy I must make him my heir. Molech requires this of me. Who am I to dispute his will? And now, the letter . . . ." The astonished Ushna spread the document before Ahaz, then brought the sealing wax for the impression of the king's ring.

Ahaz glanced at the letter. "I am your servant and your son," it began. "Come up and rescue me from the hand of the king of Israel and the king of Syria who are besieging me . . ."

"Give me ink, Ushna," Ahaz said. "I would have that Assyrian see that I can write as well as press wax." It was an unusual request, for the King's seal was all that was necessary, but Ushna did not question him. Obediently, he brought the writing materials, watched wonderingly as Ahaz seized the quill, and then gasped in astonishment as the young man signed in his large, uneven handwriting: Jehoahaz the King, Ben-Jotham Ben-Uzziah.

"There," said Ahaz, affixing his seal, "and may all the gods of heaven bless its delivery."

"And now does my king still want the potion?" Ushna inquired.

Ahaz did not even answer, but turned and, with step light and swinging, strode across the inner court and up the stairs towards Abi's bedchamber.

* * * * *

In later days, Abi would look back upon that unforgettable night in wonder. She would never know what had impelled Ahaz, who that afternoon had been burning with fury, to return to her and in ecstatic whispers to sigh: "The child . . . our child . . . it is the gift of Yahweh." He pressed her close against him. She only knew that her prayers seemed to be answered and in the brief hours they spent together that night she felt complete happiness which even the thought of the enemy armies could not mar.

Long after Abi slept that night, Ahaz lay wakeful. Thoughts he scarcely dared to think raced through his brain. For the first time in his life he dared to despise Molech; that bloodthirsty creature had tried to trick him into destroying Abi's child. And it would have been done had Yahweh not intervened. It seemed that Yahweh was on his side after all. Who could understand the workings of the gods? Ahaz only knew that he wanted help and protection, and in the strange incidents of the day Yahweh seemed to be reaching out to him. Perhaps these things were all signs that the God of Judah would continue to help Jerusalem through the siege. Perhaps this was the true explanation of what Isaiah had meant by the sign of Immanuel, "God-is-with-us." It was a magnificent name, worthy of a great prince. *Perhaps I could call my child Immanuel, after all,* Ahaz thought. *No, that would be bending too much to Isaiah's wishes.* Ahaz tingled as he thought of his impulsive signing of his own name as "Jehoahaz" on the letter to the Assyrian.

141

For the first time ever, he regretted having changed his official name to Ahaz. He wished instead that he had kept the name his father gave him, with its clear token of dedication to Yahweh. Ah well, it was too late to change it back again. He would not have people thinking he was inconsistent. But he would surely give a Yahweh name to his and Abi's child. What did Abi always say: *we must not ask Yahweh for favors, we must ask him for strength to bear whatever must be borne.* "Lord Yahweh, give me courage to endure this siege and I will name my child Hezekiah," Ahaz prayed. "Yahweh-is-my-strength."

The spring night air was cool. Silently Ahaz eased himself from the bed where he lay, tossed a light coverlet about his shoulders, and strode out to the open rooftop beneath the boundless sky where Yahweh dwelt. "Lord God of Judah," he said softly. "Hear me! I am grateful to you for everything, but I dare not let it be known as yet. I will wait, and when the New Year comes this fall, provided we endure the siege, then I shall acknowledge your help before all the nation." Ahaz's spirit was wondrously light from the removal of the great burden that had oppressed him that day. He felt a powerful confidence that the siege would be lifted, that Yahweh, who had helped him once, would continue to do so. But what of Molech? And Ushna? What of Ahaz's solemn vows to the great god of the Ammonites? Could there be any permanent escape from the hold that the bloodthirsty god of the glowing fires had upon him since early childhood?

No, thought Ahaz, *there is no escape, but perhaps I can placate him.* "You shall have your glory, Molech. When the siege is over, I will build you a public shrine in the valley of Hinnom and you shall have more worshipers than ever before."

* * * * *

The next morning, just at daybreak, while the armies of Pekah and Rezin set up siege outside the walls of Jerusalem, Isaiah the prophet walked alone up the slope of Mt. Zion to the Temple.

142

A few early rising citizens peered out at him from behind the shutters of their homes and wondered what strange business the prophet was about now, but otherwise the city was ominously still.

Barefoot and clad in his usual sackcloth, Isaiah was carrying an unusually large wax tablet in his arms. He and Naamah had worked late the night before preparing the tablet from an old piece of lumber on which they had applied a thick coating of wax. The load was heavy and bulky, but Isaiah was not one to allow minor hindrances to stand in the way of accomplishing a task once he had set his mind to it. There was an unquenchable sense of finesse in the character of this prince of the royal family, a finesse that his calling to Yahweh's service had not mitigated. The tablet . . . ah, already he could visualize the crowds gathering and hear their clamor for an explanation of the inscription which he had carved upon it: Maher-shalal-hash-baz, which meant, in the language of Judah: "The spoil speeds, the prey hastens."

When he reached the Temple courtyard, Isaiah sat down on the steps and laid the heavy tablet flat down beside him. It was most necessary to get priestly witnesses to seal the tablet, he reminded himself. *The great failure of so many of our prophets has been their inability to win support from the organized cult of Yahweh at the Temple. When priest and prophet work together the people are much more likely to be impressed.* There would be no trouble in getting the priest Urijah to cooperate, Isaiah knew. Urijah was a remarkably agreeable man.

When at length the priests arrived at the Temple to perform the morning ritual, they found Isaiah waiting for them. With a tone of great urgency, he called aside Urijah and also Zechariah (for everyone respected the king's father-in-law) and explained to them the purpose of the tablet. "I want to assure the people that Pekah and Rezin will very shortly find their lands despoiled and plundered by Assyria," he said simply. "The folk of this city have no real idea of the strength of Tiglath-pileser. They must be told that their fears of the anti-Assyrian league are needless. And they must be shown also," the prophet's voice dropped to a whisper,

143

"that what shall happen to North Israel and Syria may happen to Judah as well if our king entangles us in the web of foreign alliances."

It was a mystifying thing, Urijah sighed to himself, the way this young Prince Isaiah thought he was serving Yahweh through interfering in politics. In all his long life as a man of God, Urijah had scrupulously avoided controversy whenever possible.

"If you would just lay your seal to the tablet," Isaiah was saying, "and you too, Zechariah."

The elderly priests looked at each other wonderingly and then again at the earnest face of the young prophet. Isaiah is wealthy, Urijah thought, and any other rich man seeking a favor from the Temple would offer a little gift. "What do we receive from this?" he said smoothly.

"You will have the assurance in your hearts that what you have done is pleasing to our God." Isaiah's reply was startlingly simple. Something within Urijah's soul trembled and fresh remembrance of the night when the newly committed prophet had first come to Jotham's banquet hall swept through him. "Isaiah," he said, pressing the seal of his priestly office into the yielding wax, "I have heard tell that you are writing a record of your work for Yahweh." The prophet nodded and the priest continued. "Well, then, there is something which you can do to reward me beyond measure; write of Urijah that he was proud to be your witness."

"Indeed, I shall," Isaiah promised, "and you, also, Zechariah," for by now Zechariah too had fixed his seal upon the tablet of Maher-shalal-hash-baz. "And I trust you both will pray for my success."

The priests assured him that they would, and with that he lifted the heavy tablet in his arms once more and started down the hill to the waiting crowds.

* * * * *

As Isaiah had hoped, the days that followed brought a great number of curious persons to stare at the tablet which he set up in front of his house, and when they came he was always ready to speak to them. "Syria and North Israel will lift their siege very soon. The lands of Pekah and Rezin will be invaded by the Assyrians, and the two kings of whom we stand so much in dread will fall."

But when?

The long weeks of the siege wore on: outside the walls, Pekah and Rezin's men could be observed building huge ramps of earthwork, designed ultimately to bring them level with the top of the wall. Day and night, defenders of Jerusalem remained positioned on their ramparts, with piles of large stones to drop down on the head of any enemy who ventured near. Meanwhile, there were frightening reports that some of Rezin's troops were attempting to dig a tunnel under the city wall, though Ahaz's forces could find no traces of such a mining operation. Daily the king and his advisors walked the circuit of the walls. Ahaz watched the enemy's ever-growing earthworks with mounting apprehension, but to his people he presented a calm, reassuring facade. "Our allies are on their way to deliver us," he often said. "We will be rescued."

Because Jerusalem was full of refugees along with the usual inhabitants, food supplies were running low. King Ahaz opened the royal grain warehouse, and rations were doled out to the hungry. "It could be much worse," people were heard to comment. "It *will* get worse," said others. "At the siege of Samaria in the days of King Jehoram, women killed and ate their own children."

"It can't happen here. Yahweh will protect us."

"Yahweh or Molech or Assher of Assyria; maybe we need them all."

"If Tiglath-pileser is coming, he had better hurry."

"He will come," said King Ahaz, at every opportunity. "We will be delivered. Jerusalem cannot fall."

"Jerusalem cannot fall," repeated Isaiah. It was strange to find himself in agreement with his cousin Ahaz, but he was, at least in this one surety. "Jerusalem will not fall," he added, "because Yahweh still loves his city, and his remnant, undeserving as we may be of his mercy."

The people were less confident than the king and the prophet.

145

"How long must we endure this siege?" Their cries were incessant. Isaiah should know; Isaiah who was Yahweh's prophet. Every day there was a mob of them outside the prophet's house, demanding to know if there was any word from Yahweh. Naamah, pregnant again, very weary, frantic with worry about their country house which was no doubt in enemy hands and perhaps destroyed, sighed deeply. "Can't you tell them anything, Isaiah? Anything at all?"

"The spoil speeds, the prey hastens: Maher-shalal-hash-baz." Isaiah pronounced the same strange sentence to the clamoring people daily. "And then we must take care that Judah, too, does not fall prey to the destroyer, the king of Assyria."

While the common folk clamored over Maher-shalal-hash-baz, there were also those who recalled Isaiah's pronouncements that day at the conduit. As the siege dragged on, the sign of Immanuel remained a frequent topic of conversation. There seemed indeed to be more versions of what Isaiah had actually said about Immanuel's birth than there were listeners who had actually heard him. Since Abijah's pregnancy was by now a secret no longer, the people's first inclination was to assume that "Immanuel," whose birth would be a sign of Yahweh's disapproval of the Assyrian alliance, was none other than the King's own child.

But when this interpretation was mentioned to Ahaz, he protested vigorously. "Whoever said I would call any son of mine 'Immanuel'?" he demanded. "An absurd name! Why, anyone would be a fool to name a child 'God is with us,' when God might be with us one day and against us the next!"

Then when it became known that Isaiah's prophetess was with child again, the rumors started all over. "Doubtless Isaiah was speaking of her. They'll call their baby 'Immanuel,' just wait and see!" A logical explanation this was, but not one to satisfy the King.

"When Isaiah said 'young woman,'" Ahaz declared, "he could have meant anyone. If he had meant my Lady Abi or his Naamah either one, he would have said so." Everyone who valued his standing at court decided to agree with Ahaz.

But then, to everyone's consternation, another rumor got started, one which persisted despite the king's efforts to put it down. One

146

of the workmen who had been in the gang detailed to go out to the reservoir that day declared that he had distinctly heard Isaiah mention a virgin mother. Immanuel was to be no human child at all, but some miraculous infant god, who had nothing to do with the offspring of Abijah or Naamah or any other young wife. To the siege-weary people of Jerusalem, this story had great appeal. The dream of Immanuel as a heavenly deliverer sent from Yahweh captured their hearts. They repeated the tale to each other with rising hopes, and the disputations went on.

Isaiah himself could not be prevailed upon to clarify the problem. "What was said, was said," he proclaimed sternly. "My people have ears to hear, but they understand not."

As spring turned to early summer and news reached the city that aid from Tiglath-pileser was on the way, the whole incident of Immanuel seemed to drop into oblivion. Still, Abijah did not forget. Indeed during the long, lonely days, the tingling unrest she felt over the prophet's remarks intensified. Of the very few people who knew why Isaiah had inserted the name of Immanuel in his prophecy, Abi alone was willing to face the matter as it was. She was confident that she was the "young woman" of Isaiah's prediction; she gloried in the rumors that Immanuel would be a heavenly deliverer and pushed from her mind the related comments that his birth would somehow be related with disaster for Ahaz. Then she heard rumors of the virgin mother and new doubts began to assail her.

The summer passed slowly for Abi. She saw Ahaz not nearly so often as she would have liked, for he toured the wall daily, inspecting defenses and heartening the defenders and many hours more were spent in the council hall with his advisors. Usually he came to her only in the evenings, if then.

Abi tried to keep herself busy preparing things for the baby. *He will be born in the winter,* she reminded herself over and over, *and we must have plenty of warm cover for him.* She did not doubt it would be a boy. True, little girls were precious and dear, but Ahaz's first child had to be a son. The prophet had said so.

And suddenly, quite without warning, she became possessed with a burning longing to talk with Isaiah by herself, and to hear from his own lips an explanation of his prophecy of Immanuel. "Every afternoon without fail," she said aloud though there was none to listen, "he comes from the Temple to the palace. Now, if I should be waiting on the royal walkway in between, I could see him alone." The thought was so exciting that the woolen baby blanket which she had been embroidering slid unnoticed to the floor.

Abi rose, smoothing the folds of her soft green linen dress. The bells tied about her ankles jingled softly, and Abi remembered how recently, at a court banquet, Isaiah had launched a vigorous attack on woman's fashions, and declared that Yahweh detested such frivolous adornments. *It is a foolish style*, she thought, *an absurd thing, but everyone is wearing bells now. Besides, Ahaz gave them to me and I'll not take them off for that prophet.* Resolutely, she pinned a veil of soft yellow over her dark hair and moved toward the hall. The jingling seemed to grow louder; her ears rang, but she tried to ignore it.

I'll just say to him: "Isaiah, you must tell me if the Immanuel in your prophecy is my son," she resolved. *I must know if you think he will be king and reign in peace or if we will all be defeated . . . Isaiah . . . Isaiah*, her brain whirled. *I know he will be kind to me*, Abi reassured herself, and again she heard the noise of her anklets, a noise that seemed somehow more like the clanging of brass gongs that the tinkling of tiny silver bells. Impulsively she bent and removed them, then laid them carefully out of sight behind one of the great pillars of the walkway. Now across the inner court, through another covered walkway, and down the long hall of the palace Abi went. At last she came to the private walkway used only by the royal family and their household to cross from the king's house to the Temple.

Aching with tension, Abijah leaned cautiously against one of the great pillars. She could feel the chill of the stone through her linen garment, and she shivered though the day was warm. *Certainly*, she told herself, *he must come this way soon.* Each minute seemed an eternity as she listened for footsteps in the distance. Then at last she saw him approaching from far down the walkway. The prophet was walking slowly, his eyes downcast in meditation. He was dressed in the peculiar style which he so often affected,

149

his coarse, short skirt of prophet's sackcloth was an incongruous contrast to the jeweled pendant sparkling upon his bare chest and the heavy gold bracelets on his arms. An elegant blue cloak with tassels of gold hung about his shoulders.

As he came nearer, Abi spoke his name softly, so softly she doubted he would hear.

But he did hear, and he looked up obviously startled. "Lady Abijah! You should not be here unattended," he said.

"There is something I must ask you. Everyone has been so curious about Immanuel . . . ." All the carefully planned demands that she had thought to make left her, and she felt herself looking into Isaiah's deep set, compelling green eyes with an expression of servile pleading.

"Ah yes," Isaiah replied. "They wonder, do they not, what I meant." A certain awareness came to him that the young woman who was looking up at him with such earnestness was clearly beautiful and radiantly lovely.

"Certainly we wonder. But if you could just tell me . . . ." she hesitated. Her voice was softly musical.

Isaiah felt an uneasiness of a sort he had never felt before. "As long as I live," he said evasively, "nay, as long as people remember Isaiah ben-Amoz, they may wonder over my words."

Abijah's face was a mirror of disappointment. "It is just that I had hoped . . . ."

"That your child would be the prince of the peaceable kingdom?"

The peaceable kingdom. Abijah had not heard that expression used before but the sound of it was beautiful. A sense of unworthiness penetrated the very depths of her being. "If I was wrong, forgive me."

"My Lady Abijah does not need to feel she is wrong. The child who shall be born to you has been greatly blessed by Yahweh, believe that." He looked directly into her eyes and for the second time in those few moments the disquieting thought came to him that she was unusually lovely. "Our God has placed you in a position to mold the future of our nation: do not ever forget it," he said. Without waiting for her comment, he turned and walked away.

150

* * * * *

Abijah rushed back to her apartment fairly glowing with happiness, having quite forgotten the little silver bells that she had left on the walkway.

"Tamar!" She had to tell someone about Isaiah. "I have seen the prophet and talked to him about my child!"

The slave woman dropped the armload of Abi's clothes—filmy veils, belts, scarves, and the like—which she had just neatly folded, and ran to throw herself at her mistress's feet. "Abijah, my Lady." Her old hands were on Abi's knees; her eyes looked up imploringly. "How could you dare to do such a thing? Suppose the king had happened to find you out there talking to the prophet, unattended and unwatched? It might have meant severe disfavor for you and Isaiah both!"

"You exaggerate terribly, Tamar!" Abijah said with a little laugh to cover her nervous uncertainty. "Now get up and stop worrying. Ahaz would have been very angry, no doubt, but he never stays angry for long. Besides, he didn't find out."

Tamar rose and Abijah motioned her to the bench beside her.

"Let me just say this, my Lady. The king tolerates Isaiah because he believes he has to, but he hates him more than you realize."

"Why?"

"Well," Tamar hesitated. "They have been enemies ever since they were just boys. Why, they used to fight like wild Scythians out in that very courtyard." The old slave nodded in the direction of the window.

"Really, Tamar?" Abi smiled. "Don't you suppose they were just playing more than fighting? My brothers were always carrying on that way." Boyhood scuffles certainly did not seem a cause for life long enmity. "But tell me about it anyway," she added lightly. "Who won?"

"There was one time I remember especially," Tamar began. "Amoz, Isaiah's father, had sent him to visit the court for some festival, I suppose. Anyway, my Lady Jerusha sent the boys out into the courtyard and I was sitting out to watch them. Maaseiah

151

was just learning to walk and I was busy enough keeping my eye on him. Isaiah and Prince Ahaz were sitting on one of those benches at the other end of the garden. Isaiah's almost three years older than Ahaz, you know, and he was always such a well-mannered child, I wouldn't have thought he'd start a fight. But the first thing I knew, I heard Ahaz screaming at the top of his voice and I looked over in their direction and those two were really going at it, hitting and scratching and hair pulling."

Abi closed her eyes. It was not hard to visualize little Ahaz, fury aroused, attacking a playmate. But Isaiah? "Did you find out what caused it?" Abi questioned.

"I did," Tamar sounded proudly self-satisfied. "Well, that is, I think I did. By the time I reached them, Isaiah had Ahaz down in the grass and he was pounding him hard. Well, I put a stop to that, and I grabbed one of them with each hand. Ahaz was crying, but Isaiah just looked at me with a serious look like he gives now when he's preaching. I said, 'Isaiah, you will be punished for this! The very idea of picking a fight with your little cousin! Whatever made you do such a thing?' And do you know what he told me?" Tamar paused, with obvious enjoyment of the dramatic effect.

"Go on," Abi said eagerly.

"Well, Isaiah said, 'I had to,' and when I asked why he told me, 'Ahaz said something too terrible to repeat.' So I asked Ahaz what he had said and he pouted and sulked a little but he didn't deny what he had said."

"What was it?"

"Oh, my Lady Abi, pardon me, but if you must know, I'll tell you: he told Isaiah that he hated Yahweh!"

Tamar fully expected to produce an expression of shocked horror on Abi's face, but the younger woman appeared unmoved.

"Before I had a chance to do a thing," Tamar went on, "Ahaz got away and ran to his grandma and she didn't punish him at all. Lady Jerusha was like that. Some days she would love him half to death and some days she would punish him so severely he would cry for hours. Anyway, she didn't do anything to him this

152

time. Isaiah got a thorough beating for it, though. I can't help but say it seemed a bit unfair."

Abi sat silently listening to Tamar's tale. In her mind she could see the two boys: Isaiah, proud and sturdy champion of all he had learned was right and little Ahaz, defiant and petulant, seeking the refuge of his unpredictable grandmother's arms. "They've been enemies ever since?" she asked.

"Yes, I think so," Tamar replied thoughtfully. "But Isaiah has always been a kindhearted soul. I think he would be grateful to have the king's friendship, but you know how Ahaz feels about him."

"I do not think that it is Isaiah himself that Ahaz hates. It is just that they have such a different outlook about most things," Abi said. A strange awareness came to her mind that old Tamar had known Ahaz so much longer than she had. In her vast store of unspoken memories perhaps lay keys which would help Abi understand him better. "And I certainly do not think that Ahaz hates Yahweh," she added. "Do you?"

"Aye, I do." Tamar replied. "And I suppose it was his grandmother's fault more than anything else." The slave woman spoke with cold finality. "And then too, he has been influenced by that Ammonite Ushna ever since he was just a tiny boy. Molech is a fierce god, but he is the protector of the Ammonites, and Ahaz is very conscious of being half-Ammonite himself. His grandma used to torment him about it, always called him "half-breed." But really I think he's proud of it. He loved his mother, and his Ammonite blood is his gift from her."

Abi nodded. She knew all this herself. "You know when I first met him, I called him Jehoahaz, and he told me then that he was not really a follower of Yahweh," she confided. "But lately, just this spring and summer he's made me feel that he was going to change his mind. He hasn't said much, but clearly he is not so antagonistic toward Yahweh as he used to be. All I can do now is pray. Oh Tamar, I do pray so much."

"Aye, my Lady, I too." Tamar said.

For a moment both women were quiet. A vague discomfort

nagged in Abi's mind, an awareness that perhaps she had said too much. "We will not speak of these things again," she said at last, and was moving toward the doorway of her bedchamber, when a sudden shout broke out in the courtyard below, a loud clamorous noise of many voices.

"What on earth?" Tamar exclaimed, and the two of them rushed to the rooftop. A crowd was gathering in the outer courtyard, and the shouting rose to a feverish pitch. Breathlessly Abi darted across the rooftop, Tamar close at her heels. *The bells,* Abi thought guiltily, and her heart pounded with the wildest fears. *Someone has found my ankle bells on the walkway and told Ahaz.* Scarcely knowing why, she rushed on toward the section of the roof over the king's audience chamber.

It was at that moment that Ahaz, with Ushna and a crowd of courtiers following him, appeared at the landing. With the king's appearance, the clamor in the street below increased to an almost deafening pitch. Ahaz was gesturing emphatically, trying to silence them. "Yahweh has granted us a great favor," he shouted above the noise of the crowd, when suddenly he caught sight of his wife standing a short distance away. Obviously she had no inkling of what had happened; indeed she looked very frightened. All awareness of the crowd left Ahaz. He had never been one to be overburdened with royal dignity and now, when there was joy to share with his beloved, what did it matter if all of Jerusalem saw? "The siege is lifted!" he exclaimed, rushing to embrace her there before all the people of the city. "They are withdrawing! Today! Now! Tiglath-pileser has invaded Syria!"

And Abijah, who had never fainted in her life, collapsed in Ahaz's arms.

* * * * *

Through the long, hot summer months that followed, more and more good news was brought by the Assyrian couriers to the King in Jerusalem as defeat after defeat continued to be inflicted upon

154

Ahaz's troublesome neighbors by the armies of Tiglath-pileser. In token of his alliance with Assyria, Ahaz sent a small force of Judeans to join the Emperor's hosts on the distant Syrian frontiers. The land of Judah was at peace, and the young king who had allied with the mighty emperor had placed his country on the winning side in the blazing turmoil that was sweeping all the rebellious Westlands.

Ahaz found himself engulfed in waves of popularity. There was nothing so exhilarating as a journey down to the city gate where he would address the eager people who thronged to see him. "The gods have granted us another great victory!" He had but to say those words and the crowd would cheer even more wildly. Ahaz's sense of the dramatic was sparked to a feverish pitch. He could speak of the conquests of Tiglath-pileser as if they were Judah's own, and the people, in turn, seemed now to love him fervently, even those who had been very dubious about him at the beginning of his reign. After all, it is not hard for a nation to love a handsome and dramatically gracious young king.

"You have saved us! The Lord's anointed one!" "You have delivered us from destruction!" The cries of the masses thrilled the depths of Ahaz's soul. Clearly it mattered little to the people during that wonderful summer which gods inhabited Ahaz's heaven. His newly noticeable lack of antagonism toward Yahweh was welcome even if somewhat perplexing. Indeed it was a very good sign. But at the same time, the king's known recognition of the existence of the other gods had an appeal to the masses that Jotham's inclination toward monotheism had lacked. Ahaz was generously tolerant of Baal and Ashtoreth, of the serpent god Nehushtan, and any other diety his people cared to worship. Of course, it was a widely-accepted fact that Molech was the king's special patron. And as Ahaz's popularity mounted, his subjects, thinking to please him, began to turn in great numbers to his Ammonite god. It was at this juncture that, true to his plan, Ahaz ordered construction of a public shrine to Molech in the valley of Hinnom, a short distance south of Jerusalem and designated Ushna to draw up detailed plans.

Ushna should have been in his glory. For was not the king making a greater display of outward devotion to the Ammonite god than he had ever done before?

But even as Ushna sat in the seclusion of his study, the plans for the shrine spread out before him, he could not banish the uneasy premonition that Molech's apparent triumph was in truth far from being the victory it seemed.

It was in the fall, when the New Year came and the first cold winds began to blow across the Judean hills, that Ahaz, according to the vow he had made months before, was at last to deliver his public announcement which would attribute to Yahweh sole credit for the nation's escape from the enemy. The New Year, the first day of Tishri, was the greatest of Judah's festival days. By a happy coincidence it was also Ahaz's birthday. What better time could there be for him to acknowledge openly before all the nation his gratitude to Yahweh? Unlike the impromptu speeches he had made so often during the summer, this one was carefully written and rehearsed days before the day of its delivery. He had allowed no one to help him. In the quietude of his private apartment he had repeated the striking phrases over and over again until he knew the words by heart.

And now all Jerusalem knew that on the first day of the New Year, King Ahaz was to make a speech upon the royal platform before the Temple where all the kings since Solomon had stood to address their subjects upon high holy occasions. Everything had been prepared to perfection. Word had been circulated throughout the city for days of the importance of the king's forthcoming pronouncement and the crowd that gathered was tremendous.

"Oh gods of heaven, oh Yahweh, give me strength!" Ahaz, magnificently garbed in splendid new robes and bedecked with jewels, mounted Solomon's royal platform, trembling but determined to overcome the cold waves of fright sweeping through him. "Hear me, oh my people: Yahweh our God, Yahweh is one." Ahaz began

157

with an oft-repeated pronouncement as old as the nation itself. The words, so carefully practiced, did not come easily. Those who stood closest could clearly see the tension in Ahaz's face and the nervous wringing of his hands, even though they could not feel the frantic pounding of his heart. Deep within Ahaz's soul other words than those of his speech were echoing, words of a frightened child kneeling before his lost mother's god: "If I turn from you, I shall expect no mercy; if I fail you, may I be smote with misery and early death."

Ahaz swallowed hard. "Many have asked which of the gods has helped us to defeat our enemies," he proclaimed. "And now in reply let me ask you: Who among them all is Protector of Judah?" A half-moment of shocked silence fell over the multitude, a silence which seemed to Ahaz an eternity. Then someone started the cry, "Yahweh! Yahweh!" and the crowd took up the chant almost as if with one accord. "No, Molech!" someone shouted, and Ahaz gestured wildly for order.

"Who brought our forefathers up from slavery in Eygpt?" he shouted. "Who gave the land of Judah into the hands of King David and his descendants forever? No other god is so great in his love for our nation as Yahweh our Lord, not Molech, not any other!"

By now the crowd was roaring and cheering mightily. "Silence! Listen! Listen to me!" The color was rising in Ahaz's face; his voice which, at times could be so magnificently forceful, merely sounded harsh and angry. No one was listening; indeed by now they were singing and dancing in the streets. It was a day the people would never forget, a day that in later years they would look back upon as the greatest and most beautiful day of Ahaz's reign over Judah. But to the king himself, the event was a failure. Hastily he concluded his remarks, stepped down from his platform, and strode across the Temple porch to the private royal walkway. An unspeakable cloud of uneasiness hung over him. In the great banquet hall of the palace preparations for the New Year feast were already beginning. *It will be a long, long night,* the young monarch thought wearily, *and they will all talk about today and expect explanations.*

Suddenly, the ubiquitous Ushna was beside him. Ahaz expected to hear reproaches; he might even have welcomed them, but Ushna was plainly in no mood to dispute with him. "It is not too early to dress for the banquet," the Ammonite said in his smoothest voice. He was not going to mention his master's speech; that was obvious.

"Yes, it is too early," Ahaz replied. "I am going up to see the Lady Abi."

Abijah, who had watched the festivities from one of the nearby palace balconies, was waiting for Ahaz when he came. Her heart was singing. The words that her husband had spoken before his people were almost too wonderful to be true, and she could scarcely wait to tell him so.

* * * * *

"What did I do wrong?" Ahaz sighed a sigh of utter weariness. He moved toward the window, closed the lattices, and sat very still, peering through the cracks into the garden below. "They would not listen," he said in a half whisper. He did not look at her.

Abi eased herself down on a small stool at her husband's feet. "Oh my darling, when they heard you acknowledge Yahweh, there was no need to listen further. You were wonderful . . . magnificent! Oh, Ahaz, Ahaz, I love you so!" Her hands sought his and pressed them fervently. *The thing I have prayed for from the beginning has come,* she thought. *Oh God, my happiness is complete!* Adoringly, she gazed up at her husband's face. His dark eyes were pools of mystery and she sensed that he was no more conscious of her presence than if she had not been there at all. She spoke hesitantly. "My darling, tell me, do you really believe the things you told them today about Yahweh?"

"Yes." His voice came as if he were in actual pain. "I believe. I think I believe." He closed his eyes and breathed heavily, a deep

159

frown of concentration furrowed his brow. Abi's hand crept up to a tiny golden amulet suspended from a slender chain at Ahaz's throat. The charm was engraved with sacred symbols of Yahweh. Abijah pressed it between her fingers and felt shivers of joy.

"I had never thought to see you wear such a thing as this," she said.

He brushed her hand away almost roughly. "Here, if you want it, you take it," he muttered, unfastening the little token. "You have more right to it than I."

"Oh Ahaz, no! Keep it!" Abi said, her fingers closing about the proffered ornament in his hand. His whole body became tense, but he sat motionless, saying nothing.

"Tell me about yourself and Yahweh," she added after a moment, oblivious to the warnings of the gathering storm.

"Abi, for the sake of all the gods, will you never learn when to let me be?" He rose suddenly, freeing himself from her grasp. "Is it not enough for you that you bear the fruit of my body? Would you own my soul as well? Great gods of heaven, will you ever learn a woman's part?"

"Ahaz!"

"A wife is property, don't forget it! Abi, you are my possession." The anger was rising in his tone. "More completely mine than anything else I own and yet you seem to think *I* belong to you. I could be rid of you whenever I wished it! I am free, Abi!"

He did not mean what he said, and deep in his heart he knew it. He loved her. Even in moments like this when she provoked him, trying to make him explain the fears he dared not explain, he loved her. He was bound to her forever; she with whom he had shared a thousand joys, she who even now carried his child, she who was not only his wife but his dearest friend. And yet he was also bound to Molech by the solemn covenant of his childhood and by his desperate vow at the beginning of the siege. He had spoken against Molech, and he was afraid.

"What have I done?" Abi, the innocent victim of Ahaz's abuses, stared at her husband in horror, completely oblivious to the agonies of soul that had precipitated the outburst save only for a certainty that whatever was amiss was far beyond her. In a moment such as this there was nothing in her to make her want to argue in her own defense. "Whatever I have done to offend you, forgive me and let us be at peace again. After all, would Yahweh want us to argue?"

"Oh, for the sake of heaven, Abi, who really knows what Yahweh wants?" He leaned against a chair. "Don't try to tell me. You don't know," he muttered. "You don't know anything about it."

Abijah had seen Ahaz angry before. She had seen and felt the full force of his temper let loose upon her, but such episodes always culminated in his stalking away in silent rage. Yet now he made no effort to move. His eyes were focused upon the little fire burning in the brazier upon the hearth. *Merely a few pale blue and orange flames,* Abi thought, *yet he stares as if he is watching the secrets of the future,* and she felt a chilling wave of fear. *There is so much about him that I do not know . . .* and all the dim, haunting memories that she longed desperately to forget rushed into her consciousness: that strange night when he had spoken of his childhood vows, his inexplicable anger over the name Immanuel . . . .

"Ahaz," she whispered, forcing herself to be brave, "It is the greatest joy of my life that I do belong to you."

"Abi, my darling, my precious one." In a moment he had become all gentleness. Words of love had never come easily to him. Though he adored her and longed desperately to protect her from all the dark, shadowy evils that threatened to engulf them both, what was there to say? His arms were about her, tender but powerful. "I swear to you, Abi, it will be well with the child and with you. Do you believe me?"

"Of course I believe you, dearest," she replied and an uneasy sense of wonder swept over her. "I know you will always protect me."

"Yes, Abi, yes," he said. "And now, promise me we will speak of this day no more."

"I promise," said Abi, "if that is what you wish."

161

In the gray, shadowy light before the sunrise, Abijah's child was born. The agonized screams of the young mother rent the cold, still air while aged Tamar with several young maids brought the child to birth. "Yahweh! Ahaz! Help me!" Abi moaned from the mists of a semiconscious world where her God and her husband both seemed to have deserted her.

When she awakened again, it was midmorning. "Is it a son?" she asked weakly.

"Indeed it is," Tamar replied as she propped Abi up in bed with a mountain of pillows at her back. Warm winter sunshine streamed in from the inner garden and a gentle breeze stirred the soft transparent draperies. Abi smiled. "Oh Tamar, for a while I thought I could not endure the pain. But now that the baby is here, I am so happy I can forget all the hard part."

"So it always is, my lady. And now I shall bring him."

With her newborn son in her arms, Abi was a picture of radiant motherhood. "My baby! I can scarcely believe it yet!" Abi gazed at the tiny bundle she held, tears of gladness hovering at the corners of her eyes. "He is mine . . . a son at last! Ahaz will be even more pleased than I, if such is possible." With all the fiercely burning joy of a new mother, Abi cuddled the child to her breast, lovingly inspecting his tiny brown fingers. He was a little angel, with big dark eyes and a few wisps of wavy, jet black hair. "Some babies are so ugly, but mine is beautiful," she said aloud. That he did not have Ahaz's red hair was a matter of small consequence, for his tiny face seemed to her the perfect image of his father.

Suddenly as if reading her thoughts, Tamar spoke: "There will be no mistaking whose child he is. He is exactly like the king— remarkably so."

"Which should please Ahaz all the more," Abi smiled.

It was at that very moment the king strode in, trying hard to look dignified. He had dressed splendidly in his finest robes of purple wool. A heavy gold chain with a brilliant pendant gleamed upon his breast. The jewels on his narrow headband twinkled against the gleam of his coppery hair. Abijah looked up at him and her heart loved him beyond all measure.

"Abi!" All dignity forgotten, he ran to her and threw himself down on a little stool by her bedside. "I must hold our boy," he said, reaching for the precious bundle in Abi's arms.

There could be no doubt that he was delighted with the baby. "Abi, I worried so about you," he said as she cautiously handed him their son. Ahaz held the infant awkwardly. "I'm new at this, you know," he continued. "When my brother was born my grandmother would not let me hold him, and there have been no other babies in the family since."

"Well, I've had plenty of practice myself!" Abi replied. "They were always so glad to have me to help!" And she and Ahaz both laughed delightedly.

"What shall we call him, Abi?" he said after a moment.

Abi smiled. "If all our traditions did not forbid it, I would call him 'Ahaz.'" She glanced at her husband's name carved upon the ring which she wore constantly. "There is no name in all the world so precious to me."

"We cannot do that." Ahaz dismissed this unprecedented remark promptly. No prince of Judah had ever borne his father's name, or, for that matter, the name of any of the kings who had gone before. Many months ago he had decided on his son's name but he could not explain his feelings to Abi, so instead he spoke lightly, as if on a sudden impulse: "It has occurred to me that in honor of our victory over the enemy, we should give him a name which honors Yahweh. Something like 'Hezekiah,' maybe. Do you like that, Abi?"

"'Yahweh is my strength,'" Abi whispered. "It is beautiful. Ahaz, darling, I thank you."

"Say no more of it," he urged. "If I can make you happy with such small favors, my life shall be easy indeed. Besides, if he doesn't like it, he can certainly change it when he gets older."

"As you did . . ."

"Ah yes, as I did. Sometimes I wish I had kept 'Jehoahaz' for *official* purposes."

163

It was a highly charged comment, and Abi felt it best to ignore it. "Hezekiah," she whispered, reaching out to grasp the little one's hand. "Prince Hezekiah ben-Ahaz."

Ahaz laughed again, a little nervously. "Prince Hezekiah ben-Ahaz," he repeated. "Heir to the throne of Judah. And now, my Abi, I must be going."

"Don't go, darling." She reached out a restraining hand. "I'll call Tamar and she can take the little one for a while. I just want to talk to you. I've missed you so."

"No, Abi, I've a conference to meet with some emissaries from Tiglath-pileser."

"Couldn't you be just a little late?"she said.

"You would have them think my sun-clock was not accurate?" he laughed, moving closer to the doorway. This was far too perfect a day to spoil by letting Abi know of the latest developments in his dealings with Assyria. There would be time enough for that some other day.

* * * * *

Ushna sat with the Assyrian envoys in the council chamber nervously awaiting the king's arrival. A clay tablet in a clay envelope sealed with the seal of the great Tiglath-pileser lay unopened before Ahaz's place; a demand, as Ushna plainly knew, for the New Year's payment of tribute to Assyria, already too long overdue. It was no secret among the King's close counselors that Ahaz's appeal for Assyrian aid had placed Judah in the irrevocable position of a tributary state and that an annual payment would be expected from now on. "You must make allowances for my king's tardiness," Ushna was saying. "There has been a child born to him this morning."

"A son and heir," Ahaz said entering. "A prince to inherit the throne of Judah, and his name is Hezekiah."

* * * * *

Hours later, when the meeting with the Assyrians was over and Ahaz had completed arrangements for his tribute payment, Ushna

164

called him aside. "My King, I must commend you on your magnanimity in accepting the bastard. You have put on a wonderful performance. I know it has not been easy, it can never be; but Molech must be grateful for your obedience."

Ahaz sighed convincingly. "At least," he said, "the child has the royal blood of the House of David in him. I think I shall have our Isaiah to write a commemorative ode for him," he added, with an enigmatic smile.

The next morning, Ahaz carried little Prince Hezekiah out on a balcony of the palace that the crowds in the street might see him. The cheering was almost deafening, and the proud father felt a warmth of happy exhilaration through the crisp chill of the winter morning air.

"I have called him 'Hezekiah' because Yahweh has strengthened our nation against the enemy," Ahaz explained at length when the noise died down. With this announcement the people cheered anew. Ahaz smiled down at the bundle in his arms. "Yahweh also has strenghtened me," he whispered in a voice so low that no one could hear.

* * * * *

"How I wish that Isaiah would be more careful with his things," Naamah sighed as she stared at the cluttered array of potsherds which he had spread out on a table in their great hall of their country house. As soon as the siege had ended the previous summer Isaiah and his family had returned to the house that Naamah loved. They were relieved to find it still standing, though somewhat the worse for having served as the headquarters for King Pekah.

Slowly Naamah lifted some of the pottery fragments Isaiah had left on the table. The hastily written black characters upon them were a scramble to her eyes. She could not read very well. True, Isaiah had been teaching her when they were first married, but since Jashub was born, and now with another child on the way, it was hard to find time for lessons.

Suddenly, something on one of the potsherds caught her eye.

"A child is born." The letters seemed to leap up at her from upon the brownish clay. "Unto us a son is given." The words were not hard; Naamah made them out slowly. "His name shall be called Wonderful Counsellor . . . Prince of Peace." There was more; words she did not know and she made no effort to read it farther. *It is for me! For my child!* she thought. *My son to be born!* Delight filled her heart. *Isaiah will read it all to me when it is finished.* Carefully she restored the potsherd to its place on the table, and then her eyes lighted upon something else, a sheet of papyrus, carefully inscribed in Isaiah's most beautiful handwriting. On it were the same words she had seen on the potsherd, only more— much more.

"If only I could read better!" Her fingers traced over the lines, looking for words she recognized. " 'The Spirit of Yahweh shall rest upon him, the Spirit of wisdom and understanding, the Spirit . . . .' "

Naamah was startled by a loud pounding on the door. Closer to it than any of the servants, she rushed to open it.

It was a messenger from the palace. "My lord King Ahaz has commanded me to fetch your husband's poem in honor of the new Prince."

"The new Prince?" Naamah was taken aback. "Lady Abijah's child has been born already?"

"Certainly. Yesterday morning. Did Isaiah not tell you?"

"Why, no." Naamah felt ashamed. *There are so many thing he forgets to tell me,* she thought. "He was very, very busy yesterday evening, writing something." she added aloud.

"Well, that matters not. I just want the poem. Is your husband here?"

"No, he went up to the city, I think." Naamah felt another wave of embarrassment that she really had no idea where he was.

"Ahaz expects to receive the poem today."

"It was for the birth of the prince . . . Oh yes!" Naamah's mind flashed back to the beautifully written papyrus. "Is this it?"

The messenger grasped the papyrus and read, smiling a pleased smile. "I'm sure it is," he replied and was off to deliver the precious poem to the king.

"You gave him that sheet of papyrus off of this table!" Isaiah was closer to anger than Naamah had ever seen him before.

"It was not for Ahaz's son? Oh Isaiah, when I first saw it, I thought it was for our child. When the messenger came, I just knew it was for the baby prince. I'm sorry! Then it was for me after all?"

Isaiah did not answer; he seemed to be lost in thought, unaware of Naamah's existence.

"My Lady Abijah will surely think it is as beautiful as I did," Naamah said. "Surely there can be no harm in that. You will forgive me?"

Isaiah scarcely seemed to hear her. For eternally long seconds the room was completely quiet. "What is done, is done, Naamah," he said at last. "God knows the meaning of those words, so why should it matter what Ahaz or Lady Abijah or even my own wife should draw from them?"

"You do not love me, Isaiah." The frustrations stirring inside Naamah reached their peak. She had never spoken to him in such a tone before. "You do not ever tell me anything. If you really cared about me, you would explain things better." She was sobbing deeply. "And I . . . I have always loved you so."

Isaiah held her head against his chest and ran his fingers in her long hair. Her sobs subsided. *She is so little and so helpless,* he thought. "I do love you, my Naamah, more than anything on this earth," he said. "I'm just going to have to teach you to read," he added after a moment.

* * * * *

As Naamah had predicted, Ahaz and Abi were delighted with the poem. Ahaz sat by his wife's bed and read the beautiful, stirring lines over and over.

> "The people who walked in darkness have seen
> a great light

those who dwell in a land of deep darkness, on
     them has light shined.
Thou, O Yahweh, hast multiplied the nation,
     thou has increased its joy.
For unto us a child is born,
     unto us a son is given;
and the government will be upon his shoulder,
     and his name will be called
Wonderful Counselor, Mighty Lord,
     Everlasting Father, Prince of Peace.

"Of the increase of his government and of peace
     there will be no end,
upon the throne of David, and over his kingdom
     to establish it, and to uphold it
with justice and righteousness
     from this time forth and for evermore.
The zeal of the Lord of hosts will do this."

"It is hard to believe that Isaiah meant it for our child," Abi
said in wonder. "It is almost as if it were for some heavenly deliverer—the Prince of Peace."

"The prophet would not send us anything he did not want us
to have," Ahaz replied, and that was that.

When Abi spoke again it was not of the poem. "The eighth
day will be here before we know it," she said. "We must start
making plans."

Ahaz nodded. The eighth day after his birth was a day of great
importance to every boy born in the land of Judah, for on that
day he would be circumcised as the sign of Yahweh's eternal covenant with Abraham, when first he selected his chosen people.

"I was hoping," Abi said, "that we might ask my father to perform
the circumcision."

"Of course," said Ahaz. Zechariah was a priest and this rite
was a priestly prerogative. "I would not think of having anyone
else."

168

"Then one of these days you will want to put the royal Star on his wrist."

This, Ahaz knew, was the father's task, but the prospect of it terrified him. "He is far too little yet, Abi," he said hastily. "We don't do that till he is about five or six. In fact I see no need to do it at all." He spoke with fumbling hesitation. "It is such a difficult thing, and it will hurt the little one so."

"Ahaz!" Abi was surprised. "Every true prince of Judah has borne David's Star. Of course, I'm sure it hurts, but not for long." She had always treasured the fact that Ahaz bore this ancient sacred sign upon him, and now she grapsed his arm and touched the mark in his flesh. "Aren't you glad your father did it for you?" she asked, tracing lightly over the Star with her fingertips.

Ahaz shifted uneasily. "I suppose so, Abi, though really I never think about it much at all. It has been a part of me almost as long as I can remember. I do recall I screamed very loudly when my father put it on me," he added with an artificial laugh. "I must have been five years old. It was before my mother died. She was there, and I remember her telling me to be braver. I don't think I really understood what they were doing to me, or I would have cried even harder and tried to keep them from doing it at all."

"You mean you have never felt proud to bear positive proof that you belong to the House of David, something that no one can ever take from you?"

"My little Abi, who needs proof?" Ahaz smiled and squeezed her hand gently. It was so like her to be filled with highminded sentiment which turned the obligations of tradition into something holy and beautiful. "If it means so much to you, our son will surely have the royal Star upon him," he said, "as soon as he is old enough. But five years is a long time."

"And you will cut it yourself?"

"Yes, yes," Ahaz spoke loudly to cover the cold wave of fear that was sweeping through him. "When the time comes, I'll even get our prophet to write us another poem for the occasion," he added, hastily changing the subject. "As long as he continues to stay around the court, we might as well keep him working at the thing he does best."

* * * * *

It was less than a month after Abijah's Hezekiah was born that Naamah the prophetess gave birth to her second son.

"His name shall be Maher-shalal-hash-baz," Isaiah announced at the court, and the people who heard him laughed uproariously.

"The prophet is finally learning to make sport of his own foibles," Ushna was heard to remark. No one believed that Isaiah was serious.

No one, that is, but Naamah. And when Isaiah told her the name he had selected, she grasped the infant tightly against her breast as if someone had threatened it with physical harm. "You mustn't, Isaiah," she pleaded, her eyes filling with tears. "I did not care when you called the first one Shear-jashub, for Jashub is a real name after all, but Maher-shalal-hash-baz! How would you like it if your parents had named you that?"

"I would be proud if I thought that through my very name I might proclaim a message from Yahweh," he replied.

"And so you do!" Naamah countered. "Everyone knows that Isaiah means "Yahweh is my salvation." It is a wonderful name, and yet it's not the least bit peculiar. And the baby prince, Hezekiah, "Yahweh is my strength." There are hundreds of nice, sensible names like that."

"So nice and so sensible that people do not stop to think about what they signify. We must make people think."

"But the siege is over."

"Yes, my dear, but the Assyrian danger is far from over."

And Naamah could see that argument would be of no avail. "Very well," she sighed in resignation, "but don't expect me to call my baby Maher-shalal-hash-baz every time I call him."

Isaiah bent, kissed his wife's forehead, and grasped the infant's tiny hands in his own large, strong ones. "I and the children whom Yahweh has given me shall be as living signs," he said.

"I will just call him Maher," said Naamah. And Maher it was.

170

Winter passed and spring came. In far-off Syria, Tiglath-pile-ser's mighty forces set up siege around Damascus, the city to which Rezin, the wily ally of Pekah and the last surviving leader of the plot against Judah, had retreated. Already that winter had come the news that the arch-plotter Pekah had been assassinated by one of his own men, while the crafty Judean traitor Ben-Tabeel had been captured and beheaded by the Assyrians.

Safe in peaceful Jerusalem, Ahaz contented himself with the thought that he had saved his country while he secretly worried about the obligations of tribute payment which would press upon him for the rest of his life. Taxes would have to be raised and tax collectors sent out in greater numbers. Ahaz and Ushna planned the matter with careful detail, if not with enthusiasm. Even some of the treasures from Solomon's Temple would have to be given up, Ahaz knew. The twelve magnificent bronze oxen that stood in the courtyard of the building, supporting the great laver, the Moulten Sea, were shipped off to Assyria, along with gold and silver ornaments from the Temple treasury. The ordinary people complained loudly, but Ahaz's officials were quick to point out that by giving up these treasures from the national shrine, the king would not have to demand quite so much directly from his subjects.

And in faraway Damascus the siege dragged on. People began to say that Rezin's city was invulnerable, that in time the Asyrians would capitulate and withdraw. A year passed, and two years, and then at last came the news: Damascus has fallen. Rezin is dead.

The kingdom of Judah rejoiced with a great rejoicing and polite courtiers congratulated Ahaz as though the victory had been his own.

It was not until several days after the arrival of the good tidings that Ahaz let Abi know that the victory entailed more than was apparent on the surface. Abi was reclining lazily on her couch in the dusky twilight. It was late summer, with a distinct touch of autumn in the air and one of the maids had tossed a light silk coverlet over her feet. On a little table, a short distance away, stood a lovely Phoenician brass bowl piled high with fruits, big luscious grapes and some choice summer figs. Ahaz would probably be hungry; he often was.

"I am going to Damascus, Abi." The words dropped like hailstones in the gentle stillness of the room.

"Ahaz! Why?" Abijah sat up. Her husband stood in the doorway and for the first time the thought crossed Abi's mind that he was beginning to look older, or was it just weariness?

"There is to be a meeting with Tiglath-pileser," he was saying. "Victory celebration and that sort of thing, you know." His attempted cheerfulness betrayed plainly that he was covering his real feelings.

"How long will you be gone?" she said.

"I don't know," Ahaz replied moodily. "As long as Tiglath-pileser decides to keep me there, I suppose. Who can say how long that will be?"

Abi tried to ignore his mood. *He must pay tribute in person,* she thought, *and he is ashamed to say so.*

"Ahaz, darling, take me with you."

"No!!" he practically shouted.

"But why not?" Her voice was soft and pleading. "I'll never have another chance to go to Damascus. Besides, it would be something we could remember together for years."

"Abijah, I have said no. Is that not sufficient?"

"But, Ahaz . . ."

"I'll hear no more from you on this matter," he said, gloomily slumping down in his chair. "It is not a woman's place to question

172

her husband's decisions. Have you never learned that?"

Abi sat motionless. She could feel the anger that was burning within him and for long moments she did not speak. "I will miss you," she said at last. "If there is any opportunity to write, you will write?"

"I suppose so," replied King Ahaz.

*   *   *   *   *

Less than a week later the royal Judean caravan departed for Damascus.

In later days when Ahaz looked back on that memorable journey, he could find no adequate words to describe his distaste for the experience. Day followed day in dismal, monotonous succession, night after night in the discomfort of the stuffy hot tents. For the most part Ahaz traveled on horseback, and though he was skilled enough in horsemanship, it was all too evident that he lacked the stamina of the battle-seasoned guards who rode with him. Under Ushna's coaxing he had once retreated to a litter, which was some slight improvement. He might have continued for the rest of the journey in that fashion had he not awakened that very night to the voices of guards outside his tent:

"I tell you he is a weakling. The kings in the old days weren't like that. They knew what war was. They knew how to put up with hardships, and some of them carried on till they were way up in years. And now look at our young Ahaz! How old is he, anyway?"

"Twenty-three, I think."

"Twenty-three, and there he goes riding along in a litter like his old grandma used to do. Wonder what King David would think if he could see what his House has degenerated into? or Uzziah? or even old Jotham?"

Ahaz lay still, clenching his fists angrily. Other kings, he knew, would rush out, take the prattling guards by surprise, and order them at least to be tortured and beaten, if not killed. That was something Ahaz could not do.

173

For the rest of the journey he rode in the saddle, scorning the litter with loud, open contempt. His body ached with a hundred unaccustomed aches but he said nothing. At the end of the road, he assured himself, lay Damascus and rest and accommodations befitting his kingly station.

* * * * *

It had not entered Ahaz's mind that Damascus lay largely in ruins. The palace where once King Rezin had dwelled was still partially standing, to be sure, but practically everything of value had been stripped away to fill the coffers of the Assyrian conqueror. Tiglath-pileser had no intention of lavishing any more of his newly acquired wealth than was absolutely necessary upon the tribute-paying kinglets who were gathering from all over the Westlands to do him homage. Kings they might be in their own territories, but to the Assyrian they were little better than slaves.

Established in a cramped, meagerly furnished suite, Ahaz found time hanging heavy on his hands. From the anteroom outside his bed-chamber he could hear the voices of his guards engaged in a game of dice, or entertaining each other with tales of war and fair women. Ahaz was the king and he held himself aloof from such amusements. He did not know how to join them if he would, for whenever he came near, his men immediately grew silent and seemed concerned only with showing him the proper respect due their sovereign.

He was wretchedly lonely and wished a hundred times and more that he had brought Abi. Ushna was little company. Indeed for many months now he dreaded moments of privacy with Ushna alone lest the Ammonite begin to question him concerning Molech and to pry into secrets and fears which he preferred to keep buried. The days were hot and still; there was nothing to do but wait until the summons might come to present himself to the Emperor. Ahaz stared sullenly from the window at the ruins of Rezin's once beautiful courtyard below. And inexpressible sadness filled his heart.

174

* * * * *

"Your Majesty, my Lord the king of Israel would see you . . ." Ahaz looked up with a start. In the doorway stood a cringing slave, head bowed, a little papyrus scroll in his hand.

"Certainly." Ahaz took the scroll and read it hastily. "King Hoshea . . ." he mused. "Is he the fellow who stabbed old Pekah last spring?"

The slave was too surprised to smile. "My Lord Hoshea delivered us from the hand of the tyrant some months ago now," he said somberly. "The emperor of Assyria has conferred the kingdom upon him in reward."

"Tell your master I would like very much to meet him," Ahaz replied.

* * * * *

"My brother of Judah . . . ." If the sturdy youth who had gained his crown by killing his predecessor in cold blood felt any discomfort in the presence of the scion of a dynasty which had ruled for three centuries, he did not show it. Hoshea of North Israel, peasant born, younger than Ahaz but already the hardened veteran of several years in Pekah's army, held out his hand to the king of Judah as to an equal.

Ahaz stared back at him with steady gaze and clasped his hand in welcome. "My brother of Israel."

For the few moments they exchanged proper courtly civilities, Ahaz scrutinized his visitor carefully. Hoshea was making a real effort to appear kingly. His coarse black hair had been carefully set in the popular Assyrian manner. His elegant blue robe was a copy of the style worn by Tiglath-pileser's highest officials. Large loop earrings, similar to those the emperor himself reportedly wore, hung in his pierced ears, a fashion that few men of Israel had ever adopted.

"You are well named, Hoshea," Ahaz remarked, smiling. The name "Hoshea" meant "deliverer." "I owe you a debt of gratitude

175

for disposing of our enemy, Pekah."

The young king of Israel laughed and his eyes sparkled wickedly. "Pekah was easy enough to be rid of; he was lying in his tent roaring drunk with a woman beside him, and I was on guard duty that night. You should have heard him scream when I plunged my knife into his fat belly."

Ahaz winced. "Yahweh was with you, no doubt," he said.

"I rather think it was Assher," said Hoshea. "The great god of Assyria."

"What of the woman?" Ahaz asked after a moment.

"Her? Oh, I sold her. She was impossible. I kept a whole flock of them though, Pekah's women. Brought a few of them up here to keep me company. And then too I've got a few little items laid aside for the emperor. Say, there's one of them you would like. A little thing from Judah. Pekah got her on his ill-fated expedition into your kingdom three years ago, but she's just now getting old enough to enjoy. I'll tell you what, Ahaz, she's yours. Tiglath-pileser will get enough of them without her."

Ahaz sighed. To refuse Hoshea's gift would be rudeness. When practically every kinglet of the Westlands kept a harem full of women, how could he explain that there was only one woman, and she in faraway Jerusalem, to whom he already belonged heart and soul? To have spoken to Hoshea about Abi would have been impossible. "Thank you, my brother," he said at last. "Send her on."

* * * * *

The woman Hoshea brought was a mere girl and as beautiful a creature as any monarch could desire. Her hair was a rare fiery auburn like Ahaz's own; her eyes a dancing, restless green. Beneath the almost transparent garment she wore, he could plainly see her lithe and shapely form.

"My lord and king!" She dropped to her knees on the little rug beside him and pressed her lips against his hand.

"What is your name, girl?"

"Ishtarah, if it please my lord."

176

"Look at her hair, Ahaz," Hoshea urged. "Like yours. I could not help but think of the handsome children she can give you."

"I am half-Ammonite, you know," Ahaz said, proudly admitting a fact that most any man of Judah would have tried to hide had he been in a similar circumstance. "Maybe you are too, Ishtarah." He touched the soft auburn curl that hung entrancingly upon her forehead.

"I . . . I . . . don't think so . . . my lord . . . my family never told me . . ." She giggled nervously.

"For the sake of heaven, girl, if you're going to live with me, stop calling me 'lord.' My name is Ahaz."

"My Ahaz! My possessor!" Her curly auburn eyelashes fluttered enchantingly. Without waiting for his sanction, she eased herself up to the bench beside him and pressed her cheek against his shoulder. Hoshea smiled and withdrew.

"Since I was a little girl, I have loved you," Ishtarah whispered. "There is no greater honor could come to a woman of Judah than to give herself to the king."

Ahaz drew himself up erect. He did not look at her. She was pretty, entirely too pretty, but there was something about her that repelled him.

"How old are you, girl?"

"Fifteen." A soft, small hand crept over his and began toying with the stone of his seal ring.

"You should be betrothed to some young fellow who would love you as a husband ought," he said.

"Ahaz!"

"You know that I will not marry you."

"That does not matter. I am nothing and you are the king and I have been provided for your pleasure. Do to me what you will." Even as she spoke she had unfastened her belt and now her hands were reaching for the brooch on her breast.

"She-devil!" Ahaz screamed, and in a powerful blow he knocked her to the floor. "Swine! Filthy swine! Get away from me!"

"Ahaz! My king! What have I done!" The brooch had fallen from her hand and her dress had come open to the waist. Ahaz's eyes focused on the amulets of Yahweh and Ashtoreth that hung from a fragile chain about her neck. "Get out!" he shouted. "Here," he said, unfastening a wide gold bracelet on his wrist. "Take this as a memory of your king and be gone!"

Ishtarah grasped the bracelet eagerly and fastened it on her own arm. "I have nowhere to go," she pleaded. "Oh Ahaz, please let me stay, even if only as your slave. I love you!"

"Do you think I believe that?" He rose and stalked impatiently before her. Suddenly the hatred in him melted into compassion. "Come here and tell me about yourself. Have you any family left in Judah?"

She shook her head sadly. "Pekah's men killed them all, only Pekah took me as a slave. I was just twelve then; I was too little to provide him with pleasure, but believe me, he was keeping me till the time came. And then Hoshea killed him, thank God, and I was spared. I think I would have rather died than have had to lie with that horrid man."

"I think we are all grateful that he is gone," Ahaz said.

"But then, Hoshea was about to give me to the emperor," Ishtarah went on. "And I had no hopes of ever seeing my own country again or anything. And then you came and you have saved me. Ahaz, my rescuer! Is it any wonder I love you?" Once again her head was nestled against him; once again her soft hands grasped his and squeezed them longingly.

"You shall see Judah again. I promise it," he said.

* * * * *

Ishtarah was pregnant with Ahaz's child and disgustingly nauseated most of the time. Ahaz spent the long days lolling around, drawing designs for a copy of an Assyrian altar he had seen and admired in the inner courtyard and wondering what he would ever do with Ishtarah when they got back to Jerusalem. He wished a thousand times that he had not taken her. He wished now that there was somewhere to put her to get her out of sight. But in the crowded suite the Emperor had assigned him, her daily presence

178

was not merely an inconvenience, it was inescapable.

Now at last the Emperor had set the date for the ceremony of tribute, and even though it was several weeks away, Ahaz began to count the days with a new spirit of hope. At least he knew *how long* he had to wait before he could leave this despicable place. Somehow when he got back to Judah, things would have to be better. He would get a house for Ishtarah in Gibeah, her native town, and see to it that she and the child were well provided for. Abi would never need to know.

Abi. At the thought of her, uneasiness filled him. He stared at the plans for the altar spread out before him, together with a carefully composed letter to the chief priest Urijah instructing him to have a replica of it built for use at the Temple. The missive had been ready to dispatch for several days, though Ahaz had postponed sending it, telling himself that he needed to recopy the plans for the altar.

"That's it," he said half-aloud. "I cannot send a courier to Jerusalem without a letter for Abi." Determined he rose, gathered up his writing supplies, and seated himself at a little nearby table.

"What are you doing, Ahaz?" Ishtarah called faintly from her place in Ahaz's bed.

"I am writing to my wife, my Lady Abijah in Jerusalem." Ahaz's voice was cold.

Ishtarah giggled. "You're the only king I ever saw who knew how to write. I'm glad you're not writing to me because I can't read."

* * * * *

"Jehoahaz of Judah." At last the dreaded but long awaited day of the tribute-oath had come. Ahaz heard his name called . . . his name as he had impulsively signed it on that letter of appeal more than three years before. He heard Ushna whisper a benediction: "Molech's grace go with you." His brain whirling, Ahaz started across the porch to the improvised throne where the emperor sat at the gate of Rezin's ruined palace. "Molech . . . Yahweh

179

. . . Oh gods, whatever gods you be . . . help me now!"

Before him, between two cracked and crumbling pillars, sat the great emperor in all his splendor. Tiglath-pileser's robe of blue and purple was stiff with heavy embroidery in threads of gold. The wide bracelets on his arms and his huge loop earrings were solid gold. Hard, black eyes glared out from narrow slits beneath the Emperor's tall, jewel-encrusted crown-hat. A mass of well-curled, bushy black hair hung to his shoulders. A little beard, set in perfectly even waves, accented his chin. *The Great King, the Mighty King, the King of the World.* . . .

To Ahaz it seemed an eternity that he lay prostrate upon the leopard skin at Tiglath-pileser's feet. Fearfully he glanced up at the famous pendants of the five great gods of Assyria that dangled on a wide chain about the Emperor's neck. Actually it was scarcely a moment until the Emperor's toe nudged his shoulder and he assumed a kneeling position. Well he knew the words he must say: "Hail to thee, Tiglath-pileser, king of the World, king of Assyria . . . I, Ahaz," he paused, breathed deeply and corrected himself, "I Jehoahaz, ben-Jotham ben-Uzziah, King of Jerusalem and of the land of Judah, do solemnly swear to be thy slave forever. My nation shall henceforth be subject to thy laws. To Assher, the great God, I swear it; to Bel and Ishtar; to Senn and Shamash, I swear it. May the wrath of all the five great gods and the host of heaven fall upon the head of Jehoahaz should he break his vow."

"Arise, Jehoahaz." The Emperor spoke and Ahaz rose. "You will proceed to the altar of consecration."

And, somehow, the worst of it was over.

Ahaz walked resolutely to the altar, tossed on the required grains of incense to the five great gods, swore another powerful oath of eternal allegiance to his Assyrian overlord and to Assher, the god who had made Assyria the mighty nation that it was.

From a window high above, Ishtarah was watching, her heart singing even as was Ahaz's. *Tomorrow, tomorrow, at last, we are starting home.*

* * * * *

Every day as they walked up on the great flat roof of the palace, Abi talked to Hezekiah almost tirelessly. "Someday we will look out and see him coming. Over there, from the northeast. And he will have all his banners flying and a great company of guards, and I'm sure he'll bring us presents." Abi's voice sang with enthusiasm. "And he'll tell us about all his adventures and the faraway places he's seen. And, oh my Hezey, he will be so happy to see his big boy, three years old and going on four."

"I hope he comes tomorrow," Hezekiah would always say. "It will be the happiest day in the world."

Then at last the day came when Ahaz did return; and at last he was in Abi's apartment once again, crushing her to him in a powerful embrace, smothering her with warm kisses. Nothing that had happened in Damascus could possibly matter, Abi thought. Her beloved had come home; the long months of aching loneliness were behind her. "My dearest, it has been forever," she whispered. The moment was perfect, but it was only a moment.

Neither of them saw little Hezekiah enter. Abi had planned to get him from his own room a short while later, but he had heard the excitement. It mattered not to him that his mother was in his father's arms; he merely wanted his share of love and attention from the man who in the long months had come to seem to him more like a dream than a reality. "Father . . ." An impatient tug at Ahaz's sleeve . . .

Ahaz was visibly annoyed. "For the sake of all the gods, Abi, who let him in here?" he said icily. "Out you go, boy, out, I say!"

"Hezey, my sweet!" Instinctively Abi's arms were around him. "Your father and I want to talk a little while." Her voice was gentleness itself. "Come on now, back you go, and in just a few moments I'll come get you."

Hezekiah looked up wonderingly into her eyes and then into the eyes of his father.

"You heard her," Ahaz said. "Haven't you learned to obey?" His voice was harsh.

"You said we'd be happy," the boy said turning to Abi. He

181

began to cry. Abi sat down on her couch and gathered her little son in her lap.

"Hezey has been looking forward to your return," she said. "Hasn't he grown, Ahaz? And talk! He talks all the time!"

"Hmmm. Come here, boy." Ahaz fumbled in his girdle and drew out a small box. "Give this to your mother." Hezekiah obeyed, already smiling again.

The little box contained a beautiful set of jewelry, necklace, bracelets, and earrings of sparkling amber beads. "They're lovely, dearest," Abi smiled.

"And what did you bring me?" Hezekiah was at his father's knee again.

A look of dismay came to Ahaz's face. He had completely forgotten the matter of a gift for his little son. "Don't ask so many questions!" he said roughly.

Abi gasped. *Oh Ahaz, how could you?* she thought. "Look, Hezey, you can play with my beads," Abi said, slipping the sparkling necklace over the little boy's head. "Do you like it?"

"No, I hate it! It's ugly!" Angry little hands tugged at the fragile strand and the next instant a shower of beads cascaded to the floor. Hezekiah screamed.

"Oh, Hezey!" Abi sighed. "It's all right. Mother can string them together again." She bent and began gathering them up.

"Get up, Abi! Let the boy do it! Pick them up, Hezekiah!" Ahaz was shouting.

The boy did not obey. Altogether astounded at the way his mother's beautiful promises were failing to come true, he sat on the floor with his head against the couch, sobbing softly.

"Pick them up, I said!!" Ahaz rose, pulled the boy up from the floor, and delivered a resounding slap on his cheek.

Hezekiah bent to the task and as soon as he had gathered a little handful of the sparkling amber beads, Abi carried him off to bed.

For the mother, as well as for the unhappy little boy, the day was utterly ruined.

In her hideaway at Gibeah a few months later, Ishtarah died giving birth to a frail little daughter. Ahaz received the news with a mixture of sorrow and relief. It would be easy enough to place the child with some family in Gibeah; to give her away and then to forget that Ishtarah had ever existed. Hesitantly he began trying to compose a directive on the matter, but the thought nagged at his consciousness: *The infant is mine as much as she was Ishtarah's. She is a little princess with the blood of King David in her. She is my responsibility.*

There was nothing to do but to tell Abi, and to hope she would not be too hurt.

* * * * *

"I will provide nursemaids for her," he explained. "We will install them in another wing of the palace. She will not be any bother to you."

"Ahaz, Ahaz!" Abi interrupted. Already the first look of dismay that had crossed her face when he broke the news was fading. "Listen to me. Nursemaids are fine; we need them. But every little child needs a mother, too. That little girl is yours. I am your wife, and I will be her mother. I have prayed so long for another child; perhaps this is Yahweh's way of answering."

"I thought you would hate her."

"How could I hate your little daughter when I love you so much?

183

Hezey will be happy, too. You know, Jashub and Maher have a little sister now, and he'll be so pleased to have one, too."

"I think we should call her Gibeah, since she was born there," Ahaz said.

"Well enough," Abi replied. It was a cautiously neutral name, attached to no god. Yet, since it was the name of the town that had been the kingdom's first capital before King David ever took Jerusalem, it was heavy with significance.

Ahaz sent word that his daughter was to be brought to the palace without delay, while Abijah and her maids prepared a nursery.

But the little Princess Gibeah never reached Jerusalem. On the journey the infant suddenly sickened and died.

There was none who wept as sincerely as Abijah, for this child whom she had never even seen. "I wanted her, Ahaz! I want another child so much."

"We shall have one of our own, perhaps," he answered, "someday."

Yet as the years that followed Ahaz's return from Damascus began to slip by softly one after another, Abi's prayers for another child were not answered. The common people talked about it: it was unlucky for the whole country, they said, to have a king who had not begotten many sons. He should take other wives. Yet it had been the same with old Jotham, who had had his bevy of concubines and yet had sired only Ahaz and Maaseiah, both by his Ammonite princess. The kings' inability to produce numerous offspring was clearly a sign of Yahweh's disfavor. Hadn't King David and his several wives had twenty-three sons and a great number of daughters as well? Ahaz heard these mutterings and seemed unmoved.

After all, the land was at peace. There were few serious problems to disturb the king, save of course the inescapable reality of annual tribute, and even this was of little direct concern to him since he had trusted officials, headed by Ushna, to work out the details of the unpleasant matter each year. "The gods are good," Ahaz was frequently heard to remark, and no one seemed to question the fact that among his heavenly patrons he now included the

184

Assyrian war god, Assher, whose altar, under orders from the Emperor Tiglath-pileser stood in the courtyard of Yahweh's Temple. True, Ahaz seemed none too enthusiastic about the foreign deity from the land of his overlord, but he gave him due respect and that was all that was demanded.

Little more could be said for Ahaz's attitude toward Yahweh. To the people of Judah, the stange fervor which their King had once exhibited had become a misty memory. Now Yahweh, like Assher, was accorded polite respect by Ahaz, but nothing more. Though Abi was puzzled and saddened by Ahaz's behavior, she had lived with him too long to expect explanations, or to try to question him. They talked freely of most things; they were still deeply in love and delighted in each other as much as they had when they first met, but despite their closeness, there were matters that Ahaz could never bring himself to discuss with her. Abi had learned that this unbridgeable gulf lay between them; that no human being can enter completely into the soul of another, no matter how beloved. Ahaz was afraid of the gods and more afraid to admit his fears. He thought that Yahweh had failed him, though he would not have dared put the thought into words. If Yahweh had truly been on his side, he would not have had to suffer the humiliation of going to Damascus and the inescapable annual tribute payments. The best he could do, he reasoned to himself, was to treat all the gods with cautious respect but not to hope for too much from any of them.

Perhaps strangest of all were Ahaz's dealings with Molech. Though he fought hard to conceal it, sometimes he felt dizzy spells when he was sure the hand of Molech was upon him for ill; and transitory pains sometimes tore inside his chest. *Molech knows how I've cheated him of my son,* Ahaz often thought. *But I can bear his chastisement, as long as it does not become too severe. And I can placate him.*

So he heaped favors upon the shrine in the valley of Hinnom, just outside Jerusalem, as an outward indication that Molech stood as high as ever in the king's favor, with no hint of the reasoning which underlay his actions. A statue of Molech, larger than life-size, was commissioned by the king. The bronze Ammonite god, seated in splendor, held his arms outstretched to receive the burnt offerings of his devotees, while in his innards burned a fiery furnace. Ammonite priests were imported, and on high festival days Ushna himself officiated as high priest, magnificently garbed and surrounded with display which dazzled the worshipers. Occasionally, some devotee of Molech, in desperate straits and longing for the god's favor, would bring his child and place him in Molech's arms to be offered as a human sacrifice, and Ushna presided over this rite whenever required with fearless fanaticism. The shrine was doing a thriving business. But King Ahaz himself was never there.

Isaiah had his words to say about the valley of Hinnom. The rites of Molech, he declared, were an outrage and abomination in Yahweh's eyes, as bad as following after Baal and Ashtoreth. He said it often and loudly. And Ahaz never tried to curtail Isaiah's freedom of speech. It was as if there were an unspoken compact between them. On matters of the gods they agreed to disagree, for each knew he could never change the other.

Strangely enough, on matters purely political, the royal cousins were in close agreement, though for widely different reasons. "We must submit to the yoke of Assyrians," Isaiah declared. "We must pay our tribute, for Yahweh has brought this chastisement upon the sinful nation. Tiglath-pileser is the rod of Yahweh's anger. It is no more than we have deserved."

"We must pay our tribute," said King Ahaz, galling as it was to see his land's treasures whisked off to Assyrian coffers, "because rebellion would result in Judah's total destruction." Ahaz was determined to hang on to the throne of Judah, even if its luster was somewhat tarnished; to preserve the kingdom, and to pass it on to Hezekiah.

Hezekiah. Ahaz was always ill at ease in the presence of his child. He never knew how to talk to him; he never understood him. Whenever he came to Abi's apartment and found Hezekiah there, Ahaz would send the child away as rapidly as possible.

His only son: the son he had promised to Molech and then refused to give him. Hezekiah looked so much like Ahaz that Ushna had to suspect the truth, but Ahaz vowed within his heart that he would keep up his network of lies to protect the life of his child.

* * * * *

When Hezekiah was six years old, Ahaz declared the time had come for the cutting of the royal Star of David upon the little prince's arm. As the day for the solemn rite drew near, Abi thought back to how Ahaz had earlier tried to convince her to forego this ancient custom altogether. That had been when Hezekiah was first born, and if Ahaz felt any such qualms now he certainly was not showing them. Though he ordinarily had little to say to his son, he made a special effort to talk with him about the meaning of the sign and the importance of being brave during the ceremony. Hezekiah, fortunately, seemed eager to comply.

"Isaiah has the star on his arm, too," Hezekiah explained to Abijah, when Ahaz was nowhere near. Among his many other duties, Isaiah had recently started acting as the prince's tutor, and it was obvious that Hezekiah idolized him. "Then on his other hand, he has a Yahweh sign branded. He said he was already grown up when he got that, and that it hurt something awful when it happened, but not anymore. When I grow up, I want to get the Yahweh sign on my hand, too."

"We'll see about that when you grow up," Abi said. "Not everybody can be a prophet like Isaiah." (*Oh, but what if he should be?* she thought. *Wonderful Counselor, Prince of Peace* . . . so the poem had read that Isaiah had sent her when Hezekiah was born. No, one must not dream too much. He was just a little boy. He might be, someday, a great and good king, but a prophet also, certainly not.) She hugged him close. He was her treasure, she who had hoped for so many children, and had but this one.

When at last the day for the rite came, a great crowd gathered in the central audience hall of the palace to witness the cutting of the sacred sign in Hezekiah's flesh. All of Abi's family were there, together with a collection of courtiers, officials, and royal

187

cousins. Little Prince Hezekiah, looking very serious, sat in a chair in the center of the room. His left arm was bound firmly to the arm of the chair to prevent involuntary flinching when his father should make the mark that would distinguish him forever as a prince of Judah. Already, Abijah had drawn the royal Star on the child's arm with ink, now Ahaz had only to make the cuttings and to rub in a specially prepared powder. Near the prince's chair stood a table upon which the implements to be used were laid out. There seemed every promise that the occasion would be one for great rejoicing.

The time had come. Ahaz glanced from his son's face to the sharp little knife on the table. He lifted it and turned it over and over in his hands. *Once they did this to me*, he thought. He stared down at the mark upon his own wrist which Jotham had placed there long ago, faded a little but still plain. *Truly*, he told himself, *I suppose am I proud of it. It is a fine and noble thing to bear the sign of my great predecessor, King David. If nothing else, it is a token of my love for Judah*. He was trembling.

"Aren't you ready, Ahaz?" Abi was saying. Ahaz placed his hand on his son's arm.

"I can't do it!" he whispered softly so that only Abi and Hezekiah heard. "I won't do it!"

Hezekiah said nothing, but a look of disappointment crossed his face.

"Ahaz," Abi spoke in a faint whisper, but the room had suddenly become very quiet and she felt sure that everyone heard. "Everyone is watching us. You know that you must do it. You must not deny our son his birthright! He will hold still. It will be over soon."

There could be no escape, though Molech would be displeased, most assuredly. *Oh, if only one could escape Molech forever*, Ahaz thought, as slowly he drew the little knife across Hezekiah's soft flesh. The boy's fist clenched and his whole body tensed, but he was being very brave. Mechanically, as if it were not himself but someone else performing the rite, Ahaz saw himself making the six cuts that formed the design of David's Star. "The powder," he requested, and Abijah handed him the specially ground powder.

"There, 'tis done," Ahaz was saying, "and none will ever be able to deny he is a prince of Judah, and a part of Yahweh's covenant with King David. May Yahweh's blessing on David's House be with him forever." His voice shook.

Abijah untied the cords that bound Hezekiah's arm to the chair and now was wrapping a strip of soft white linen around the boy's wrist. "My Hezey, you were extremely brave," she whispered softly. "It will not hurt very long." She held him close, while Ahaz grasped the back of the chair. The whole room seemed to be moving, but his wife and his son both looked very happy.

The next thing Ahaz knew solicitous courtiers were bending over him and he was struggling to raise himself from the floor. "Abi," he gasped. "I am ill. I must go back to my apartment." Ushna the Ammonite, he noticed, was beside him, helping him to rise.

Ahaz forced himself to address the gathering. "Go on with the feasting and celebrating! I am ill, I say, I am leaving!" And leaning heavily on Ushna's arm, he withdrew from the hall.

For several days thereafter Ahaz lay abed, very real pains tearing at him from inside his chest. *Molech is angry that I marked my son with the sign of Yahweh's covenant with David,* he reasoned. *Oh, Molech, I had to do it! Does it really matter?*

And Abi never dreamed of the mental anguish or of the very real physical pain Ahaz suffered. To her it seemed the fact that Ahaz found the shedding of blood so difficult might indeed be an encouraging sign, a sign of deep-rooted gentleness, of unwillingness to inflict hurt. She thought of the cruelties of Molech worship of which she had heard. She assured herself, as she had many times through the years of their marriage, that Ahaz surely would never bring himself to take part in such rites. Within a few days Ahaz seemed well enough and Abi resolved never to mention his sudden show of weakness after such effort on his part to be brave, for she sensed that he had lost a deep inner struggle within himself and was ashamed for it.

As for Hezekiah, the cuts on his wrist healed rapidly. In spite of his trepidation, Ahaz had done the task well. The Royal Star

189

was cut deep and even and Abijah was proud that her child bore it.

In time, she thought, *we can all forget Ahaz's behavior at the ceremony, but my son will have the sign of the House of David on him forever.* And she took consolation in the thought.

* * * * *

It was about a year later that Ahaz again fell mysteriously ill and this time remained so for many days. It was a burning, scorching summer, with scarcely a breeze to bring even a breath of relief. The royal physicians were sure it was the weather that had made the King ill. Ushna, on the other hand, openly attributed the strange sickness to Molech's wrath. Ahaz, as he lay tormented by recurring dizziness, aching head, and pain in his chest, was inclined to agree with Ushna.

They spread wet cloths over his body, they fanned him, they muttered mystic incantations over him, but he burned with fever. He was unable to eat; he was repelled by the very sight of food. "Tomorrow . . ." he would mutter over and over. "Tomorrow. . . ."

From behind the thin curtains drawn around his bed, Ahaz could hear anxious whispers. "If he lives, it will be a miracle," Ushna was saying. "There is nothing much can be done for them when they get like this. I've seen it happen before."

Ahaz's brain whirled. "Ushna!" he called, and the curtains parted.

"My King, I thought you were sleeping," the Ammonite muttered apologetically.

"I must talk to you, Ushna," Ahaz said. Fierce longing to live raged within him. "I lied to Molech long ago and he knows."

The Ammonite bent solicitously over Ahaz's pillow. "Confess, oh my Ahaz, confess, and he will help you! I know he will! I promise!" His voice was very solemn.

The king was obviously in deep agony, and when he spoke it was only in a bare whisper. "Hezekiah is no bastard. He is my own child."

190

Ushna gasped, speechless for a moment, as fantastic prospects shaped in his mind. "You speak the truth?" he said after a moment. Ahaz nodded.

"Then pray, Ahaz, and I shall pray also. Of course, you will have to make reparation. You will have to offer up Hezekiah."

"Ask him to have mercy, Ushna."

"Molech is not a merciful god, my King. Doubtless he appreciates your confession, though, and if you show yourself willing to make amends, I believe . . . I strongly believe . . . he will make you well. I shall go now and seek his guidance."

* * * * *

It was a strangely disturbed Ushna who appeared moments later at the door of Abijah's apartment. For years he had suspected that Ahaz was Hezekiah's true father, but he was powerless to act on suspicion alone. Now that he had the king's confession, he suddenly possessed the power to destroy forever Abijah's love for Ahaz by seeing to it the king sacrificed their child. And if Ahaz recovered from his illness he would no doubt return to Molech with new fervor. Alienated from Abi he would rely more heavily upon Ushna.

Yet, there was the very real danger that Ahaz was dying and if Hezekiah died too, the throne would go to Isaiah. This was a risk that Ushna could not permit.

Silently the Ammonite stood in the doorway of Abi's apartment, watching her as she sat sewing, and he hated her from the depths of his soul. "Lady Abi," he said, after a moment.

Abijah looked up in surprise. "Ushna, how is he?"

"I speak bluntly, my Lady. He is dying."

Abi uttered a weak cry. Little Hezekiah, who had been sitting on the floor at her feet, rose and buried his head in the folds of her mantle. If Ahaz were to die he would be king. Abi's protective arms wrapped about him, holding him tightly.

"My Lady Abi," Ushna was saying, as devious wheels turned in his mind. "There is something you can do. Your husband's

191

life may depend on it. But before I tell you what it is, you must promise you will not refuse."

"I swear it, Ushna, to Yahweh himself I swear. Anything, anything on earth."

"All I want is that you answer one question. I want you to tell me the truth. Do not be afraid. You will not be harmed regardless of what the answer may be. But you *must* speak the truth, or I assure you heaven itself will take vengeance." Ushna's voice rose to a feverish pitch. "Who is the father of this child?"

Hezekiah looked up in horror. The Ammonite's accusing finger was pointed straight toward him. "Who, Lady Abi, who? Isaiah the prophet?"

"Oh no!" Abijah screamed. "Ushna, how dare you say that? I have never in my life been unfaithful to my Ahaz! Oh, Ushna! Look at my son! Look at his face, he is just like his father!"

Ushna sighed. The boy did bear a striking resemblance to the king. He had noticed that himself long ago and had mentioned it to Ahaz, only to have Ahaz rebuke him with the reminder: "Isaiah is my first cousin. After all there are family traits."

"Listen to me, Ushna," Abijah continued. "I don't know where you got your despicable idea, and I don't care to know. It is a lie, a hateful, dirty lie! Isaiah is a good man, a wonderful man, and I respect him from the depths of my heart. But Ahaz is my love, my *only* love. And let me tell you something else! Right now I am carrying another child. Oh Yahweh! I did not want to tell it yet!" A sudden sob shook her and she buried her face in her hands.

Ushna turned silently and withdrew. When Abi looked up again, the Ammonite had vanished like a figure in a terrible dream. He had gained more than he hoped from their encounter. Could it be that Molech was helping him?

* * * * *

Molech's will was conveyed to Ahaz in several steps in the days that followed. The night after he made his confession the King

192

had spent long sleepless hours in which the memories of his promise to Molech hung over him like oppressive weights. Fears waged war with equally unspeakable hope. *I must offer up Hezekiah! Molech, Molech, I will do it, only restore me to health!*

When Ushna came that morning and asked Ahaz if he were ready to sacrifice the child, the King could only nod weakly, "Yes."

The day following, Ushna returned with a second revelation. "I besought Molech for mercy," he said gently, "and he spoke to me clearly, as clearly as I have ever heard him in my life. He said 'Ahaz has proven to me that he is willing to fulfill his obligation to me. For that I grant him respite. I will not take his only son, so long as he has but one.'"

"Yes, yes . . . ." Ahaz's face brightened. "Oh Molech, my blessed lord!"

"Now should another son be born to you," Ushna said, "Molech will expect you to fulfill your obligations."

"Gladly," said Ahaz. "Gladly."

That very day, the King's fever broke and he ate a hearty meal.

* * * * *

In her happiness over Ahaz's recovery, Abijah could ignore his sudden fervor for Molech worship. It did not make her feel any better, but she had learned to endure much in silence that was inwardly disturbing. But his reaction when she told him she was pregnant again was something she could not accept unquestioningly. Why, oh why, had he looked so horrified when she had imparted the news to him? Why, after eternal moments of gloomy silence, had his only remark been: "I hope it is a little girl"? Why since that day did he come so rarely to Abi's apartment and when he did come, what made him so edgy and sullen? Abi scarcely dared to think, yet thousands of times during the long, lonely days of autumn and winter, the questions returned to vex her. She longed to talk it out with Ahaz, but Ahaz was unreachable. Even on the rare occasions when he came to her, he could not be brought to explain himself. All her attempts ended in his stalking away gloomily, perhaps not to return for weeks.

"When the little one comes, things will be better. You will feel differently," Abi said at last, on his last visit before the child was born.

"Indeed," said Ahaz angrily, "It would be better for the little one, if he were never born at all." He turned and walked quickly away.

"Ahaz! Oh Ahaz my darling, what is wrong?"

But Ahaz was gone.

* * * * *

Abi's second son was perfect, equally as delightful as newborn Hezekiah had been. "After all these years," Abi cooed, holding the little one to her breast, "God has sent me another child." With the infant in her arms, she was happy, banishing the dark memories of the past months from her mind. Her soul fairly sang as she observed how the baby's tiny face seemed to reflect the features of Ahaz. Even his few wisps of curly hair promised to be auburn. *"Ahaz will be delighted. He cannot help but be,"* she assured herself.

Eight-year-old Hezekiah was thrilled with his new brother. "When he is bigger," he said reaching out to touch the infant's tiny fingers, "I'll teach him everything I know and we'll have such fun together, like Jashub and Maher. I'll never be lonesome again. Let me hold him, Mother."

Abi smiled. For several years, ever since the prophet Isaiah had started teaching Hezekiah his lessons along with his own sons, Abi had heard the refrain of how glorious it was to have a brother. She handed him the squirming bundle carefully. "Be gentle," she warned.

"What are you going to name him?" Hezekiah queried, rocking his brother in his arms with a naturalness that made Abi tingle joyfully.

"I don't know yet. That is for the king to decide," she answered. Though it was usually the mother's prerogative to select the names for the children, she had not forgotten Ahaz's violent reaction when she wanted to call her first child Immanuel. "And surely he will come to see us soon," she added. "Probably today."

* * * * *

But the hours turned to days and Ahaz did not come. Then when the infant was four days old, a note came, brief and without emotion:

"Greeting and health from Ahaz the King to my Lady Abi. I shall leave it to you to decide on a name for the child. Let me know your choice."

Abijah read the note to Hezekiah, trying hard to conceal the shocked surprise she felt over her husband's strange behavior.

"Let's call him Isaiah," Hezekiah suggested, his eyes sparkling with enthusiasm.

"Oh dear, no!" Abi was horrified to think what Ahaz's reaction to that suggestion would be.

"I thought it would be nice," the boy replied, temporarily dejected. In a moment his face brightened again. "You could call him Azrikam, for that man you told me about, the one who saw you at the well and then got killed in the war."

"Azrikam . . . ." Abijah closed her eyes, trying to envision the face of the man who had been kind to her long ago. "He was a good man. He brought me to Ahaz. Had it not been for him, I might never have come to the palace. And he gave his life in the service of his king. It is a good name. Azrikam—'help has arisen.' I hope Ahaz will be pleased with it."

She sent a note telling Ahaz of the name and begging him to come and see the little one, but the king did not reply.

* * * * *

Why doesn't Ahaz come? The thought began to haunt Abijah's every waking moment. She could talk of little else. Even the joy of the precious baby's arrival was clouded by her husband's long absence. She sent him notes declaring how she missed him but they remained unanswered. "He must be very busy," she would say over and over, but her heart knew that something was dreadfully amiss. "Oh Yahweh," she prayed, "send him to me!"

Young Hezekiah saw his mother's grief and heard her prayers, and he determined to help Yahweh in answering her supplication. Abijah had no idea that the boy would try to find Ahaz. Hezekiah always seemed so uneasy around his father. Had she known his plan, she would have certainly restrained him. But on the afternoon of the sixth day while she was resting, he slipped away. She did not know he was gone.

* * * * *

Not daring to think of the possible consequences, little Hezekiah climbed up the steep steps toward the tower of Ushna's apartment where King Ahaz met so often now with his Ammonite prime minister. Hezekiah had never seen the inside of the place. In his wildest fancy he did not guess that the walls of that room housed a shrine to Molech far more imposing than that up on the roof. It was to this shrine in Ushna's apartment that Ahaz since his illness went often to worship the Ammonite god of the glowing fires. This was also a fact of which his young son was unaware.

The great, heavily carved door of the chamber was shut, but the little prince could hear the subdued voices of his father and Ushna. *I will wait until they come out,* he thought, leaning against the wall.

"No, Ushna, no, I cannot do it!" A scream of agony rent the air. It was the voice of Ahaz lifted in pleading. The boy outside in the corridor started with fright. The thought crossed his mind of running back to the safety of his mother's apartment, but a weird fascination held him.

"You cannot escape your vow another day," Ushna was saying with fearful solemnity. Behind the barred doors, the room where they sat was in total darkness save for the fire that burned before the idol of Molech. The Ammonite god seemed to survey the room with menacing gaze. Two fiery red rubies in his eyes glowed

196

eerily. His hideous stare appeared to be fixed upon Ahaz.

"When you were a child, I saved you from Yahweh's wrath and dedicated your soul to Molech. Then nine years ago before Molech's altar, you made your vow, your bargain with him to preserve you through the siege. You cannot deny it. You tried to escape; you lied to the god and in time he struck you. You would have died last summer had you not confessed and repented. And now the time has come when the vow must be fulfilled." Ushna's voice was loud and angry.

"Ushna, please, is there no other recourse?"

"None. I have prayed. I have besought him to be merciful, but Molech is an unbending god, demanding his just due." The solemnity in the priest's voice was terrifying. "From the time Hezekiah was born, Molech has been growing increasingly displeased. Who made you a vassal of Assyria? Who forced you to yield up so many of your possessions into the treasury of that foreign despot? Molech! And why? All because of your failure to give him what you swore to give him long ago! Last summer, who brought you to the edge of the grave? But now, he has also sent you a second son. This is your final chance, Ahaz. Humble yourself before him and give him what you promised, or I declare he will snatch everything away from you."

"But even if I do what you say, how can I know he will be pleased?" Ahaz protested.

"Think of all his mercies toward you already. Is it not Molech who has protected you thus far from the disease which smote your royal grandfather? Was it not Molech who saved us from the hand of Rezin and Pekah? I know you tried to ascribe that to Yahweh. When you consider your failure to keep your part of the covenant with Molech, you must admit that he has always been overly gracious to you. But his patience cannot hold out any longer now that Abi has borne another child. I am giving you the warning, Ahaz, because I have always loved you as if you were my own son."

"When shall it be?" Ahaz sounded defeated.

"It should be tomorrow morning in the valley of Hinnom. You and the Lady Abi shall. . . ."

197

"No!" Ahaz interrupted. "No! Abi has made no oath. Besides, she is the daughter of a priest of Yahweh. I cannot make her go! Anything but that, Ushna! Anything!"

Trembling, yet too fascinated to flee, Hezekiah pressed his ear against the wall. He did not comprehend the matter of which his father and the priest were speaking, but he sensed plainly that there was tremendous danger in the air and that in some strange way, he and his new baby brother and mother were all involved in it. Suddenly the voices within the room dropped to whispers.

Then, "No! Ushna! No!" Another scream from Ahaz, accompanied by what sounded as if the King were pounding his fists on the furniture.

"At this moment, Molech sees you," Ushna shouted dramatically. "Would you have him know your unwillingness to give him what he demands? You're already risking the loss of his favor! Ahaz, you must listen to reason! Do you want to die?"

"I will do it. There is no escape."

"Swear it!"

Ahaz knelt before the altar. His voice dropped low and the boy in the hall could not hear his words: "Molech, God of heaven, I shall bring the son you have given me to the valley of Hinnom. I swear it, I, Ahaz the King."

* * * * *

Suddenly and noiselessly, the door opened and Ushna came out alone, his soft slippers making no sound in the carpeted hall. Too late, Hezekiah looked up. He darted toward the staircase, but the priest of Molech was too quick for him.

"Come back here, you cursed little spy!" Ushna's powerful hands gripped his shoulders and shook him vigorously. "How long have you been here?"

"Not long."

"What were you doing?" Ushna growled, fury burning in his eyes.

"Uh . . . ah," the frightened child was far too terrified to answer.

198

"Spying! I know it! I'll teach you not to spy on me!" The Ammonite grasped a handful of Hezekiah's hair and pulled it with all his strength.

The prince's cry of terror rent the air. "Ushna, please!" he gasped. "I was just looking for my father."

"When the king wants you, he will send for you. And believe me, he will not have you bothering him." Ushna's tone was the epitome of cold cruelty. "Now or ever!"

Tears hovered at the rims of Hezekiah's eyes but he held them back. "You cannot hurt me. I am a prince of Judah and you're just an old Ammonite!" he burst out.

"I am your elder, and I will have your respect!" Ushna delivered a resounding slap on Hezekiah's cheek. In another instant, he had shoved him against the wall. The palms of the priest's hands pressed hard against the boy's shoulders.

Hezekiah was not aware of his father standing in the doorway behind them until Ahaz spoke. "Ushna is far wiser than you'll ever be," the king said. "If you are insolent to him, he will call down the wrath of Molech upon you." His voice was not cruel like Ushna's, only indifferent and distant.

"I'm not afraid of Molech. He is not the god of Judah and he has no power over us. My mother said so, and Isaiah too," Hezekiah replied defiantly. "Isaiah says he's just an idol that people have made and they pretend he's a god but he isn't really."

"I'll not hear another word out of you, child," Ahaz said gruffly. Then turning to Ushna he added, "We'd better keep him up here, or he will go running back to his mother and give her the warning."

And they led him into Ushna's apartment and shoved him down on a hard couch somewhere in the darkness.

"Of course the decision of which one you give is yours, Ahaz," Ushna was saying. "But it seems to me that Molech has led Hezekiah to his altar. You know the firstborn is always most pleasing to the gods. Perhaps my king will consider. . . ."

199

18

Hezekiah lay very still, too frightened to cry. "Yahweh, Yahweh!" he whispered, but no other words of prayer would come. After long moments he heard Ushna withdraw, then Ahaz moved over to the couch where Hezekiah lay and sat down beside him. "You are going to kill me?" the young prince's voice trembled.

"No," Ahaz said softly, and for a moment Hezekiah felt a wild hope that he had misunderstood the whole matter. "No, my son," Ahaz continued. "It shall not be you. I have decided. It shall be your brother instead."

"Oooh!" A gasp of dismay and pained surprise. Then, "My father, please don't do it! Please, please!" and Hezekiah's tears, so carefully held back, began to flow.

"I must do it," Ahaz answered, rising quickly. "And you must not ask me to do anything else. You will stay here until after your brother is brought here," he added sharply. Then he withdrew and Hezekiah heard the door being bolted behind him.

After that, Ahaz went straight to Abijah's apartment, to the outer chamber where a young nurse maid, Tirzah, sat rocking little Azrikam in her arms, while old Tamar hovered attentively near. "My king," Tamar rose, but Ahaz motioned her to silence.

"Come with me and bring the little one," he whispered to Tirzah.

Astonishment was mirrored all over the girl's face. "Do as I say," Ahaz commanded. "I want to show the child to some officials from Samaria," he lied, talking rapidly in order to conceal the nervousness in his voice. "Do not look so frightened, Tamar," he added to the old slave whose penetrating gaze seemed to pierce into his inner thoughts.

"Would you not see Lady Abi?" she suggested meekly. "She talks of nothing but you."

"I'll see her when I return," Ahaz replied evasively, moving toward the doorway. The astonished Tirzah followed without a word, never dreaming of Ahaz's true intentions.

So it was that little Prince Azrikam and his nurse were brought to Ushna's apartment and Abijah saw her baby son no more.

* * * * *

Before the statuette of Molech, Ushna paced restlessly. "It will have to be tomorrow morning," he was saying. Tirzah listened uncomprehendingly. The wife of one of the palace guards, she had borne a child of her own and lost it less than a month before. The opportunity to serve as nurse to the baby prince had helped to ease the ache in her heart. With fierce possessiveness, she clutched the infant to her breast. The room was hot and stuffy; Azrikam was napping. In the dim light, she fastened her gaze on his tiny features and smiled. Ushna and Ahaz had withdrawn to the far end of the room and were talking in subdued whispers.

"I will not tell Abi," Ahaz was saying. "You'll have to tell her yourself. I can't. I won't. And I'll not see her either."

Meanwhile a faint voice at the nurse's back whispered, "Tirzah," and a tiny tap on her shoulder made her turn nervously. "My Prince Hezekiah! I did not know you were here. It is so dark in here!"

"They're trying to kill him!" Hezekiah eased himself noiselessly to a place at Tirzah's side. "Let me have him!"

"Child, what are you saying?"

"Really, really, let me have him!" Hezekiah reached out to lift his sleeping brother. Azrikam awoke and squealed at the top of his voice. Tirzah moaned.

In an instant, Ahaz and Ushna were beside the would-be escapees. "Hezekiah," Ahaz said sternly, "You may go back to your mother now."

"My king," Ushna interrupted. "Let him tell her. Hezekiah, tell your mother that the king's son will be offered to Molech

201

tomorrow morning in the valley of Hinnom. Now be gone with you, be gone!" and he shoved him roughly toward the door.

* * * * *

Hezekiah could not return to his mother. He could not bring her the news alone. He must tell somebody else; he must have help. Isaiah! Swift as the wind, the prince ran through the corridors of the great palace. It was late afternoon; he might be at the Temple! Across the wide covered walkway he flew, his heart beating furiously. "Isaiah will help us! He will, he will!"

But Isaiah was not at the Temple.

"Where is he?" Hezekiah demanded breathlessly of his grandfather, Zechariah. "I have to find him! I just have to!"

"Now, now, don't be in such a hurry, child." Old Zechariah who had aged considerably in the last few years did not know the meaning of *hurry*. "You look like you've been running as if somebody was chasing you," he said, gently smoothing his grandson's dishevelled black curls. "Just sit still and catch your breath a minute. Now whatever you want to tell Isaiah, you can tell me, can't you?"

Hezekiah shook his head. He loved his grandfather, but he couldn't imagine Zechariah's being any help whatsoever. "Please take me to Isaiah."

"Isaiah's out at his country house, as far as I know," Zechariah replied.

"Oh." It was sigh of utter defeat. "Well, then, I guess. . . ."

"Tell me," Zechariah interrupted. "How is that baby brother of yours?"

"Oh, that's it, Grandfather! They're going to try to kill him!" In a few swift sentences Hezekiah poured out the whole incredible story.

The old man listened, his face turning almost as white as his snowy beard. "Hezey, my child, I'll do what I can," he said soberly. "We must tell your mother."

Zechariah held his grandson's hand tightly as the two of them

202

entered Abijah's apartment and sat in the outer hall to await her. "Hezey, where have you been?" Abijah entered the moment she heard her child's voice. "Oh, Father, I'm so glad you have come. Tirzah took the baby to show somebody, but they should be back soon. Have I told you, we decided to call him Azrikam? You remember Azrikam, Father? Hezey thought of it." Abijah bubbled with happy excitement.

Moments later, the fatal message delivered, she was racing through the halls of the palace, frantically shouting her husband's name. Hezekiah and Zechariah followed helplessly behind her.

"Ahaz! Ahaz! Answer me!" But there was no answer except the astonished gaze of a few assorted slaves and guards. Abi's carefully upswept hair had come loose and flew behind her in a wild black cascade. Her eyes were burning pools of fury. "Ahaz!" Her cries held all the fierce hurt of a lioness deprived of its young.

"They were all in Ushna's apartment," Hezekiah ventured. And in moments Abi was at Ushna's door, pounding with all her strength against the hard, unyielding wood. "Ahaz! Open it please, open it!"

From inside she could hear her infant shrieking piteously. "Ahaz, you must open or I will stand here all night! Father, Father, take Hezey and run, I won't have us all in danger," she added, turning distractedly to the two who loved her but were powerless to help.

The old man hesitated. "My daughter . . ." his hands were on her shoulders, his eyes searching hers with pleading, gently urging her to come away, to abandon the hopelessness of her cause.

"You two must go," Abi said, almost sternly. "But I will stay here till I see Ahaz again."

The next hours were interminably long. Abijah beat at the door and implored until a weird sensation overtook her that she had spent her entire life in that spot. "I must be dreaming. I will awaken and Azrikam will be safe in my arms." But it was no dream. The sobs of the infant behind the locked door were those of her child, so drastically and suddenly taken from her. Inside too, she felt sure, was Ahaz, and Ahaz did not answer.

Within the dark chamber, the king slept oblivious to the screams of either his wife or his child. The Ammonite had seen to that. No sooner had Hezekiah left them that afternoon that Ushna had urged Ahaz to drink a cup of wine heavily drugged with a sleeping potion. And now while Abijah cried, Ahaz lay motionless.

When at last the door opened, Abi practically fell into Ushna's arms. His powerful hands grasped her and she struggled wildly. "Where is my child, you foul creature? Let me have him! Let me go!" A small, sandaled foot kicked violently at Ushna's shins. "Let me go!"

He heaved her up into his arms, heedless of her struggle. He did not speak. Once again, Abi made the long trip through the corridors of the palace, this time in the relentless grasp of the Ammonite priest. When at last they reached her apartment and Ushna released his hold upon her, he spoke tersely: "You realize that the king did not answer you, even though he was with me in my apartment."

Abi lay slumped on a soft cushioned bench, her head against the wall. She seemed almost lifeless. Ushna turned to make his exit. "It will be no use for you to try to escape," he said. "There will be guards posted in the halls everywhere."

Abi moved slowly as one awakening from a long sleep. "You will have no peace ever again, Ushna," she said.

* * * * *

Early the following morning, Abijah's mother and father had sought to enter their daughter's apartment and were denied admission by Ahaz's special guards.

And now, as the time of the sacrifice drew near, the palace was deathly quiet. Ahaz had insisted that almost all the slaves attend the ceremony. All of Abi's maids had gone, even old Tamar, who at Ahaz's command had taken Hezekiah. Alone in her room, Abijah lay weeping, her head buried in the soft silk pillows of her bed. The events of the last few hours were still like a terrible dream to her. The ache in her heart was so unremitting that she felt it would never cease. To know that even as she lay there her husband

was placing their child in the arms of that hideous idol Molech
. . . "If only I could quit thinking," she moaned, but she could
not. The wildest of thoughts ran through her mind. "I will take
Hezekiah and leave here. I'll run away; I'll go somewhere Ahaz
will never find me." But even as she thought, she knew that such
a plan was impossible. She might seek out one of her brothers
but she would be searched for and endanger the whole family.
"Even if Ahaz does not care for me, he would search for Hezekiah,"
she thought. And Abi knew that by all the laws of the land she
was bound to Ahaz forever. Right or wrong, he was her master;
there could be no recourse. Life held no other alternative for her
but to remain the wife of the man who killed their son, to lie
with him when he demanded it, perhaps even to bear him more
children.

A shudder of repulsion ran through Abi's body and she felt chilled.
"Ahaz! Ahaz!" she sobbed wildly. "How could it be?" The piercing
thought of how she had always loved him crossed her mind, and
this was the most painful of all.

Then when she had wept so deeply that she could weep no
more, she lay perfectly still, almost as one dead. "Yahweh, Yahweh,
grant me peace!" Over and over her mind echoed this fervent
hope, the only prayer that she could pray.

* * * * *

It seemed hours before Abi heard the first faint sound of the
returning procession in the distance. Gradually the sounds became
louder. She became aware of the scurry of feet on the steps outside
her bedchamber and the loud clamor of the dozen or more excited
voices of her maids.

At length the door of the outer chamber opened, but she did
not stir. "Where is my mother?" she heard Hezekiah asking imploringly. Abi felt a sudden, intense longing to see her remaining child
and to hold him in her arms.

Tamar was trying her best to placate him. "I have told you,
Hezekiah, she is ill. She must not be disturbed."

"But, Tamar," the young prince protested, "if I could see her, maybe I could make her feel better."

"No, Hezey, I just can't. Maybe tomorrow."

"Let him come in, Tamar," Abi called. "Hezekiah, come here."

It never occurred to her to think about her appearance, but to Hezekiah the change in his usually beautiful mother was all too apparent. Her lovely long hair hung wild and tangled about her shoulders. Her face was flushed, her eyes rimmed with red from much weeping. There were a few ashes streaked upon her forehead as a sign of mourning.

Hezekiah's young heart was filled with sympathy, but suddenly he felt utterly unable to think what he might do to cheer her. "I have missed you so much, Mother." He spoke gravely and carefully, afraid he would say the wrong thing. He wanted desperately to make her happy again.

"Sit down here by me, Hezey, and tell me about the sacrifice." Abi felt herself saying it almost unconsciously. Hezekiah sat down on the edge of his mother's bed. His eyes were swimming with tears, but he felt he must try to be brave. "It was very sad, Mother," he said. "It was the saddest thing I have ever seen."

"To them who serve Molech it was not so," Abi commented.

"Oh Mother, that's what Ushna said. He said it should be a happy day because my father, the king, had proved his devotion to Molech. But Father did not think so."

"He didn't? How do you mean?"

"That's what made it so sad," Hezekiah explained. "When it was over Father went back to the royal pavilion and he cried and no one could stop him. I never saw him cry before. Ushna tried so hard to stop him, but it didn't do any good at all. Then Ushna got very angry with me and Tamar and told us to go back to the women's tent. I did not see what happened after that. Oh Mother, I don't understand why Father had to do it, anyway," he added after a pause.

Abi had listened wordlessly to Hezekiah's story. The boy's words were like a healing balm to her broken spirit. Ahaz had wept. She could scarcely believe it, yet one look at her son's earnest face told her he spoke the truth. Ahaz had loved the little one too. The deed which he had done this day was to him the supreme sacrifice. He had given his most precious possession to his god and now the horror of it was too much for him. Abi's heart ached for Ahaz.

She clasped her son's hand tightly. "Hezekiah, this had been a very, very sad day. The king did what he felt he had to do, but it has not made him happy. Now you and I know that Molech is a false idol and that Yahweh, our God, the true God, has never wanted people to do these terrible things. But your father doesn't think this way. I cannot explain why because I can't understand it myself. But someday you will be king and you can be an example for all the people of our country. When that time comes, I want you to remember this day and lead our country back to the true God."

"I will, Mother. I promise I will," Hezekiah said.

"And one more thing, Hezey. Even though you and I know that the king has made a terrible mistake, we must never speak of it. We are not in a position to judge him, but more important still is this, no good could come from it if we did."

"Mother," he hesitated.

"Yes."

"I will try to be so good to you that you won't even miss him."

The well-meant offer of childish love sent a new shudder of pain through Abijah's heart. "I will always miss him, Hezey . . . just as I would miss you if the king had taken you." With a deep sigh she sank back upon the pillows of her bed.

Hezekiah could not bear to see the tears which he knew would come. Wordlessly, he pressed his young mouth against his mother's hand and kissed it. Then he slipped away to the garden of the inner court, fiercely determined to be brave.

* * * * *

Ahaz's head was splitting with pain. Ushna the Ammonite, who had followed him unbidden into his private apartment, was as

207

smoothly solicitous as ever, but there was a note of warning in his voice. "Ahaz, you must not grieve so. It will negate the good effects."

"Who are you to tell your king what he must do?" Ahaz turned furiously. "Now begone with you, Ushna!" he screamed, delivering a resounding slap on the Ammonite's cheek. Bowing meekly, Ushna retired without another word, and Ahaz was left to face by himself the grim realization of what he had done. He was trembling all over. His heart beat so rapidly it seemed almost that his breath would stop. "I'll kill him!" he shouted, flinging a little silk pillow against the wall with all his might. "I'll kill him tomorrow!"

Before him in realistic vividness hovered the terrible scene of that morning. He threw himself on his bed, buried his head among the pillows, but still the infant's screams echoed in his ears. He who had always tried to find an excuse for staying away from battle, he who had always hated the sight of blood, how could he have plunged the knife into the living body of his own son? "Why did I do it?" he moaned aloud. "Abi, Abi, I am sorry!"

But she was lost to him forever. This realization was only too clear. In his headstrong determination he had destroyed the one beautiful thing in his life: Abi's love for him. *The child I killed was her son.*

"Oh God," Ahaz sobbed. "Oh Yahweh, give her back to me and I will give her whatever she asks!" Almost unconsciously his hands began to claw at the breast of his robe. The scarlet cloth gave way. There was something vaguely gratifying about it and he began to tear wildly at the splendid garment.

She will hate you as long as she lives, a little inner voice seemed to whisper to him. *She can never forgive you. As long as you live, Ahaz. . . .*

"Other kings in other lands have given their sons," he rationalized with himself, but it did not ease the pain. He knew that what he had done this day would remain with him forever, a reality which could never be escaped. The realization brought with it waves of agony surpassing the deepest grief he had dreamed possible. *You have always feared the things you cannot change.* Ushna's

208

words long ago echoed in his mind. Fitfully he tossed among the great soft pillows. His golden bracelet, one which Abi had given him, pressed hard against his flesh. He peeled it off and hurled it against the opposite wall. A violent shudder ran through him; his teeth began to chatter; he was shivering.

Better it would have been had I died myself than for me to have taken the life of my own child.

His frantic hands continued to tear at the fine scarlet fabric of his robe until the garment hung in shreds about his chilled body.

In desperation, Ahaz struck the gong beside the bed. "Yes, my King." The slave who answered the summons was clearly frightened.

"Bring me," Ahaz spoke slowly, "a goblet of wine and get some sleeping powder from Assher-dan the Assyrian, not from Ushna, mind you."

The slave stared at Ahaz in amazement. He had never seen the King except in faultless array, and the sight of his master clad only in the torn shreds of his robe was startling. "Yes, my King."

Ahaz was sitting on the edge of the bed when the slave returned with the wine. Wildly he grasped the goblet in his hand and raised it to his lips.

"Does not my King wish I should taste it first?"

"It doesn't matter," Ahaz replied bitterly, gulping down the strong potion. "Now help me take off my shoes and then let me be." The trembling slave bent to obey his master's orders.

"Does my King wish I should draw the bed curtains?" he asked meekly.

"Oh no! Do not close me up in the dark," Ahaz replied.

The slave withdrew, and Ahaz slept a sleep of death-like stillness.

* * * * *

Early evening twilight had settled over the palace when Hezekiah came in again and sat wistfully on the edge of Abi's bed. "Mother?" He reached out a frightened little hand, seeking hers.

"Yes, Hezey."

"What if he comes and tries to take me too?" His eyes swam

209

with great tears. "Oh Mother, I don't want to die and go down into Sheol. I want to live to be very old."

Abi reached out and pulled her son close to her, holding him tightly. "He cannot take you from me, Hezekiah. I would never let him."

"But what if he sent soldiers?"

"They would have to kill me first." It was almost impossible to be reassuring when her own lips were trembling, but for her child's sake she must try. Abi held him until the sobs subsided. "Come now," she said at last. "It is getting late and you need to be safe in your own bed."

It was a tremendous effort but she raised herself and walked hand in hand with her son to the little room where he slept. "Mother will stay with you till you go to sleep," she promised.

Abi pulled a little stool to the side of Hezekiah's bed and all through the long night she sat there beside the bed where he lay. A tiny oil lamp burned in the anteroom outside and she did not extinguish it, for there was always something comforting about light.

The little boy did not sleep much. He breathed heavily and tossed about, but he did not keep talking. Frequently she reached out her hand to touch him, as much to reassure herself as to comfort her child. "Oh Lord Yahweh, deal kindly with him!" she prayed silently. "The child of my body and Ahaz's. Oh Lord, make him better than either of us."

"Your mother loves you, Hezey," she whispered whenever he stirred. "More than I could ever say."

When early morning came, Tamar found her asleep, her weary head leaning against the side of Hezekiah's bed and her son's small hand clasped tightly in her own. The slave's footsteps wakened Abi from the brief respite. The reality of Azrikam's loss rushed upon her, as it would every morning for the rest of her life. She was indescribably weary. Hezekiah was asleep, and she was grateful for that.

The objects in the familiar room somehow looked unreal in the early morning light. There was little furniture: his bed, a pair of large wooden chests for clothing, a few little stools, and a long bench beside a writing table where he often sat to study the scrolls Isaiah gave him. The bed was in an alcove against the wall. Around it hung bed curtains of red, Hezekiah's favorite color, which Abi herself had lavishly embroidered with threads of gold. On the opposite wall were windows and the ledge where the boy had placed some of his dearest treasures. Abi's gaze fastened on a pretty greenish-brown rock that Isaiah had brought him from his country estate. *Hezey always talks so much about visiting Isaiah in the country,* she thought. *The prophet has promised to have him. Perhaps now would be the best time for it. It is not good for him to be here with me in this terrible time.* Impulsively, she wakened the sleeping child. "Hezey," she spoke in a whisper, "tell me, how would you like to go out and stay at Isaiah's house?"

"Oh Mother, can I really?" He seemed delighted. "Jashub and Maher and I can play all day long. And Isaiah has a cave, too, and we can go exploring."

"Of course," Abi added, "we will have to ask permission of the king."

* * * * *

Ushna! What will I do with Ushna? It was the first thought to penetrate Ahaz's consciousness when he awoke in the cold prelight of early morning. "I'll have him stoned to death outside the gate." But there was not even a shred of comfort in the thought. The picture of Ushna who had befriended him in his lonely childhood flashed through his mind. Ushna, who had told him the stories of the beautiful land of Ammon and the mother he had lost; Ushna, who had tended his wounds when old Jerusha hurt him, who had helped him to build the wonderful sun-clock. The thought of that magnificent structure sent a new little pain through Ahaz's mind.

He was terribly cold. He pulled the bed covers tighter around him, but it was a coldness that no coverlets could alleviate. *It is not even Tishri yet,* he thought. *How long must I live with the knowledge of what I have done? I am twenty-nine years old. I could live forty or fifty years yet. Oh God! Oh Yahweh, have mercy! Yahweh and Assher and all the host of heaven!* He buried his head beneath the covers and prayed to die. And, utterly exhausted, he slept again, the effects of the potion still hanging heavy upon him. And he dreamed that Abi lay in his arms.

It was midmorning when the old nurse Tamar came to Ahaz's apartment with a tiny scroll from Abijah. A slave admitted her to the outer chamber and went to announce her presence to the king. Still abed, still dazed from the sleeping potion, he forced himself to rise. "Let her come in," he groaned weakly. He was still clad in the shreds of the magnificent robe he had worn yesterday; his feet were bare, his long, thick hair hung wild and uncombed about his shoulders. Tamar was visibly startled to see him like this, but she knew better than to comment. Wordlessly she handed him the scroll, which after all was the purpose of her coming.

"Is it from my Lady Abi?" Ahaz asked, grasping it eagerly.

Tamar nodded, watching with weird fascination the emotion in Ahaz's face as he unrolled the message and read:

"To my Lord and King, greeting from Abi. If Isaiah consents, it seems good to me to let Hezekiah spend two or three weeks at his country home. Do you agree?"

"Is this all?" Ahaz asked, not even trying to conceal his disappointment.

Tamar nodded. "I am to await your answer if it please you."

His heart was almost bursting with the things he longed to impart to her but there were no words to write them. Slowly he walked to the little writing stand in the next room with Tamar following and watching his every move with penetrating intensity. His hand wavered for a moment before he wrote simply across the bottom of Abi's note: *Do as you wish.*

Nervously he twisted the little roll between his fingers. "Tamar," he began, "Is she . . . I mean, has she said anything about me?"

The old nurse looked at him with withering coolness. "What is there to say?"

"You know well enough what I mean, Tamar."

"Her heart is broken, but women have often learned to live

212

with a broken heart." Tamar bowed low, then moved swiftly toward the door.

"Come back! Ask her . . . no, tell me yourself, do you think she would see me?"

"If the king commands an audience, who can refuse him?"

"Tell her then," he said, "I will come to her by midafternoon."

* * * * *

It seemed that the appointed time would never come.

Abi spent the rest of the morning in preparation: a long, cooling bath, brushing and arranging of her hair, lengthy pondering of what to wear. The dress she selected was brown, not especially pretty. Dark-haired, dark-eyed Abi had never cared much for brown, but now it seemed most appropriate, for it was most akin to the sackcloth she would not have dared to wear.

Tamar wrapped her long hair in a crown of braids. The array of face paint was left untouched. She was very pale and there were shadowy dark circles beneath her eyes.

"Let him see what he has done to you," Tamar clucked lovingly. Abi did not reply.

* * * * *

He had promised to come by midafternoon. Time dragged by. Abi tried to embroider, but her head ached and her eyes were weak and watery. There was nothing to do but wait, and as she waited she talked with forced cheerfulness to Hezekiah about Isaiah's estate in the country and the many delights of the forthcoming visit. At last they heard Ahaz approaching, and Hezekiah scurried away, while Abijah moved to the bench before the window. Beyond her, through the filmy, almost transparent draperies, Ahaz could see the inner garden wrapped in the serene hues of late afternoon. Abi herself, in her brown robe, seemed a part of the day, serene and still. *Never has she been more lovely. Now that I dare not touch her.* It was a disturbing thought crowding the already all

213

too many waves of discomfort that continued to sweep through Ahaz's brain.

Abijah rose to greet him. "Peace and health unto my Lord the King," she said quietly, without emotion, in the formal language of the court.

Pained surprise crossed his face. *What does he expect of me?* she thought. He did not move or speak. "Sit down, Ahaz," she said.

"Yes," he nodded, with eyes downcast, unable to meet her gaze. "I was going to say that I will leave it to you to make the arrangements with Isaiah about the boy's trip. It will be a fine thing for him to see how life is in the country."

"Hezey will be so happy about this. Would you have me call him to thank you?"

"No!" Ahaz almost shouted. "That is, I think it would be just as well not to."

She did not reply and the silence was oppressive.

"I suppose that is all we need to say about it," Ahaz said rising. "He may stay there as long as the prophet wishes to keep him."

"I will tell Hezey and I know he will be glad. We both appreciate it, Ahaz." Such calmness, such unruffled placidity. Her voice was as soft as in those moments, never to come again, when she had whispered her love. He longed to take her in his arms, but he would not have dared to do so. *She hates me and yet she feels that she must be kind. Would that she would scream at me, curse me, strike me. That I could understand, but not this.*

And astonished by her bravery and overwhelmed with admiration for this noble lady who was his wife, he walked slowly away. It would be many weeks before he attempted to see her again.

There was nowhere to go. As he walked with downcast eyes through the halls of his palace, Ahaz thought suddenly of his grandfather, Uzziah. "I am an outcast now, too," he murmured. The palace guards who stood at their customary posts in the hallways saluted him with proper decorum when he passed, yet he sensed cold hatred in their eyes. Something in him longed to cry out, "I know I have done wrong! Forgive me!" but he knew that was not the way a king conducted himself. Besides, who was there to forgive were he to admit his guilt? Abi? Hezekiah? The nation? God, or the gods, whoever they were? No, there was no hope. He straightened his shoulders and walked with a regal pace. "I am Ahaz the king," he said aloud, "and no one shall dispute what I have done."

"Your Majesty . . ." a breathless slave appeared it seemed from nowhere and cast himself at Ahaz's feet. "Ushna the Ammonite is dead!"

Ahaz motioned for the man to rise. "When did this happen?" he said coldly. He could see in his mind's eye the choice array of powders and potions which Ushna had kept always in his apartment. There was little doubt as to what had happened.

"He was found dead a few moments ago."

Ahaz sighed deeply. "His attendants may bury him in the valley of Hinnom," he said. "I will not be disturbed any further on the matter."

By the next morning the news was all over Jerusalem that the king had killed Ushna. Ahaz did not bother to deny it.

215

*****

How can these things have happened? Isaiah the prophet thought to himself. That Ahaz should have sacrificed his infant son to Molech was a horror almost beyond the prophet's comprehension. For years he had known and spoken against the terrible rites in the valley of Hinnom. His common sense told him that there was always the possibility that Ahaz *might* act as he did, and still the deed was incomprehensible. That anyone could believe that *any* god would require such a dreadful act, that any father *could* kill his own child to placate an idol was unthinkable! *I could not have stopped him,* Isaiah thought. *Even had I known what he was planning. No more than I could stop him from seeking help from Tiglathpileser.* It was discouraging, but Isaiah had learned that Yahweh works through discouragement.

This present age is a dark time for Judah. The hope for Yahweh's people lies in the future, he thought. *And perhaps in the child Hezekiah.*

The prophet's two sons, Jashub and Maher, had been greatly pleased that Hezekiah had come to stay with them. At the moment, as Isaiah watched them from a distance, the boys were sprawled beneath a tree a short way from the house. It was morning of the day after Hezekiah's arrival. The children, Isaiah guessed, were planning their day's adventure. It was most likely a trip to the cave they had discovered on the estate. The cave was Jashub and Maher's favorite hideaway.

It was a beautiful, clear day. The countryside, though dry and dusty as Judah invariably was in the summer, was still wrapped in the serene hues of the early morning hour. It was hard to realize how in this beautiful world, little Prince Azrikam had lost his life.

"Sometimes, on days like today," Isaiah said aloud, "it almost seems as if the peaceable kingdom has already come." He was standing in the doorway of his house with his arm around the shoulders of his little daughter Hephzibah. She was six, and she was a lovely child, with Isaiah's green eyes and fair skin. He had let Naamah name her, since he had had his own way with the

216

boys' names. "Hephzibah" which meant "My delight is in her" suited her perfectly.

"I don't think," said Hephzibah solemnly, "that Prince Hezekiah likes us."

"Oh, of course he does," Isaiah dismissed the child's suggestion.

"You know, Isaiah, she may be right." Naamah had joined them at the doorway. "I'll declare, he is the *quietest* child! Of course he's been through a lot, but honestly I haven't heard him say a word since he got here, except greeting me when he first came in last evening and thanking me for his breakfast." Naamah's voice registered no little complaint. "I don't know what I'm going to do with him. He seems so sad."

"Why is he sad?" asked Hephzibah.

"Because he had a little brother, and he died," Isaiah explained. There would be time enough in later years for his children to know the full impact of the recent tragedy. "Poor little fellow," he added. "He will brighten up in time. Don't worry. The boys will see to that." His eyes turned to the group beneath the tree just in time to see Jashub rising in disgust.

"You don't want to do anything, Hezey," the older boy exclaimed. "You're no fun."

"Jashub and I wanted to show you the cave," Maher put in. "We were going to go exploring and everything. Don't you want to, really?"

"No," said Hezekiah. "I don't want to."

"Then you ought to go home," Jashub exclaimed.

"Even Hephzibah plays better than you do," Maher added. "And she's so little and a girl besides."

"Go play with your baby sister then, and leave me alone. Go on, I don't care! I don't care about anything."

Maher's face was a mirror of disappointment. He and Hezey were friends. They had often played and studied together at the palace, but this was the first time Hezekiah had ever been allowed to visit him. Slowly he turned his back on the listless prince.

"Come on, Maher," Jashub said. "Let's tell Father to send him back to the palace."

217

"No!" Hezekiah shouted. "No! Not that!" Like a flash of lightning he was off up the path to Isaiah. "Don't send me home," he panted. "Please, Isaiah!"

The prophet's strong arms held the boy closely. "Of course not, Hezey. You just got here. Jashub! Maher! What is all this about sending Hezey home?"

"He won't play," Maher said.

"He won't do anything," Jashub added. "He just lies under that tree and says he doesn't care about anything."

Isaiah sighed. "You boys run on by yourselves," he said. "Now Hezey, I am going down to the cave where I have stored some things that I need. Do you want to come with me?"

The boy shook his head. "I just want to stay here."

"I'll show you my rock collection," offered Hephzibah.

"Not now."

"All right then." Isaiah said. "This evening when I come back, I'll bring some scrolls and we'll have stories. You'd like that, won't you?"

"Oh yes," cried Hephzibah, but the boy said nothing, and Isaiah went on his way.

* * * * *

Late that afternoon Hezekiah still sat under the tree near the front gate of Isaiah's house. "As soon as he comes, I will ask him," he told himself, "and tomorrow, oh, maybe even tonight, he can get it off." As he had done a thousand times or more in the last two days, he stared down unhappily at the design in the shape of David's Star which Ahaz had placed upon his arm long ago. His heart beat with uneasy excitement. He remembered the day when his father had put the mark upon him, explaining that the Star was a sign to show that he was King Ahaz's son and that he was a prince forever. At the time it had seemed wonderful. Even though the process had hurt more than he'd expected, the ceremony was thrilling. But now the Star was an altogether different matter. "I must get it off," Hezekiah thought. And in this one thought all the diverse sorrows in his young heart seemed to concentrate themselves. Indeed he felt he could never be happy again unless the despised mark could be removed.

"Isaiah!" At last he saw the prophet approaching and ran to meet him. "Isaiah, I have to ask you something very important!" There was a plaintive note in the young prince's voice. "It's a secret!"

"Here; let's sit down." Isaiah motioned to a large rock by the side of the path. "Now, don't make it too hard," he said good-naturedly.

"Is there . . ." Hezekiah faltered, "I mean, could anybody ever get this off of me?" He extended his arm and pointed to the clearly imprinted sign of Judah's royalty in his light brown flesh.

The question took Isaiah completely by surprise. Did the little prince fear that someone would try to rob him of his birthright? "Why, no, Hezey, certainly not," Isaiah said. "It will be there as long as you live."

There was a merciless finality in the prophet's words and cold shudders of unhappiness gripped at Hezekiah's mind. His lips trembled. Big tears welled up in the corners of his eyes. "I had hoped so much that you could take it off," he said, making an effort to hold back his tears. "You can do almost everything. Oh, Isaiah, please try! I don't care how much you hurt me!"

Isaiah's heart ached for the unhappy little boy. Gently he placed his broad hand over the mark on his small cousin's wrist. "Why do you want it off, Hezey?" he said at last.

"I cannot tell!" Hezekiah shook his head.

"You can tell me."

"Because . . ." and now the boy did not try to hold back the tears, "because it is like my father, and I hate him! They always say 'Honor your father' but my father wanted to kill me, and he did kill my little brother. And he's made my mother sick, and he worships idols, and oh, I hate him! I despise him!"

The boy's outburst, Isaiah knew, was an offense against the laws

219

of both God and nation, yet he could not hold it against him. Would it not be futile to try to prove Ahaz worthy of his son's loyalty and love?

"And that's why I don't want to have his sign on me," Hezekiah went on, "because I don't want to be his son."

Isaiah sighed. It would have been easy to remind Hezey that he, Isaiah, was also born a prince of Judah, that he too bore the sign upon his arm and had never dreamed of having it removed. It would have been easy too to tell him that almost any child in Judah, Jashub and Maher and Hephzibah included, would be delighted to have the privilege of bearing the royal sign. Isaiah's own children were not born descendants of the reigning monarch and the strict custom regulating the right of bearing the royal mark had prohibited their receiving it. But these matters, Isaiah knew, were not what Hezekiah needed or wanted to hear.

"Hezey, think with me now," Isaiah said gently. "Has anyone ever said this is the Star of Ahaz? It is the Star of David, is it not?"

The boy nodded.

"Then let us talk about David for a little while," Isaiah said.

Of course, Hezekiah had heard stories of King David from his earliest childhood. He knew that David was the best king, the one whom Yahweh loved most of all. Something about David seemed too good to be true, and Hezekiah had never cared much for him. But now Isaiah began to speak of David, not as the mighty monarch that he eventually became, but as a youth at the court of King Saul. Hezey closed his eyes and it seemed that he could almost see the scenes that Isaiah described: the frightened boy playing his lyre before the unpredictable king, never knowing when Saul's insane rage would break forth against him, or again, David an outlaw in the wilderness, forced to hide from the king who wished to destroy him.

"Now Hezey," Isaiah went on, "when David was having such hard times, do you think he was ever worried or sad? Certainly he was! But even at the same time, he trusted that Yahweh would

220

always love and protect him and in time would make him a great king."

"But . . ." Hezekiah protested, "Yahweh loved David better than he loves anybody now. There can never be another king like him."

"But that is not Yahweh's fault . . . nor David's. Hezekiah, every man who ever wears the crown of Judah has equal chance, if only he loves Yahweh as David did." The prophet lifted his eyes toward heaven. "Someday, someday, I feel it, there will be another king fully as great as David."

Hezekiah was very still. Thoughts of the future, of the kingship which would someday be his, stirred within him. It was strange how he had never thought much about it before, for suddenly the future seemed very close indeed. "Do you think I can be the one?" he said at last.

"Yes, oh yes, my Hezekiah! You can be." Isaiah clasped the boy's wrist tightly. "You can be the greatest and best king that our nation has ever known. And I want you to think of David's Star that you bear on your body as a sign of this goal, a reminder that Yahweh loves you just as much as he loved David long ago, and that it is by his help that you shall be a great king." Slowly the prophet released his hold on Hezey's wrist. Slowly, thoughtfully, the boy's fingers rubbed the mark. He did not speak immediately, for there was an indescribable feeling of happiness stirring within him, a wonderful feeling unlike anything he had ever known.

Isaiah broke the silence. "Now, if you still want me to," he said matter-of-factly, "I can get you some berry stain to rub on it. It will not take it off, but it will cover it, more or less, for a while."

The prophet's words broke the boy's reverie and he gasped in surprise. "Oh no!" He could not put the indescribable feeling into adequate words. "I would not ever want to have it off now," he whispered softly, looking into the prophet's eyes, "even if I could."

And Isaiah could see that he had planted a seed of glorious hope in the heart of Hezekiah ben-Ahaz.

221

Was this child Yahweh's chosen one who would bring to Judah the new golden age? Isaiah did not know. *But it is possible,* he thought as they sat there side by side in the late afternoon shadows. *Truly it does not matter what his father is like.* There were other prophets, other spokesmen for Yahweh, Isaiah knew, who would say it did matter: that the children were punished for the sins of their fathers, that good could not come out of evil. *But that is not so,* thought Isaiah. *Every soul has an equal chance in Yahweh's eyes. It must be so, and this child must never fail to believe it.*

* * * * *

The weeks that followed were happy ones for Hezekiah. With Maher and Jashub, he explored the wonders of Isaiah's lands. There were numerous trips to the cave, and on one occasion when Isaiah stayed with them, they even spent the night in its dark recesses. As much as the boys loved the outdoors, there was time set aside every day too for study, reading from Isaiah's vast collection of scrolls and talking with him about a thousand different things. And, of course, there were Isaiah's stories and his beautiful songs to listen to in the still of the evening. Sometimes Isaiah sang of the peaceable kingdom; a fanciful, wonderful song that was the children's favorite, a song of the time when:

"The wolf shall dwell with the lamb,
    and the leopard shall lie down with the kid,
and the calf and the lion and the fatling together,
    and a little child shall lead them.

"The cow and the bear shall feed;
    their young shall lie down together;
and the lion shall eat straw like the ox.

"They shall not hurt or destroy
    in all my holy mountain;
for the earth shall be full of the knowledge of Yahweh
    as the waters cover the sea."

222

"Will it really be like that?" Little Hephzibah, secure in her father's lap, looked up at him in wide-eyed wonder.

"There are no words that can tell the glories of the time when peace, true peace, comes to dwell in the hearts of men," Isaiah answered.

Hezekiah's love and admiration for the prophet, which had always been deep, grew deeper. If he had any sorrow to cloud those happy days it was the thought that Maher and Jashub and Hephzibah belonged to Isaiah and he did not. "I wish you were my father," he confided to him at last, to which the prophet answered simply and directly, "I love you as one of my very own, Hezekiah. Do not forget it." That reassurance Hezekiah locked in his heart together with his ideal of being like David. And somehow, when he thought upon these things, it no longer mattered very much that he was in reality the son of Ahaz.

The days passed swiftly. After two months, Ahaz sent word saying that Prince Hezekiah had stayed long enough and must return to Jerusalem.

Back in the city, Abijah awaited Hezekiah's return with mixed emotions. Her days, ever since she lost Azrikam, had been indescribably long and lonely while the nights brought little that was real rest. Often she would awaken sobbing from a fitful sleep. The dreadful awareness of what Ahaz had done never left her. Every waking moment it haunted her consciousness. Even the few brief hours she was able to sleep were filled with nightmares. She would see little Azrikam in Molech's arms, hear him crying helplessly. Sometimes, she would even dream that she had been there, that she had snatched him from Molech's fiery embrace, and that he still lived. Or again, and this was the hardest of all, she would dream of Ahaz as he was in the days before and awaken with unbearable longing and love for him burning within her. He did not come to see her, and she was glad, for she could not, she told herself, have borne his presence.

The days turned to weeks, slipping away in monotonous succession. Time stretched ahead into eternity in which she knew she would never be free from the realization that the man she loved had killed their son. These were the days for learning to live with a broken heart, a time for gathering up the shattered fragments of life and searching for some reason to keep on living. Abijah found this reason for existence in the person of Hezekiah. Now, after two months with Isaiah he was coming back to the palace. Abi knew that for the sake of her remaining son, she must force herself to overcome the tragedy that had come upon her marriage. She thanked the Lord for Hezekiah and vowed to do for him what she could to make his life a happy one.

* * * * *

And now, he was home, his brown eyes shining with youthful excitement. His arms about her were not those of a frightened child craving comfort, but of a strong boy whose love for his mother had something of the element of protection in it. "I have so much to tell you," he said. "So many wonderful things have happened."

"My Hezey," she smiled, for the first time in many weeks. "I want to hear every word."

In the still summer evenings of the weeks that followed, Hezekiah would sit with her on the flat roof above her apartment. Often he spoke of his days in the country, or again he would find Maher and Jashub, who now had resumed daily lessons with him at the palace, and bring them to listen to Abi tell the stirring stories of their nation. The children all loved to listen to Abi's stories, and she seemed never to tire of telling them. Her voice would ring with expression as she recounted the ancient tales reflecting Yahweh's watch over his people. Ever since his visit with Isaiah, Hezekiah loved the stories of David best of all. "Do you think David was ever afraid of King Saul?" he would ask her. It was so interesting to discover what one's mother thought about questions like this one. He did not tell her how sometimes he pretended he was David and that Ahaz was Saul. Would a mother really understand that?

Then sometimes, on evenings when the air was clear, Abijah would spread out coverlets on the roof and she and her son would

224

lie still and gaze at the boundless sky which Yahweh had created. During that summer, Abijah taught him the names of many of the stars in the heavens, fiery Arcturus, clear, bluish-white Vega, and a host of others that she learned from Ahaz in a happier time long ago.

They never spoke of Azrikam. If his memory remained forever in Abi's consciousness, she was determined not to say so.

* * * * *

On the day the prophet came, Hezekiah was alone up on one of the latticed porches that opened out from his mother's apartment and looked down to the main courtyard. He was reading quietly when he heard an uproar from below. Cries of "Be gone!" mingled with the cheers of an excited mob.

Hezekiah peered through the lattice work to the outer courtyard below. There before the palace, on one of the lower steps of Ahaz's famous sun-clock, stood a remarkable sight. The man was clearly a prophet; his sackcloth robe indicated as much. Surely he was a stranger to the city as well, for what man of Jerusalem would have dared to mount the king's sun-clock? The prophet's arms were upraised in an attempt to silence the mob that pressed around him.

"Mother! Come!" Hezekiah bounded back into the great hall of the apartment where Abi sat. "There's a prophet! We can look through the lattices!" She followed without a word.

The man was speaking when they reached the porch. It was difficult to understand him because the crowd was still noisy. Suddenly Abi became aware of the fact that he was talking about Ahaz and the sacrifice of Azrikam, asking the crowd if Yahweh, if any god, demands such a sacrifice from any man.

> "With what shall I come before Yahweh
> and bow myself before God on high?"
> Shall I give . . ." he cried, "the fruit of my body
> for the sin of my soul?"

225

The prophet's voice was very clear, and suddenly the crowd fell completely silent. As if in answer to the question he raised he continued:

> "He has showed you, O man, what is good;
> And what does Yahweh require of you,
> but to do justice, and love mercy
> and to walk humbly with your God?"

Was it the words the prophet spoke or was it some mystic quality in his voice? Abijah leaned her head against the framework of the lattice and wept. "Oh God, oh God, if Ahaz could only have lived by that." She felt Hezekiah's hand squeezing her own reassuringly. "Oh Yahweh, forgive King Ahaz!" she cried.

That evening a palace slave went in search of the prophet to tell him that Lady Abijah requested a written copy of his words. But the prophet was not to be found.

* * * * *

One morning in late summer Ahaz came to Abijah's apartment. It was the moment she had both dreaded and longed for. She thanked God she was alone. Hezekiah was having his lessons with Isaiah's sons in a distant part of the palace and would not be in all morning.

"Ahaz. . . ." Now that he was with her she could think of nothing to say. What could she say? Her eyes met his and she could see in them the expression of a man who was fighting a fierce inner battle and was determined to win. "Ahaz . . ." she repeated his name. "My lord, my king."

"I have come to talk about the New Year," he said slowly, cautiously. It was as if he addressed a total stranger.

"And your birthday," she ventured. Ahaz's birthday conveniently fell on the New Year day, the first day of Tishri, the first day of autumn.

"My birthday makes no difference," he said crisply. "The New Year festival does. The court will expect to see the king's wife

226

beside him at the feast. I expect it of you, Abijah." His voice rose angrily. "And you'll not say no to me." His hands were on her shoulders, his eyes blazing fires.

"No, Ahaz, I'll not say no," Abijah replied.

"Thank you, my wife," he said and he walked away.

* * * * *

For weeks, months, thereafter, Abi felt that Ahaz would try to say something to her about Azrikam, something to heal the hurt. He came more often now, always in the mornings, perhaps twice a week, perhaps a little less. At last it became clear that there was an unspoken agreement between them never to mention that terrible day. After a while, the uneasy tensions began to fade a bit. After a while she could think without pain of the days before, even talk of them to him. But still there was an unbridgeable gulf between them. He never touched her, except occasionally to shake her in anger. He never called her "Abi" as he had done in the days before. She was always "Abijah" or even "Lady Abijah."

And so the months turned into years. The hot, still summers and rainy, gray winters passed in monotonous succession. No more, so far as anyone knew, did Ahaz prostrate himself before the god of Ammon. Not that this really made any difference, for now he had turned more strongly than ever to Tiglath-pileser's Assher. The Assyrian god whom he had once resented so strongly, he now worshiped with an outward show of zeal. Before the Temple of Yahweh stood Assher's magnificent altar. There Ahaz himself offered cereal offerings. Sometimes Abijah prayed that he would return to Yahweh, but even as she did so, she felt little hope that her prayers would be answered.

Publicly, Ahaz showered Abi with all the attentions a king's wife could ask for. She had the finest clothes, jewels, and bangles to satisfy her every fancy. She had a place beside the king in his banquet hall whenever she wished to attend him.

Ahaz took other women to his bed, Abi knew, and she accepted the fact without emotion. After all they were only concubines, she

227

told herself, but even had he taken another legal wife she knew she could not have protested. "One thing you must promise me," she told him. "Whatever happens, Hezekiah is still your heir," and Ahaz swore it with an expression of vast relief.

None of the girls he took bore him a child and at length it was rumored that the king had lost all interest in women. What was the joy of holding a soft, yielding female in his arms when it was not his Abi, the woman whose soul was still, unexplainably a part of his own? Physical pleasure, perhaps, nothing more, and even that left hauntingly disquieting memories when it was over.

And it was said by certain of the concubines that while he slept, Ahaz was often heard to cry the name of Abi.

* * * * *

Prince Hezekiah grew to young manhood. On his twelfth birthday he had been granted a separate apartment and Abi saw him not nearly so often as she might have wished. His days were spent in learning the military and political skills expected of every highborn youth.

By his early teens he had already surpassed his father in stature. Now at seventeen he had grown to be a strikingly handsome young man. His wavy, jet black hair was without doubt his heritage from his mother, but his features were distinctly those of Ahaz. The dark, penetrating eyes, the well-formed mouth were as clearly a testimony of his royal birth as was David's Star on his wrist. He was a thoughtful, serious young man. Apt enough in the art of swordsmanship and a superb charioteer, he gave every promise of being an able warrior should the need arise. Nevertheless, few things delighted him more than the composing of songs. Unfortunately, he had inherited Ahaz's inability to sing. But he had learned to play the lyre with some skill and would recite his verses against this musical background. Whenever he had a new poem that especially pleased him he would go with it to his mother, to the benches in her private garden, and recite it for her.

Abijah's love for him was boundless. It was the love she could

228

have given to a dozen sons had the Lord wished it, a love that went deeper because of the little lost one. If he had any faults, his mother's eyes did not see them. Sometimes, indeed, Abi wondered how she and Ahaz could ever have produced such a marvel. But then who would try to explain the ways of Yahweh?

"Someday he shall be king, he must be king." How many times Abijah thought it! "Oh Yahweh, my Lord, do not let anything interfere with his destiny!" No prayer that she had ever prayed was so deeply felt as this one.

In the nineteenth year of the reign of King Ahaz, the year that the King reached the age of thirty-eight and his son seventeen, there came a letter to the court of Judah from the Assyrian King Sargon. Tiglath-pileser, the mighty conqueror to whom Ahaz had bowed in the ruins of Rezin's capital, was dead now these several years. But his death had meant no relaxation of the tributary bond which bound Ahaz irrevocably to Assyria. Sargon, indeed, as Ahaz had learned in the past few years, was a master even more to be feared than his predecessor. The Assyrian king's reign, he remembered, had begun with the fall of the great city of Samaria. King Hoshea had broken his loyalty oath, sought aid from Egypt, and refused to make the tribute payment. The ultimate result of all this was the complete desolation of the once-splendid northern capital. No king at all now ruled in the Northern Kingdom, Ahaz recalled with a shudder. North Israel as a political entity had vanished, incorporated into the Assyrian Empire. Vast numbers of Hoshea's subjects had been rounded up and deported to distant lands, and already the men of Judah were beginning to speak of their former northern neighbors as the "lost tribes of Israel." Now, only Judah remained of the once-proud Hebrew sister states, and Judah would remain only so long as Ahaz the King was loyal to Sargon's demands.

So when Sargon's letter came—the particular letter which was to cause such commotion in the royal household before the full force of its impact was spent—Ahaz's first thought was simply of pleasing Assyria.

230

"The great king is sending a delegation to our New Year feast. The honor of our great protector Assher must be very much in evidence." Ahaz had gathered his counselors, not for the purpose of asking advice, for he knew well enough what he was going to do, but because he felt that the sooner he announced his plan publicly the more difficult it would be for him to revoke it. "I thought until this morning that I had done sufficiently for Assher and for Sargon. Have I not erected an altar for the Lord Assher in the court of Yahweh's own Temple? Have I not provided ample burnt offerings, celebrated his feasts with diligence, maintained his priests in suitable style? Indeed is his chief priest Assher-dan not also my most trusted advisor?" Ahaz nodded to the Assyrian who had taken Ushna's place as prime minister and who was seated at the king's right hand. "Yes, I would say," he went on, "that I have proved myself a willing servant of the lord of Assyria. Yet, according to this letter which was brought me this morning, there has been one requirement which up to this time has been over-looked. It will be rectified at once, for as a servant of the great king, it is my pleasure to do whatever the great king commands of me." Ahaz's tone became very self-effacing. "Would you hear his words? Here, Assher-dan, read this thing to them." Ahaz had never learned to read the Assyrian cuneiform script, and, with an unspoken twinge of dislike for a people who couldn't write sensibly on papyrus, he handed the little clay tablet which had arrived from Sargon that morning to the smiling Assyrian at his side. Assher-dan had been prime minister now for nine years, and if he had not won the King's devotion as had his predecessor, Ushna, at least he had his respect.

"It is the desire of the great king," Assher-dan read, "to learn of the progress which our servant Ahaz of Judah has made in establishing firmly the worship of Assher, the great god, the lord of heaven. It is the great king's special concern to learn the identity of Assher's high priest among the native sons of Judah."

An involuntary gasp went up from around the council table. Assher-dan himself had served as high priest ever since the cult of the Assyrian god had been introduced, but he was an Assyrian

231

himself, one whom Tiglath-pileser had sent in with the special purpose of establishing the ritual as he would have it done. "Sargon has forgotten our Assher-dan," Ahaz broke in. "That is obvious. But if he wants a native son of Judah, a native son he shall have. The consecration of the new high priest will be the high point of our New Year. Sargon's officers cannot fail to be pleased." Ahaz paused. "Of course, we must have the right man for this role, one of whom I, King Ahaz, can proudly say to Sargon's delegation: 'This is the man whom I have given to Assyria's god.'" Ahaz's dark eyes darted around the council room. Everywhere the silent, unresponsive faces of his courtiers met him; there was not one smile of approval. At the far end of the table, opposite Ahaz, sat Prince Hezekiah; his features, usually so expressive, seemed devoid of all emotion. Beneath the table his hands were clenched tightly into fists. In the heavy moment of silence, it was as if something told him what his father was about to say. Then he heard his father speak his name. He heard the stunned gasp of the courtiers, and saw Isaiah, his face livid with anger, rise and leave the hall without a word.

"Hezekiah, prince of Judah and high priest of Assher," Ahaz was saying. "Of course, he will need to select a new name, something not so obviously attached to Yahweh."

The prince said nothing. Inside him was a fiery torrent of rage longing to let itself loose, but he had seen Isaiah's example and he knew that if he were to remain true to Yahweh, he must for the moment be quiet. "Oh God," he prayed silently. "I do not want to die. But if I must, I shall, rather than submit to this." He moved toward the door.

"My son!" Ahaz called him back. "If you should need help in selecting a name, I asked Assher-dan to prepare this list." Nervously the King twisted a piece of papyrus with the list of names into a tight scroll. "We will need to begin training you in the ritual soon, perhaps early next week." Obviously to Ahaz the entire matter seemed as routine as any other business of daily government.

Hezekiah could not stand before the King without any answer.

He spoke slowly, his voice cool and even: "Why are you doing this to me, Father?"

"Because I know you shall do as I command of you," Ahaz answered. "It is your duty as a son to help me without question. I want to preserve this nation, and to do so we must please Assyria. You know that. And we do not please Assyria by bowing to our provincial God. Sargon wants a Judean Assher priest, and surely no choice can be more pleasing to Assher and Sargon than a prince of royal blood. Hezekiah, someday you will have to try to develop a little political sense. Someday you will be the king of this country. I am trying to help you." There was genuine sincerity in Ahaz's tone, but it was not unmixed with anger and frustration.

"You would help me by forcing me to serve a false god!" Hezekiah shouted, all his careful reserve of unspoken resistance shattered. "I cannot! I will not!"

"You will!" Ahaz screamed. "Now go!"

* * * * *

"I cannot! I will not reject my God! I would sooner that my father should kill me than this!" Hezekiah had returned to his apartment and found Maher waiting there for him. The prophet's son, who had no inkling of the dire pronouncement which Ahaz was to make at the council meeting, had come to the palace with the pleasant intention of suggesting to his friend a morning ride in the country. Now, all of a sudden, all hopes of peaceful leisure were vanished and he found himself confronted by a very disturbed but very resolute Hezekiah. "I will not be forced into it," the prince muttered vehemently, more to himself than to Maher. "No power on this earth will make me do it!"

"Start at the beginning, Hezey," Maher urged, visibly confused. "How can I know what you are talking about?"

Hezekiah nodded and in terse sentences began to relate the story of the morning's events. Maher noticed that his friend's eyes were burning with a fire very like Isaiah's when the prophetic spirit

233

came upon him. "My father will probably kill me," Hezekiah concluded calmly, the telling of the awful pronouncement seeming to have steadied him. "I shall not be afraid to die."

Now it was Maher's turn to be excited. For the present he could see only the two alternatives which Hezekiah had so vividly described, submission to the King's will or martyrdom. And, personally, Maher was not of the stuff of which martyrs are made. "Hezey, you must not risk your life!" he implored. "You can serve Yahweh much better living than dead. When you are praying aloud to Assher, cannot your heart be praying to Yahweh? Let King Ahaz consecrate you. Let him change your name if he wants to. It will make no difference really."

The young prince's heart beat faster. "Yahweh is my strength," he said—the literal meaning of the name that Ahaz had given him when he was born. "Oh Maher, can you imagine me as 'Asshernasipal' or 'Assher-pileser' or some such, standing out there muttering all that nonsense that Assher-dan goes through? Making the people believe that Assyrian idol is stronger and greater than the true God who chose us? Would you have me live such a despicable lie? If only, if only my father and all the rest of them could see that Assher is nothing, that Yahweh is everything." Hezekiah's voice was filled with the fiery fervency of youth. His devotion to his God was unquestionable even though he sensed how poorly he had expressed himself.

"Hezey, remember you are crown prince of Judah. You are the only hope this nation has for better days. If you die you may destroy all that."

"If I die, I leave your father as heir to the throne," Hezekiah countered. "Isaiah would make the finest king this nation has ever had. It may even be Yahweh's plan to dispose of me for this very reason."

"Oh, no!" Maher gasped. Isaiah's family had always lived in awareness of their close proximity to the throne, yet none of them had ever dreamed of envisioning the prophet as Ahaz's successor. The idea struck Maher as if it were a physical blow and it took him a moment to recover his composure. In the intervening moment

234

he allowed himself to envision his father as king and to feel a fierce anxiety as to whether Yahweh were indeed planning to take Hezekiah's life with this end in view. When he spoke again, however, it was with complete calm. "What will it do to your mother if the king kills you?" The words seemed to shatter in the air. In the minds of both young men echoed the cries of a child long dead.

"Hezey, we will hide you, my father and I." Maher broke the silence at last. "You remember the cave? You will be safe there, I'm sure of it."

"But for how long? Would you have me spend my whole life in hiding, a hermit in a cave?" Hezekiah protested, though already he had inwardly accepted the idea of his escape as soon as Maher suggested it.

"Certainly not. We'll get you out of Judah, over into one of the Philistine cities if the need be."

"I shall leave here tonight." Hezekiah's imagination was fully awakened, and with the fearless excitement of youth his mind had transformed what was to be the most perilous act of his life into a glorious adventure. "In disguise. They'll not even know I'm gone until morning. Of course, I remember the cave. It won't be hard to find."

So he spoke, for had he not in his dreams relived the golden summer at Isaiah's home hundreds of times? It would be easy to find the cave.

* * * * *

"Mother, I had to see you." The long hours of the day had passed since he and Maher had formulated his escape plan. Now Hezekiah swung open the little gate to Abijah's private garden and stood before her looking marvelously handsome in the dusky twilight. Still, the mother's eyes were quick to notice that something about him seemed very unlike himself. Suddenly it occurred to her that there was nothing about him to bespeak the fact of his princely birth. He was clad in a coarse brown robe such as any

235

country fellow might wear. His only adornment was a plain leather bracelet upon his left arm, a bracelet which carefully covered the royal sign upon his wrist.

"Something is wrong," Abi said, holding out her hand to him and motioning him to the little bench where she sat.

Hezekiah scarcely knew where to begin. He was worried that his mother, with her strange sense of loyalty to Ahaz, would urge him to do as the king commanded. Yet, he would not have considered leaving without telling her that he was going. "Has the king told you about his plan?" he asked, half hoping she already knew.

"Ahaz scarcely ever tells me anything, my son. You know that," Abi said. She sighed deeply.

"Well, the king is planning a great Assher festival to be held at the Temple at the New Year festival when the Assyrian inspectors come."

Abijah accepted the news wordlessly.

"And that is not all. He wants to have me consecrated as Assher's high priest." In brief, emotion-charged sentences, Hezekiah related the details of the morning's scene. Abi shuddered, sickening, cold fears grasped her—an agony much akin to that she had felt when she had lost little Azrikam.

"You will not submit?" She spoke questioningly as if dreading to hear his reply. What if he had already reconciled himself to serving as minister to that foreign god? He, Hezekiah the hope of Judah. But why did she doubt him even for a moment?

"You know I will never bow to any god but Yahweh. I am leaving the city tonight."

His last statement took Abi by surprise. A sudden motherly fear for her son's physical well-being eclipsed all other concerns. "Hezekiah, you cannot! Where would you go?"

"Don't worry about that, Mother. I know a place where I can find safety." He spoke with such determination that Abi knew that nothing she could say would change his mind.

"Just tell me where you are going," she repeated.

"I cannot tell you. *He* will ask you and it will be better that you do not know."

Hezekiah was right, Abi realized. Indeed, he was splendid. But, if this venture should be a failure, and there were so many things that could go wrong. She threw her arms about him and held him tightly, loving him with all the protective intensity that she had felt for him when he was a small child. "Hezey, my Hezey," she whispered. She was intensely proud of him, but she could find no words to tell him so. "May Yahweh go with you," she said at last.

"I will come home," he said, "when the time of danger has passed." He kissed her lightly on the forehead.

"You will be with me always in my prayers," she replied.

And then he was gone, out into the twilight.

*　*　*　*　*

Abijah could not fight back the thoughts which kept pouring into her mind. Would she ever see her son again? His hasty action, even if it did not cost him his life, might lose him his chance for the kingship. Oh, why must he decide things so hurriedly? Why had she not even tried to convince him to let her intercede with Ahaz?

"Oh, Lord, Yahweh, be with him and protect him!" She sank to her knees and buried her head in her arms. Her cheek pressed against the cold stone of the bench where she had sat with her son only moments ago. Fears of the worst sort laid hold of her. "Lord, I love him too much to lose him! He is my only son, and he will make such a splendid king! Take care of him and bring him home!"

Abijah rose from her place on the ground and gazed up at the boundless sky. The lonely silence of the night pressed in upon her, yet in that loneliness she felt a great surge of power and unshakable confidence that Yahweh had heard. Clearly as if the words had been spoken came the prompting: "It is for you, Abijah, to make Ahaz change his mind. You alone can do this, for you are the one person on earth who has truly loved him."

The next moments were filled with a sort of feverish activity

237

that left Abi's young servant girls completely bewildered. What had possessed Lady Abijah to come dashing into her apartment almost breathlessly and to write a hurried note for immediate delivery to the king? Whatever had happened to inspire her at this hour of the night to send one maid scurrying to prepare a bath of sweetly scented water, while others rummaged through her dresses and veils for "the very prettiest thing I have in green. . . . the king's favorite color, you know." It was no secret to the palace staff that King Ahaz and his lady, while outwardly on good terms, rarely saw each other alone. Yet now, obviously Abijah was attempting some sort of reconciliation. There must be a reason for it. Abijah herself smiled enigmatically and did not attempt any explanation.

* * * * *

"Why?" King Ahaz bellowed to the frightened maid who delivered Abi's note. "Now what do you suppose she is up to, wanting me to meet her on the roof in an hour's time?"

"I really don't know, my king," the girl stammered, "but she looked very excited and very beautiful."

Ahaz had intended the question as simply rhetorical and the girl's answer took him by surprise. "Tell her I shall meet her," he said coolly, indicating the girl's dismissal. Within him a strange reawakened longing throbbed almost violently, and he remembered when he and Abi had been alone together for the first time on that selfsame rooftop and the joy he had known when first he held her in his arms. Could that have really been more than twenty years ago? Could it be that this same radiant creature still wanted him? He rose to prepare himself for the rendezvous and was almost happy.

* * * * *

Abi was on the roof waiting well before the appointed hour. Ahaz would be late, she felt sure, but that didn't matter. He would come soon enough.

The wind seemed cold for this time of year. Abi felt an unmistakable tinge of fall in the air that well matched the icy apprehensions she was beginning to feel within herself. Lost in thought, she was startled to hear Ahaz's voice.

"Well, Abi, what do you want from me? Out with it now; I haven't time to listen to a long discourse." Uncertainty made Ahaz gruff in spite of his deep-seated desire to make his wife happy.

Abi realized it would be best to get to the point immediately. "About this matter of the Assher ceremony at the New Year festival and Hezekiah's consecration," she began with a remarkable calmness in her voice.

"You've heard about it? Who told you?" Ahaz seated himself on one of the marble benches and motioned Abi to his side. "Who told you?" he repeated.

"I suppose practically everyone knows by now. You realize there are very few secrets which can remain hidden here at court even for a day." Abi was evasive. "Was there perhaps a reason why you wished me not to know?"

"No. You had to know eventually. After all, you will be expected to attend. But I hadn't wanted to tell you any sooner than I had to. I know this will be hard on you, Abi." There was a note of genuine sympathy in the King's voice.

"Oh, Ahaz, not just me!"

"You are right," Ahaz sighed. "On us all, especially Hezekiah, but I will make him understand me. He will do it."

"Ahaz, why must you do it to him?"

"I have to. You can't understand it. You never will. You're too devoted to Yahweh. But I, well, it's different. Once someone is committed to Assher, he has to fulfill his obligations. Abi, Abi, can't you see he is the god who has made the Assyrians great and made Judah what it is as well? Assyria's fate is in Assher's hands, and Judah's fate lies with Assyria. The great king and his god must be given preference over all else, any personal feelings we might have." This was Ahaz's reasoning; it was clear and it was all he could offer. To tell Abi that deep in his soul he hated Assher even as she did would be unthinkable, for it was a reality

239

that he would not have admitted even to himself. Assher was powerful, of that he felt certain, and Assher and his earthly representative were realities with which Judah had to reckon. "Hezekiah's consecration will be the greatest gift I can give," Ahaz concluded. "Assher and King Sargon will be very pleased."

"You gave our other child to win a god's favor and did it help you?" In one instant Abi had shattered the nine years of silence regarding that dreadful subject, the subject that had long ago erected an invisible barrier of fear between them. Nothing but utter despair could have made her do it, Ahaz knew.

"Oh no, Abi," he sighed in deep anguish. "It was to the wrong god."

"And is Assher the right god?"

"Oh, Abi, I don't know! I've tried all my life to find peace with the gods and with myself, and I never have. I have never known what I should do to please the gods. Now it has come to the point where pleasing the gods does not matter so much as pleasing Sargon."

"Ahaz, don't say those things."

"No, let me say on. Abijah, you know that I mean well. My people say I have a hard heart, I know. They even say there's no good at all in me."

"Those who say that have never seen you as you really are. There is so much that is good and wonderful in you."

"Now you are trying to flatter me." Ahaz was unmoved.

"No. I say it because I love you. True, you've hurt me so deeply that I can never forget it, but still I love you."

"Why, Abi, why?"

"Because I need you, and you need me."

"Abi, my darling, you cannot know how many times I have wished that I might call back our child from Sheol."

He had said it: the words that for almost ten years he had longed to say and that Abi had longed to hear. Yet now was no time for dwelling upon their significance.

"Yet you would take our living son and dedicate him against his will to a god more cruel than Molech?"

240

Ahaz was motionless and only vaguely was he listening. He had fixed his gaze on a distant star and for the first time in many years he felt a marvelous sense of peace. Abijah had been able to forgive him, to tell him that she loved him. Suddenly his arms were about her, powerful, passionate. "I will never hurt you again, my beloved. I swear it," he whispered. "Even if I must defy King Sargon's wishes. Don't worry. I will change the plans about Assher."

He made no explicit promise, but Abijah was happy. "Ahaz, my Ahaz," she whispered, great tears running down her cheeks. And she knew that though she had come to her husband that night with only the thought of rescuing Hezekiah, something far more marvelous had happened. "Please believe me that I love you," she said.

And Ahaz replied, as one answering to the ritual formula prescribed for the worship of some great deity, "I believe."

* * * * *

The next morning Abijah awoke with a singing feeling in her heart. "Ahaz. . . ." she breathed his name and reached out to him, but he was gone. Unwillingly, she sat up, rubbed her eyelids, and wondered for a moment if she had really lain in his arms all night and heard him speak to her in words that she had never dreamed she would hear again. Yes, it was true, she assured herself. He had risen early and slipped away while she slept. Surely before the day was over she would see him again.

"My lady is happy this morning?" One of the young maids tiptoed in cautiously to help Abijah dress.

"Oh yes," Abi smiled. "It is a wonderful day. Find me something pretty to wear."

"Abijah!" It was Ahaz's voice, and he was angry. Startled she rose and turned to see him standing in the doorway.

"Come in," she said softly.

Ahaz strode in and seated himself on a little bench beside Abi's bed. "Leave us;" he glared at the servant girl.

Abi trembled. She felt a dozen fears at once. He had changed his mind about his plans for Hezekiah or regretted their scene of last night.

When the girl had left, Ahaz spoke. His voice was cold. "Prince Hezekiah is gone."

The look of amazement on Abi's face was, she hoped, convincing if not genuine. "Gone? Where?"

"I think you should be the one to supply that information."

"Why, Ahaz, I don't know where he is any more than you do. How do you know he's gone, anyway? Have you searched the palace?"

Ahaz ignored these remarks. He rose and placed his strong hands on Abi's shoulders and looked straight into her eyes. "He is gone, and I have every reason to believe you know where he is."

"I don't see why you should think that," Abi protested.

He released his hold and began to pace furiously back and forth before her. "Oh, Abijah, I can see it now. You telling him not to compromise his vows to Yahweh by giving in to me. You're the sort who would do a thing like this. You've filled his mind with Yahweh ever since he was born, and he's just as bad now as you are about how there can only be one God in Judah."

"Ahaz!" Abi gasped.

"Don't contradict me. Everything I say is the truth and you know it. You knew Hezekiah was gone, didn't you?" He was scowling.

"Ahaz, I told you; I don't know where he is."

"But you've known all along he was gone," Ahaz repeated. "Last night you knew!"

"I hadn't seen him recently. But what conclusion can I draw from that?" She was not adept at lying.

"Abijah, either you tell me all you know about this matter, or I will revoke my promises of last evening."

Abi trembled. "You wouldn't." It was only a whisper. He made no answer, but the furious look in his eyes bespoke the worst. *Last night I gave both my body and my soul to this man, and he loved me,* Abi thought. *And now this.* The magic of his reawakened

242

love for her had not changed him. Things were no better than before.

"I'm waiting," Ahaz said.

"All right, I knew he was gone." Abi's voice was cold. "But I didn't tell him to go and I don't know where he is. You must believe me. It was not my idea, but he has a far braver heart than I have, and a firmer devotion to Yahweh. Ahaz, you know I love Hezekiah better than my own life and if anything happened to him I believe I'd die. But he was determined to leave and there was no stopping him. And I do believe Yahweh will be with him."

Ahaz listened attentively. His eyes now held a look of deep sadness. "What I wouldn't give to have the courage that Hezekiah has!" His anger had vanished. "I am proud of our son; he will make a good king. I would call him back, if I knew where he was, that is."

"Give him time, Ahaz. Let it be known that he is not to be Assher's priest and he will come home of his own free will."

The king sighed deeply. He realized that his recent outburst of anger had been intense and, in view of his promises to Abi of only the night before, unpardonable. It would not be easy to explain the reason that lay behind his concern, but he knew he must try. "Abi," he said carefully, "I don't think you understand how bad it is for me to have him disappear like this. If I should die, perhaps, and he is not here to claim the throne, you know what would happen—Isaiah would become king."

"Ahaz! You are too young to speak of death!" She laid a consoling hand upon his arm. "You are not even forty yet!"

"My father died when he was not much older than I am now," Ahaz went on, staring at a far wall and not daring to look into her eyes. "I too have felt the pains that he felt, like a knife under my heart."

"Not all the time?" she said, as if in saying it she could wipe away the pain.

"Oh no, just sometimes, but more often now than it used to

243

be. I am not afraid, Abi. Why should anyone fear to go down into Sheol?"

Abi ignored the question. "Ahaz, my love, I believe the pains will pass." What else could she say? "We must believe it. It has been a long summer, but when autumn comes. . . ." Her words hung in the empty air for a long while.

"Yes," he said at last, "when autumn comes. . . ." Suddenly he caught her in a fervent embrace. "My Abi loves me; I should live forever!"

21

The driving rain beat hard upon the earth. That it should come at this time of year—with the fall rainy season still several weeks away—was ominous. It must be a sign from Yahweh, Hezekiah thought, but why Yahweh should choose such a sign was beyond him. The fugitive prince huddled against a boulder; his teeth chattered; he was drenched and miserable. Sadly his eyes scanned the horizon for the scene he had hoped would be so familiar, but there was nothing in view except the brown, rain-soaked earth and the huge rocky crags. Last night when he set out and early this morning he had been so full of hope. Then the sudden rainstorm had come and with it came the realization that he was lost. Disconsolately he leaned back against the wet, clammy rock. The wind was cold and he pulled his coarse robe tighter about him. He looked down and saw mud, deep and slimy, oozing through the open toes of his sandals. He looked ahead and saw a world in great gray sheets of rain. "My Lord, Yahweh, help me," he groaned aloud, and trying to ignore the storm he plodded on.

He was not sure when he first noticed the slender figure in a long cloak on the trail ahead of him. But suddenly he was aware of the presence of another human being within shouting distance. "Stop," he called above the roar of the storm. "Stop!"

The stranger heard, no doubt, but instead of stopping began to run, clearly frightened. An instant later, Hezekiah saw the rain-soaked wayfarer lose balance and fall headlong into the mud.

As fast as rain and mud and rocky ground would permit, he was at the stranger's side. There he found himself looking into the eyes of a young girl, a girl who even here, rain-drenched and spattered with mud, was undeniably attractive. "My foot," she said weakly. "I cannot get up."

In another instant she was in Hezekiah's arms. "You should not have run," he said.

"I was afraid." She looked up at him with deep, expressive green eyes, as if to say "I am not afraid now." This calmness of face was belied, however, by the rapid thumping of her heart, which Hezekiah could feel against his own body. "Take me home," she whispered. "It isn't far; I was nearly there."

"You have only to point the way," Hezekiah answered. *She is amazingly light,* he thought, for she had seemed tall when he first glimpsed her on the trail.

She smiled. "You'll see it, the other side of this hill."

It was impolite, he knew, to ask a stranger's name. As much as he would like to know her identity and her reason for wandering in the wilderness in this weather, years of training in courtly etiquette had taught him to avoid the direct question till the other party volunteered information. "My name," he said after a moment, "is Hezekiah." Surely that was safe enough, for were there not hundreds of young men in Judah named for the crown prince?

The girl nodded. "The same as our king's son," she said matter-of-factly. She did not offer her name and for a time that seemed an eternity they were both silent.

"There, there look!"

They had reached the top of the little hill and in the valley below them was a rambling grey stone house. "I told you we were almost there!"

Hezekiah said nothing. The house in the valley was Isaiah's house—and the girl in his arms, no doubt of it, was Isaiah's daughter. He sighed deeply, trying to remember little Hephzibah as she had been in that magic summer long ago. But that was nine years ago and that was the last time he had seen her, for though Isaiah brought the boys to the palace frequently, Hephzibah had never come with them. A strange joy possessed him that the girl did not know him. For the first time in his life he was completely free from his identity as the son of King Ahaz. The descent to the house seemed short indeed. If Isaiah or Naamah, Jashub or Maher were there, of course he would have to give up his ruse immediately. Otherwise there could be no harm in continuing the mystery a while longer.

The stillness pervading the old house told him as they entered that there was no one to greet their arrival. The place was almost as dark and dank as the inside of the cave he had sought. Hezekiah placed the girl gently on a rug before the dead hearth. Her ankle, he could see, was badly swollen and she was shivering. "Let me get a fire going and then we'll do something about your foot," he said.

With a fire on the hearth, the house immediately seemed both warmer and brighter. Hezekiah seated himself at the girl's side, took her foot in his hands and began to massage it gently.

"My mother and my brother Jashub are in Jerusalem," she said softly, "at our city home. But Jashub should be here any moment."

Hezekiah did not answer.

"I didn't tell you," the girl added. "My name is Hephzibah."

"A pretty name."

"I don't know how to thank you for saving me. If you hadn't come, I might still be lying there in the mud."

"If I hadn't come," Hezekiah said, "you would not have run and you would not have fallen. You are the one who has rescued me, Hepzibah. I was lost and you have given me shelter."

"The rain is a sign," Hephzibah said. "I thought as soon as it started. . . ." She was speaking cleverly, for now a great number of doubts were beginning to cross her mind. For one thing there were the strange events of yesterday. Her father and Maher had come dashing in, talking rapidly and in excited whispers, and in a few moments were off to the cave, with word to Hephzibah and Naamah that they might be gone indefinitely. Under no circumstances were the women to reveal their whereabouts to anyone. In their frantic rush, they had departed with only a goatskin bag of water and not even a morsel of food. Hephzibah and Jashub, the latter of whom was still in Jerusalem but who was due to

247

appear at any moment, would meet them at the cave the next morning with a well-stocked basket and "any news Jashub may bring in from the palace." For her own safety, Naamah was to return to the prophet's city home along with the family servants. In the days to come, she would send messages of further news from Jerusalem. These plans made, Isaiah and Maher had hastily departed for the cave.

Morning had come at last (after a night that seemed interminably long). Naamah and the household servants rode off for the city, leaving only Hephzibah behind. Hours dragged by; still Jashub did not arrive. Hephzibah dawdled over the preparation of the basket, hoping fervently for her brother's arrival. At length, when he failed to come, she set out alone.

It was on her return trip from this mission that the storm had come up, she had fallen, and now was sitting at her rescuer's side while he bathed her swollen ankle and wrapped it in strips of linen. She looked into the young man's eyes. "Hezekiah," she said slowly, "Have you ever seen the prince, your namesake?"

"Who in Jerusalem has not seen him?"

"Do you think he will make a better king than his father?"

"I should hope so," he answered.

"You speak as if you do not admire King Ahaz."

"He has been a great disappointment to many people," Hezekiah said. For long moments Hephzibah did not answer.

"When I was a little girl, I saw the prince," she said at last. "My father brought him here to be with my brothers that summer when King Ahaz offered up the other little prince. I was so excited when he came, but he and my brothers paid me no attention at all."

"That was long ago. You were too young to remember." Hezekiah looked straight into Hephizibah's lovely eyes and with equal steadiness she returned his gaze.

She knows, he thought.

But if she knew, she was enjoying the game of his anonymity.

"It is so strange," she said, "about the prince. My father has always had great hopes for him—even when Hezekiah was just a

248

little boy. But something has made my father very sad now, and I have a feeling it has to do with Hezekiah. He would not tell me. I don't know why I am telling you all these things except that your name is Hezekiah too, and I am worried about him."

"I know what is wrong, Hephzibah. Everybody inside the city knows, I suppose. Would you have me tell you?" She nodded and in a few brief sentences he revealed King Ahaz's plan for the prince's consecration. He spoke cautiously, careful not to reveal his identity.

Far from registering the look of dismay which he expected, Hephzibah's face radiated a smile. It was time to end their little game. "He will not submit," she said. "He will escape from the court and seek refuge with some kinsmen of his in the country in a cave." She paused but her companion said nothing. "Only he will lose his way in the storm and wind up rescuing his cousin Hephzibah from the mud. Hezekiah ben-Ahaz, do not think you can fool me." Her pretty, deep green eyes twinkled with merriment.

"I did for a little while," he countered, smiling back at her. Then suddenly he was completely serious. "It may be years before I can admit to anyone that I am Ahaz's son—maybe forever. Hephzibah, your father and Maher are going to help me escape over into Philistia, I think."

Outside the wind howled furiously, as if moaning for all the woes of the kingdom of Judah. The rain poured down in sheets. "You cannot go to Philistia in this," Hephzibah said. Her heart was beating with an unaccustomed sense of urgency. She had known Hezekiah for only a few moments, and now he might be going forever into the land of the Philistines. She wanted him to be safe from Ahaz's wrath, but she dreaded to think of his going.

"When King Ahaz dies, you will come back?" she said and realized immediately that it was not the thing to say.

"The king is still a young man. Yahweh will probably give him many years more: I do not know. There are some things which one does not think about."

Hephzibah's lips parted as if to speak. Her face bore a solicitous look, and he felt sure she was about to comfort him in advance for the loss of his father.

249

"Don't think I love him, Hephzibah," he burst out, "either as my father or my king. I cannot, not after all he has done. Yet I will be sad when he dies, for I know my mother loves him still and I will mourn with her. Certainly, I want to be king, and if Yahweh wills it, I shall be eventually. If not, then I must accept whatever he does will for me. That is all anyone can do, really, I think. And I will pray that he will grant me strength and patience if I must be disappointed."

Hephzibah did not answer. She longed to reach out and grasp Hezekiah's hands, to hold him in her arms, to speak a thousand words of encouragement. She longed to say, "I will go with you to Philistia or the ends of the earth." *He is actually a distant cousin,* she thought. *Father would give me to him, but would he want me?* It seemed too much to hope for, and she was silent.

She could feel his eyes studying her but she kept her own eyes downcast. "Little Hephzibah, so grown up," he said after a moment. His voice was warm and wonderful and happiness welled up in her. Still she could not speak. No words would come to her.

"Listen, the rain has stopped," Hezekiah said suddenly.

"Yes, yes it has." Hephzibah made an effort to rise but remembering her wounded foot sank back to her place on the rug. Hezekiah had sprung up and flung open the door. Outside sunshine pierced through an atmosphere still heavy with mist and wrapped the world in a strange, almost mystic, light. "You must get up to the cave," Hephzibah said.

"And leave you here all alone, with your foot like it is. No indeed, Hephzibah. Besides I need you to show me the way before I get lost again." As he spoke, he had scooped her up into his powerful arms and in moments they were off on the trail to the cave.

The next few days, though spent in the narrow confines of the prophet's cave, passed for Hezekiah with a speed he had scarcely dreamed possible. On the morning of the second day, Maher departed for a secret investigation of the Philistine border area, instructed by Isaiah and Hezekiah to search out a likely place where the fugitive prince might settle and live for years, if the need be, incognito. Maher promised to return in a week's time, if at all possible, with his report. In the meantime, Jashub arrived from

250

Jerusalem, with the news that as yet no word had been released by the palace to the effect that Prince Hezekiah was missing. Apparently Ahaz was planning to keep his son's disappearance a secret, lest popular reaction be such as to put the king in a very uncomfortable position. Returning again to Jerusalem, Jashub promised to send word should any sudden change occur at court.

After that, Isaiah and his daughter and the crown prince of Judah were alone. It was an unreal situation. The prophet could clearly see his daughter's eyes shining with attraction for the young man. Moreover, he felt, or thought he felt, something of Hezekiah's fierce inner battle to conquer his longing to return Hephzibah's love. In the still afternoon of the second day at the cave, Isaiah watched them and reflected, while pretending to be engrossed in the contents of one of his scrolls. Hezekiah was docilely sorting reeds for Hephzibah's deft fingers to weave into a mat. Hephzibah was singing. She had inherited her father's talent for music, and the song she sang was a sad one of unrequited love. *My two beautiful children,* Isaiah thought for a moment, his eyes shifting from Hezekiah's dark, handsome face to the lithe figure of Hephzibah and the cascade of light brown hair that tumbled gracefully about her shoulders.

Isaiah remembered a time years ago when he had held little Prince Hezekiah in his arms and assured him, "I love you as one of my very own." He knew that there was no man in Judah to whom he would rather give his daughter. Still there were qualms in him. Would Hephzibah, reared in a home which had never known hardship, be able to cope with the situation which would be hers as the wife of a fugitive prince? Would Hezekiah, beset as he was sure to be by the new role of nonroyalty thrust upon him, be able at the same time to learn to live in peace and harmony with a wife? He sighed and resolved at the moment to say nothing.

* * * * *

Hephzibah's ankle healed swiftly, and in a few days she was up and about with her usual vigor. For hours at a time she would be gone from the cave on expeditions back to the homestead for food and supplies, and Hezekiah found himself longing for her return whenever she was gone. *Still*, he told himself, *in my situation I have no right to think, even to dream, that I might have her for my wife. I could not expect Isaiah to give his daughter to an outlaw, a fugitive.*

* * * * *

"Time is going by forever," Hephzibah said aloud as she walked the long path toward the cave, "and soon he will be gone and he will never know . . . ." Thoughts assailed her of a future with some other husband, some stranger of her father's choosing, a life settled and secure perhaps, but without the joy that could be hers with Hezekiah. "Oh Lord God of Judah, help me! Do not let me lose him!" It was a cry of despair, but no sooner had she spoken it than she felt a quickened sense of hope. Her step grew light and it was almost as if she flew to the cave.

It seemed as if the long hours of the evening would never pass. Isaiah and Hezekiah ate slowly, talking little. Hephzibah's heart was pounding frantically, "Oh! If only I could get either one of them off to himself." The plan in her mind had crystallized clearly.

But nothing happened. After a while, as the cave grew dark, Isaiah said he was very tired and Hephzibah rose to spread their bedrolls. Hers was in a tiny nook at one side of the cave, the place that afforded the maximum of privacy that such a makeshift dwelling could offer. Isaiah and Hezekiah slept in the center of the cave, close by the entrance, where they would be ready to defend themselves and Hephzibah should an intruder venture in.

The menfolk were sleeping soundly, but the long hours of the night passed and Hephzibah lay sleepless. "Lord Yahweh, now or never," she whispered. "I cannot let him go without ever telling him." Rising soundlessly, she tiptoed to the mat where the prince of Judah lay and knelt at his side.

"Hezekiah, I must talk with you, now." She touched his hand and he awoke, startled.

"What's the matter?"

"Shhh! You'll wake Father. Come outside." He rose, mystified, and the two of them slipped outdoors. The wind was delightfully cool; the sky a perfect sea of stars. In the faint moonlight, Hezekiah looked at Hephzibah's face, so lovely and now apparently so frightened. "Dear Hephzibah," he said gently. "Whatever is wrong?"

"Nothing is wrong, only . . . Oh Hezekiah, I love you and you are going away."

He caught her hands in his. "Would you go with me?"

"Oh yes!" Tears of joy ran down her cheeks.

Hezekiah pressed her close against him. "Hephzibah, my dearest, I never dreamed, I never hoped . . ."

"Father can write out the betrothal contract for us in the morning. Oh my darling, wherever we go, whatever happens, I'll be happy just to be with you."

And for hours that passed as moments nothing existed for either of them but the sudden reality of their love for each other.

* * * * *

"I, Isaiah ben-Amoz, give unto you, Hezekiah ben-Ahaz, Prince of Judah, my daughter Hephzibah." Slowly, in the beautiful elegant script with which he recorded his prophetic messages, Isaiah's hand now traced the words of the betrothal contract. "For as long as life endures." The first rays of morning sunlight had just filled the cave when Hephzibah had awakened her father to listen to her and Hezekiah explain the sudden realization of their feelings for each other. Isaiah had smiled, and, without a moment's argument or hesitation, he had bestirred himself and produced the required document. He looked at his daughter's radiant face and could see a reflection of the expression of his own Naamah when she first gazed at him long ago. He felt a sense of security, of confidence, that Hezekiah and Hephzibah would have each other to care for, to protect, to cherish. *It will be good for both of them,* he thought. And yet, he pondered with a small twinge of regret, there could be no traditional ceremony, no public celebrating, feasting, and singing, with crowds of relations and friends to wish them

253

a happy life together. Even Naamah would miss the chance to see her only daughter as a bride. And as for the parents of the bridegroom—Isaiah sighed deeply.

"You are worried that we are not able to have a great celebration," Hephzibah commented. So often she seemed to guess her father's thoughts.

"Yes, a little. There should be more witnesses at least. But that is not important to you, is it?"

Hephzibah shook her head.

"Yahweh knows, and *you* know," Hezekiah said, as he signed his name on the papyrus scroll Isaiah had prepared. "And someday, if ever I am king, all of Judah shall know. Is that not enough?"

Yes, thought Isaiah. *It is more than enough.*

* * * * *

Late in the afternoon of that same day, Maher returned from his expedition. "I have found a prophet." He entered the cave exuberantly. "In Moresheth-gath, on the Philistine border. He's not a Philistine, he's a Judean. He will take you, Hezey. He and his wife are poor but they've got a little place and their children, they only had daughters, have all married and left home. He doesn't know who you are, but I told him who I was, and I told him you were a kinsman of Isaiah the prophet. He said he would be glad to do what he could to help." Maher spoke breathlessly. "You can decide for yourself how much you actually want to tell him after you see him. Oh yes, his name is Micah."

"Will Micah and his wife take Hephzibah too?" Isaiah broke in, and in moments Maher had been enlightened with the whole sudden development of Hezekiah and Hephzibah's betrothal.

"They are kindhearted folk. They ought to be happy enough to take Hephzibah." Maher sounded confident, though he was not unperturbed by inner qualms of uncertainty. "There is nothing to do now but go on," he added, "for as I came through Jerusalem today, everyone in the city was talking about the fact that Prince Hezekiah was missing from the palace. The king has sent out an

254

appeal for him to return home. I feel sure it is a trap."

Hezekiah and his bride arrived in Moresheth, footsore and weary, two days later. The journey had not been easy; travel on foot over the mountainous Judean roads was difficult at best, and for the young couple the hardships of the trek were compounded by fears of their discovery en route and of the uncertain reception that awaited them at the end of the journey. Nevertheless, Hephzibah, her husband soon discovered, was an excellent traveler. She never spoke a word of complaint or discouragement. For her it was enough simply to be with Hezekiah and to trust that somehow Yahweh would provide for them in the future. In the crisp autumn nights as the prince of Judah and his bride lay in each other's arms beneath the open sky, Hephzibah was completely happy.

* * * * *

Now, as the long tedious weeks in Moresheth wore on, Hephzibah looked back longingly to those days on the road when she had had Hezekiah all to herself. Things were different now. The prophet's house was a one-room hut. There was never any chance for the young couple to be alone together, never a time to speak words meant for each other's ears alone. Through the dark stillness of the night, they lay huddled close together on the pallet that was their bed. But when dawn came, Hezekiah rose and was off to the fields with Micah to help with the autumn planting, while Hephzibah spent the long hours with Micah's wife, busy at a thousand housewifely chores. "This is the hardest time of the year," Micah's wife would often say. "Wait till the crops are sown."

Yes, then comes the rainy season and the cold winds of winter, Hephzibah thought, but she did not give voice to her feelings. *The prophet and his wife have been good to receive us at all*, she reminded herself. *They are giving us all they can give.*

Winter came with heavy rains and wind, as cold a winter as the land of Judah had seen for many years. Micah's house was almost as cold as the fields outside. The menfolk stayed indoors now too, most of the time, and all hovered close about the hearth.

255

Hezekiah and Micah frequently spent their time reading, for poor as he was, Micah had managed to acquire a collection of scrolls, some of them of his own writings. The prophet's wife and Hephzibah, more often than not worked at spinning, weaving, and sewing.

And the long winter days wore on.

How long will things go on like this? Hephzibah thought. She thought it a thousand times, and she, who had been so patient, began to feel restless, uneasy.

"Hezekiah, my precious. . . ." The hut was completely dark; the fire extinguished for the night and on their pallet Hephzibah and her husband huddled beneath the all too meager coverlets. Her voice was a mere whisper, for across the room Micah and his wife lay, perhaps sleeping, perhaps listening.

Hezekiah held her tightly. "You are so cold, dear one."

"I feel like something is going to happen. I am afraid."

"Yahweh is with us, and we have each other," he said. "There is nothing to fear."

She longed to ask him if when spring came and the harvest was gathered, they might then search for a different place, a place of their own, but she could not. *I wanted to come with him,* she thought, *and I must not let myself be a burden to him. I could be at home now, safe, warm, unafraid. But I would have lost him, and rather than suffer that loss, I can bear anything.* Consoling herself by the warmth of his body and the tenderness of his care for her, she closed her eyes and fell asleep.

Ahaz rose on the morning of the day he was to die as he had every morning for many months, determined to ignore the sudden chest pains and spells of dizziness that sometimes assailed him. There was work that must be done. It was time to send a report to King Sargon concerning the New Year festival, to tell him in as glowing terms as he could discover, how Assher had been served by the consecration of a new high priest. True, he was an obscure volunteer from among the ranks of the palace guard, but to the Assyrian inspectors and now in his report to Sargon, Ahaz would describe him as "kinsman to the king of Judah." "To Sargon the great king," Ahaz dictated slowly. The inlaid cypress squares in the floor of his council chamber seemed to be whirling. He closed his eyes and pressed against them with his fingers. "The mighty king, the king of the world, the king of Assyria . . . from Ahaz ben-Jotham ben-Uzziah, thy servant and son, greetings. . . ." He opened his eyes. The little wooden squares in the floor were still dancing about. *It is not as if I had been drinking over much,* he thought to himself. A bolt of pain shot through his chest. ". . . greetings, and may the great king live forever . . ." he said, grasping the edge of a table. *I am too hot; all I need is a little fresh air.*

Joah the scribe looked up wonderingly. "Yes, my King," he said, indicating he had written all that Ahaz had dictated.

"Ohhh. . . ." A sudden little groan of agony fell from Ahaz's lips. Frantically he groped for the wall. "I . . . am . . . falling," he gasped.

257

Joah dropped his pen and rushed to the king's side, but before he could reach him Ahaz had collapsed. The spark of consciousness within him told Ahaz to get up. He made a weak effort to rise, but it was no use. *I have died and gone down into Sheol,* he felt. *What will become of me?*

In a moment he was in the arms of a strong eunuch from the palace household staff who ordinarily would not have dared to touch the royal person of the king. With Joah to guide him, the eunuch made straight for Ahaz's private apartment and would have placed him in the great ivory bed with its deep purple canopy had something not stirred in Ahaz which caused him to whisper, "Not in the dark." So they placed him on a couch in one of the anterooms. He lay still, on the edge of consciousness, while attentive courtiers came and hovered around him. "He is burning with fever," Assherdan remarked, pressing his hand against the King's forehead.

"Abi, Abi!" Ahaz's voice was a mere whisper. It seemed an eternity before she came. But as last she was there.

"Please leave us, all of you," she was saying, so sweetly that no one could have been offended. "You may all wait in the hall if you wish." She motioned to the long corridor which was separated from the room where Ahaz lay only by gauzy, almost transparent curtains.

"Tomorrow I will be better, I know," Ahaz said, mustering all his strength and reaching for her hand.

"My love, my darling," she whispered, "do not try to talk. You must rest."

"You talk to me, Abi. About Yahweh . . . and why he made you so good and me so . . . so . . . ." he broke off.

He is dying, Abi thought. *Oh God, help me to help him!* She swallowed hard. "Ahaz, our Yahweh knows you have always been a seeker after truth," she said, "and I have confidence that he will remember it in your favor. For what we are all really seeking, I believe, is the same in the end. There is only one God, the power that rules all the nations, God who gives us life and strength . . ."

"Yahweh holds fast," Ahaz sighed. That was the meaning of

his name, his true name, Jehoahaz. "I never really believed it until now. Yet all these years, Abi, through your love, he has held fast to me."

"That is one of the most beautiful things you have ever told me, my beloved," she whispered.

He did not answer. His eyes were closed. Somewhere out in space he could hear the screams of little Azrikam lying in Molech's arms. He could see the hurt and anger that had so often reflected in Hezekiah's eyes as his elder son grew to manhood. And he could hear Isaiah's stinging reproach by the conduit so long ago: "Is it too little that you weary men that you must weary my God also?"

Abi's cool hand pressed gently upon his burning forehead. "Ahaz, Ahaz, I love you so."

She never knew if he heard her, for he spoke no more. The hours wore on: she could hear his breathing, faint, as if from another world. As the gray hues of twilight crept into the room, he died in Abijah's arms.

Abijah sat almost motionless, holding him close to her; her fingers buried in his thick auburn hair. Over and over she whispered his name and the silent tears rolled down her cheeks. Outside in the hall, Abijah could hear the anxious voices of guards and servants. *I must tell them. Let the mourning begin. Let the women moan and slash themselves and lie in sackcloth and ashes. Let the mourners come and wail outside the palace. Let the people light funeral fires.*

She rose, placed a pillow under his head, and then pulled back the curtains and the flood of the curious rolled in to gaze upon the lifeless body of their king. Many wept, for weeping was considered proper at such times, but Abijah realized suddenly, kneeling there at Ahaz's side among the crowd of mourners, that she was not weeping at all. The man she loved was dead. Her son, who should be king, was missing, and her own thoughts lay too deep for tears.

Outside the palace, no one seemed to doubt that Ahaz's son would return. Already, from the open courtyard below the main gate of the palace cries rang out "Long live King Hezekiah!" Then too, there was talk, ugly talk, in the streets of the city. "It would serve old Ahaz right if Hezekiah refused him a tomb," people remarked. "If I were his son, I'd cast his body beyond the wall." But Abijah, in her vigil beside her husband's bier, heard none of these things. The long night passed, and Judah was without a king.

* * * * *

It was Maher the son of Isaiah who took the news of Ahaz's death to Hezekiah in Moresheth, dashing from the city that very evening on a swift horse, galloping across the Judean hills in the dead stillness of the winter night. To Maher, Ahaz's death could be regarded as nothing but a blessing. Now his friend would be king. Now there was hope for better days.

Hezekiah and Hephzibah, Micah the prophet and his wife, received Maher's news in stunned silence; a stillness so heavy that it seemed to crush in upon them all hung over the room. Maher watched his sister's hands tighten on Hezekiah's arm. Hezekiah himself looked dazed and almost uncomprehending.

"He was still young," Micah's wife said at last. "He wasn't much, but he was our king."

Maher dropped to his knees before his brother-in-law, his childhood friend. "And now we have a new king," he said. "May I be the first to swear my loyalty to you, my lord King Hezekiah?"

Hezekiah nodded gravely. "My brother Maher, you have convinced me of your loyalty already."

Micah and his wife looked at each other in astonishment, then dropped to their knees before the prince whom they had sheltered unawares. "Yahweh bless you forever, my King," Micah said, tears filling his eyes. "Seek him and serve him and he will make you great."

* * * * *

In the audience hall of the king's palace, Isaiah and the Lady Abi, both clad in the traditional mourners' garb of sackcloth, sat

260

on the steps before the empty throne of Ahaz. Isaiah had acted speedily when news of the king's death had reached him. Dispatching Maher to Moresheth, the prophet himself had headed straight for the palace. There he had taken his place before the King's chair, announcing to the astonished guards and courtiers that he came as "temporary regent for King Hezekiah." Isaiah spoke with authority and with his usual air of finesse, and no one dared to say him nay.

In the morning Abijah came to join him. She came silently and sat on the steps at his feet without a word. Her long hair hung loose and disheveled; her eyes were heavy from lack of sleep. She looked tired and old.

"My lady," Isaiah reached out and touched her shoulders. "I have sent Maher to bring Hezekiah home."

"Today?"

"Last night."

"Where is he, Isaiah?"

"In Moresheth. He should be here today, maybe tomorrow."

"Isaiah . . ." Abijah did not look at him when she spoke. In her lap her slender fingers toyed with the only ornament she wore, the ring on which was engraved Ahaz's name.

"Yes, my lady."

"Should I stay with you, or should I go back to the mourners?"

"Stay here, Abijah, for the sake of the living."

She nodded and they lapsed into silence, to keep their vigil of waiting.

Some while later, Abi spoke once more: "Isaiah, what is going to happen? You would not tell me before: please tell me now: is my son the chosen one, the Prince of Peace?"

"Truly, my lady, I do not know. Often I fear that the peaceable kingdom is farther away than I dare to contemplate, off across the centuries. But this I do know; it will come *someday*, in Yahweh's own good season. And I also know that Hezekiah is a part of Yahweh's plan for great good, and so are you, Abijah, for the good that is in him, he has from you."

"Not from me alone," said Abi.

Isaiah wondered, but he did not ask what she meant. His mind was full of the future: of dreams he scarcely dared to dream and fears that the greatest of these visions belonged to a future that neither he nor Hezekiah would live to see. Yet whatever happened, the immediate future promised to be better than the past. Hezekiah would be a dedicated king; he would serve Yahweh to the best of his abilities. A new age was about to dawn.

"Hezekiah will reign in righteousness," Isaiah said softly. "He will be like a hiding-place from the wind, like the shade of a great rock in a weary land."

"You care about him, I think, as much as I do," Abijah said.

"As much as if he had been my own child."

Abijah said no more, but the prophet's words she would treasure in her heart forever.

Then at last, late that evening, Hezekiah came home with Hephzibah beside him, and the palace once more was filled with the flurry of activity. The next day King Ahaz was buried in regal splendor, in the garden of Uzziah, beside the tomb of his grandparents. This had been his wish, and though Hezekiah would have laid him in the tomb of the other kings, it was better, he thought, to do what Ahaz had wanted.

A few days later, on the porch of Solomon's Temple in the pale winter sunshine, Hezekiah was crowned king of Judah. Before the very building where his father had planned to have him consecrated to Assher, he knelt and swore the royal oath of eternal covenant to loyalty to Yahweh, who had made him what he was. And Isaiah the prophet lifted the holy vial of oil, which had been used at the coronations of the land's monarchs through the centuries and anointed Hezekiah ben-Ahaz king of Judah. Below in the vast open courtyard, great multitudes of his subjects watched in reverent admiration, while from a window in one of the Temple side chambers, so close they could watch every expression of his face, Abi and Hephzibah clasped each other's hands and unashamedly let tears of inexpressible pride roll down their cheeks.

The anointing done, Hezekiah rose, mounted the king's platform, and began to speak. His voice was strong and confident. "My people,

262

Yahweh our God has seen fit to make me king over Judah. I am young and with the Lord to give me strength, I have a long life ahead of me. I do not know when my days are done what shall be written of me in the annals of this kingdom. But one thing shall be written of me before all else, that I am the son of Ahaz the King."

A moan, a gasp of astonishment, went up through the crowd. Why did the new king choose to mention this?

"Many a time I have asked myself why I was born Ahaz's son," he went on, "and I can find only one answer, that Yahweh willed it so. But, my people, I also believe truly that Yahweh shall neither condemn me nor vindicate me on the basis of how my father lived and ruled, but rather on what I, Hezekiah, shall do. Now Yahweh has put it in my heart to make a covenant this day, a new covenant of service and dedication to him. And I ask you, my people, to join with me, to swear with me your loyalty to Judah's God, and no other."

A wave of agreement echoed through the audience. Cries of, "We swear! Praised be Yahweh!" mingled with shouts of, "Long live the King! God save King Hezekiah!"

In her place before the Temple window, the Queen Mother Abijah dropped to her knees. "Yahweh, oh Lord," Abijah spoke simply, her upturned face reflecting an almost holy rapture. "Accept him, I pray, Lord, as the gift to thy people from his father, Ahaz, my beloved."

Hephzibah listened, for a moment taken aback, her eyes fixed on Abijah's radiant features. *Oh God,* she thought then, *if a mere woman can love so deeply, what must divine love be?* "Lady Abi," she said, "Yahweh has heard your prayer."

"You believe?" Abi asked.

"I know," said Hephzibah.

And the two women rose and went forth to join Hezekiah's subjects in their oath of loyalty to the God of Judah and to the king they loved.

Afterword

The story of Ahaz, as related in the preceding pages, is based closely on the biblical narratives found in the books of 2 Kings, Isaiah, and 2 Chronicles and on archaeological evidence and ancient traditions from extra-biblical sources.

To those readers who notice in Ahaz's world an absence of many of the practices of later Judaism, the author urges recollection of the fact that our story is set in a very early period of Jewish history before many of the characteristic customs of later times were strictly observed. Ahaz's world was one where the many gods still vied with the one God for man's allegiance, and Ahaz himself, half-Judean, half-alien, was very much the product of his heritage and his environment.

In the unfolding of any biblical story in the form of a novel, there are areas where the author's own imagination and intuition must be freely invoked. In the years that the story of Ahaz evolved in my mind and heart, I came to feel very close to this tragic, misguided king of so many centuries ago, and to love him. That my readers may also feel compassionate empathy for him is the sincere hope of

CONSTANCE HEAD

Cullowhee, N. C.
1979

264